Where the Cricket Sings

D T Murphy

D1319827

Where the Cricket Sings

An imprint of D T Murphy(eBooks)
Copyright © 2022 by D T Murphy

All rights reserved.
First published in Ireland by D T Murphy 2022

This book is subject to copyright and no part may be copied, reproduced or transmitted in any form or by any means, without the written permission of the publisher except for a short evaluation in a book review.

While some of the events and places in this work are based on actual events and places, the characters are purely fictional and any resemblance to real persons is purely coincidental.

Where the Cricket Sings / D T Murphy – 1st edition

Website: www.dtmurphyauthor.com
Email: mailto:dtmurphyauthor@gmail.com

eBook ISBN No: 978-1-3999-3257-8
Paperback ISBN No: 978-1-3999-3566-1

Cover Design by designforwriters.com

Lo que sois fuimos nosotros
Y lo que somos sereis
Cuando menos lo penseis
Rogad por nos, y lo haremos por vos

What you are, we were
And what we are, you will be
When you least think about it
Pray for us, and we will do the same for you

Anonymous

Chapter 1

The Basque Country, Spain, 1936

Luken propped the butt of the Lebel rifle against the table and placed the muzzle into an enamel basin on the floor. He poured a kettle of hot water through a tin funnel and let it run down the inside of the barrel, washing down the dirt and residue from the last expedition. He finished the clean-out by pulling a piece of flannel on a string through the tube.

Just after sunrise, he closed the door gently behind him, paced down the grassy hill, across the Eguzkitza Valley and up into the forest. His home side of the valley was too close to the town for decent sized game and he needed to bag a sizable boar or better still, a deer.

After five kilometres through the mixed beech and pine forests, he rested in a depression in a meadow, where a group or party had seemingly been sitting around.

About to move on, he picked up a spent bullet casing. Someone else had been out hunting, he thought, probably cut up the animal and buried the entrails in the nearby plot that had been dug up, just as he might have done himself. And yet? He rolled the spent cartridge around in the palm of his hand and then closed his fingers around it. A pistol cartridge? Nobody uses a pistol for hunting.

He rooted through the dirt and grass with his boot. Suspicion crept over him as he scraped away further to discover a txapela, a black beret. Immediately, the size and shape of the dug-up area took on a new meaning. A shallow grave?

He cast off his jacket. Raking the ground with his hands, his fingertips became chafed and his fingernails blackened.

Luken paused for breath, sweat dripping from the tip of his nose. He looked towards the wood and listened, reassuring himself that he was alone.

He pressed on, then, staring coldly up at him was a face he recognised. Ander Ybarra.

'Cristo!' He slumped backwards. 'Jesús, no, it can't be. No! Who could have done this?'

He sat on the ground, unable to move, with a feeling of incredulity that soon turned to helplessness. Brushing the earth from Ander's face, he thought of the man he used to play soccer with, always up for fun and a joke. Someone he'd known all his life. Who would want to kill such a decent man, only a few years younger than himself? A man who others in the liberal Casa del Pueblo movement suggested might have betrayed other volunteers because of his contrary political arguments. But Luken didn't believe that, those squabbles were just him being difficult, he loved an argument.

Luken examined the shot in the chest and the skin puncture over the left eye, where he had been struck, possibly with a rifle or pistol butt. Already the smell of decaying flesh pervaded his nostrils. He put his own shirt over Ander's head and drew the soil back over him. He picked up his rifle and jacket and hurriedly started back.

Breaking the news to his father, Estebe, was going to be difficult, he thought. Even though a tough man, it had to be heart-rending, receiving surely the worst news of his life. He tried to think of the best way of explaining what he had found but soon abandoned the idea and reckoned the only way was to choose the most appropriate words at the time. He hoped in a way that Estebe's wife, Arossa, wouldn't be present. No doubt she'd break down. Although not a weakling either; he recalled her arguing at length with a vendor at a market stall when she had been short-changed. And, despite being a small woman, as a school teacher she had to deal with teenage impudence.

The sweat ran down his back as he hastened back home through the forests, oblivious to any wildlife or game that might cross his path. They would have to bring a car or van around the mountain past Arakoa village to recover Ander, a perilous time to be caught with a dead body. Retrieving game was one thing but human remains? Dangerous.

Back at the cottage, his wife was on her knees, cleaning out the stove. 'You're home early, did you get anything?'

Luken attempted to speak but hesitated, feeling a sense of dread. He leaned against the sink, took a breath, and said, 'Something terrible has happened, Miren. Ander Ybarra has been killed.'

'What?' she said in alarm, putting down the dustpan.

Luken explained at length what he had found and, as she got to her feet, saw a tear forming in the corner of her eye.

'Poor Ander. He was so good to his mother. Why would anyone want to kill him?'

Luken embraced her. 'I don't know. I'm assuming it was one of the right wing death squads.'

She poured a kettle of water into a basin to clean his hands. He used a splinter of wood to pick the dirt from his fingernails while she cut up pieces of flannel and wrapped them around each fingertip oozing blood.

'We have to go over to Estebe and Arossa straight away. Where's Kasen?' he asked.

'He's down playing with Matias. I better go down and tell Señora Pérez to keep him until we get back.'

***

The Citroën van coughed and started on the second attempt as Miren climbed into the passenger seat. Luken swung the vehicle past their gate and out onto the road.

Countless times over the years men must have been faced with such terrible tasks, he thought, though that didn't help him now. The murders had come to Euskal Herria, the Basque Country, and they just had to face up to it.

The van left a flurry of dust in its wake and he made a point of slowing down as he passed through Durango, unaware of pedestrians walking around town or people sitting outside a café. Turning left, he drove up into the lower rises of Mugarra Mountain.

Estebe and Arossa's two-storey cottage, located on a slope, faced rolling hills at the front, while a rugged limestone mountain dominated the view to the rear.

Arossa turned from putting bedsheets on the clothes line as they pulled in. After greeting each other, Luken said, 'I've bad news for you, Arossa. Is Estebe at home?'

'He's inside.' She gestured towards the cottage as he noticed her observing his face.

Sitting in an armchair by the window, Estebe was engrossed in a book.

'It's Ander,' Luken said, his visage dropping while Miren sat down on the sofa next to Arossa.

'What of Ander?' Estebe asked.

'He didn't come home last night,' Arossa said. 'Has something happened to him? Was he picked up by the Guardia Civil…'

'I'm sorry, Arossa.' Luken shook his head. 'It's much worse than that. Ander is dead.'

The book fell from Estebe's lap and thudded on the stone floor. After a brief pause he removed his glasses. 'How?'

Arossa had stiffened but said nothing.

'Shot. I found him on the south slope of the mountain near Arakoa, in a shallow grave. It was miraculous that I found him.' Luken noted Estebe's reaction from clasping the armrests of the chair to standing up full height, gripping his forehead. Arossa started to weep.

'Had he been tortured?'

'I don't think so. He had a cut over his eye but I only partly exposed his body. I'm sorry to be the messenger of such terrible news, Arossa.'

'Why did he have to go out to those training sessions?' she asked. 'He's only twenty-two — '

'He's the same age or even older than the other men who volunteered,' Estebe interrupted. 'And he has a mind of his own as you well know. He wouldn't sign up for any organisation that he didn't believe in.'

Miren put her hand on Arossa's shoulder. 'He was a good man and a good son.'

Estebe took out a bottle of brandy from a cupboard and poured out four glasses, including a large one for himself. He swallowed the contents and poured himself another. He stood rigid in the middle of the floor, lost in thought before declaring, 'I've seen my whole life pass by in the last few seconds. I've heard it said that when men are confronted with death they have that experience.'

Nobody spoke for several minutes and Luken thought of the strangeness of what Estebe had said.

'It's as well not to pander to such thoughts, Estebe,' Miren responded softly. 'It could drive you mad.'

'He was just coming in to the prime of his life,' Arossa reflected. 'When he was a child I remember showing him the sunflowers engraved on the stone lintels, explaining how they were looked on as God's eye, protecting us against bad luck and misfortune. Every year he brought me a bunch on my birthday.'

Estebe motioned for Luken to follow him outdoors.

'We'll have to recover Ander after dark. Can we use your van? It'd be as well if there were just the two of us, the fewer people who know about this the better. For now at least, until we retrieve the bullet and see what type of gun was used which should give us some idea about the killers, probably some right wing militias. Just as important, we don't want the Guardia Civil to find out. They'd be coming around here asking questions, wanting to know who Ander's acquaintances were, what his movements were, and what our own political affiliations are. We'll get Doc Lopez to do the death certificate. How far is it from Arakoa?'

'It's not that far but you can't see it from the village. I found this at the scene,' Luken replied, handing Estebe the cartridge.

'Six millimetre,' Estebe said. 'Just to make sure, we'll ask Doc Lopez to remove the bullet and confirm that a pistol was used. If we handed Ander over to the police we might never find out, depending on the loyalties of whoever was doing the investigation.'

'Agreed.'

Walking around the smallholding, Luken noticed Estebe straightening up, his nostrils flared while clenching his teeth as he continued, 'The killers could have been from here and left him at Arakoa to avoid local suspicion. Whoever did this has to be found and killed, Luken, however long it takes.'

'Maybe we should bring him to our house and ask Doc Lopez to do a post-mortem there,' Luken offered.

'I'm glad you suggested that, I don't want his mother to see him until he's been cleaned up. When we've confirmed what kind of weapon was used, we can make an educated guess as to who carried out the murder.' Estebe paused. 'I might look as though I'm coping with this, Luken, but underneath I'm raging.'

'I thought as much,' Luken replied. 'Nobody could expect you to feel any other way. I remember the times Ander loved getting into an argument and fighting his side until the last. He was like you in many ways. Dogged.'

'There's a fine line between torture and a beating,' Estebe said, looking up towards the outline of the mountain against the sky. 'I wonder what he might have told them.'

'No more than what they probably knew already,' Luken guessed while considering then dismissing the possibility that Ander, despite being a liberal activist, might have been in league with them and ran foul over a disagreement.

***

Neither Luken nor Estebe spoke much as they drove down the valley, skirted around Mount Artxara and passed through the tiny Arakoa village – more a crossroads than a village. Despite driving slowly, the unpaved mountain roads tested the shock absorbers on Luken's van to the limit, bouncing the two men in their seats as it hit numerous potholes. The slope up to the burial site steepened dramatically. Unable to force the vehicle all the way, Luken stopped and reversed onto a level patch of long grass.

In semi darkness, Estebe stood back to let Luken do the digging, seeing as he knew the exact positioning. The body was uncovered in minutes.

Estebe knelt down, brushed the earth from Ander's face, pushed back his hair and clasped his head in both of his hands. 'My son, my one and only son.'

He peered at the wound at the side of Ander's face. Luken saw tears forming at the corner of Estebe's eyes, but he didn't sob. Through tightly clenched teeth he declared in a loud voice, 'They'll pay for this. God help me, they will pay for this!'

Luken reflected that it was the only time he had ever seen Estebe display such an outburst of emotion.

***

Hours later, at Luken's house, Miren and Doctor Lopez heard the van approaching and went to the window in the spare room. A table now stood in the middle of the floor; cloths, sterilising fluid and medical instruments were stacked on a side cabinet.

Luken and Estebe brought in the covered body and placed it gently on the table. The doctor drew the blanket down to Ander's chest and shook his head in dismay. 'It's getting out of hand. To be confronted with a healthy young man like this just isn't right. I pray that it will stop soon. Were you close, Estebe?'

'We were, generally. Though we had our arguments. Who doesn't?'

Miren began cleaning Ander's face, while the doctor ushered Estebe and Luken out of the room, closed the door, and set about tidying up the facial wound.

Though an experienced nurse, Miren realised it was the first time she'd assisted in the post mortem of someone she knew. Previously, it had always been a hospital patient, where she kept a detached approach. She fetched a second basin and washed the dirt out of Ander's hair. In spite of her best efforts she couldn't hold back a tear.

The doctor noticed and asked, 'You knew him well?'

She nodded, wiping her face. 'He used to come around with Endika, Luken's brother, for dinner. Afterwards, we'd play Mus, the card game. Good fun.'

Later, Doctor Lopez called in Luken and Estebe, and handed Estebe the bullet. 'Six millimetre. Same as the cartridge case.'

He filled out the death certificate, declaring that Ander had died from a fall from the roof of Estebe's house while repairing roof tiles. 'Just make sure the police don't get to see him before he's buried…'

'I can guarantee you that, Rafael,' Estebe interjected.

***

Located close to Durango, the cemetery occupied a picturesque location on a plateau surrounded by rolling hills, with the Cantabrian Mountains in the distance.

Three Guardia Civil hovered outside the low peripheral wall, watching the mourners. At the graveside, Luken spoke quietly to Endika. 'Has anyone in the Casa del Pueblo asked about Ander?'

'Of course they have, wanting to know every detail. There'll be a full investigation soon.'

'Normally, it'd be Estebe leading the investigation,' Luken said, 'but since it was his son it'll be someone from outside. It was a brass bullet that killed him, probably a military one, which could've come from any number of different makes of pistol. Estebe was disappointed that we couldn't establish a particular type of gun.'

Endika looked over at the officers. 'I wonder what those zipaioak are doing over there. I know two of them to see but the third I've never seen before.'

'Neither have I. But the casual way they asked about Ander's death is a sign they don't know or care what happened.'

Under the late morning sun, they returned through the entrance archway and out onto the quiet road. Friends and neighbours approached Estebe and Arossa, offering their sympathy.

Luken noticed Arossa's paleness and her eyes bloodshot from crying, yet she still kept a gracious, upright presence. Estebe was expressionless as he thanked each person for coming.

Miren remarked, 'How does Estebe stay so calm? He looks unmoved…'

'He's anything but unmoved,' Luken interrupted. 'If you'd seen him at the exhumation, he was like a spitting devil. I've never seen him so mad.'

***

Situated in the Ametzagaña district, the hospital sat close to Donostia city centre, in an area bounded by a curve of the Urumea River. Built just before the Great War, it stood five floors high in spacious grounds, surrounded by shrubs and young larch trees.

Unfazed by the long bus journey from Durango, Miren usually struck up a conversation with a fellow traveller to help pass the time. Today, however, she didn't feel like talking to anyone and nodded to familiar faces and avoided sitting next to them.

She was gathering her thoughts, trying to set her mind at ease over the events of the previous days. She thought of her son, Kasen, who had been spared seeing Ander lying dead. Though Kasen knew Ander from the board games, she felt it wise not to have brought him to the funeral in case he overheard a careless word about Ander's demise. Kids were always the first to pick up on contradictions. Who knew when he might say the wrong thing at the wrong time. What would the country look like when he grew up? Since the liberal government had been elected last February there'd been no sign of reconciliation between them and the rightist factions. When would the killings cease and peace prevail? Estebe seemed to be dealing with Ander's death alright but Arossa was clearly heart-broken. Beyond sympathy what else could she offer her? Just spend more time with her when her friends and relations had departed and the dull light of sadness had settled in.

Many patients had arrived at the hospital that evening needing urgent surgery. Miren donned her scrubs and went directly to the emergency operating theatre.

She took over from another nurse who had been working continuously for twelve hours.

A man undergoing treatment for a gunshot wound lay unconscious under sedation; a large puncture showed where the bullet had exited his body. Compounded by her preoccupation with Ander's killing, and not having worked in theatre for some time, she had difficulty remembering the names of the instruments requested by the surgeon.

'Are you okay, Miren?' Doctor Eguren asked, and helped by pointing to the devices on the tray.

'I'm fine, just a bit tired.'

Given the severity of the wound, she contemplated the patient's good fortune to be alive.

'He was shot from behind,' the surgeon said. 'Bullet went right through him, missed his lungs. You're looking at the exit wound, much worse than the entry wound, as usual. We've already treated that.'

After the operation, she wheeled the patient to a male ward where, except for one, there were twelve occupied beds and, with the summer heat, each patient had just one sheet. The stringent smell of camphor prevailed and a single light bulb gleamed overhead. A storage cupboard sat by the side wall and a table stood by the curtainless windows. Above it, a picture of the Sacred Heart of Jesus looked down.

In the dim light, one of the sisters pointed out the updates to the treatments that patients had received, running through the notes on clipboards stacked on the rail behind each bed. Even in the gloom, Miren noticed the spotless, polished wooden floor.

She carried out the regular tasks of dispensing drugs, recording temperatures and the amount of fluids being taken. Unusually for a male ward, she sensed a strange quietness; few of them spoke; even the younger ones, who'd normally be keen to start up a conversation, said little.

On the bus home the next morning, she nodded off intermittently as tiredness swept over her.

***

The following evening, she made a point of first attending to the man who had had the operation the previous night and surprisingly saw him sitting partially up and in good spirits.

'You're Luken Abaroa's wife, aren't you?' he asked.

'I am. Have we met before?' Miren searched his face for familiarity.

'Don't think so,' the elderly man replied, introducing himself as Juan Joseba. 'Luken comes into my shop to get his hair cut. I see you out on your horse, galloping by our place sometimes. You look like a wild figure with your scarf flying in the wind.'

Miren smiled, unaware of the colour change in her face from embarrassment. 'I love being out on that horse – a mare, actually. You get such a great sense of freedom.' She inspected his dressings. 'You're a lucky man to survive that bullet wound.'

'At my age, Señora Abaroa, every day you live is a lucky one.'

'No need to be formal; call me Miren.' She thought better of asking how he had got the wound but instead enquired, 'Have you a family?'

'Just a wife and myself. She was here earlier. You used to help your father with the festival.'

'Ah! That's right. Strange we never met, seeing as we don't live so far from each other.' She handed him the painkilling tablets and a glass of water. 'It's very quiet in this ward.'

He beckoned her closer. 'Some of us are here because of "war wounds" and won't say anything without knowing where loyalties lie. Be careful what you say and to whom.'

She paused momentarily, thinking that she should have expected to see conflicting attitudes in such a place. For the rest of her rounds she kept conversation to a minimum, focusing on the work in hand – nonetheless feeling a tense, cold atmosphere throughout the hospital.

***

Back home the following afternoon, Miren wore a loose red cotton dress and tied her hair in a bun at the top of her head. By way of a head-dress she wore a white section of the same fabric around her head and tied it into a knot at the nape of her neck. Using a hoe, she dug up the weeds around the pepper and onion plots.

Despite her normal cool-headedness, she damaged a few large onions with the tip of the hoe before sensing the jitter in her movements. She stopped momentarily and thought of the tit-for-tat killings being reported in the newspapers. Maybe now someone else will their life in retribution for Ander's murder.

She took a firm grip on the hoe and made a concerted effort to avoid further damage.

Unlike springtime, the growth of weeds had almost come to a standstill and she reckoned this was her last hoeing session for the summer. She topped up the water bowl in the hen run next to the barn and dropped a handful of grain into the feeding trough. Refilling the pail, she returned to the barn and dropped it into the stall.

'How is my Yulene, the most lovable mare in the world?' she asked, petting her muzzle. Of all the chores, attending to this animal was what she enjoyed most, talking softly to her while brushing her silken chestnut coat before taking her out for a canter.

She secured the saddle on the mare's back and fastened the bridle around her head. A car stopped on the road. The doors slammed and the vehicle drove off. Surprised at the sudden commotion, Miren went to see Endika walking down from the top of the garden. As he came closer she saw that he was holding a blood soaked cloth against the side of his head; the swelling stood out and blood oozed from the wound on his cheek.

'What happened to you?' she asked, guiding him into the cottage.

'I've been questioned over Ander's murder. Our own people seemed to think I might have had something to do with it.'

'How could they think such a thing?' She washed his face while allowing the wound to bleed a little to purge any small particles of foreign matter. 'Who were they?'

'I didn't know any of them. Whenever there's an investigation, the practice is to use a team from outside in case of any local involvement.'

'Why did they beat you?'

'To make sure I got their point. It's their way of making sure I understood that whatever I said was to be taken as definite truth, on pain of death. In a law court I'd have been swearing on the bible.'

'It's all so extreme,' Miren said while applying the gauze and taping the wound on his cheek. 'I don't understand why they have to use such brutality.' She made coffee and handed him a cup. 'I'm going to get Luken.'
Drinking the coffee, he followed her out to the stable and helped her mount the mare, then watched as she set off at a steady trot towards Durango.

Chapter 2

The overnight rainfall had little effect on the dusty roads, the summer weather had been so dry. Luken's black van splashed through the occasional evaporating puddle as he drove to his garage and parked up. He moved the new Citroën Traction-Avant out of the service area, deliberately placing the car beside the petrol pumps, tempting customers, waiting for fuel, to look and sit inside. A potential sale.

He reversed the van into the rear of the service area. Three cars and a lorry were in the process of repair. He put on a brew of coffee as a short man of medium build wearing a short-sleeved jacket and a collarless shirt walked in. Luken regarded Kerbasi, his senior mechanic, as his most dependable and skilled worker.

'How was Estebe?' Kerbasi asked.

'He kept a brave face but drank a lot back at the house. Arossa was inconsolable as you might expect.'

'They'll be after me too, I'm sure,' Kerbasi said while gesturing to a newspaper he had thrown on the table. 'There's a short article in that about Ander.'

'Are you bearing up okay? You're going to miss him,' Luken reflected on how close the two of them had been. The three of them, when he included Endika.

'Badly. A great friend and ally,' Kerbasi picked up his coffee, lost in his thoughts.

They left the office, donned their overalls and set about the repair work. Three more men arrived shortly afterwards, two of whom immediately set about installing a new exhaust pipe and silencer on the lorry while the third started removing the hood from one of the cars. Luken reflected on how different it was to just a few years before when there were three more men engaged. The atmosphere had been full of wisecracks and mockings, the perennial indulgence of men engaged in mutual lampoonery. Humour was becoming rare nowadays and politics even rarer as though allegiances were hardening. Nobody wanted to voice their opinion about political events anymore. While the economic downturn wasn't helping, he reckoned jobs were being completed quicker, something he could hardly complain about. Importantly, however, cordiality prevailed whenever talk on a technical matter was unavoidable.

He removed the driver's seat from the van and set up the acetylene equipment. He cut out a plate in the steel turret that ran laterally under the front seats to make a compartment then fitted a hinge and lock to the plate before securing it back in place.

At lunchtime Luken picked up the newspaper and read Ander's obituary:

With a sad heart, we report the death of a young man, Ander Ybarra.

Ander was a man well-known and respected in his local community. He participated in sports, notably Jai Alai, and represented his town in many tournaments. His future was to have been in Law where he was at an advanced stage in his studies. Ander's father Estebe, now back living in Durango, fought for France during the Great War and later represented Action Française.

Police statements indicate that the death was a tragic accident.

His death is even more tragic since he was the only child of Estebe and Arossa Ybarra, to whom we offer our sincerest condolences.

The newspaper had got its facts wrong, Luken reflected, about Estebe representing Action Française, a rightist group; he wouldn't be happy with that.

He went to the storage room at the rear of the office and switched on the printing machine then locked the door. Among the workmen, only Kerbasi knew of his involvement in the Casa del Pueblo. Word was that the printing machine was used to create invoices, reminders and other papers to send out to customers. But it was also used to print leaflets, essays and lectures given by pro-worker academics encouraging wage earners to stand up for their rights.

He printed out a batch of leaflets for covert distribution to factories and for display in appropriate public places, then locked the boxed leaflets in his safe.

Luken heard the echo of his name being called from the service area. Unlocking the door, he saw Kerbasi directing Miren to the office.

'Slow down,' he said, sensing her breathlessness and state of agitation as she hurried into the room.

'Endika has been beaten badly. He was interrogated about Ander's murder.'

'Where is he now?'

'At our house.'

***

Endika watched Miren dipping a cloth pad in cold water while advising him to hold it over his eye and refresh the cold water periodically. 'And use two pillows to keep your head up when you go to bed. It should help reduce the swelling during the night.'

Luken drew up a chair and sat down. 'What did they ask you?'

'They wanted to know when I last saw Ander, and what we'd been up to. I told them we'd been digging out the cave further, the one on Mount Miloatza, making it bigger. Kerbasi was there too, as you know. Didn't he tell you? We buried more tinned food and ammunition there in case we have to leave here at short notice.'

'It was too busy this morning for Kerbasi to tell me anything,' Luken said. 'That place is a long way from here...'

'It needs to be,' Endika interjected. 'They kept asking me, when was the last time I saw him. And clobbered me every time I answered.'

'That's the way they do it,' Luken said with a sigh. 'Like it or not.'

Miren handed each a cup of coffee and put down a plate of biscuits.

In a while, Endika took a deep breath. 'Luken, I was thinking, you used to beat me up when we were kids.'

Miren gasped. 'What?'

'Yes, Miren,' Endika continued. 'He was a bully boy. I'd be lying down in our bedroom reading a book then he'd come upstairs from playing the guitar and beat the shit out of me.'

'I don't believe it!' she said.

'It's true,' Endika replied. 'Your brother doesn't count, you see! He probably forgets, if it was someone out on the street he'd remember that all right.'

Miren turned to Luken. 'How could you do that?'

'Look who's talking!' Luken retorted. 'You used to beat Gechina, you told me so! Remember?'

Miren's face coloured with embarrassment.

Endika burst out laughing. 'Beating up your sister doesn't count either by the looks of things! Looking back over our years growing up, Luken, you took up boxing, whereas I went for what might be called intellectual sports, chess and the like. It's interesting, I went for the military side of the Casa del Pueblo and you went for the social side. It seems we've done an arse about face!'

Luken gave out a short laugh. 'I've grave doubts about using armed force as a way of changing things.'

'When you met Miren, you went your separate way really. Softened up.'

'I did not soften up! I'm just more…considerate, that's all. You don't begrudge me Miren, do you?'

Endika looked up wistfully at Miren and paused. 'She reminds me of someone, I can't think who. Of course I don't begrudge you Miren. She's a lovely woman. Sometimes I think I'm in love with her myself.'

Miren laughed mockingly. 'Ha! To think, I might have married either of you! If only I'd known.'

She went on to recite a childhood rhyme, 'Flowers in the garden, fishes in the sea, if you want to pick one, please pick me!'

***

Next day, Luken instructed Kerbasi to follow in the van as he drove a Citroën Rosalie to the customer's engineering business. The owner, a keen racing enthusiast, had bought the two-door coupé version. Luken opened her up and soon left his colleague far behind. Nearing the factory, he slowed right down, and after a wait, Kerbasi appeared in the rear-view mirror. The owner came out as they both pulled into the yard.

'Kaixo, Carlos,' Luken said. 'Looks like you've been waiting for us?'

'Kaixo, Luken. I certainly was waiting for you. How did it work out?'

'We skimmed a millimetre off the cylinder head to increase compression, you'll find it's an improvement.'

Carlos Etxartea started the car and turned his head either way to listen to the engine.

'Bikain! Magnífica! I can't wait to give her a good run now and hopefully get her into the next race at Montlhéry.'

'I wouldn't push her too far just yet, Carlos,' Luken replied. 'You'll need to run her in for a good three hundred kilometres. Let me know when you have and we'll tighten up the head. Don't go racing until I've done that or you might blow the head gasket.'

'Of course,' Carlos replied, nodding. 'Well, if you fellas aren't in a hurry this time, I'll give you a tour around the works.'

He showed them into the factory and pointed out the newly installed presses alongside the older lathes and forges for producing pipes and castings. While some of the machines were in operation, many lay inactive. For such a big enterprise, Luken expected more noise and hustle. And yet there was noise, but muffled, distant, hard to make out.

'It wasn't such a good idea buying those presses,' Etxartea said, pointing to the idle machines. 'The depression since the Wall Street crash is still having its effects here. The demand for industrial and household stuff has dropped way off.'

They ambled to the far end of the building where Etxartea took out a key to gain entry through a heavy steel door in a partition, then beckoned Luken and Kerbasi to follow.

Inside, Luken was startled to see forty, maybe fifty men in brown overalls operating row after row of lathes, deafening with the noise of their grinding metal. Sparks flew, and the concrete floor around each machine glistened from a carpet of metal filings. He sensed the warmth of the air mixed with the familiar smell of lubricating oil.

'I don't have to tell you what we do here,' Etxartea said.

Luken and Kerbasi observed, among other things, the barrels and pin mechanisms for firearms being turned out.

Etxartea gestured to the caged area where material was issued and completed items returned and said, 'Stock has to be strictly controlled coming in and especially going out. And "work in progress" to make sure any off-tolerance parts are recycled or destroyed.' He pointed to the finished-goods area, stacked with stout wooden crates.

Luken instructed Kerbasi to wait for him in the van as he had to go over the accounts with Etxartea. They went into a small office where he made a point of closing the door behind him. He gazed at photographs on the wall of Etxartea's exploits at racing events, and wondered if he manufactured arms for the Fascistas Españoles. When handed a cheque, he asked as casually as he could manage, 'Is it impertinent to ask who your main customers are?'

Immediately Etxartea stiffened and looked him seriously in the face before returning the question. 'Why do you need to know that?'

'With the murder of Ander Ybarra it makes me wonder what's going to happen next.'

'Luken, this is a commercial operation and with the downturn I can't afford to be choosy.' He gestured towards the immediate area outside. 'If it wasn't for what's going on there most of the men would be out of work and if it gets much worse, everyone will be out of work including myself.'

'We've known each other a long time,' Luken replied. 'And I wouldn't want you to give away any trade secrets but I'm concerned that the murders are getting worse.'

'That might be and you know I'm a sympathiser with the Euskal Herria cause but, let me put it this way. I was approached about two months ago by, let's call them intermediaries, and told that regardless of what happens if I didn't supply to who they represented that this business would be destroyed and me with it. So, what am I to do? Take a moral stance, close down and walk away? It's not the inanimate weapons that kill people but the men who fire them. I'm not a quitter and if the time comes when I'm forced to make a choice between Euskal Herria and Espania, you know the answer.'

They sat back and reflected.

'It'd be irresponsible of me not to consider my family in all this and I have to make plans,' Etxartea said.

Luken took this to mean that he would take his family abroad. He took out the cheque he had been given earlier and asked, 'Could you do something for me, I need a six millimetre pistol but I want it off-record, no name, address or serial number, can you do that?'

He offered the cheque back but Etxartea waved it away, asking, 'What do you want it for?'

'Protection only. I've no intention of participating in military operations.'

'Give me a week.'

Kerbasi drove the van back with Luken in the passenger seat. The late afternoon sunshine had diminished and the temperature cooled. Luken looked back over the things that Etxartea had said and realised that the fellow was trying to run a dangerous middle path between the viciously opposed factions. Let's hope he doesn't fall foul of either, he thought. Come to think of it, was it really such a good idea to ask him to make that pistol? He dreaded the thought that it would draw him into taking an active part in the killings. Sure, he hunted and killed the occasional wild animal but in a humane way that made no difference to the overall population of such creatures. But killing a man was an act of betrayal to his race. Surely there was an alternate way to resolve the ideologies or, at least, a way for them to live side by side in some form of compromise. He thought back to his conversation with Endika. They were twins, so alike, yet there was truth to what Endika had said about him. He had changed since being with Miren. Had he gone soft or was he being wiser, more judicious in his thinking?

Breaking the silence, Kerbasi said, 'These motors are a big improvement on the old AC series…'

'That's for sure,' Luken replied, glad of the distraction. 'Like all machines, each generation gets better. Especially when it comes to killing machines. Look at how sophisticated the equipment is that Etxartea is turning out now. Where is it going to end?'

Kerbasi stroked his chin and said, 'It probably isn't, there is no end to it.'

Passing through Urkiola, Luken noticed what looked like a small warehouse with the doors open. He glanced into the building to see two motor cars in various stages of repair. He signalled Kerbasi to pull over. Nobody appeared as they wandered into the building, quiet except for their own footsteps. Two more cars were parked at the rear section of the warehouse, awaiting repair, by the looks of things. The building is being used as a repair shop, just like my own, Luken thought. And looks well-equipped. He examined several tool cabinets by the wall and numerous items that lay on a bench undergoing inspection, including a stripped-down wiper motor. Whoever owns the place seems to be doing a decent trade, he reckoned.

The thumping sound of a motorcycle grew louder as it approached. The rider pulled up outside the open door and shut down the engine. He walked in, helmet and goggles in hand, a slightly suspicious look on his face. 'Can I help you? Customers aren't allowed inside.'

Luken introduced himself and Kerbasi, mentioning that he owned a similar garage on the outskirts of Durango.

'I've heard of you. Good reputation by all accounts. Pleased to meet you. My name is Robinson.' They shook hands and Robinson explained the work in progress for each vehicle and his efforts to procure spare components. 'This industrial trouble in France is causing havoc. Every day there's another bloody strike. I'm forever waiting on Renault parts. I expect you find the same?'

'I certainly do. When I'm badly stuck I just drive over myself. What brought you to Euskal Herria?'

'The sunny climate which takes me away from the inclement English weather, the beautiful countryside, and my wife happens to be from these parts. I came over about twelve years ago to set this up. Unfortunately, I've had the greatest difficulty holding on to my mechanics. As soon as they broaden their experience, off they go.'

'Your Euskera is good,' Luken remarked.

'My wife insisted I learn the language and it was a good idea. I can speak Española but having Euskera has made me amenable to local people. Made a difference to the business.'

The man looked tired with his steel-rimmed glasses and white hair and Luken reckoned he was well past sixty and probably seventy years. He invited them into a small office and offered a cup of coffee. 'We've considered going back to England, but I have a good business here, and I couldn't bear to close this place down. Not after all the hard work I've put in.'

'Would you think of selling it?' Luken asked.

Robinson's eyes brightened, 'Interesting that you should ask me that. I'd just been thinking about it over the last few days.' He sat back and after a moment continued, 'Tell you what, I'll talk to madam and go through the books. Give me your number.'

Before his visitors left, Robinson took them for another inspection of the vehicles, explaining who the owners were and where they lived. Motorcycles were his first love and he pointed to the one he had just arrived on, an Ariel Four Square, as his own, his pride and joy.

Further on the journey back, Kerbasi spoke. 'That was a quick decision you made.'

'An opportunity not to be missed,' Luken replied. 'You could see he wanted to retire. Did you notice that he didn't check to see if any of his tools were missing? That's the first thing I'd have done. He went off on the bike for a break and never even closed the door.'

Luken reflected that no firm commitment had been made and he could always change his mind. Nonetheless the days of the horse were well and truly gone and his future was in motorised transport. And one service station was not where he intended his whole working life to begin and end. The real money and opportunities were in the cities, where the numbers were. In the meantime he would build on the available business in the outlying areas to establish a base and enable him to launch into the market place of Bilbao.

Midway between Urkiola and Durango, Luken turned and asked, 'Kerbasi, old friend, how would you like to run

Robinson's set-up for me? I mean, if the numbers look good.'

Kerbasi looked across at him, and smiled. 'Are you serious? Of course I would.'

The two men shook hands across the steering wheel but before they could say anything further, a police checkpoint appeared and they were flagged down.

Three officers emerged, each armed with a carbine. One approached Kerbasi who passed out his papers without hiding his irritation. Luken passed his to another who looked the senior of the three. The officers instructed them to step out of the van and casually looked them up and down.

'Aren't you the owner of that service station?' the superior asked.

'What's that to you?'

'We like to know who might be starting trouble,' the officer said as he stared face to face with Luken, who replied, 'The only people starting trouble around here are you.'

The officer's face flushed red in a temper and he attempted to punch Luken. The bulk of his carbine obstructed his swing and Luken intercepted the attempt with his left hand. The second officer, a tall, robustly built man, struck Luken in the jaw and sent him flying on his back. Kerbasi, though keen to intervene, was held at gunpoint and could only curse them under his breath.

'Here's a man who has no respect for the law,' the superior officer said while throwing Luken's papers on the ground. The lawmen emptied the van, threw out the tools and boxes of nuts and bolts over the road. The superior examined a bundle of screwdrivers and a set of spanners. 'You could be thrown in jail.'

'What for?'

'Obstructing officers of the law.'

'What law? There is no law as far as I can see.'

The officer put the tools in the police vehicle, indicating to the others that it was time to move, as though they'd had their fun for the afternoon. Luken watched them climb into their car, slam the doors, and drive off, and from the laughter inside, felt the loathing in his veins for all three of them.

'That was a bit risky, wasn't it?' Kerbasi looked sideways at Luken while they painstakingly picked up the washers and clips, the nuts and bolts and returned them to their boxes and trays in the van.

'Maybe it was but since Ander was murdered I find it hard to keep my mouth shut with those kabroiak. I got those spanners in France and they cost a fortune.'

Luken twisted his jaw feeling the soreness and hoped that his lip wouldn't swell.

'How's your head?' Kerbasi asked.

'A bit dizzy.'

On the rest of the journey Luken wondered about the hidden compartment he had made earlier in the day and what he might have done had a pistol been there. The realisation caught him off guard. Courting trouble was unwise, he should have known that. He berated himself – he had a young son to consider and Miren would never forgive him if he foolishly brought grief to their door. It would have to stop, it wasn't doing him or anyone else any good. He shuddered at the way he'd addressed the lawman. He'd been no better than a loutish youth. Maybe he deserved the punch. He glanced across at his friend. Kerbasi might have got the same treatment, just for being there. Worse, they both could have ended up behind bars.

The pistol was for defensive purposes, nothing else, thus he had justified it to himself. He realised that Ander's murder more than anything else had unsettled him. Such random killings meant anyone could be targeted. And the murder squads were making things ever more worrying. So much for those bloody elections earlier in the year, the new liberal government still hadn't managed to rein in the fascists, or anyone else for that matter.

As a business owner he could be targeted by the leftists yet as someone with liberal views he could be regarded as a target by the right. And, the extreme rightist position of the Catholic Church was making matters worse. Unlike Miren he wasn't religious but, in fairness, some of the priests did good work for the poor and downtrodden. The church itself was a different matter with its condemnation of any form of worker's rights or land reform.

Going through the mountain passes, he stared up towards the craggy peaks poking their white limestone heads towards the heavens, the luxurious forests and the meadows stretched out below. He contemplated the hatred that existed in such an idyllic country. He remembered how, in his teenage years, his father had been killed in the conflicts at that time. How many more years would it take before a lasting peace came?

Luken thought of Kerbasi again as they continued the journey in silence. Kerbasi was a sympathiser and an active one, making him vulnerable. Living with his elderly mother, at least he didn't have a young family.

***

That evening, Luken left home and drove back to his garage where he opened the store room and removed the package of leaflets he had put in the safe earlier.

A short time later Endika arrived. They drove to the rear of the Erhardt Steel Company in Bilbao and parked in a nearby street. Luken opened the box of leaflets and gave half to his brother. They stuffed the papers into shoulder bags and made their way to the factory gates as the evening shift ended.

The factory disgorged its three hundred and seventy-two employees. The two men mixed in with the crowd, handing out the leaflets to workers willing to accept them and encouraged others passing, by calling out, 'Stand up for your rights!' and, 'Demand better conditions in your work!'

Some men stopped to read the pamphlets, others just pocketed them and walked on. Luken wondered how many of those men could actually read. Hopefully, a young family member at home could enlighten their father or uncle who didn't have the ability.

After some twenty minutes, as the crowd dwindled and thinned out, he noticed two security men behind the factory fence observing himself and Endika. One of the officers went to a cabin next to the gates and picked up a telephone while staring at him.

'Time to go,' Luken said, tapping Endika on the shoulder while gesturing towards the cabin.

They rushed back to the van and sped off, not in the way they came but in the direction of the city. After a few minutes, they laughed at a police car, with its siren flashing, going in the opposite direction. Considering the roadblock incident earlier in the day, Luken felt he'd gained his revenge of sorts.

They went to the Azenari Taberna on Barrenkale in the old quarter. The bar, hundreds of years old, stretched the length of the room with an ancient oak counter. Light came from glimmering gas lamps. The end of four large casks with dispensing taps peered out from the opposite side of the bar, each with a sign indicating a different type of wine, Tempranillo and Airén. A steel urn at the end of the bar for making coffee boiled up periodically while several men of mixed ages sat scattered at the bar and at tables, drinking wine and smoking. The aroma of coffee and cigar smoke permeated the room.

'No lady friend with you tonight?' the barman asked.

'Not tonight, relations only. Brother, in fact,' Endika replied, introducing Luken.

Luken leaned over and shook hands with the barman who took a good look at the two of them and said, 'Well, you're not identical but similar maybe?'

'We've been told that many times before, Ramon,' Endika said without sarcasm.

'So who is this lady friend?' Luken asked when the barman went on his way.

'It's a woman I met when out delivering timber. You wouldn't know her. I wonder how effective those leaflets are?'

'In themselves they'll hardly convince anyone to do anything drastic,' Luken replied. 'But at least they should get the message across for workers to get together and negotiate as one rather than trying to do things individually.'

They ordered more wine and smoked a cigar before going home. On the way Luken recalled how quickly Endika had changed the subject when his 'lady friend' had come up.

Chapter 3

The following Saturday night Endika sat in the kitchen of his ground floor apartment reading a newspaper by the solitary electric light. He heard a gentle tap on the window by the door; Kerbasi's face appeared.

'Have you got it?' he asked, opening the door.

Kerbasi delved into his rucksack and unravelled a colourful specimen of the Ikurrina, the Basque national flag.

'Good,' Endika said in admiration. 'Much bigger than I expected. Where'd you get it?'

'I bought it.'

'You bought it!' Endika said, jeeringly, 'Where'd you rob it?'

'I bought it from someone who "procured" it from a police station!'

'That's a good one, there's a good chance it'll end up back there!'

The two men gave a short laugh.

'This'll look good flying over the Donostia Cathedral,' Endika said.

'Let's hope we can get it up okay.'

Endika looked at the bruises on his compatriot's face. 'I don't think the "committee" did you over as badly as me in the interrogation, did they? We didn't have much time to talk yesterday, what else did they ask you?'

'They just kept repeating the same questions over and over, they must have asked them at least fifty times. How long were we there? Did anyone see us? What exactly did we do? As they went on, they hit me harder each time. The bastards.' Kerbasi shrugged. 'The men in the garage stopped asking where the injuries came from when I told them that the two of us got into a late-night drinking squabble over the money you owe me – which you still do by the way – and ended up sorting it out physically. One of them was surprised that I got the better of the fight since I'm smaller than you.'

'Ha! Wishful thinking. Did you ask Luken to come along?'

'I did, but he said that two of us should be enough considering that it's just a flag we're putting up.'

'I wonder,' Endika replied, thoughtfully. 'I hope he's not losing his cojones.'

'Don't forget that he's the man who publishes and prints the leaflets for better pay and conditions for workers. That's something that marks him out for assassination.'

***

Etxartea is as good as his word, Luken thought, as he reflected on the hidden pistol. Once he'd assured him that it was only for defensive purposes, he was happy to hand it over. Well-engineered, no sharp edges and lightly lubricated and yet he only wanted a token amount of money.

Luken turned into a copse and parked the van so that it couldn't be seen from the road. He walked into the wood and hung a section of cardboard on the branch of a tree. Listening to make sure that he was alone, he took three practice shots to gauge his accuracy. He buried each spent cartridge and, satisfied that his aim was as good as it could be for a handgun, refilled the empty chambers from his box of cartridges. He returned to the van, wrapped the pistol in a piece of cloth and replaced it next to the cartridges in the hidden compartment. Before moving off, he heard a passing vehicle. A lorry, he thought and waited a full five minutes before firing up the engine.

Out on the open road, he assumed the vehicle was going in the same direction and drove slowly to avoid catching up. But after a few kilometres his expectation was frustrated when he came up behind a local military truck with a canvas cover. The soldiers in the back pointed their weapons at him and gestured to move back and slow down, forbidding him to overtake. As if the day wasn't long enough, he pondered, here I am plodding along. And to make it even worse, from the registration number, he knew the lorry had been serviced in his own garage.

The back door of the house lay wide open when he got home. The stove had gone out and vegetables lay in the sink, uncut and with soil on the roots. Tomatoes had fallen on the floor. He looked through each room but there was no sign of Miren or Kasen. Ordinarily, he would have assumed that they were visiting their nearest neighbour and think nothing of it but today Luken had misgivings and ran down the field to check.

'No, I haven't seen either of them today,' Señora Pérez said, scratching her forehead.

He went to another neighbour. Nobody there.

Walking slowly home, he tried to think, where could they be when she'd explicitly said she'd be at home all day? He went to the stable to see that the cart was there but no horse.

Re-entering the house, he turned sharply on his heels on hearing a clattering, only to see Miren and Kasen mounted on the mare at the gate. Both called out and waved.

'Kaixo, Papá!' Kasen called out. 'We had a great ride!'

'Where did you go?' he asked, noting his son's delight.

'We started on a canter around the field but got fed up waiting for you,' Miren said. 'Kasen liked it so much I took him out on the road. He loves it, as you can see.'

Luken lifted the boy down and reflected on the doubts he'd had earlier. The frown on his face eased into a smile as the tension of the day left him.

***

The wind had picked up by the time Luken had eaten dinner and ventured outside. With the purchase of Robinson's garage on his mind, he shifted a rock behind the stable and retrieved a tin hidden underneath. In the stable, he unwrapped the waxed paper from around a bundle of banknotes and counted them out, then returned the tin to beneath the rock.

Sitting at the kitchen table, he looked up invoices and statements from suppliers and his bank. He ran a check on which bills had and hadn't been paid and made a list of those unpaid, so he could make a call on each customer. He went through the bank statements to ensure that all cheques paid in at the bank had cleared, and made a final tally to clarify his financial situation.

At the bottom of the paper pile, he picked up a business card he had been given by a garage owner by the name of Padraig, whom he had met some time back in Paris during the unveiling of a new car model. Luken remembered the elderly Irishman as an affable individual who had invited him to pay a visit whenever he might be in Dublin. He recollected the joviality of the evening as the two had left the Citroën party and traipsed around Paris while the others went back to their hotel. The inevitable visit to the Folies Bergère and the memories of the late-night tour through the bars and cafés on the Boulevard San Michel remained vivid. One quiet bar was about to close as they arrived but the owner, after a short argument, agreed to give them one drink. Padraig broke into a song and passers-by walked in when they heard his voice. The owner's mood changed as the bar and the till filled up. He took a few drinks himself and broke into a few French chansons. What a night that had been. He put the card back wondering how Padraig was and how his business was doing.

***

Luken drove up the mountain to Robinson's garage at Urkiola. Situated near the peak of a hill and surrounded by a deciduous wood, he savoured the sunshine, the quietness and sniffed the early morning air. He noticed a grass snake wind its way across the forecourt and into the undergrowth while contemplating the deal he hoped to finalise that day.

Robinson was buried in the bowels of a large saloon car.

'Kaixo, Luken. People think these things are complicated but we know better, eh?'

'True but there's always room for carelessness and sloppiness. Have you given further consideration to selling the business?'

'I have and I think it's the right time – for the right price, of course.'

They proceeded to the office and went through a folder of documents, evaluating the assets of the company. Over coffee, turnover figures, customer lists, goodwill and inventory of spare parts were thrown into the mix and eventually the two men after a lot of to-ing and fro-ing agreed a value. Most of the consideration was to be paid by a bank draft, with an initial cash deposit and a final cash amount that was off the books.

Robinson poured a shot of Scotch into each of their coffees and soon the smell of cigars filled the office. 'Will you run this place yourself?'

'Kerbasi is the man, you met him the last time we were here. From your list of customers and work I'd expect to have two men here. I have another man available over at the other workshop and if it's busy in one outlet they can always switch around. What will you do now?'

'Don't know for definite, I'm getting too old for the heavy work. I'll have to take a hands-off approach for any new business. Now that I'm no longer a business owner I'm less worried about the political situation with the leftist government, especially being a foreigner.'

'I don't let politics interfere with the daily push,' Luken replied. 'Otherwise we'd never do anything. The political situation is still a mess but, you know, it's always been that way.'

On his way back, he reflected on the terms of the deal and wondered if he should have held out for a better price. On balance, he thought, no, it was just about the right value.

***

That weekend, Luken took Kasen on a fishing trip to the river near Estebe's house. The pool was situated below a short run which carried down the effervescent water from the mountain. They had waited until early evening to come and after unpacking the rods, reels and other tackle, he showed Kasen the techniques, as he fitted the reel to the base of his own fishing rod. He pulled out and threaded the line through the eyelets, then tied the end of the line to an artificial fly.

Kasen, after several attempts, fitted the reel to his rod and attached the fly to the line.

'Is it okay, Papá?' he asked, as he watched his father inspect the fly.

'The knot needs to be tighter. Other than that, perfect! Well done.'

'How many will we catch?'

'Just one will do for today. Provided it's a big one.'

With practice, Kasen began to get the technique of casting the fly. He stood back from the water's edge with the rod held high and the line drawn out behind him, then swung the rod over his head and let the fly drop into the water. He gently issued out more line to let the fly drift towards the far bank and then downstream, before repeating the exercise.

None too bothered with his own attempts, Luken subtly observed his son's efforts. Other than the sound of the water breaking over the stones at the riverbank, quietness prevailed. He reflected that this form of relaxation was life at its best, being out with his son on a summer's evening, the best time for fishing. He relished the environs with all the worries of the world left behind and looked back at the times he, at Kasen's age, had spent at this same pool with his father and Endika. Competition was fierce for whoever could catch the biggest fish, though Papá only offered a few Turkish delights for the winner. An argument usually broke out with each claiming their specimen was 'easily' the biggest. Only later did the boys realise that their father had made each of them a winner on alternate trips, regardless of the size of the fish. In years to come, he hoped Kasen would be doing the same.

As the sun went down, the breeze dropped and flies started hovering over the river.

A fish jumped to pluck the fly from Kasen's line but, in his excitement, he lifted the rod too abruptly. Luken put his own rod aside and rushed over to help, but it was too late. The fish hopped off the line and escaped.

'Don't be disappointed, Kasen,' Luken said, noticing the upset on the boy's face, 'There's plenty more where he came from.'

Not until the third attempt at reeling one in did Kasen keep calm, lightly taking up the slack on the line then tightening up in time and gently reeling in the fish. A substantial catch, he jumped up and down with delight. 'Look at the size of him, Papá! He's huge!'

'Great, Kas! Not many boys of your age could have done that!' Luken replied, having gaffed the trout.

He noted the look on his son's face, smiling from ear to ear, his earlier frustration completely forgotten. 'There you are, you've even caught one before I did!'

'Did you catch many fish when you were a boy, Papá?

Luken stopped and looked at the curiosity in his son's dark complexion and brown eyes, so similar to his own, and said, 'I caught loads of them, as I know you will, but you know something? None of them were as big as the one you just caught.'

'Really? I bet it's a prize trout!'

'I think you're right! We'll have to get you into a competition. I think that's enough for today.'

They packed up and walked the short distance down the track to Estebe's house.

Sitting out on his veranda, Estebe was smoking his pipe when they arrived. Arossa and Miren came out on hearing their greetings.

'Did you catch anything?'

'A big trout,' Kasen replied, taking the fish out of his bag. 'See!'

Both families went inside and, after congratulations from everyone, Arossa invited Kasen into the kitchen where she made lemonade and took out a plateful of homemade biscuits. She handed him a package. 'I was going to give this to your Mamá but I'll let you do that for me.'

Kasen unwrapped the parcel to reveal a framed photograph of his parents and himself taken several years previously. After a cursory glance he passed the picture to his mother and went back to admiring his fish.

'That's beautiful, thanks so much, Arossa,' Miren said. 'You must have spent so much time making this?'

'I do it as an occasional pastime, as you know. My father showed me how years ago. We must get a few photos of Kasen at this age, with yourselves of course, so I can make a current one.'

The men went out and talked quietly on the veranda, listening to the sound of the river while sensing the scent from the maturing wheat fields on the breeze. Anxiety crept across Estebe's face as he spoke.

'I see the big landowners and bankers are throwing their weight behind the fascist movement. You only have to browse through the right wing newspapers to see that. And I'm sure they've been talking to the generals, those with the same dogmas at least. If this breaks out into a civil war and you want to get out, you won't have much time, especially if the road to the French border is blocked.'

'What?' Luken exclaimed. 'Do you really think it's that bad?'

'Nobody expected the Great War to happen and suddenly, it was upon us. It'd be naïve to think that those in the right wing camp aren't aware of your opinions. You'd need to plan in advance. Don't leave it too late, especially with a young wife and son. If it comes to it, that's what they'll blackmail you with.'

'I haven't thought ahead like that,' Luke replied, feeling as though he'd been left behind on an important trip. 'Where would we go? I can't think of anywhere I'd fit in. France is in turmoil. Germany is out of the question with that fucking lunatic in charge. Where could I get work? England? I don't want to leave this country, anyway. As my father used to say, down through the centuries there's always been a threat of invasion here. Anyway, I hate the idea of giving up our homestead especially after all the work and time we put into it. Do I walk away and let someone else – some conquistador – walk in and take it?' He turned to Estebe. 'What about you?'

'I'm not going anywhere, not that I'm too old but I'm not prepared to run. I still think you should plan for Miren and Kasen to move abroad at short notice. Just in case. Make sure she always has a valid travel visa, for France at least. By the way, how did your recent circulation of those leaflets work out?'

'We gave nearly all of them out but we had to run when one of the guards called the cops.'

'Did the guards get a good look at you?'

'I don't think so, it was late,' Luken replied and paused before continuing. 'With your experience you could do a lot abroad. A government in exile maybe?'

'I've been out of politics for so long now, Luken,' Estebe said. 'I'm hardly representative and few people in

Euskal Herria would look on me as that either.' He took a deep breath. 'Looking out across the fields you'd think that all is right in the world. A lot of people have come here from different parts of Espania and they're welcome as far as we're both concerned. How can you deny a penniless man work? They work for a pittance in the industrial areas and I'd hoped that over time even they would benefit from better conditions, especially after the recent elections. Your efforts to encourage unionisation should help. But now, both sides are digging in and the strikes are getting more violent. Likewise, the big landowners aren't moving an inch with the farmworkers. And on top of that, the church isn't helping with their condemnation of the strikes. They're afraid the communists are going to take over and they'll be at the loss of a livelihood. I think serious conflict is on its way and it can only get worse.'

On the way home Luken considered Estebe's words and a deeper perception of the political situation came to mind. He looked in the rear-view mirror and saw Miren sitting in the back of the van with Kasen asleep, his head on her lap. A family is worth dying for but is a country worth dying for?

At home, he locked the doors of the van, something he was aware of never having done before at the house. Anticipating future events after the discussions with Estebe had put a tightness in his chest.

When Kasen went to bed, Luken put his arms around Miren and held her tightly. He kissed her lightly at first then intensely as she responded. Miren smiled and drew back. He held both of her hands and without moving, they stared at each other for several moments without speaking before moving to the bedroom.

In the quietness of the room they peeled off each other's upper clothing, his bronzed appearance in contrast with her lightness of skin. His brown eyes as against hers' blue. He recalled her laugh when he said that the colour of her eyes was so intense they were almost luminous in the dark. They removed the rest of their clothes and climbed into bed. She stroked his chest while he softly caressed her breasts and the tightness that he'd felt earlier eased away.

Beyond the gentle love making they spoke in whispers as though they might be overheard by a ghostly listener.

'What if I become pregnant again, this is not a good time.'

'There might never be a good time. Let's try and be a little positive,' Luken said, surprised at how optimistic he sounded. In a while they drifted into a sleep.

They hadn't bothered closing the shutters and he awoke just after sunrise. He looked down at Miren slumbering, her arm over the sheet she had pulled up to her chest. She had a square jaw and a pleasant if not beautiful face and he saw in her a strength that showed through her look of innocence when asleep.

After breakfast, Luken said, 'I think we should go and get your travel papers updated. You never know when we might have to leave this country.'

'Are you telling me you want to leave? Just after you bought another garage!?'

'Of course not. It's just ... you never know what's going to happen for sure. The whole of Europe, if not the world, is in a mess. I met an Irishman in Paris at that last Citroën unveiling and I think I should write to him, just to keep in touch. You never know.'

Miren shrugged. 'If you think it's important, okay.'

He tore out a sheet from a writing pad and sat at the kitchen table. She sat while they wrote in French.

Cher Padraig,

I do hope you are in good spirits and that your business in Dublin is doing well especially with the new Citroën models.

You know I often think of the evening we had in Paris and the sport we had afterwards, especially in that bar. Do you still sing?

How is the situation in your country now? I read about the changing events in Ireland and I hope that now with your independence you will prosper in the years to come.

It is worrisome here in Euskal Herria now because we are going through political upheaval and we don't know for sure what the outcome will be. Already many people have been killed.

Write to me when you can and let me know how you are.

I wish you and your family the very best of health and prosperity.

Luken Abaroa

He faced Miren and said, 'Good thing you helped with that. I couldn't have expressed it so well.'

Chapter 4

Later that morning Luken worked on a Renault Nervastella sports car. Endika entered the garage as he was fitting a radiator and Kerbasi had an electric dynamo in pieces on the workbench. The other men were working on a Berliet lorry.

'Nice looking car,' Endika said, inspecting the two-toned convertible.

'Nice looking owner too,' Luken replied. 'Fabulous woman. If you stay around for a while you might see her, a widow. Husband died of cancer two years ago. You might do all right! Hey, what about your flag-hanging escapade?'

'I'll get my own women if you don't mind. We got the flag up, looks great flying in the wind. You should have come too. I rang El Día, there should be a photograph of the flag in tomorrow's paper. Let's hope more people get the message, especially the bigwigs and the bible-fanatics, we want our independence.'

'I must go into town and have a look before they take it down.'

'What'll be on the agenda at the Casa del Pueblo meeting this week?' Endika asked.

'Depends on the latest reports about the Fascist activities, the "disappeared" and how many have been killed by the murder gangs. Six months ago, the big issue was water, but now it's been side-lined. I'm sure the meeting will end up going around in circles, as it usually does, talking about the same thing over and over, never mind the agenda. I'm only staying for a while, but I expect Estebe will be bringing up the subject of Ander.'

'What good will that do?'

'What do you mean?'

'What will they know that we don't know already?'

'It's worthwhile asking the question at least. You never know, something might come up.'

Despite being in a quiet section of the garage, Luken lowered his voice and, alluding to the military side of the Casa del Pueblo that Endika was committed to, asked, 'What about the other meetings?'

'I was hoping you could tell me,' Endika replied with a shrug. 'We were told not to attend any further until we were given permission.'

'Our meeting this week will be a closed one, the first since Ander was killed.'

'Where will it be?'

'Don't know yet. One place it won't be is Estebe's house, not with Arossa there.'

'Wish I was coming along. I better get back,' Endika said and left.

***

One of the well-built mechanics approached Luken, spanner in hand and with a glum expression. 'There's a fault on the head of that 402.'

Luken detected nervousness in his mechanic. 'What's wrong with it, José?'

'The plug in the second cylinder won't tighten.'

Luken's face froze and his body flinched. 'Don't tell me you've sheared the threads?'

They went to the other end of the garage where the Peugeot was gutted, the engine sitting on a work stand. Luken took a plug spanner and tried tightening the spark plug. No good. 'Did you screw it in at the start by hand?'

'I couldn't, it was too stiff…'

'How many times have I told you never to screw in a plug without starting it by hand? It's the sure way of knowing that it's on the right threads.'

The mechanic gestured openly with his hands. 'I tried.'

'Did you clean the threads and put some oil on them?' Luken knew by the sudden change of expression on the man's face that he hadn't. He felt the anger all over his body so badly that he started to perspire and then, raising his voice, said, 'Do you know how much it costs to replace one of these? Of course you don't and you don't care either, do you?'

'I made a mistake…'

'That wasn't a mistake, it was just carelessness!' Unaware of the silence he had created among the other men, Luken stood back from the engine, paused for a moment then turned to look the mechanic straight in the face and quietly said, 'If you do something like that again you're finished here, José.'

He called Kerbasi over. 'See if you can recover that. Try and get a sleeve made up.'

With his hands still shaking, Luken went to his office, made a point of not slamming the door shut, and made a cup of coffee, thinking that no matter how often he emphasised correct practice, that wastrel mechanic never took his advice. And, unlike the rest of his staff, he was not going to be intimidated by the man's large physical presence or his attitude.

He thought back on losing his temper, comparing it to the incident with the police officer, where his inability to restrain his impulse was self-indulgent and ill-judged. Losing it with the mechanic, on the other hand, he decided, was fully justified, no other way would the man take his words seriously.

Later, he sat and watched as the lady owner of the Nervastella appeared outside. She stepped out of a taxi and although older than himself, stood upright and decorous. The intensely coloured silky blue dress, contrasted by the bright sunshine, added to her elegance. As she walked into his office her appearance and fragrance lifted his spirits.

'Have you finished the repair on my baby, Luken?'

He gave a little laugh. 'Your baby is almost ready, Señora Serrano. Would you like some coffee while it's being done?'

'Only if you can spice it up.'

Luken unlocked a drawer and poured a dash of brandy into an empty cup before topping it up with coffee. He dropped in a sugar lump, stirred the cup and said, 'I know you also like a little sweetness.'

The woman's eyes lit up and she tapped his hand. 'You remembered! You're sweetness itself, Luken. So, did you find much wrong with my car?'

'Just a leaking radiator, that's why it was overheating. It's been repaired and is now being refitted. Why don't you take your coffee and follow me out? You can sit in your baby and talk to me while I finish it.'

The men looked up at the stylish lady as she accompanied Luken across the floor and sat in the driver's seat.

'We haven't seen much of you recently. Don't you drive it much nowadays?' he asked, as he bolted down the radiator and filled it with coolant.

'I try to go out for a spin as often as I can, especially in the summer like this. There's nothing like sprinting up and down the hills to clear the head. My sister lives near Gorliz, beside a beautiful beach, and that's a drive I adore. It's a long run and I'll be on my way there first thing tomorrow morning. It's her birthday, you see, and I'm looking forward to the celebration. She always puts on a good get-together.'

Luken wiped the coolant from his hands with a rag. 'Start the engine and let it run for a few minutes.'

Señora Serrano did as instructed and the car burst into life.

'Do you still miss Ramon?' he asked.

She gripped the steering wheel tightly. 'I do, of course I do. This car helps me get out and about. But in the end, you always come home to an empty house.'

He topped up the coolant and screwed down the sealing cap. 'It'll be due a full service in about a month's time, bring it into me then. Do you want me to move it out for you?'

'That's okay, Luken, I can manage. Don't forget to send me the bill.'

He watched as she effortlessly manoeuvred the car around the other vehicles, past the lorry and out into the sunshine. A self-assured woman, she moved that car out better than most men would have done, he noted. He went out and watched her disappear up the road and wondered if she realised how much potential danger she was in, a wealthy woman taking a long trip away from home at a time like this.

***

An abandoned house – a *suhil* – vacant for many years and regarded as community property was now used to accommodate tug-of-war and other country competitions and festivals. The dwelling had been big enough for perhaps two families but now the ground floor, which had been used to accommodate farm animals, had been cleared and used as a hall. The upstairs rooms, split over three floors, were mostly empty. Rectangular in area, the house was located in a quiet valley and not visible from the road.

Luken drove to the rear of the building for the clandestine meeting where an armed sentry checked his identity and waved him on. He wondered why a covered lorry, parked alongside a few cars, would be brought to a meeting like this. He reached under the driver's seat to remove the pistol but then changed his mind, realising that he'd probably be searched and have the weapon removed.

Another sentry, smoking a stump of a cigar, recognised him and waved him through the archway door on the ground floor.

Inside, thirteen men stood around, indulging in loud conversation. He saw Estebe and went to join him at the side of the hall. Three other men sat around a table at the top end, apparently talking about matters relating to various papers spread out in front of them. Luken knew the men only by sight and that they led the military wing, not the political wing, of the Casa del Pueblo. This wasn't what he was expecting, the meetings must have been switched around, he decided. The Ikurrina flag was visible on a pole behind the table. He thought of Endika and Kerbasi and their antics at the cathedral.

Luken sensed a strange tension in the air, one of expectation. It seemed the meeting had been called at short notice, and he knew that usually meant something urgent had to be dealt with. He whispered to Estebe, 'What's going to happen here do you think?'

'I don't know, we'll have to wait and see. Look, it seems as if they're ready to start.'

Blindfolded, with their hands tied behind their backs and with make-shift shackles about their ankles, two Catholic priests and a police officer were pushed into the hall by three armed militiamen. Luken recognised the officer as the senior cop who'd recently stopped him at the checkpoint and confiscated his tools.

One of the men at the table, who Luken knew only as Xavier, stood and addressed the meeting. 'These men are traitors. The priests have been preaching about the "evils of leftist principles and the perverse iniquity in sticking to them". They urge their congregation to turn away from their evil ways and to embrace the values being advocated by the traditional forces now re-possessing Spain, the forces of Fascism determined to defeat Democracy. These sermons are not new, they've been preached for a long time now. They would have us accept the most oppressive and tyrannical forces that we have ever seen and to accept the union of the Catholic Church with the Spanish Nationalists. We would have expected a more humanitarian outlook from men of the cloth, as many others of their faith have shown. Of course, they have a personal interest, being in collusion with the rich and wealthy, as you know well enough. They think we're all communists who don't believe in God and would take their property and send them to prison.'

Luken and Estebe moved towards the front of the crowd where they watched the prisoners' reaction. The clerics were dressed in full length black cassocks, buttoned from their white collar down to their shoes. He recognised neither and reckoned that one was mid-fifties, from the school of fire and brimstone by the look of him, while the other was probably late thirties, possibly his novice. The younger one seemed edgy, turning his head from side to side as though he could see something despite being blindfolded, while the older man stood rigidly still. The police officer was also probably late thirties, in uniform but without his peaked cap. Like the elder cleric, he seemed unmoved. In spite of their apparent stoicism, Luken reckoned they had to be frightened.

The hubbub among the men was positive towards Xavier's speech with an occasional encouraging shout. Alarmed, Luken felt his mouth go dry as, all of a sudden, he suspected that the two priests were about to be executed. Something he never imagined the Casa del Pueblo would indulge in and could scarcely believe. And yet, what Xavier had said was true, these men in black were in positions of power and influence, intent on preventing the country from becoming a more equanimous society. And all just to preserve their own position of privilege.

The spokesman stared at the policeman. 'This so-called police officer has been less than forthright in his duties. He stops travellers and if they happen to be wealthy or of a rightist reputation he treats them favourably. If they are poor or of a non-rightist reputation he mistreats them and steals their property. Isn't that right, officer?'

No response came from the policeman, as if he didn't hear or care what was being said.

A man in the crowd went over and punched the officer in the mouth, knocking him to the ground. He fell heavily. Two militia guards pushed the man back and lifted the officer to his feet. Blood ran down his face and Luken reckoned that he had a few broken teeth while the attacker had a wildness in his eyes that struck Luken as full of hate.

'Worst of all,' the spokesman continued, thumping a fist on the table, 'this man has no principles. He takes bribes! If you get thrown in jail that's okay if your family can get hold of money, a lot of money. Otherwise you're in for a hard time and a long one at that.'

The spokesman gestured to the guards, who promptly removed the three prisoners from the hall. The crowd fell silent. Xavier asked, 'Does anyone want to say anything?'

Luken raised a hand. 'Can we give the cop a chance to redeem himself? If he gives back the money and the things he took, and we make it clear what'll happen to him if he doesn't mend his ways, then isn't that enough? A dead cop will bring us a lot of trouble. You know what they're like. Close-knit, they'll want revenge.'

'What interest have you in this?' the spokesman asked.

'He took a set of tools off me,' Luken replied and the crowd burst into laughter.

A show of hands was called for and the officer was narrowly reprieved. Xavier called for the officer to be brought back. 'You have an opportunity to redeem yourself. If you undertake to return all stolen goods, including money, to their rightful owners you may go free. Provided, of course, it never happens again.'

The lawman remained unmoved for several seconds as though expecting to hear more, maybe further conditions being laid down, then shrugged and nodded in the affirmative.

The officer was again removed from the hall, the two priests brought in, sentenced, and then pushed outside into the dark. Two cars were manoeuvred to face the building with their full headlights turned on. The clerics were still blind-folded; the younger one had difficulty standing. A militiaman went over and told him to lean against the wall. The elder priest's lips were moving as though in prayer.

Three of the militiamen took aim and Luken wondered if one of the rifles was fitted with a blank. As they fired at the behest of their superior he felt a numbness creep over him as though his internal eye had closed to shut out the repulsion of what he was seeing, two priests being shot in the chest.

He thought he saw a puff of smoke as they were hit but then maybe it was from a bullet that had passed through one and ricocheted off the wall. The two clerics fell into a heap.

'Are you shocked?' Estebe asked.

'I am. What will they do with the bodies?'

'I don't know, I don't want to know and neither should you. I'm not sure that was such a good idea, you asking for leniency for that cop. They might think that you're in collusion…'

'Without giving him a second chance, I think to kill a man for being a thief is too ruthless. A step too far.'

'It's more to do with the fact that he doesn't steal from the wealthy or those in sympathy with the Nationalists. He's gone to the trouble of establishing who's who so when and if the Fascists come to town he'll be able to point the finger. And, if you don't know, in other regions a lot of priests have been naming liberals, those they regard as socialist or anti-Catholic, who've subsequently been tortured and killed.'

Luken drove home playing the events of the evening in his head and wondered whether the things that Estebe had said were true. He had avoided reading newspaper reports of such events as there were conflicting stories as to who was to blame, with each side accusing the other.

Chapter 5

Miren gazed down the hill from the kitchen and watched her husband and son build up a pyramid of timbers for the bonfire. Already she sensed the excitement about the forthcoming festivities. She looked out for her sister and her two daughters who were expected to arrive soon. Her only sibling, Gechina, was younger and they wrote to each other on a weekly basis. Before putting the marmitako, a tuna fish casserole, on the stove to stew she prepared the starter plates. For dessert she had already baked a goxua cake, sponge with a cream base topped off with custard. Luken and Kasen had a savoury taste and for them she had made a few cheese tartlets with walnuts and quince jam.

When the preparations were finished she looked down the western side of the hill to see the taxicab make its way up along the winding bends.

Luken opened the doors and helped Gechina out of the front seat while the two girls, Errita and Sabine, immediately jumped out and ran down the field when they saw Kasen. They presented him with a toy soldier they had made out of fabric, buttons and pieces of wood. The elder sisters embraced and exchanged greetings.

'How's things in Otxandio?' Luken asked.

'Quiet, as usual, Luken. How are you getting on with the garage?'

'Wish I could say otherwise but it's just ticking over.'

The women set out the food and beverages on the outside table under the shade of a grove of pine trees. They brought out three glasses of cider, a bottle of txakoli wine and a large jug of lemonade along with the starter plates of cold meat, cheese, bread, and olives.

Luken went down to the children and drew them away from the waterwell where they had been throwing in stones, leaning over the edge, eagerly waiting to hear the splash at the bottom. He then started a game of tag.

'How's the job going, I hope that new boss of yours is not too pushy?' Miren asked.

'He's not bad once you get the work done,' Gechina replied. 'There's plenty of orders for the costumes and uniforms but it's tough. Long hours. Supervising the younger women can be a problem later in the afternoons, they get distracted so easily. I have to keep a tight watch on them at the sewing machines, he gets really annoyed when the uniforms have to be de-threaded and done again.'

'So, tell me all the latest. All the scandal.'

They tucked into the food and drink and the party atmosphere prevailed for the afternoon. In early evening the occasional dark clouds floated across the sky. Miren and Gechina sang and recited a few otoitz txikiak, little prayers from their childhood.

Farewell Holy Sun until tomorrow
Rise tomorrow as today
Now and forever may it be that way.

'When are we going to light it, Papá?' Kasen asked.

'As soon as the sun goes down,' Luken replied. 'We're not allowed to light it before that.'

'What happens if we do?'

'It'll go out after only one minute.'

'Why?'

'Because fires start better in the dark, and anyway they look much better in the dark.'

Kasen looked puzzled at the answer and Errita, Gechina's elder daughter was smiling, aware that Luken was joking.

At sunset, fires became visible down the valley and the children made sure that theirs was set alight too. The moon appeared casting its ghostly light on the surrounding countryside. They sat on the ground, around the crackling flames, and sipped more wine and lemonade, content to chat away and stare into the fire.

Too excited to sleep that night, Miren thought about the Sun Festival, taking place the following day. Responsible for organising the event, she recounted the arrangements she had made, trying to think if she had forgotten anything. It was a social convention that she cherished, a tradition that had been handed down from previous generations through her father; only in recent years had she, as a woman, been given such authority. She turned to Luken, who was reading. 'What did you think of Gechina today?'

'The same as I always do. Lovely. It's just a good thing I met you before her. Who knows what might have happened.'

'When we were young I used to push her around, as you know. It didn't bother her until one day when she got a piece of coal and fired it at me. That's where I got this mark.' Miren pointed to a small scar on her left temple.

'You told me that was from the branch of a tree when you were out on horseback?'

'That was a lie.'

'So, you didn't push Gechina around anymore after that?'

'We became close friends after that.'

The following morning, Miren, Gechina and her daughters dressed in traditional costumes for the festival. Driving into Durango, they remarked on the red, green and white buntings hanging from the townhouse windows and various specimens of the laubaru, the national motif, a Celtic cross with four petal-like symbols stemming out from the centre, also on display. The van had been cleaned and decorated in the same manner. Endika helped as they alighted from the van while Gechina fastened the brilliant red sashes around the girls' midriffs.

The rest of the young danzarines arrived and gathered excitedly in the town hall. Miren checked that they each had their costumes in trim. All wore the same white dresses, tiered with striking red hems and sashes, while the boys also wore red berets. Gechina placed Errita and Sabine along with girls according to their age group. Miren looked on as the pride showed in Gechina's face.

One of the younger dancers' mothers had arrived to ensure her daughter had not been left alone but Miren had already appointed an older girl as her guardian and helper.

'Are you sure you don't mind keeping an eye on Terese, Katarin?'

'Sure. I know Terese, she's a friend of my little sister.'

'There you are,' Miren said, turning to Terese's mother. 'She'll be well looked after.'

The procession moved off, dancing their way through the streets to the church where the youngsters placed themselves along the side aisles while a young town councillor waved the Ikurrina flag around in a ritual before a statue of the Blessed Virgin, the annual homage to the mother of Jesus. The hymns began with Franck's Panis Angelicus and soon the intense choral singing reverberated around the walls and side chapels. Some of the elderly ladies wiped tears from their eyes with their handkerchiefs.

When the ceremony finished the congregation applauded enthusiastically then dispersed and gathered around the food stalls now erected in the square and side streets where pintxos, tapas-like treats, and other local delicacies were given out along with glasses of txakoli.

Miren realised she had a grin on her face, thinking that it couldn't have gone better and felt the tension ease away. Light-hearted Basque music filled the air with skilled accordionists, flute and guitar players in action, adding to the celebratory atmosphere.

Miren and Gechina helped themselves to a few pintxos and a glass of wine then sat on stools in the shade. An elderly gentleman with a white moustache, a cane and txapela, sitting nearby, said, 'That was a nice presentation. Well done.'

'Esskerik Asko, Ramon,' Miren replied, thanking him, while munching on a mouthful of hake and tomato. 'They did exactly what they were supposed to do.'

'Do you miss your father?'

'Of course we do, especially at this time,' Gechina said. 'He loved days like this.'

'He was a great man for organising the festivals, just like his daughter.'

Miren tapped him on his shoulder in recognition of the compliment. 'How's Carla?'

'Not so good on her feet these days. She couldn't come this year.'

'I'm sorry to hear that.'

'I'll bring her back a few pintxos, she'll be happy with that.'

The two sisters walked through the busy streets to a field at the edge of the town and spotted Luken and Kasen in the crowd watching Endika participate in a tug-of-war contest. They waved, then made towards a children's outdoor crafts competition, where Errita and Sabine were taking part, making model dragonflies and spiders out of colourful fabric. Gechina was about to offer advice but was halted by the supervisor. 'Sorry, no helping. The children must do it themselves.'

Afterwards they went back to the town square over which a canvas shelter had been erected to shield the musicians from the sunshine. A wooden platform had also been set up for the experienced, costumed performers, the men and women performing the Dance of Arms before going on to the Dance of Light.

Onlookers joined in and Gechina and Miren couldn't resist participating.

When they took a rest, a young priest, Father Garai, appeared beside them. 'Are you enjoying yourself, Miren?'

'I am, it's wonderful, Father.' She saw a nervous look on his face.

'I shouldn't be here,' he said. 'You've heard about the two priests who disappeared?'

'Any word about them since?'

'Nothing. Father Mikel thinks these dances should be put off as a mark of respect.'

'For the times that we live in, who knows what might have happened, Father,' Miren replied. 'Let's hope they're all right. Would you like to dance?'

The cleric hesitated before saying, 'You'll have to show me what to do. Just for a few minutes.'

At the end of the dance, they sat down to watch other dancers participate and Miren reflected that maybe it had been insensitive to have asked Father Garai to dance. Especially with the disappearance of the two priests.

***

Luken and Kasen stepped down from the cart while Miren tied the reins of the mare to the bar at the rear of the church. The pews were almost full and they squeezed into the centre of one at the front. All women and children were on one side of the main aisle; all men on the other.

She followed the mass with Kasen, through the introductory rites and liturgy and went to receive communion. For the sermon, the parish priest took to the pulpit and delivered his lecture on the national confrontation in loud, forthright terms.

'My dear people, Catholics see this conflict as a religious crusade against atheism. Either it is won or Catholicism will disappear from the country. Those who take up the Republican cause are the enemies of God and of the nation. They will be forever subject to his wrath by being condemned to the torture of hell!'

Father Mikel raised his voice further and pointed a finger at the congregation. 'In this part of the country such a deadly poison has been spread and it has not gone unnoticed by the sacred powers. Two practising priests have disappeared, one of whom I knew myself and a more dedicated and revered man you could not meet. There are probably individuals in this church who know the perpetrators or are the perpetrators themselves! Let me tell you, your time at liberty will soon be over. I am holding everyone in this community responsible for the disappearance of these dedicated priests and it is incumbent upon you to come forward and name the criminals! The Nationalist armies are now starting the redemption of these lands and no mercy will be shown to those who have either participated or are aware of those who carried out these deeds and failed to come forward.'

The cleric cleared his throat and continued. 'It has come to my notice that certain films of a lustful nature have been shown in private theatres here in the province of Vizcaya. These have been brought in illegally from France and shown to male audiences. Watching such filth is an act of mortal sinfulness and the gates of hell are wide open for such sinners. If any man here has been indulging in this wickedness I order you to desist. As the Almighty begat Jesús Cristo as his only son on earth, the act of procreation is purely to bring children into this world.'

Father Mikel finished his vitriolic discourse, blessed his parishioners and stepped down from the dais.

Father Garai appeared before the girls' choir in the apse to initiate the sacred hymns. Despite the parish priest's caustic speech, Miren felt excitement at the part of the mass that she loved. She knew all the girls and her only regret was that she wasn't there singing with them.

Afterwards, Luken went off to visit Estebe's house while Miren waited outside to chat to some of her neighbours, the topic of nervous conversation being Father Mikel's sermon. Had anyone seen the missing priests? Or heard what had happened? Nobody offered any news, nobody had heard anything. Nobody had seen anything.

As the girls in the choir came out she noticed that Katarin wasn't wearing the coloured pink sash around her waist. The sash was a representation of good standing among girls within the Saint Francis Girls Sodality Society, a religious confraternity dedicated to a particular saint. The missing sash wasn't just a bad sign, but a punishment. The girl had a sullen look and while the others were chatting in groups, Katarin stood alone. Before Miren could talk to her she disappeared.

Father Garai came out and explained that Katarin had been seen dancing cheek to cheek with a boy. Father Mikel as parish priest had decreed that the girl be forbidden to wear the sash. Physical touching between boys and girls, of all ages, was absolutely forbidden for all unmarried couples.

Immediately, every other notion disappeared out of Miren's mind as she felt herself starting to rage at the idea. 'How could he do such a thing!? Katarin of all the girls who was always so devoted and so helpful. Now she's going to be ostracized and subjected to all sorts of gossip.'

Father Garai was taken aback by her reaction. 'You know how strict the church's teaching is on girls and boys touching.'

'That's ridiculous! Dancing is just harmless fun.'

The cleric said nothing more, seeing that Miren was not to be mollified. She took a disappointed Kasen away from playing with his friends and went home. On the way she made a deliberate effort not to exercise her anger on the mare as she felt it coming in waves. Next morning, she visited Katarin's family to offer support.

'I don't understand why he was so harsh with her,' her mother said. 'He could have told her not to let it happen again. Her father is very annoyed, saying she should have known better; now he won't speak to her.'

Not to be placated, Miren decided to pay a visit to the parish priest. She took the cart to town, tied it to the bar at the rear of the church and knocked on the door at the priests' house. The house-keeper gestured to the office at the top of the stairs. Miren gently tapped on Father Mikel's door and entered quietly when called. He stopped writing, looked up, smiled and invited her to sit and, given the welcome, she suspected that Father Garai had not spoken to him about the matter.

'Do you not think that it was severe, removing Katarin from the Saint Francis Girls Sodality?' she asked.

'Certainly not. It's lucky she wasn't also put out of the choir altogether.'

'So you left her in the choir so she could be seen as an example?'

She noticed him sitting back in his chair while considering the young woman before him, someone he regarded as a staunch supporter and ally of his church.

'Miren, you know there are rules laid down that we're obliged to follow. The church is quite clear on what can and cannot be accepted as moral behaviour…'

'I've difficulty believing that two young people enjoying a dance can be construed as not being moral, Father Mikel. Could you give her another chance, withdraw the order and if not at least let her attend the sodality meetings?'

'Young men and women must never touch each other. We've no choice but to accept these teachings.'

'I don't see why. I mean Katarin's reputation has now been ruined, her school companions won't talk to her. This is a reputation that will follow her, even as an adult. It's completely unjustified. Katarin who has always been such a good—'

'Now you listen to me, Miren. Maybe if you had impressed on her the importance of acting in a proper manner this would never have happened…'

'I'm not her dancing teacher and even if I was I still wouldn't see anything improper in what she was doing.' Miren felt the blood rush to her head and saw that Father Mikel was amazed at her, a woman, responding so indignantly to a parish priest.

The senior cleric took a deep breath as if to temper his reaction and said, 'I've been told that you invited Father Garai to take up one of those regional dances last Saturday. I'm instructing you not to encourage any priest to—'

'I suppose that's not moral either, asking a priest to dance!'

Father Mikel ignored her remark and returned to writing, an indication that as far as he was concerned, the conversation was over. Miren left the room and closed the door but not in the quiet manner in which she had entered.

She walked out into the streets and made a point of staying on the shaded side to help cool down, both from her temper and the heat of the sun. At the Ibaizabal River she sat under the overhanging branches of a larch tree, listening to the lapping waters, recollecting the conversation. She considered whether she had overstepped her position as a lay person, saying what she had to a representative of the Catholic Church and a senior one at that. After a good twenty minutes Miren decided no, whatever rules they had, Katarin was of good character and deserved forgiveness. And on her way home she stopped to reflect at the Kurutziaga Cross, the very symbol of forgiveness and hope.

***

Before dawn Estebe donned a traditional txapela and took a staff and rucksack that Arossa had packed. Inside was a canister of water, sandwiches and olives. He threw them into the back of the car and drove towards Oñati. He did the solo hike annually as a pilgrimage, the only time of the year when he felt at least partially spiritual and at times wondered whether it was the breath-taking views that gave him the uplift rather than the otherworldly reflections. Despite having read several theological works, the sacred theses never quite stood up to scrutiny; at heart he had difficulty with faith. He was a man of politics and of the real world. Nonetheless, he was not expecting this year's trip to be as uplifting as previous years; another expectation occupied his mind.

He parked at the Aránzazu Basilica, noticing that the dew had started to evaporate. After a walk, he came upon a tavern, a converted shepherd's hut where already there was a jovial din. It was like the middle of the day here, he thought, and the sun scarcely up. Tempted though he was to partake of a tankard of cider, he instead opted for a mug of coffee. Plenty of time for alcohol on the way down. There was a mixture of families, individuals and a group of what seemed initially like teenage boyscouts but in fact were Mendiogoizaleak – mountaineers who were devoted to Euskal Herria and the Blessed Virgin. Not wishing to socialize he sat for a time, ate some of the refreshments then proceeded up one of the Aizkorri Mountain trails.

Having been passed down from his father, the staff was worn smooth and it helped to keep his balance when leaned on through the steeper inclines. He pressed on through alternating patches of beech forest and meadow intertwined with narrow trails through the ascending slopes. He came upon a pagan era dolmen, a large flat stone perched on upright rocks which, he supposed, had been erected either in praise of the sun or as a tomb for a local ruler. Resting for a time, he mopped his brow and took a drink of water. The memory of his tough fighting days in the Ardennes with the French in 1917 came to mind. The killings in which he had participated weren't difficult to think about, knowing that the men he had killed were in equal measure out to kill him. Whoever was better at killing was all that mattered. What was not so easy to think about were the women he had seen abused and for whom he had done nothing. The rapes and beatings.

Back home he never spoke about it. Even when Ander in his teenage years pestered him incessantly, he never uttered a word other than to say he went to fight for a cause he believed in. And in time, everyone stopped asking. Now it was a tragic period buried in the past, one that he couldn't go back to nor do anything about only to feel remorse and shame that he could have done something at the time, but didn't.

After two hours he reached the rocky summit and although having been here on numerous occasions he still felt lifted by the view. In the sunshine the vista seemed like looking down from the heavens, a god-like perception across the valley and into the depths below, across the mountains and forests. On the far side of the valley he saw a goat standing at the peak of another Aizkorri Mountain top, even higher and much more precipitous than the one he stood on. How sure-footed goats are, he thought as the creature looked down the sheer rock face into the depths of the valley, hundreds of feet below.

A short distance below the summit he came upon two young mountaineers sitting on a grassy patch off the trail.

'You must have set out early?' he asked.

'We've been here since yesterday,' they pointed to several bivouacs at a clearing some distance below. 'We're on a retreat.'

'Are you being inspired?'

'We're fasting, water only for twenty-four hours. The only inspiration we're getting is a dream of a plateful of food.'

Estebe opened his rucksack and took a drink from the can of water. He ate the olives and offered one of the sandwiches to the boys. They agreed that either both or neither would partake. They decided after a short deliberation, to pass on the offer since there were only four more hours to go on the fast.

He finished the rest of the food and started on the alternate route down. Though not as difficult as the ascent, the walk had its own snags, and much of the path was over broken stony ground.

Arriving at a sanctuary church dedicated to the Blessed Virgin, he checked the time and realised he was slightly late. Inside with his beret removed, Estebe appeared to say a prayer below the statue of the Mother of Jesus. In fact, he was thinking of his dead son, Ander.

As he left the church his peripheral eye noticed a figure following him, his old colleague, Gabirel Araña. The two men sat on a tree trunk at a distance from the rear of the building.

'Do you still come up here regularly?' Estebe asked.

'I do but not to visit the church, as I used to. It's just to get out for a time. Can't remember the last time I saw you praying, Estebe.'

'Lip service on my part, literally. Have you anything for me?'

'Wish I had, the investigation into Ander's death is inconclusive —'

'Murder, you mean,' Estebe replied with impatience.

'Murder, apologies. We spoke to everyone and anyone who had any connection with Ander, including Kerbasi and Endika as you know. We talked to them separately and each confirmed what the other had said. The three of them had been working in the cave on Mount Miloatza and nothing out of the ordinary happened. It was thought that maybe the Requetés had followed them up there but if they had why would they single out Ander and let the other two go? We've been up there since and everything is intact.'

'We prevailed, with vigour, on the weapon and ammunition suppliers to give a full account of themselves. Anyone we spoke to will remember being asked.' Gabirel paused to let the implications of what he had said sink in. 'The pistol was probably a standard issue Eibar. Which doesn't necessarily mean it was an Espainola who did it. We spoke to a few people in Arakoa, which as you know, is the nearest village to Mount Miloatza. They said that there were some Requetés in the area at the time. Without anything more concrete it looks like they're most likely responsible.'

Estebe responded, 'I can't understand why Ander was singled out.'

'There's no way of knowing for sure where he was killed, they could have moved the body as a decoy. Maybe he was in the wrong place at the wrong time.'

The men sat in silence for a time.

'How are you coping, Estebe? I know this is the worst of fates that could befall a man.'

Estebe shrugged. 'It's difficult. Had he been killed on a battlefield, as we expected might have happened to us those years ago, I could understand and reconcile myself to it. But this … this cowardly, underhanded business of targeting an individual man, as those damned murder squads are doing, causes me no end of grief. What about you, Gabirel, how is it with you?'

'My home life is fine, but when you work in administration you're at the mercy of the political winds.'

Estebe nodded in acquiescence. 'Who knows what the future will bring. It's getting late and I better move on. Thanks, Gabirel for letting me know.'

'We'll still keep our ears and eyes open for any information that comes our way, Estebe. Give Arossa my regards.'

The men split up and Estebe started on the trail home. Though not having expected much in the way of news, he was disappointed at being no wiser after the conversation than before and although he trusted Gabirel, he felt there was something he wasn't being told. Anytime he had been involved in such interrogations himself, some new information had usually surfaced.

Estebe rested on the descent and noticed a mature red kite, a bird of prey, with wing-tip feathers splayed out as it soared above the open ground below. Perhaps a foreshadowing of things to come, he reflected, and regretted having told his wife the other purpose of his pilgrimage; now he'd have to face a questioning himself. As if things between Arossa and himself weren't bad enough.

Chapter 6

One afternoon, Señora Serrano and Robinson, the Englishman, with his helmet and goggles in hand, appeared at the door of Luken's garage.

'My motorcycle broke down a few kilometres out on the road to Bilbao and I was hoping you might fix it for me, Luken,' he said with a smile. 'This lady was kind enough to give me a lift.'

'What's wrong with it?'

'Can't select any gears, it's locked in neutral. It's a damn nuisance because I've to catch a sailing from Bilbao this evening.'

'I'll leave you gentlemen to it,' Señora Serrano said and departed.

They drove out to where the motorcycle had been abandoned and after starting the engine Luken observed, 'It looks like gearbox trouble right enough; the clutch seems okay.'

They removed the pannier cases and loaded the motorcycle into the van.

Three hours later with the gearbox stripped they examined the fractured primary shaft.

'We'll have to have a replacement sent from England,' Robinson said. 'If it's okay with you could I leave the bike here? Would you mind?'

'Not at all. What about your sailing?'

'I'll have to catch a taxi or something. I'm going to Bordeaux and on to Portsmouth.'

Glancing at a wall clock, Luken shook his head. 'You'll have trouble catching a taxi now.' He looked through the service book to see what jobs were scheduled and found nothing urgent. 'I'll drive you.' He went to the office and changed into his everyday clothes.

The mist had descended on Bilbao port when they arrived. Iron ore was being hoisted by dockside cranes into the cargo ships; barrels of oil, sacks of grain and other commodities were also being winched aboard. Ocean-going vessels floated alongside smaller craft, moored beside each other in the wider stretches.

Time was running short and Luken raced the van along the dockside until he came to the ship bound for Bordeaux. Robinson removed his bags. 'It's very decent of you doing this. I'll send you the shaft as soon as I can get my hands on one.'

A dockside officer checked Robinson's documents then hurried him up the gangway, which was hauled up no sooner than he'd reached the deck. A burst of smoke billowed out of the chimney stack as the ship tooted its farewell; the vessel cast off and turned about one hundred and eighty degrees to make its way to the open sea. Robinson gave a final wave and moved along the deck. Too late to return to work and to ease his limbs, Luken locked the car and took a stroll.

Walking along the dockside, he noticed rowing boats ferrying stevedores to the far bank or onto ships. He pressed on as far as the iron mills, picking up the repellent smell of burning coal and smoke until he came upon the massive foundries with their open, doorless work areas. From a distance he reckoned they were hundreds of metres high and felt the heat from the blazing furnaces. Men with goggles, dressed in leather overalls, used lengthy tongs to pour the molten metal into castings. It looks like hell, he thought.

He drove into the city, parked and went looking for a coffee shop. He saw delivery boys carrying supplies into shops and offices and pedestrians including pretty nannies dressed in white uniforms pushing prams along the elegant boulevard of Gran Via. Electric trams passed up and down, all clattering, and he felt a tiny sense of excitement at the bustle; how much busier it was compared to his own small town. Several years had passed since he had been to Bilbao City and he had forgotten what it was like.

He wandered into the Café La Granja in the Plaza Circular and ordered a coffee. Like the Parisian cafés, he recalled, where people came to while away the afternoons. He sat in a booth and took time to observe the high ceilings, the wrought iron columns, the long wooden bar and the art-deco lamps. Ladies in their finery took afternoon tea and cakes and gentlemen in their expensive suits smoked cigars with their coffee and brandy. How different the pleasant atmosphere and the clientele were here, he thought, in comparison to the scenario of the men in the steel factories, men working long hours every day with little time off and paid a pittance. A short distance away but worlds apart.

***

Luken was sitting in his office catching up on paperwork when an officer of the postal service appeared at the door carrying two packages.

He opened the packages to find one was a replacement shaft for Robinson's motorcycle while the other contained the tools that the police officer had stolen at the checkpoint. He examined the tools to find that they were all intact.

So, the cop did as he was asked, Luken thought and wondered if he had returned the money he had extorted from other people. Must ask around.

He spent most of the afternoon fitting the shaft and later took the motorcycle home. As he arrived, Miren and Kasen had taken out the mare and were about to go for a canter when the boy rushed over to admire the Ariel. 'Where did you get that, Papá?'

'It broke down and the owner asked me to fix it for him.'

'Can I go for a ride with you?'

'Of course you can.'

Miren looked at the bike, mounted the horse and asked, 'Fancy a race?'

'Why not. Kasen, climb up.'

The boy got onto the rear seat and wrapped his arms around his father. They headed out onto the road and although the motorcycle was faster, Miren took a side turn and guided the horse through rough open ground. Luken came upon a lorry that was going in the opposite direction and had to pull in.

The mare was tied to a tree while Miren sat on the grass waiting when the boys arrived, their hair blown out in all directions.

'Hard luck, you can never beat a woman on a horse. How did you like that, Kas?'

'It was great, it goes so fast. Could I go to school on it?'

'Someday maybe.'

The three of them stood around the mechanical wonder and Miren asked, 'Could I drive one of those things?'

'Well, you could always try,' Luken replied, surprised that he should have been bowled over by his wife's gumption.

'You could bring me to school on it,' Kasen said.

'What a picture that'd be,' she said, while Luken wondered whether the people in the town would accept a woman motorcyclist as normal. Probably not, he supposed, thinking of how so many seemed stuck in their ways, with outdated views. It would be looked on as unseemly.

***

Luken lay awake on Sunday morning and sniffed the coffee. He noticed a brown powder sprinkled on the bed covers while Miren made breakfast.

'Where did that come from? Maybe it's talcum or something,' he asked when she brought in a pancake and coffee.

'I've no idea. There's no such thing as brown talcum,' Miren replied while examining the powder. She looked up and pointed to a spider's web in the overhead beam peppered with the same powder.

Luken stood on a chair to get a closer look and declared: 'Woodworm. *KaKa, Zaharra!* Shit. Just when I was looking forward to having a rest. This has to be sorted straightaway.'

'Ah well,' Miren said as she removed the bed covers and dressed. 'I'll say a few prayers for you at mass. By the way, have you heard anything about those priests who disappeared?'

Luken flinched. 'No, I haven't. Maybe you could ask around after mass.'

'It's strange that two priests just disappear off the face of the earth and nobody seems to know anything about it.'

'Maybe they jumped over the wall when they discovered that celibacy is not for them and went off to a house of mala reputación in Barcelona.'

'Luken, for God's sake!' Miren grabbed her jacket and made for the door. 'See you after mass.'

He stared out the window after her, wondering when the truth about the two clerics would emerge.

Next day, waiting at the sawmill, an enterprise in which Endika had a part ownership, he watched as his brother arrived in a Berliet lorry.

Luken pointed to what looked like a prayer book in Endika's hand. 'What are you doing with that?'

'I was at mass.'

'Turning more religious as you get older?'

'I was always religious.'

Rather than argue the point further and since he was in a hurry, Luken said nothing while his brother removed the padlock and opened the barn-sized door. Inside, he went in behind the trade counter and switched on the electric light. 'What do you want?'

'I need to replace two flooring beams in the house.' Luken handed over the measurements. 'The same as what's already there. Woodworm got at them, bloody nuisance.'

'That'll be quite a job. Do you need help?'

'I will when I get the cavity open in the back wall. I'll let you know.'

'Of course. We'll do you a special deal, sir. Cash customer?' Endika jibed.

'I'm not going to answer that,' Luken replied while trying not to look up to the heavens.

At that point he noticed Father Mikel cycling across the open yard at the front of the mill and recalled Miren's recent description of his anti-liberal tirade and his ostracism of the dancing girl. 'Here comes Fire and Brimstone.'

The cleric parked his bicycle against the door and walked in. 'Ah, the terrible twins I see. Endika I need you to repair some furniture for me. One of the pews is quite shaky and the lectern needs looking at.'

'I could call down this evening?'

After agreeing to Endika's suggestion Father Mikel drew Luken aside. 'I didn't see you at mass yesterday?'

'I wasn't there.'

'Why not?'

'I'd something important to do. Woodworm in the ceiling beams which have to be fixed before it gets out of control—'

'Nothing is more important than attending mass!' the priest thundered. 'If a child had to be rushed to hospital perhaps but a household repair hardly makes an excuse!'

Not to be spoken down to, Luken replied in an equally firm voice. 'If you don't mind, Father Mikel, I'll decide on what's important in my life and what isn't …'

'It's not up to you to decide on what is the will of God! I'll expect to see you at mass next Sunday. And it will not go unnoticed.'

Father Mikel stormed out, took his bicycle and pedalled away.

'What the hell is bothering him?' Luken asked.

'That's the first time I've seen someone arguing with a priest,' Endika replied.

'It's about time everyone did. That way we wouldn't have to kowtow to them. Here we are taking advice from men who get everything handed to them and their wisdom from a two-thousand-year-old book.'

'So you don't believe in God anymore…'

'I do but it doesn't matter whether I do or not. Do you have much dealings with them?'

'From time to time. I go to mass and get on fine with Father Mikel, we have the occasional chat. And they pay well—'

'Well they might. Since when did you get so religious?' Luken asked.

'I've always been fairly religious.'

'Who are you kidding?'

Afterwards Luken was satisfied at the way he had stood up to the cleric. As for Endika, he reckoned he was sniffing out as much business as he could get from the church. Best of luck to him.

Luken went to the builders' suppliers where he collected a box of terracotta roof tiles and drove to Estebe's house.

Estebe brought a ladder from a storage hut at the back of the house and they climbed onto the roof with the replacement tiles in hand. They removed the cracked tiles and the few fasteners wherever they were fitted.

'You should put a hat on that bald head of yours,' Luken remarked as he observed Estebe's mahogany-coloured crown in the bright sunshine.

'Don't need one.'

'In the heat up here, you need to be careful.'

'Speaking of being careful it's you and Miren who need to be. I heard about her argument with the parish priest.'

'That makes two of us.'

'What do you mean?'

'I had a row with him this morning.'

'What about?'

'Mass. I told him I'd only go when I'd nothing important to do. He wasn't happy with that.'

Estebe laughed, 'I'd say he wasn't. Luken, you need to recognise the all-pervasive influence of the church in this country. As the saying goes, "Cristo and Caesar live hand in glove." They have their hand in everything and you need to be cautious.'

'Miren is a woman ahead of her time,' he continued distractedly. 'Perhaps too far ahead of her time, arguing with a parish priest. The few rights women have been given in recent years are easily taken away.'

They finished the remainder of the tiles and climbed down from the roof. Luken returned the ladder to the outbuilding while Estebe poured out two tankards of cider. They sat in the kitchen.

Estebe said, 'I've been told that the police called to the council offices and demanded to see records on some individuals, what property they own and statements they'd made at meetings. I don't know who they were after but I'll find out. I'm not happy with the police just marching in and getting copies of records, we'll have to do something about that. You can help me. Maybe there'll be a fire.'

'And the fire brigade will be late getting there, I'm sure,' Luken said.

'No doubt. By the way, make sure I give you that list of safe-houses for our old friend Guillaume before you go to St Jean.'

***

Miren tied up the horse and cart at the rear of the church and sang to herself as she traipsed around the building. Despite the trouble with the parish priest she still loved conducting the choir and coaching individual girls, especially those turning up for the first time.

Father Garai was tidying up the sacristy when she walked in. He turned with a solemn face and explained that he had been given instructions to henceforth prepare and conduct the choir himself.

'Was that on Father Mikel's instructions?' she asked, feeling the spirit drain out of her.

'Sorry about this, Miren, but he believes that it's important to preserve the traditional values of the church.'

'It's probably more like he doesn't want to have me around stirring up what he thinks is trouble.'

'That might be part of it but he has also forbidden me to participate in any form of dancing.'

'That wasn't your fault, it was mine,' Miren replied, feeling the disappointment go even deeper. 'I'm sorry to have caused you all that trouble.'

'You did it in all innocence, Miren. Don't lose any sleep over it.'

She went out into the nave where the Saint Francis Girls' Sodality were gathering to practice singing for the solemn mass. She saw the girls' faces lift on seeing her and forced a smile while explaining that Father Garai would now be their choir master and urged them to do as he asked. She also noticed Katarin's dejected expression lift when she also urged them not to be unkind to her; she had made a mistake and after all, it wasn't all her fault, there was a boy who had made the same mistake as well.

A noteworthy citizen had died during the week and the mass was dedicated to his memory. Miren sat in a front pew and, during the singing of Mozart's Rex Tremendae, observed Katarin looking towards her while singing at the top of her voice.

Afterwards at the front of the church grounds she commended the girls' singing when Katarin approached. 'I know the mass is devoted to God but I sang that just for you.'

Miren baulked momentarily in surprise and resisted an urge to reach out and embrace the girl. Instead she just thanked her, regarding it as unwise to be seen publicly engaging in such an act of fondness. The other girls might look on Katarin disapprovingly, leading to even further ostracism. She suggested that they take a ride together to her parents' house.

Father Garai drew near. 'That was really good singing by the girls and it's thanks to you. I've only just arrived at this and it's obvious they knew what to do.'

'Don't thank me, Father, it's a natural gift that they have. Just needed to be teased out. I'm going to miss those rehearsals; I don't suppose there's any point in me asking Father Mikel to reconsider?'

'Not at the moment. Leave it for a while. I'll sound him out over the coming weeks. You know he's regarded as one of the more moderate parish priests?'

'I know, and God help those who have to live under traditional ones.'

'All things change in time, Miren.'

Most of the congregation had dispersed and Katarin and herself made their way home on the cart.

'I heard that you asked Father Mikel to let me wear the sash again,' Katarin said.

'It didn't do much good. The penance is so ridiculous.'

'My mother was hoping that you won't get into trouble.'

'I can deal with that, Katarin, don't worry about me. What does your father think about it now?'

'He still won't speak to me and I have to be careful what I say in front of him.'

'Like what, for example?'

'I can't say anything bad about anyone, especially my friends. Or those who were my friends. They won't speak to me either. The only one who will is Izarra and only then when there's nobody around.'

'That's a start, isn't it? Over time the others will follow,' Miren replied, trying to restore the girl's confidence even though she scarcely believed her own words.

***

Miren wasn't keen on working the night shift but at least it was quieter than daytime duties. At the nurses' station she signed in and chatted briefly to the matron, Sister Alicia, before starting her rounds.

Orderlies were removing the remains of the evening meal and cleaning the floors. She methodically went through the medical record on each flipchart before dispensing the fluids and tablets. This evening there was an unusually relaxed air in most of the wards. Some patients were playing dominos, others backgammon. The overall atmosphere at the hospital had in fact improved in recent weeks, she thought. At one contest of checkers she was invited to act as mediator. When could a player revoke a move he had made but not yet completed?

'I think once you move your piece into the next square and take your finger off it, that's it. If you don't remove your finger, you can still move it back. How about that?'

'That's just what I said,' one of the men replied. 'You took your finger off it so I win.'

'That's my last few céntimos gone, so,' the second man said glumly.

Darkness fell outside and the electric lights were switched on. Quietness descended when visiting time was up and friends and relations had departed. Some patients read newspapers and books in spite of the poor-quality light.

Sister Alicia switched off the ward lights at ten o'clock, leaving only the corridors and the nurses' station illuminated. She sat with Miren while they discussed and made note of the progress of individual patients and updated the hospital records.

'It's great that I have someone experienced like you here to help. I have to educate the younger ones,' the sister said.

'Well, they seem enthusiastic,' Miren replied. 'I'm sure in time they'll be quite able.'

They drank tea and settled into a quiet night, taking it in turns to visit each ward on the hour.

Around four o'clock, Miren awoke out of a minor doze and realised it was her turn; the sister was asleep. She went through the wards to find one man missing. Hesitantly visiting the men's lavatory, she looked down to see a man lying face up, in a pool of blood. It was Juan Joseba, the barber. Instinctively, her hands flew up to cover her mouth in shock.

Why would anyone want to kill Juan Joseba? Jesús, what on earth had he done to deserve this?

He'd been stabbed. She checked his pulse even though she knew he was already dead. She rushed to the nurse's station, roused the sister and together they inspected the body.

'Who, in God's name, could have done this?' Sister Alicia said after a close examination of the wounds. She whispered a prayer into the man's ear then stood up and blessed herself. 'We have to call the police.'

Miren placed a towel over Juan Joseba's face. They positioned two chairs in front of the closed door to prevent anyone from entering.

Neither said anything on the way back to the station and Miren noticed that the woman, like herself, was shaking. She thought how cowardly the act was, stabbing a man while attending a toilet and wondered who might have been responsible. The injuries were to the abdomen and neck so he must have seen his killer. He, or they, must have known about him prior to his hospitalisation. Although he'd been on cordial if not friendly terms with the men around him, he kept mostly to himself. Whoever it was, had had to use a knife, of course – a pistol shot would have woken the whole hospital.

At the station the sister called the hospital chaplain first, then the police.

The chaplain was only partly dressed when he arrived and Miren immediately took him to the scene of the murder. Expressing his anger at what lay before him, he knelt down and read out three prayers from his book.

Patients had woken and wanted to know what the fuss was about. All of them expressed shock at the killing. Two men approached, asking exactly what had happened, but the chaplain sent them on their way.

Four police officers arrived and immediately cordoned off the whole hospital. Nobody was allowed to either leave or enter the building. A sentry was placed at the door of the lavatory until two technicians arrived, a photographer who took pictures of the body and a fingerprint expert who took samples from the scene. Another lawman inspected the windows and back doors on the ground floor to confirm that there had been no forced entry.

Early the following morning, one of the officers set up a temporary workplace in the matron's office. The most senior officer called each patient and hospital worker in turn, demanding information about their witnessing of events.

When Miren's turn came she waited at the table while the officer in front of her read through a series of hospital papers. Another lawman on the far side of the room waded through more papers, making side notes on what he was reading.

The senior officer introduced himself. 'Did you know Señor Aguirre before he was admitted to this hospital?'

'No, I'd never seen him before.'

'That's strange, I see from your address that you both live in the Eguzkitza Valley.'

'I know, we'd both remarked on that fact. It's a big valley.'

The officer had a dour, humourless expression. 'Did your husband know him?'

'He did, Juan Joseba was his barber; he used to cut his hair.'

'Did they ever meet, apart from Señor Aguirre's shop?'

Miren thought for a moment. 'I don't think so.'

The lawman put on a grimmer expression and asked scornfully, 'Are you sure about that?'

Feeling the anger rising in her gut, Miren retorted, 'No, I'm not sure about that. What are you asking me for anyway?'

The officer was unperturbed by Miren's response. 'We have to establish all the facts surrounding this killing. We'll be talking to your husband. Do you know of anyone in this hospital who had a grudge or bore any ill-will against Señor Aguirre?'

Miren sat stone-faced. 'No.'

'But you were the one who found him?'

'Yes.'

'Did you see anyone move about in the ward at that time?'

'No.'

'What visitors did he have?'

'None that I saw.'

Later, Miren felt disconcerted. Does he think I killed him? she thought. Or maybe Luken? Ridiculous.

Later, Miren and Sister Alicia returned to their normal duties. The day nurses arrived and were taken aback to learn of the murder. For the rest of the day each patient was called into the office, either on foot or wheelchair, to give their statement.

At the end of the on-site investigation the senior officer thanked Sister Alicia for providing the facilities. 'I can assure you, sister, we will do everything in our power to establish who perpetrated this so you can carry out your duties without fear of any such acts of barbarism in future. In the meantime, if you or any of your staff hear of anything that might be relevant to the murder of Señor Aguirre, please call us immediately.'

Overnight, the pleasant ambiance that had developed in the hospital during the previous weeks disappeared and the strained atmosphere promptly returned. And in the weeks that followed, nothing more was heard about who had murdered Juan Joseba.

Chapter 7

Luken clipped the fuel canister onto the rear mounting and kick-started the motorcycle. With his goggles on and leather helmet fastened, he turned out onto the road and rode down the mountain. The most impressive two-wheeled machine he had ever come across; Robinson spared no expense, he thought. And he must have been prepared for long runs in barren lands where fuel top-ups were few and far between.

At the main road he turned east and headed for the French border. With the new gearbox shaft he kept the speed down. Not a good idea to push it to the limit until the mechanism was fully bedded in. The last time he'd had such a run on a bike it must have been seven or eight years ago, he reckoned, and he'd forgotten what fun it was. Then he realised, Miren would be only be too glad to have a go herself. Wait now. That might not be such a good idea; she might want to keep it for herself, and besides it'd be frowned upon by the townsfolk. And anyway, Robinson will want it back when he returns. His pride and joy.

How simple it was to see the speed and oil pressure gauges while scarcely having to look down. There was even a clock; few bikes had such luxury. The sound of the four cylinder engine was smooth and he thought of it as a touring rather than a sports machine. Just as well, less temptation to speed away. He took the scenic route overlooking the Bay of Biscay, enjoying the twists and turns through the forests while the motorcycle effortlessly ate up the kilometres. He pondered on the impending meeting with Guillaume, Estebe's old comrade and a man he had become friends with. A man with an interest in motor cars, like himself. Luken looked back with disappointment on the trip to the Le Mans twenty-four-hour motor race that they had had to cancel the previous month. The race had been called off because of an industrial dispute.

He showed his passport and pro-forma invoice papers to the border guards and explained that he was visiting a spares distributor in Bayonne to get parts for his motor business. The officers took his passport to the cabin office, made note of his details, stamped the book and let him go.

Market day and throngs of people from the surrounding countryside inspected the stalls in St Jean de Luz. Preserved meats, cheeses and vegetables, a range of home-made clothing and leather goods were on display, most of which were under canopies for sun protection.

The street-side Eskualduna Hotel overlooked the Avenue Joachim Labrouche. Luken parked the bike at the rear and walked around to the front door. Inside, the busy reception area and café were up a flight of stairs. Coffee and meals were being served. A man came down from the staircase and greeted him as he walked in. 'Haven't seen you in a long while.'

'This shouldn't be a surprise, Guillaume.'

'It's not. We weren't sure who it was goin' to be.'

'Would you rather someone else?'

Guillaume looked around before answering, 'So long as it's someone trustworthy. Would that happen to be you?'

'Must you ask?'

Guillaume smiled, went behind the bar. 'You'll have a coffee at least?'

Without waiting for an answer he poured out two cups of coffee and gestured towards an empty table by the window.

Luken looked across at the older man with the rough skin and pockmarked face as they sat down. 'How are things this side of the border?'

Guillaume nodded to the stalls outside. 'Everyday life goes on here but I worry about events in Paris. The government is so fucking unstable and corrupt. There's no proper governance and they don't seem to care about the rise of Germany. What about Euskal Herria?'

'Labour trouble. I think the factory owners are too hard-bitten. Men working twelve and fourteen hours every day and hardly able to look after themselves and their families. If we weren't under Espainiarra rule I'd say we'd be better off, we'd have a better chance of sorting such problems ourselves…'

'That's what I've always maintained,' Guillaume interrupted. 'Are you active in the Casa del Pueblo?'

'When called on, I do what I'm asked, but not the military activities. And I don't want to get involved at committee level – too much to do with the garage.'

'Understandable. They've plenty of volunteers anyway. How's Estebe? I was sorry to hear about Ander.'

'Estebe's still troubled about Ander's murder, as you might expect. I reckon he'll leave no stone unturned until he finds the killer or killers.'

'That's for sure. I only saw Ander when he was a little fella. Never met him in his adult life.'

'Ander was a decent man,' Luken replied. 'He could be awkward and stroppy at times but he was dedicated to his family and friends. Arossa was inconsolable, their one and only son.'

'Of course, she could hardly be any other way. She's a kindly woman, Arossa.'

Luken handed over a folded sheet of paper. 'Estebe gave me this list of safe houses for you if you ever have to leave France in a hurry. And I need to change some money as well.'

Guillaume handed two similar papers back and they each read through a list of names.

Guillaume looked behind momentarily then leaned forward. 'The first of those lists shows the local safe-houses. Now that you're here you should find out where they are. If you need somewhere safe, the last thing you'll want is to be rushing around at the last minute with some laquais chasin' your arse. Don't get caught with the second list, eat the paper if you have to. It's a list of wealthy men and clerics in Euskal Herria who've been feeding high-level information up the line and organisin' financial support for the Fascistas Españoles who, by the way, have added a few extra people to their so-called covert office here on Rue de la Republique. They now operate mainly from a villa on Avenue Larreguy, rented by some right-wing Action Française bastard. Now you know where that list came from. We have a contact there who reckons he's still not under suspicion. I hope he's right, he'll soon be a dead man otherwise.'

'Could you show me where some of those houses are today?' Luken asked. 'I have to go to Bayonne for some parts, so maybe we could go together.'

'Sure, but I have to stay until lunchtime, can't leave with just one waitress here. We can go when Marie arrives. You can have some lunch. By the way, you'll need to be careful around town, you never know who the hell is listenin', especially in the bars and cafés. Le Bar Basque, in particular.'

Guillaume went about the morning duties and left another coffee at the table. Right enough, Luken thought, he looked like an old war horse with a big belly. Battered and bruised but still hammering on, undeterred by whatever catastrophe was thrown at him. How different he looked compared to Estebe, small and scrawny but as tough as they come underneath. And Guillaume's speech was coarse and direct, unlike Estebe's more tactful manner.

He left the café and took a stroll around the market. Miren would have enjoyed this, he supposed, great range of stuff. He negotiated for a sack of white flour, as she had asked him.

The bar area was almost full and he left the sack behind the counter. A familiar face presented him with the lunch menu as he sat down.

'Luken Abaroa. Where have you been all these years?' the waitress asked.

He paused before replying, to make sure he got her name right, realising that Guillaume had mentioned it earlier, 'Marie, what are you doing here?'

'I've been working here for years now. It helps to top up what little we make in the shop.'

Images of the coterie of old and of carefree days swam into his mind. Places they'd spent the summer days; relaxing on the beach and fishing parties in the mountains.

'How's Vincente?' Luken asked, recalling her fiancé's name.

'He wasn't getting enough work and gave up the carpenter's job. Now we've a shoe shop. He's in Toulouse for a few days to get new stock. How's Miren?'

'Miren's good, she wants to learn how to ride a motorbike.'

'That doesn't surprise me. Always one for a bit of adventure.'

He made a selection for lunch and handed back the menu.

'It's getting busy; I'll come back to you later,' she said.

Having done his apprenticeship in the town years ago he expected that he might've recognised some of the clientele but Marie was the only one. Luken watched as she went about the lunchtime duties, offering menus and returning with hot and cold plates. She seemed to enjoy what she was doing, being familiar with many customers with whom she was having a jovial rapport. She certainly hadn't put on weight, he guessed, but what a fine full-bodied woman. Dressed in a white blouse with the top buttons undone and a long tight black skirt and with short brown hair, he thought she looked unmistakeably French. Even compared to the ladies he'd noticed in the shops in the town earlier where they wore elaborate dresses from the neck down to the ground, she was simply and suggestively dressed, like those he'd seen in Paris. How much more tolerant it was here compared to home where such dress would've been regarded as loose and sluttish. On the street she'd be frowned upon. In fact, she wouldn't want to dress like that in the street.

He had the *plat-de-jour* of haddock with a bottle of beer. Guillaume came along as he finished. 'Ready to go?'

Guillaume drove his Renault Vivasport at speed and the afternoon was spent swiftly touring the outer environs of the town where Luken was shown the dwellings of the men who could be relied upon for safe transit. They arrived at the distributor in Bayonne before closing and picked up the car parts.

On the return journey Guillaume slowed to a gentler pace and looked at his watch. 'We're too late to get to the bank now. I won't be able to change your money 'till tomorrow. Should've gone there first.'

'I'll have to stop over so. Will changing pesetas into francs be a problem?'

'No, I regularly have customers from Euskal Herria spendin' pesetas.'

Twilight was in the air as they arrived back at the hotel. Luken telephoned his garage for a message to be left with Miren, saying he wouldn't be home until the following day. They sat alongside old men drinking and chatting at the bar and after booking Luken into an upstairs room, Guillaume opened a bottle of wine. Cigar smoke permeated the air. They talked more politics and drank the bottle while Marie placed an assiette des olives on the bar. Luken thought of the place as a homely kind of business.

Guillaume stood. 'I have to visit some people, Luken. And probably won't get back 'till late. I'll see you in the morning.'

Men at the bar were finishing their pastis and diners were departing after the evening meal. The noise level dropped and Marie presented Luken with a menu. 'Didn't get a chance to come back to you earlier, always busy on market day.'

'C'est okay, Marie, you've a long working day. I'll just have a Croque Monsieur and another bottle of wine.'

The bar had almost emptied when he finished the sandwich and he called Marie, gesturing to the bottle saying, 'Bring over a glass for yourself and help me with this.'

She sat opposite and took a sip. 'What brings you to St Jean?'

'I've a garage in Durango and needed to get some spare parts.'

'So you work for yourself?'

'I took the plunge a few years ago. Though not great at the moment with the recession, it's okay, I've no regrets,' Luken replied, noticing that she had stopped checking on the few remaining customers and was relaxing in the chair with her elbows on the table.

'What do you do when you're not working here?' he asked.

'Just take it easy, tidy up at home, visit my mother and so on. This time of the year I bring my daughter Brigette down to the beach.'

'Didn't know you had a daughter. What age is she?'

'Eight. Do you ever think of the times we used to go up into the mountains on those wild trips on horseback?'

'How could I forget? Even the horses must have been chastised by what they saw!'

'Strip poker, do you remember?' she laughed. 'An older couple came by and he asked to join in. His wife was disgusted but we didn't care. We had no qualms.'

He felt the friendship they had had for each other as a group of happy-go-lucky companions all those years ago. Without being aware of it they had come close to each other over the table and he unthinkingly leaned over and kissed her. She kissed him back and they went on to remind each other of the capers they had indulged in.

When the bottle was empty he asked, 'Do you want to show me my room?'

She turned to see that the bar and reception area were empty. The chef had gone home and she locked the front door. Behind the bar, she picked up the key, saying, 'Give me a few minutes to tidy it up, Guillaume isn't always so good at having the rooms cleaned.'

He soon followed her upstairs and saw that she was replacing the pillowcase. The room was long and narrow with a single bed along opposite walls and a mat on the bare floorboards in between. Luken pulled over the shutters and approached her. He saw her smile and kissed her when she didn't move back.

'I used to fancy you when I was younger,' she said.

'What about now?'

Marie stared him in the face for a full ten seconds. 'You're still not bad.'

He unbuttoned the unopened buttons on her blouse. 'That's good to know.'

They undressed, got into bed and in a while Marie handed him a small package saying,

'I can't stay too long and here, put this on. I'm not taking any chances.'

'A condom. Where'd you get that?'

'Guillaume hides them behind the bar. He thinks I don't know.'

Next morning, alone in bed and unsure what had woken him, Luken heard the sound of men in the street and the doors banging in the hotel corridor. Remorseful at having let his urge get the better of him the previous evening, the after-effects of the alcohol made him feel even worse. Don't blame the wine, he thought, it was your own fault and nobody else's. Certainly not Marie's, even if she had been a willing participant. Sitting on the side of the bed, he castigated himself, disappointed with his inability to rein in his infidelity, especially after the vow he'd made to himself at the birth of his son, to remain faithful to Miren for the rest of his life.

The banging doors suggested that guests had already dressed and departed. The darkness in the room was alleviated by a trickle of light through the edge of the shutters. He tottered over and opened a shutter to be rewarded with a burst of sunshine. A group of about forty men were standing around opposite the hotel at the square in front of Les Halles. A few carried placards declaring themselves on strike. On a banner he saw a demand for better pay and working hours for farm workers. He opened the windows and stepped out onto the little balcony, seeing individuals gathered into small groups. Poorly dressed in threadbare, well-worn overalls, two men stood up on an improvised rostrum and spoke about the inhumane conditions under which they were bound to work. They described how the demands of industrial workers at the Renault automobile plant had been met after they had gone on strike. Female workers at the Citroën factory were reported as organising themselves into a women's union. Now the time had come for farm workers to do likewise and demand legislation to improve their working lives. A march to the town hall was taking place at eleven o'clock that morning and all workers were urged to participate.

Luken poured water from the jug over his head into the basin on the washstand, washed his face and hands, took a towel and went into the bathroom at the end of the corridor. He took a quick shallow bath, dressed and went down to the bar, where he ordered breakfast.

Feeling refreshed, he contemplated the possible strike at the Citroën factory. Getting parts was a lengthy process at the best of times, so now what was going to happen? Having to cancel the trip to Le Mans was bad enough, but no spare parts for his Citroën customers? Disaster. Hopefully they'd come to some agreement.

He ate the bread roll, soft cheese and ham and knocked back two cups of coffee. Guillaume came over and went to the window to watch the strikers. 'I was thinkin' about what we said yesterday. As if they'd been let out of prison since the Great War, people have been taking to the streets. Here, Italy, Spain. After the suffering of the war, they're no longer accepting the shit that's handed them. And now there's so many factions and parties we don't know how the hell it's goin' to end.'

'What do you think we can do?'

'Stick together with people of like mind. Whatever chance we have is together, dangerous times to have no friends. I'll have that money for you by noon, by the way. If those fellas don't break into the bank!'

Filling in the time, Luken took a walk around the town and along the promenade. On the way back he passed the town hall, where the protest had finished and the men were dispersing. At the hotel he folded Guillaume's papers, unscrewed the motorcycle's front seat and hid the papers in a compartment underneath. The sack of flour he collected from the bar and strapped to the rear seat, putting the motor parts into the bike's pannier bags. He kick started the engine and drove around to the front. At reception he settled his bill with Guillaume, who said, 'Tell Estebe I'll be over in about a month's time.'

Luken came out to discover that a man had taken the flour and was running away towards Avenue de Verdun. He ran after him and soon caught up. Luken grabbed his shoulder, spun him around and punched him in the mouth. The man dropped the flour and attempted to hit back but was caught off balance as Luken intercepted the punch with his right forearm and landed a left hook on his jaw. The man was thrown back and clearly shaken.

'Malchance!' Luken said close up to his face and noticed that the thief, most of whose teeth were rotten, was about his own age and completely dejected. The fellow started to walk away and only then Luken saw that he had a little girl with him.

Noticing how shoddily dressed they were, he sighed and felt the air and the victory drain out of him. He must be one of the farm workers, he thought, and picked up the flour and went after him.

'Take it,' he said, holding out the sack.

The man hesitated with a quizzical look, then took the flour.

'Is that your daughter?'

The man nodded slightly. Luken took a few centimes from his pocket and handed them to the petrified girl. 'I'm sorry I struck your Papá.'

The girl looked at him and at her father, confused. Luken tried to smile but had to look away, not knowing what to say or do. The man gestured to her to accept the offer.

Luken turned to him and said, *'Je suis desolé.'*

The man once more nodded briefly in acquiescence.

***

On the journey home Luken recalled that the thief's face had been the colour of mahogany and reckoned he spent every hour of the day working outside on a farm. And, with a start, recollecting the girl's terrified face, he realised that she was probably the same age as his own son. The anxiety spread through him and he unconsciously let the accelerator drop. The motorcycle stalled and came to a standstill. He put his foot down and heaved the machine onto its stand.

He walked a short distance up and down the hill despairingly replaying the events in his head. A few hours ago I was feeling so self-satisfied that I was above all that misery, he thought. Think of that poor fool, he hasn't got a chance. Neither has his daughter. What must be going through her head after she saw what happened to her Papá? Imagine if Kasen saw someone do that to me. In another time and place I could have been the flour thief myself.

In a while, Luken started the motorcycle and decided to take the longer mountain road home. He turned off the main route and scooted up the Route de Souhara and onto the steep Chemin de Sainte-Anne. Despite the powerful engine some of the slopes were so steep that he had to drop down to first gear. He crossed the border, through forests then up and down the undulating slopes through Elorrio towards Durango.

On arrival at his garage he left in the motor parts, filled the motorcycle and the extra canister with petrol. He conferred with the mechanics for an update on the repairs and services carried out in his absence then drank a cup of coffee and drove to Estebe's house.

***

Miren took the horse and cart and went to offer Juan Joseba's wife, Señora Aguirre, her condolences. She had noticed the cottage before, in a picturesque location on the up-sweep of a slope, but never known who the owner was. Only at the funeral had she seen his wife for the first time. Now she felt it was appropriate to see her and offer whatever help the woman might need.

She took a bag of ripe tomatoes from the cart and after several unanswered knocks on the front door, went to the rear of the cottage. Looking through the window, she turned the handle and found the back door unlocked. Taking a quick look around inside, she went through the tidy kitchen – where she left the tomatoes – and other rooms but no Señora Aguirre; no sign of her in any of the out-buildings either. Apart from a few hens scampering around, the place was silent and looked abandoned. She waited a while, strolling around the smallholding. The stalks on the onions hadn't been turned down and were now going to seed; the bean rows were withering in the heat. The wizened lettuce plants were also dying. Miren sensed an air of neglect about the place and wondered what might have happened.

She felt it impossible not to contemplate a dreadful denouement for the woman. Had she been involved in politics? In league with her husband? Had she been taken away and killed in some sort of reprisal?

Back at home, Miren sat in the shade on the veranda and watched Kasen and Matias, their neighbour's son, playing. Using makeshift goalposts they were practising penalty shots. The height of summer was near and in late afternoon the heat was stifling.

More overbearing was the recurring thought of Juan Joseba, the murdered man at the hospital, a memory she knew that she'd have to live with forever, having been the nurse who found him. Of all the places to kill someone, why a hospital? An institution dedicated to the preservation of life. The church had been packed out for the funeral; he had been a popular man. A peaceful man who ran a barber shop and who Luken described as a gentle soul. And now his wife had seemingly disappeared. Maybe there were things about him that Luken didn't know. Or maybe hadn't told her.

Other than Ander, this was the closest she'd been to someone who had been killed. Up to now, she'd never known any of the victims personally. Someone in the hospital must have carried out the murder. Maybe there'd been two of them; they'd waited for him to go to the toilet and followed him in. Not only that but there was a good chance that someone else had seen him, or them, and said nothing. And, who knew, it might lead to yet another murder.

She asked the boys if she could join in. They told her she'd have to get in goal and save four penalties out of six shots. Kasen went first and the ball went whizzing past her.

'Hard luck, Ama. You're too slow!'

Determined not to be beaten, she made a dive and fell over but managed to catch the second shot. Likewise she caught the next two and cheered herself. 'Ha! Now who's too slow?'

Kasen put in an effort and the last two went whizzing past. She had to concede defeat. Matias started his shots but it was obvious he was embarrassed to beat her.

'Come on, Matias, kick it harder!'

Señora Pérez appeared around the corner of the cottage. 'Kaixo, Miren.'

The game was abandoned and Miren said, 'They've been playing out there ever since you brought Matias.'

'I hope he wasn't any trouble?'

'Perish the thought. Would you like a glass of lemonade?'

'I won't have time this evening, Miren, too many things to do. I'll catch up with you over the weekend.'

That game was a bit of fun, she decided, it took away my preoccupation with that murder. For a while anyway.

Shortly afterwards, the weather broke with a thunderstorm. Evening fell and torrential rain cascaded down; the temperature dropped.

After Kasen had gone to bed, the murder scene haunted her yet again. It was unlike the hospital scenes she had witnessed over the years, of people dying from diseases and accidents, memories of which had never persisted for any length of time. She wandered throughout the house thinking, *Here I am drifting about like a ghost with only the sound of the rain beating off the roof. Reminds me of Lady Macbeth walking around Inverness Castle after her husband had murdered the king.* She removed the board blocking the staircase and tip-toed up to look out the window facing down the valley. A few lights glimmered in the cottages below and on the mountain slopes beyond. She hadn't been back to work since the killing and wondered how she would react on her return. No doubt the sister would be reassuring but the enthusiasm that she had for the job was eclipsed by the unease she felt about returning; not knowing what she might find, not only in daytime but especially on night duty. *What's keeping Luken? He should have been home by now. Maybe he had to stop in France for another night. I hope nothing's happened.*

Miren went to bed but sleep didn't come for a long time and even then, only faintly. The rain stopped and soon afterwards she heard the sound of the motorcycle pulling into the plot.

'What happened?' she asked Luken in the darkness.

'Got held up in St Jean,' Luken said as he removed his wet clothes, threw them into a basket, put on fresh shorts and got into bed. 'We left it too late to change money on the day I arrived. Had to stop over.'

When they embraced, Miren sensed a hazy smell of burnt wood and asked, 'Were there any bushfires on your way back?'

'Not that I noticed.'

'I get a smell of smoke.'

'There was a group of farmhands camped outside St Jean, gathered around a fire. Maybe my clothes picked up the smell.'

'What was that about?'

'They were on strike looking for more money and shorter hours. By the way, I got your bag of flour but gave it away.'

'Why?'

He described the incident with the flour thief and his daughter.

At the end Miren said, 'Luken, the man with the quick temper and the golden heart.'

He was about to doze off when she asked, 'When are you going to show me how to ride that motorcycle?'

'How about tomorrow evening?'

'Good. It might help get my mind off that murder. I can't sleep thinking about it.'

Luken held her and said, 'You know there's nothing you could have done to stop that?'

'I know.'

'And there's nothing I can say to put your mind at rest.'

'I don't think so.'

'Do you want a glass of brandy?'

'I had one before I came to bed and it didn't help. Just lie there and be nice to me.'

The following morning Luken brought in her early coffee and mentioned that she had in fact fallen asleep before him.

Chapter 8

The public meeting of the regional council was held in the town hall and forty to fifty townspeople were seated facing the rostrum. Miren sat at the front of the hall with her neighbour, Señora Pérez. Estebe and Luken, sitting in the centre, recognised the four councillors from previous meetings. A senior police officer was also present while printed papers were handed around, outlining the matters to be discussed.

To Luken's surprise the first item on the agenda was water. The head of the council called on one of his colleagues to update the audience. The man stood and stated that drilling was well advanced in the Larrinagatxu area to improve supply and named various villages where fresh water would soon be available. Building work was progressing on the pumping station at the site. A man posed a question from the floor, asking when the work would be completed.

The head councillor said that it was difficult to be specific as unfortunately matters were not helped by the strikes at the ore plants in Bilbao which were restricting the availability of steel. He pointed out that there was indeed a lot of unrest in the Euskal Herria and all over the Espania for that matter. Only yesterday it was reported that a strike had been called in a mill demanding the reinstatement of a man who had been sacked. The farm workers' dispute in

France was likely going to spread over the border into the nearest region, Guipuzkoa. While it was understandable that workers would seek better conditions, everyone was advised to keep a substantial supply of foodstuffs in case of serious disruption.

A well-dressed man in the audience, who Luken took to be from the wealthy upper classes, stood up and, when given the attention, submitted a question for the police officer at the table, 'What progress has been made in relation to the recent murder of the two priests?'

'As you probably know,' the officer replied, 'the decomposed bodies were found in a forest near Irun. The police there believe, as we do, that they were killed elsewhere. So far we have been unable to establish their last movements. The only information we have is that the housekeeper at St Matias's saw a lorry drive off at the time they disappeared. We checked out every lorry in the area matching her description and each of their owners and drivers have an alibi. I'm sorry to report that unless people come forward with more information we cannot progress much further—'

'It's a disgrace,' the man in the audience stood up and started speaking again but was waved down by the officer who continued, 'Having said that, there's no doubt in my mind that several people must know what happened, possibly even someone here at this meeting.'

Luken observed the policeman, who was intensely watching the people during his subsequent pause, looking, he thought, for any sudden head movements, a word between two people perhaps, that might suggest complicity or knowledge of the murders.

The man stood again. 'This is the most outrageous crime I've ever heard of. I knew Father Mateo myself and not only was he a good friend he was one of the most caring men I ever came across. As the officer said, I would urge anyone who knows anything to come forward.'

The head councillor stood to express, on behalf of the town, his revulsion at the killings. He then returned to the matters on the agenda, updating the assembly on the progress of the electrification programme, which had been unaffected by the unrest, and the building of new rural roads. He went on to read aloud from his notes, 'Following the passing of the Women's Rights Bill by majority vote at the Bilbao City Parliament, women over the age of twenty-five will now be entitled to vote in all elections, both local and national.'

At that, a big cheer went up from all the women in the hall and Luken saw Miren and Señora Pérez rise to their feet and clap.

Later, as they left the hall, Estebe said, 'Strange, he never mentioned the damage that was done to the council records.'

'Yes, very strange,' Luken replied. 'Fire has a way of erasing memories as well as records. Now the cops won't know who's in the right and who's in the left!'

***

Miren walked from the church to the market at the centre of town. The conversation with Father Garai had been friendly but fruitless. Although his superior had softened on the row that he'd had with her, he was unwilling to allow her to organise the choir practice, nor participate in the distribution of holy communion. Father Garai himself was disappointed as it meant that he was now snowed under with the extra work. Miren hadn't expected any better news and missed the bustle of the church activities, especially helping the young choir. And it was so dispiriting not to have the opportunity to sing with the senior choir herself; she knew it showed on her face. To make matters worse she still had a stiffness in her left leg where she had tumbled off the motorcycle during the week.

She went from stall to stall picking out aubergines and portions of salami, but didn't bother to bargain. Even the clothes and leather stalls which she'd normally inspect were ignored. At the Post Station she picked up a newspaper and a foreign letter addressed to Luken. She inspected the title on the green postage stamps that read Eire, which she didn't recognise until she noticed the drawing of the island of Ireland below.

Luken was already at the cottage when she arrived home. She put the groceries away and sat with him as he opened the letter, written in French.

Cher Luken,

It was a surprise when I got your recent letter and I was delighted to receive it.

And indeed I do remember that time in Paris, especially on the Boulevard San Michel. It was a marvellous evening, une nuit a souvenir.

In Ireland now we are still getting on our feet since the civil war ended about thirteen years ago. Of course it takes time for a country to develop as a nation. However, things have improved in recent years and I must say I'm optimistic about the future. Motor car sales have picked up and there is also service work.

So, how are things with you, Luken? Well, I hope. We see in the newspaper articles about troubles with the communists and anarchists and so forth. But I hope that you have not been affected. And how is your automobile business?

You must come to Ireland sometime. Likewise, I must come to Euskal Herria where I'm sure you get lots more sunshine than we do!

Wishing you and your family all the very best.

Padraig

'That's a nice letter,' Miren said while moving to sit on an armchair by the window. Luken read the letter again as she browsed through the newspaper. On the last page there was an article which she read aloud:

'Durango council offices suffered an unfortunate accident last Wednesday night when the storage room used to contain important records was severely damaged by fire. Minutes of recorded meetings dating back forty-three years were destroyed along with information regarding both elected council members, staff and temporary employees. The council head stated: "The cause of the fire seems to be due to an electrical fault. The building was being re-wired, ironically to prevent such a thing happening. For historical reasons it's quite a tragedy."'

'That was unfortunate,' Luken said.

'Did you have anything to do with it?'

'Why would you think that?'

'The fire was on the night that you came back smelling of smoke.'

'Why would I try to burn down the council offices?'

'I can't think of any reason, of course! But it seems strange. Did the Casa del Pueblo have anything to do with it, I wonder?'

'This is like an interrogation, Miren. Are you okay?'

'It all seems odd.'

Miren went outside, taking a bag of grain and a jug of water, and opened the gate to the hen run thinking that she was trying to connect unrelated events. The day had brought on a bad mood at the start and maybe that was pervading everything she thought and did. Nonetheless she couldn't shake off the empty feeling. Despite being aware of having fed them earlier in the day, she threw a handful of grain into the hens' feeding trough, then topped up the bowl of water and returned to the house with two fresh eggs.

***

Next morning, Luken put a collection of small automobile parts, a box of spark plugs and an ignition coil into the pannier bags on the rear of the motorcycle. Even though she knew he was waiting, Miren took her time preparing for the forthcoming task, a long run on the bike. To make the ride easier, she dressed in a pair of Luken's trousers and placed one of her best dresses in a bag. She sliced and wrapped a goxua cake into two parts, went outside and put the dress and cakes into the panniers, on top of the motor parts.

Feeling a little nervous, she put on her helmet and goggles, stood astride the bike and tried the kick-start. The engine fired on the third kick.

'Don't go too fast now,' Luken advised as he kissed her. Miren nodded her goodbye and pushed the motorcycle off the foot-stand.

The biggest problem she had was manoeuvring the hand-operated gear change into first but, once engaged, away she went out through the gate and onto the road. Moving up through the gears was easier and the temptation to let the machine rip was irresistible. The kilometres flew past but dropping down speed was not so easy; she gritted her teeth when she got the engine speed wrong and crunched the gears.

The upward inclines brought her through the scenic Cantabrian Mountains. Traffic was light and when going downhill and changing to the lower ratios she made a point of listening to the sound of the engine to enable her to mesh the gears comfortably. She eventually picked up the technique, feeling at ease that she was at last riding the machine as it should be.

At Urkiola she pulled in to the service station where Kerbasi and a workmate were attending to a motor car. Amused to see it was a woman rider, he laughed when she removed her helmet and goggles revealing her face – red with the wind and sunshine.

'Miren, you're the first lady I've ever seen riding a motorbike.'

'I hope I won't be the last,' she replied, handing him the parts out of the panniers. 'A lot of people think it's improper for a woman to be seen on one. That's not going to stop me.'

'There's not many like you, Miren. Come on and have a cup of coffee.'

'Just a quick one.'

They went to the nearby café. 'How many times have you been out on it?'

'This is the fifth time, I think, I'm finally getting the knack of the gears. It's great fun.'

'Did Robinson not come back for it? You know this used to be his garage.'

'Luken wants to buy it but hasn't heard anything from him. I'll need to get some petrol from you before I go, by the way.'

They soon returned down the hill and filled up the tank. She looked at her watch. 'I'd better make a move, I'm visiting my sister in Otxandio, there's a festival there today.'

She started the motorcycle and left, relishing the thought of seeing Gechina and her two daughters at the festival, not having seen them since the festivities in Durango. She laughed out loud. Hah! she thought. She'll be taken aback when she sees me like this.

On the road south of Urkiola, she relaxed to savour the exhilaration of driving the machine fast on the flat straight runs.

Approaching Otxandio she heard a low-pitched hum, faint at first then rapidly increasing in volume. She looked up to see a low-flying Breguet 19, a single-engine aircraft, pass directly overhead. She slowed while the aircraft turned and flew back the way it came and then realised there wasn't one but three aircraft swooping towards the town. She saw objects being dropped from the planes and, moments later, heard the booming sound of the explosions. The motorcycle stalled and the engine cut out when she unwittingly released the accelerator. The bike leaned over until she put down a foot at the last moment to steady herself.

Incredulous, Miren watched as the planes returned again to drop more explosives. Unsure whether to drop the bike and run into a wood by the roadside or turn around and race back towards home, she sat, unable to decide.

The aircraft flew off southwards in the direction of Logroño and silence returned. She dropped the motorcycle and felt both hands shaking. Tearing off her helmet and goggles, she sat on the grass by the roadside, the palms of her hands pressing into the flat of the ground to reassure herself by touching something real. She thought of her sister and her family and her panic grew.

She saw a man on a cart drawn by two horses hurrying past, away from the town. She ran after him but unable to catch up, returned to see a woman walking slowly towards her, her face blotchy from tears.

Miren approached. 'What happened, has anyone been hurt?'

Ignoring her, the woman kept walking and didn't answer while staring into the distance. She had no obvious injury; maybe she'd been deafened by the explosions, Miren thought.

Petrol from the motorcycle tank had spilled over the road and spoiled her dress and the two sections of goxua cake that had fallen out of the panniers. Righting the motorcycle, she kicked down repeatedly on the pedal but the engine refused to start. She picked up the helmet and goggles and pushed the bike into the trees where she found a concealed grove.

Ignoring the dress and cakes, she hurried down the road and into the town, her mind filled with dread on hearing the screams and shouts. People hurried to and fro. What horror was she was going to find around the next corner? Reaching Andikona Square she stopped in her tracks at the horrific sight before her. Old women wailing as they nursed the dead bodies of their daughters and grandsons; a decapitated woman and children with limbs hanging off. Blood and bodies everywhere. Some with such terrible injuries, she thought, had been mercifully killed outright. She asked after Gechina and her daughters. The townspeople, mostly women and children, couldn't tell her but cried out for help. The windows of the houses were shattered. The buildings themselves suffered varying degrees of damage, and the temporary stage was in splinters, with bunting and tinsel strewn over the ground. The stench of cordite and smoke hung in the air. She noticed a woman with two young girls walking away from the square and over towards a side street. She ran after them. When she caught up they turned, but it wasn't Gechina and her daughters.

She went back to survey each body. Eventually she discovered her sister and her elder daughter lying on the ground, among a group of women and children who had few obvious injuries. On close inspection she saw that they had been killed by particles of shrapnel that had pierced their chests and upper bodies.

Overcome with disbelief and then shock, she knelt before the bodies and brushed the hair away from their faces, her mind in utter despair. Blood had oozed out of Gechina and Errita's ears. In a short while, she wept uncontrollably.

Unaware of how long she knelt, a numbness eventually engulfed her, her inward eye shutting out the pain and hurt. She looked up to see an elderly woman standing over her. The woman was speaking but Miren couldn't hear the words.

'What?'

'Were they relations of yours?'

'Sister and niece,' Miren replied, taking off her jacket and covering their faces. Then the thought hit her. 'She has another daughter.' Feeling completely helpless, she stood and the woman embraced her.

Two local men arrived with makeshift stretchers and diplomatically explained that they would take the bodies to a room at the back of the cathedral.

The women walked around the square inspecting the other children but there was no sign of Sabine, Gechina's younger daughter. The woman took Miren through the open door of a house and asked after Gechina's second name and where she lived. Miren struggled to describe precisely where Gechina's house was, despite knowing it well, but on speaking the family's name, the elderly woman nodded and offered a comforting smile. She sat Miren at a table in the kitchen.

'I know where it is, not far from here. Stay here and I'll check at the house.'

Before leaving, the woman poured out a glass of brandy. 'Drink that straight down, the shock of it might help.'

Miren stared at the glass while the woman left the room.

When she returned Miren hadn't moved – still staring at the glass.

'Sabine is safe and well. Come on, she's with a neighbour.'

Miren followed the woman outdoors.

The five-year-old girl was drawing in a colouring book with another girl, the neighbour's daughter, at their home, a town house ten minutes' walk away.

Sabine's eyes widened. 'Aunt Miren. Where's Mamá? We heard a lot of horrible noises.'

Overcome with emotion, Miren was unable to answer and fought to hold back the tears.

'She won't be back for a while yet,' the neighbour interrupted, giving Miren a heartfelt glance. While Sabine and her friend continued their colouring, Miren joined the two women in another room.

The woman of the house introduced herself and said, 'Children of Sabine's age can't deal with death. It's a notion that they can't understand. For the time being, I think it's best to tell her that they've gone away for a time.'

'I have to agree with you,' the elderly lady said. 'I lost a son at her age and it took three years for his twin sister to understand, before she realised what it was about.'

Miren nodded her head in agreement, sensing the reality of it all starting to sink in.

'When is this killing going to stop?' the elderly woman said. 'All my life we've been faced with war. Wars past or wars coming. Is there any such thing as peacetime?'

Miren looked up from distractedly staring at the floor, feeling as if she was slowly emerging from a nightmare. 'Where's there a telephone? I must call my husband.'

'At the square. If it still works.'

'We have to go back and help,' Miren replied.

At the square other villagers from the area had come to assist. A doctor had set up a makeshift operating table in an archway and had whatever bandages, sutures, painkillers and other medicines that were in his own practice and in the local pharmacy.

After waiting in line at the telephone kiosk Miren rang through to Luken's garage. One of the men answered and said that news of the bombing had already spread and Luken was on his way.

Outside the kiosk she saw Kerbasi wandering around in a daze. Still in his mechanic's overalls, he broke down on seeing her. 'I was convinced you'd been killed,' he said and embraced her, his eyes all water. 'I contacted Luken, he's on the road. We couldn't get hold of Endika, he's in Donostia today. What about your sister?'

Miren tried but couldn't get the words out and shook her head. She gestured for him to follow to the improvised morgue and led him to the table where the two bodies lay. She removed the face coverings.

'Oh, Jesús!' he exclaimed on seeing Errita and Gechina's faces, innocent in death.

After several minutes in silence, he turned away and Miren put the coverings back.

Back at the square, Miren introduced herself to the doctor and offered assistance. They worked through the rest of the day doing what they could, fitting splints, cleaning and bandaging wounds. Local people took in some of the injured. Ambulances arrived from Vitoria Gasteiz and Bilbao. Equally as bad as dealing with the horrific wounds was listening to the innocent agony of the children asking why they had been attacked – 'Have we been bad?'

Even some of the adults couldn't understand what had happened, unaware that a war had come to their town.

With a sense of foreboding, Luken parked the van in a side street and was aghast at what he saw as he arrived in the square on foot. Most of the dead and injured had been taken away but he saw the dried blood and, in pockets, the pools of blood that had not yet dried up. He saw a crowd trying to placate a woman who was holding the hand of a girl lying dead on the ground as she repeated, 'Come on, Isabella, we have to find Papá, we have to find Papá.'

In a stupor and without even one soldier in sight, Luken couldn't comprehend why such an attack had been perpetrated on civilians, including women and children.

He looked around and with relief found Miren, assisting the doctor stitching up a little boy's stomach. Both were speechless when they embraced.

'Gechina and Errita are both dead,' Miren said eventually, wiping away her tears.

'Oh no! Where are they?'

'At a room by the Cathedral. At least Sabine is okay.'

Luken felt that he had been struck dumb. Miren took him to see the bodies. He touched Errita's face, thinking how tender her young skin felt, and assured himself that what he was seeing was real. And then Gechina's face, trying to think of something to say but finding himself unable, realising that he was in a state of shock himself.

Back at the square, Miren returned to assist the doctor. Luken stood back to watch her, overwhelmed with pride to see that she could put aside what had happened to her sister and niece to help the other victims of the air raid. A nurse to the core.

In a while, he and Kerbasi helped other casualties, driving the seriously wounded to hospital in Bilbao and those less injured to their homes.

Late that evening, Kerbasi went home and Miren and Luken went to Gechina's neighbour's house. The woman introduced herself and husband as Christina and Jaime and, in an utterly solemn atmosphere, they discussed the horrors of the day. All agreed that it was the most shocking thing they had ever seen and could never have imagined it happening; they'd be left with the trauma for the rest of their lives. Brandy was passed around in a fruitless attempt to deaden the distress. Christina went on to say that the low-flying aeroplanes had passed over the town earlier in the week dropping leaflets and now when they'd come again, the children had run out, calling, 'Leaflets! Leaflets!' Instead of running for cover they had died greeting the aircraft that had come to kill them.

Luken and Miren stayed in Gechina's house that night, where neither of them slept. Sabine was left with Christina since hers was a household with children whom she knew well.

Next morning, in the course of conversation with Christina and Jaime, they all agreed that it was better for Sabine to stay with Miren and her family, certainly for the time being, and probably indefinitely, seeing as her father had long since been separated from Gechina and moved to a different part of the country. At least Sabine had been spared the atrocity of seeing what had happened to her mother and sister. Jaime undertook to advise the mayor and town council of Sabine's whereabouts; Miren and Luken agreed to return for the funeral arrangements.

On the journey home Miren sat in the back of the van trying to keep Sabine busy and vowed never to let her return to Otxandio. She wondered how Sabine would react to living with a different family, without her mother, and how good she, Miren, would be as a substitute.

Passing through Urkiola and noticing the closed-up garage and café, she wondered what might have happened to herself, had she not stopped there the previous day. Killed or mutilated probably.

Chapter 9

Luken walked the mare to his neighbour's field. He returned to his stable and, using a pickaxe and shovel, began digging at the point furthest away from the door. He flung the dirt onto the nearby handcart. Soon he started to sweat but laboured on, driven by his memories of the horrific events in Otxandio. He remembered the child's ear that had been torn away by shrapnel that he had picked up on Andikona Square and had been at a loss what to do with. He had finally taken the ear to the doctor, who had gestured for him to leave it on a medicine chest. He thought of the seriously injured people he'd driven in the van to the hospital in Bilbao and the less seriously injured he'd taken home. When he returned, the ear was still there and he never found out to whom it belonged nor whether the child was alive or dead.

He removed his shirt and hung it on the wall. This is going to be a lot of work, he thought, making an underground bunker. Despite the intensity of the work, he knew the images of the bombings couldn't be erased. Neither on that morning nor ever. Equally, his abhorrence for the perpetrators wouldn't go away. How could you feel anything but hatred for such men? How could you look down on a child and blow it to pieces? Whatever doubts he had about the illicit pistol from Etxartea were well and truly gone now. Maybe he should order a few more? He wondered what weapons Estebe might have, especially with his wartime experience. Within twenty-four hours his outlook had changed from the questionable morality of killing a man to the realisation that at times it was fully justified. Why had those murdering pilots changed their allegiance from the government, the freely elected government, to the Fascist Nationalist Army? And what was the follow-up going to be? When would the ground forces come to town? He'd have to get one of those radio sets. Should have got one a long time ago.

Fatigued, he set down his tools and went to the house; it was time to follow Miren and Endika to Otxandio for the funeral. After a quick wash he put on a suit and jumped into the car. On the way he drove as fast as his customer's car would take him and on the upward slopes, cursed the vehicle for its lack of power as it crawled along.

He passed the shut-up garage in Urkiola, which Kerbasi had closed as a matter of respect; he was probably in Otxandio now himself. Hardly noticing the absence of other vehicles on the road, he pushed the little Topolino recklessly on the downward runs.

As he got to the foothills the car suddenly lost power. He looked into the rear view mirror to see a pall of blue smoke billowing out the back. The car went for a hundred metres and drifted onto the verge before coming to a standstill. He knew the engine was wrecked. Emitting a succession of profanities, he stepped out of the car to see the oil dripping from underneath the engine.

A long trail of oil was visible on the roadway and he realised he wasn't going to make it to the funeral unless someone came along and offered a lift. But, after the bombing, the road was deserted. Now with the heat and the rapidly decomposing bodies there would be no postponement. He wasn't bothered about the engine damage, knowing that he could rebuild it himself, but never to see Gechina and Errita one last time was heart-breaking. Resting his head on his elbows on the roof of the car, he closed his eyes and let the emotion of recent events race through him, the gentleness towards Kasen, fast asleep in the bed beside him, and towards Miren and Sabine as he saw them asleep beside each other. And now the frustration of not making it to the funeral. Why hadn't he left the bunker until later? The emotions welled up in him and he opened his eyes but didn't weep.

He locked the door and started walking towards Otxandio, unaware of the quietness of the countryside around him.

Miren glanced at her watch, wondering what was keeping him. She sat with Endika in the Otxandio town council office, where one of the pallid-faced representatives offered his condolences and explained the funeral arrangements. 'Is your husband not here?'

'On his way – he should be here soon.'

'You may have observed that there weren't many visible injuries on your sister and niece,' the councillor said. 'This isn't to offer you any comfort but I've been told that, because of where they were located, they were probably killed instantly by the shock wave.'

Miren said nothing and waited.

The councillor continued, 'We'll go out to the mortuary where you can confirm the identity of your sister and niece before the burial. The mass will be conducted there shortly. Unfortunately, as there are so many burials to be attended to, it'll be short and there won't be time for an individual service.'

'Has anything come to light as to why these bombings took place? I can't understand why they picked a festival day, when the town was packed with civilians,' Endika asked.

The councillor shrugged. 'Franco's army has said that it intends to exterminate all communists and "red" factions in the area. They want to spread terror. That's what the commanding officer for the area is on record having said. They want to kill everyone who does not think like they do…'

'How can children think like them?' Miren interrupted.

'And how can children be "reds" or communists?' Endika asked.

'I can't answer those questions,' the councillor said.

Miren grew aware that his voice had changed and he had to stop speaking momentarily to regain his composure.

After leaving the council offices, accompanied by Kerbasi, they drove out of Otxandio and up the gentle incline to the cemetery at the Hermitage of Saint Roque. Two groups of people were undertaking the return journey, one on foot, the other on horse and cart. The solemnity of the occasion was palpable and Miren knew it was going to be difficult containing herself as they passed through the arched entrance into the room that served as a mortuary. Other families were equally quiet, everyone dressed in dark clothing.

When their turn came, the councillor instructed one of the workmen to remove the covers

from the two coffins. Miren looked in to see the faces of her sibling and niece, already shrunken and discoloured. She gently stroked Gechina and Errita's heads and kissed each on the forehead before nodding to the councillor in recognition of their identities. Endika did likewise, kissing each of them on the forehead. She put a hand on his shoulder to steady herself.

The bell rang at the small adjacent chapel. A priest entered the room and introduced himself to each of the mourners, some of whom he knew. He shook hands, spoke briefly to each family about their relationship to the deceased, then started the service.

Afterwards, Endika and Kerbasi assisted the workmen carrying the coffins to the graveside. The cleric read out a number of prayers and blessed the coffin for another family before coming by. Of necessity the prayers and blessings were short and he soon moved on to another graveside. Followed by Endika, Miren threw a handful of soil onto the coffins. Two workmen approached and partially filled the grave. When the coffins were covered they explained that they had to move to another grave and advised that they would return later to complete the fill-in. One man placed a temporary wooden cover over the grave.

On the return journey to the council office, Miren wondered what had happened to Luken. Ordinarily she'd have been angry at his non-appearance but given his fondness for Gechina and Errita, she thought something must have happened to him. A darkness swept over her. Had the Fascist Army taken over Durango? Had he been picked up on his way?

As though reading her mind, Endika said, 'What the hell happened to Luken?'

'Something serious, I'm sure.'

The councillor had returned to the office and papers prepared for Sabine's adoption were on the table when they arrived.

'With just a single signature this will be a temporary guardianship,' he explained. 'I'll need your husband's signature to finalise the application. It normally takes two years for an adoption process but under the circumstances I'm sure that'll be set aside.'

On the drive out of town, neither of them spoke. When Miren turned and said something, she saw that Endika was distracted and hadn't heard what she'd said; he seemed hardly even to notice she was there. At the same time he was nervous, his hand shaking when he reached for the gear change. This war is affecting us all in different ways, she thought.

Twenty minutes out on the road, they came upon Luken walking towards them, sweating copiously and carrying his jacket over his shoulder. He climbed on board. 'I'm sorry, and before you ask, the bloody car broke down.'

Miren thought of scolding him, for not leaving the work until after the funeral but, given the sensitivity of the occasion, thought better of it and said nothing.

Endika turned the vehicle round. They headed back to the council offices where they completed the signing off of the adoption papers.

***

Luken, Miren, Estebe and Arossa sat around the table in Luken's house.

'How low can a man sink?' Arossa asked. 'How could he look down from his airplane, see the faces of the children and do what he did?'

'There's no limit to what they'll do,' Estebe said. 'They might have expected soldiers to be there and just dropped the bombs anyway.'

'What's going to happen next?' Miren asked.

'We're in for a rough time, one way or another. We'll have to carry on with the defences, the bunkers and so on,' Luken said.

'Bit late for that,' Miren replied.

Luken looked at his wife's pale face. She had stopped eating. 'It hasn't come here yet, Miren. We can't just do nothing.'

Arossa turned at the sound of children playing outside. 'How's Sabine?'

'During the day it's not too bad. Kasen and the other children keep her busy. She keeps asking why I took her away and where's Mamá and where's Errita. I keep repeating that they've gone away and won't be back for a while. Luken has moved into Kasen's room so I can keep her in bed with me. It's hard at night-time, she doesn't want me to go to the toilet, she's afraid I won't come back.'

'I know it's early days but you're welcome to leave Kasen and Sabine with us for a time,' Arossa said. 'Just to give yourself a break…'

'We've just got her here, for heaven's sake!' Mirren snapped. 'This is going to take a long time and she'll probably never get over it.'

'Kids adapt, Miren,' Arossa said softly. 'I've seen it at the school when a child lost a parent. If they're looked after and have a warm loving home they eventually come to terms with it, at least partially. And I've no doubt that's what Sabine will get here.'

'Looks like Etxartea was right,' Luken said, sitting back in his chair.

'Is that the man who owns the armaments factory?' Estebe asked.

Luken nodded. 'A customer of mine. He waited outside the garage early one morning last week just to tell me an invasion was coming.'

'How did he know?'

'He knows someone who knows someone in the Nationalist Army. I thought he was just being neurotic.'

'What else did he say?'

Ordinarily, Luken would have thought twice about mentioning more unpleasant details but given the fact that war had arrived, he felt there was no point in being discreet any longer.

'Germany is sending the latest bomber airplanes and Mussolini is sending thousands of troops.'

'Oh, my God!' Miren and Arossa exclaimed in unison.

'What do they want from us? I don't understand it,' Arossa said.

'You should know by now, woman, I've told you so many times, total compliance!' Estebe bellowed. 'Total compliance is what they want! They've even said it on the radio broadcasts. They want us to think and believe the same things as they do. Not to even dream about worker's rights or land reform – they demand total obedience to the State and to the Catholic Church.'

After a time, Luken asked, 'When's the next meeting of the town council?'

'Tomorrow evening. Expect it to be a long one,' Estebe replied.

Miren looked up from the table. 'I'm sorry the way I spoke so gruffly to you earlier, Arossa, it's just that I'm so worked up …'

'No need to apologise, Miren. It's understandable.'

When the visitors had gone, Luken and Miren put their grief to one side as best they could and went outside to join in the children's games.

Later, Miren mulled over the conversation they'd had and reflected on how brusquely Estebe had spoken down to Arossa, something that Luken would never do. She wondered how things were between them when they were at home. Difficult, she decided.

***

Luken drove into Durango and went to the electrical supplier on Zumalakarregi to view the radios on offer. The assistant turned on a Philips 834 and a Marconi 888, suggested waiting three or four minutes for the valves to heat up, then attended to another customer. Luken selected the medium wave band on both and turned the tuning dials. The sets picked up a strong signal from the national broadcaster in Bilbao and he listened awhile to music, turning the volume up and down on each radio for comparison. Another broadcast was from a French station in Biarritz and the sound was equally good. On the long wave band on the Marconi he faintly heard a transmission from the BBC in England that wasn't available on the Philips. His mind was made up.

He picked up Kasen and Sabine on the way back and invited them to open the surprise package when they got home. He placed it on the kitchen table and the kids soon got to work.

'A radio!' Kasen exclaimed. 'Switch it on, Papá!'

Luken fitted the antenna and a big cheer went up when he tuned into the Bilbao station and the music came through loud and clear. This sounds better here than it did in the shop, he thought, it must be because we're up higher, just like the assistant said.

He went to the storage shelf in the stable and returned with a coil of wire. The youngsters were still twiddling the dial listening to the different stations. He attached the wire to the aerial and spun it out through an open window and onto a metal rod. Moving the kids to one side, he switched the selector to long wave and turned the dial to pick up the BBC. Although scratchy, the sound of speech was clearly audible.

'What are they saying?' Sabine asked.

'They're talking in a different language. It's English, in another country, in another place.'

'Like Donostia?'

'Not exactly. It's much further away.'

Miren woke earlier than usual, sat up and looked around. Sunshine streamed in around the edges of the shutters. She slipped out of bed and stood by the window, thinking of the voices that had woken her. One of the shutters was slightly open and the garden visible but there was no sign of anyone. Getting back into bed, she heard the voices again – coming from the kitchen.

She tiptoed around the corner to see Sabine at the radio turning the tuning dial and listening to what the broadcasters were saying. Rather than face her immediately she waited awhile. Luken appeared and Miren put her finger to her lips.

After several minutes she approached. 'What are you doing, Sabine?'

'I wanted to listen to the radio.'

'Why do you keep changing the stations?'

'So I can hear Mamá. You said she had gone to another place.'

'Come on and have some breakfast, Sabine, and we'll talk about Mamá and Errita.'

They turned off the radio and were sitting around the kitchen table eating when Kasen appeared. Miren decided to wait until after breakfast when she could send him on an errand. As it happened, he gulped down his food and bolted out the door to his games; Sabine immediately ran out after him.

'She's forgotten already,' Luken said.

'Not for long, I'm sure. She'll remember.'

In a while, Sabine returned. 'We found a dead bird.'

Miren followed her to the edge of the pine grove where Kasen was examining the fledgling. She picked it up and caressed its tiny head then handed it to Sabine. 'Don't be afraid. Give it a pet, it won't harm you. It's a Pardillo.'

Sabine tentatively took the brown and grey bird and stroked it gently. 'What happened to it?'

'I don't know, maybe it crashed into a tree,' Miren replied. 'Kasen, go over to the barn and bring me back a spade. We have to bury it.'

He soon returned and Miren dug a small opening in the soil. 'Put the little bird in, Sabine.'

She knelt and placed the bird in the hole and with Miren, drew the soil over the grave. Sabine turned to see that Kasen had by now lost interest and wandered off. She got to her feet and ran after him.

Miren took the spade back to the barn thinking how easily children were distracted and glad that, for now at least, she didn't have to think of an explanation for Sabine as to what had happened to her mother and sister.

Chapter 10

At his garage, Luken sat in the Renault Nervastella belonging to Señora Serrano. The sort of automobile he admired most, with an eight-cylinder engine, not only was it engineered well but beautifully styled. He kneaded the soft leather seats and felt the instruments on the gleaming white dashboard with its octagonal clock. His second garage in Urkiola was doing okay for now but his aspirations went beyond that; he wanted to become the biggest dealership in Euskal Herria so that he would have the resources to develop his own brand of motor car. But now, with the unstable political situation, his ambitions were on hold.

Nonetheless, mechanical things were his natural talent. He had the ability to do such work almost unconsciously while thinking about other things. And although the bombings and killings in Otxandio still played heavily on his mind, the daily toil went on.

He replaced the engine oil and spark plugs and topped up the coolant. Leaving instructions for one of the men to collect him, he set out to return the vehicle to its owner.

Passing through villages on the road to Amorebieta, he became aware of people stopping to gaze at the three-metre long car whizzing past. The front seats were open to the air. Pity, he smiled to himself, that he hadn't had a chance to introduce Endika to Señora Serrano. His brother could have done well there, a classy, fun-loving woman. And it was about time he got himself a decent woman instead of all that boozing and fooling around.

He turned up into the driveway, unsurprised that the front gates were open. Her husband, when he was alive, always made a point of locking the gates whether he was coming or going. Spray from the water fountain blew across his face as he stepped out of the car and noticed the red and white water lilies floating on the surface. It was such a pleasant and calming garden, he thought, as he recalled Señor Serrano explaining, in years past, that the fountain didn't need electricity to work. The house was built on a slope and a stream further up the hill was partially diverted to top up a tank. Through gravitational pressure, the water flowed down through two separate pipes, one to top up the pond, the other to create the fountain.

The front door was wide open. She's getting even more careless, he thought. Inside he realised that it wasn't carelessness but something more sinister. The hall table was turned over and its lamp smashed; vandalised pictures were thrown on the floor. The other rooms were also damaged, glass chandeliers smashed, cabinets overturned and their contents flung about; upholstery cut open with knives. And there was a smell of alcohol emanating from the wine spills on the rugs.

Although little damage had been done to the kitchen area, some of the cooking utensils lay on the floor, eggs had been thrown at the walls and bread and salami had been cut up. The glass-panelled annexe was untouched. Two used coffee cups and glasses of water sat on the coffee table alongside two padded cane armchairs.

Upstairs, the bedrooms were untouched, the beds were made and the rooms in good order. An unopened suitcase lay on one of the beds. It seemed as though Señora Serrano had a visitor who had recently arrived. By the looks of things, they were in the annexe drinking coffee when thieves turned up.

Her late husband had had an import-export business in Bilbao and Luken knew that he had a reputation for being tyrannical with his workers. Now it looked as though his tyranny might have been revisited on his widow.

Back in the sitting room he saw it wasn't just wine spills on the floor but blood stains.

A car horn sounded outside. Dominick had come to collect him. He gestured for the mechanic to follow him in. Luken waited and heard Dominick's verbal reaction as he walked from room to room. After an initial obscenity he spoke out loud, 'What the hell happened here?'

Luken explained his suspicions, suggesting that Señora Serrano and her visitor had been abducted.

'Maybe the visitor abducted her?'

'And leave the case here? Hardly.'

'Let's get away from here,' Dominick said.

'That's the worst thing we could do. We have to report it. If someone saw us?'

They drove down to Amorebieta where a passer-by directed them to the municipal police station. Apprehensive as always when dealing with the law, Luken hoped against expectation that those inside were principled lawmen. What if the cop who had stopped him at the checkpoint appeared? Would he suspect his involvement in the Casa del Pueblo? Would this be just the excuse he'd need to lock him up?

Taking a deep breath, he lumbered up the steps with Dominick and pushed open the tall oak doors of the nineteenth century building.

Inside, the duty sergeant listened to their account, went to the rear of the offices and returned with a senior officer. Luken recognised neither. The officer instructed the sergeant to send a patrol to the house, investigate the site and cordon off the area. He took Luken and Dominick to his office and brought in a novice who made notes as they recounted the events again. They both handed over their well-worn identification papers and Luken included the bill and the car keys for the work on Señora Serrano's Renault.

Silence prevailed while the lawman read through the documents. Luken reckoned he must be seventy years of age. Clearly in deep thought, the officer looked up. 'Your garage, is that just on the outskirts of Durango, on the road to Irurtza?'

'That's it.'

The lawman leaned across the desk and looked closely into Luken's face. 'I know it and I know you too.'

Immediately, Luken felt rattled. What had the old cop got on him? Were he and Dominick in for a grilling and more? A beating?

The officer continued, 'Your father's name was Ignacio?'

Luken nodded in assent.

'I knew him well and I can see the resemblance. We served in the same battalion for France in the Great War. Your Papá was great at organising men. He moved up through the ranks much faster than I did. I knew your grandfather too. He was a prize-winner at weight-lifting.' The lawman gave out a laugh. 'Nobody messed with your grandfather.'

With the joviality that the officer was exuding, Luken relaxed and sensed the same with Dominick as he slouched down in his chair.

The policeman stood. 'I vaguely remember you as a niño, running around with your brother. Follow me outside.'

They went out to the street where the officer inspected the van. 'Leave that here and give me the keys. I'll get someone to bring you back. We'll need to talk again over the next few days. Hopefully we'll find out what happened to that woman.'

On the way back to Durango in the rear of a police van, Luken and Dominick reflected on their good fortune, coming across a decent cop.

'Do you remember him?' Dominick asked.

'No, not at all.'

***

Arossa unwound the celluloid film from the Leica camera in the shade of the kitchen and took it to the outhouse in a black bag. She pulled a curtain across the door and window and switched on the red overhead light. With the baths already prepared she cut the film into three strips and placed them in the developer fluid. When satisfied that the images were sufficiently advanced she put them into the stop and fixer liquids to freeze the process. After washing and drying the strips she viewed them through an enlarger to pick out the best quality negatives. While taking the photographs she had made a point of taking not one but three of each subject with different exposure levels set on the camera. Without a light gauge it was difficult to guess the correct level so she had taken three and now selected the sharpest. She reminded herself to procure a light gauge on her next visit to Bilbao, where they'd become a lot cheaper, apparently.

In all, she chose nine negatives, six of which were to be paper photographs and three enamelled. She picked a portrait of Luken, Miren and family, one of Ander, Endika and Estebe and a third of herself and Miren.

The enamelling process was lengthier than doing paper photos so she decided to do these first. She spread pigmented gelatine on a sheet of prepared paper then applied a sensitizing solution. When this had dried she clamped the first negative and the paper together between two sheets of glass then turned on another lamp to expose the combination to light. After a time she pressed the paper onto an enamelled steel plate. Satisfied that the image had become imprinted, she washed off the paper and dried the steel. Finally, she put the plate into a small furnace where the image burnished to permanence. While this was happening she repeated the procedure for the second plate.

A skill taught by her father, she took pride in creating the photographs and presenting them to family and friends. She always thought of him when occupied in photography and pondered how he was; they had always been close and he was due a visit. Maybe pick up a light gauge at the same time.

When the first plate had cooled, Arossa took it outside and smiled at the well-defined quality of the black and white image. The last photograph she had taken of Ander. What a pity she hadn't taken a photo of just Ander himself or even one of just him and Endika. Ander, my one and only son, she contemplated and, being alone, let the tears fall freely.

She gazed at the other images and reflected. Estebe was becoming a contemptuous man. He didn't want to hear her talk about anything and treated it with derision whenever she did. She could hardly get a word out of him after he went to see Gabirel Araña about the investigation into

Ander's murder. It wasn't as if she was trying to start an argument. And she was fed up making allowances for the fact that he had suffered during the Great War. He was also obsessed with this current political conflict. The sooner the school holidays were over the better, she could spend less time at home and hopefully the tension between them would play itself out.

Arossa fetched the enamelled photo of Luken and family. Now they had a second child and she was sure that Miren would love Sabine just as much as Kasen. She was a beautiful little girl. How, she wondered, did Miren and Luken get on behind closed doors? Somehow she couldn't see Miren putting up with the likes of Estebe. But then Luken was not one to get hot under the collar about risks and the rights and wrongs of things. He got out and did what he thought was fit without going over it endlessly. Like that time when he set up the garage, she remembered him saying that he just walked out of his old job and went around to customers seeking business from them directly. They gave him their custom because he had already established his reputation with them and when he needed spare parts he just went out and bought them.

***

Outside a cave in Gorbeia, Estebe looked on as a troop of about thirty Republican partisans took part in a training session; stripping down rifles and pistols and target practice. He approached the sergeant in charge. 'How are things shaping up?'

'There's a lot more enthusiasm now that the Fascists are on the move. We have to keep movin' ourselves which means havin' to move the fuckin' ammunition as well, a dangerous manoeuvre. The captain thinks it's better to change locations every time but I'm not so sure. Being caught with the ammunition is just as bad as being caught at training. The difference is that there's only two men instead of a whole troop. And if they're unlucky enough not to be killed they can be sweated to find out who the others are. The money can be kept anywhere and we're changing most of it into francs and pounds, not knowing for sure what's goin' to happen here.'

Estebe handed over a note. 'I've been given this list of names. From our contacts in France.'

The sergeant read through the names. 'There's eleven in all. I know at least four of these fuckers. Absolute bastards who think they're god's gift to the world. I see there's a few priests as well.'

'They have to go, they've been actively finding out those with serious Republican allegiances and passing it up the line. Not only that, they've been taking note of those who know the sympathisers even though they're not sympathetic themselves.'

'When were you thinkin' of?'

'There's no time to waste.'

'Does that mean today?'

'It does.'

'Do you want to take part?'

'Just to confirm who has been killed,' Estebe replied.

The sergeant walked down to the training field and selected two subordinate officers, one of whom was Endika.

They moved into the cave that was being used for storage and meetings and sat around a crude wooden table while an orderly distributed coffee. After handing around the list, Estebe explained the urgency of the situation. The Fascist army was on the move from the south and expected in the area soon. The men on the list were Fascist activists and as such were a death risk to anyone with Republican sympathies.

The two corporals indicated their willingness to participate in the executions. The sergeant said, 'As soon as this trainin' period is over you can round 'em up and bring them to St Augustine's Church in Arzagela, where the two so-called voices of Christ give out their fuckin' bile. I remember they even brought in strike-breakers when we were out lookin' for a decent wage. We can do it in the church grounds.'

They went through the list again to clarify where the victims were to be found and finished their coffee.

When Estebe arrived at the killing scene, six of the victims had already been shot. He saw Endika order the remaining victims to drag the dead bodies to the rear of the church. The other corporal then lined them up against the wall. All the victims were men and some had urinated or defecated themselves in terror. A strong smell of human faeces carried on the breeze.

'What are you going to do with the bodies?' Estebe asked.

'There's a big grave already prepared,' Endika replied, nodding to the hills.

Estebe thought of the last executions he had witnessed and knew there was no chance of a reprieve for anyone this time. And, no blindfolds this time, either. The conflict had now become overt and allegiances were out in the open. A free for all. He noted that Endika had surprisingly taken charge of the operation. In times past, he had had reservations about his commitment to the cause, never having seemed to take his obligations too seriously. Clearly, he'd had a change of heart.

Some townspeople cautiously approached the church when they heard the shots. A few shouted abuse at those about to be shot.

Endika and two other men took aim and shot the remaining victims on orders from their sergeant.

Estebe felt neither pain nor relief when he saw those whom he thought might have had him on their suspect list being killed. I've become immune to the sight and smell of death, he thought, that's bad, it could make me careless. Not so important in peacetime maybe, but potentially fatal in a war.

'How do you feel about having killed someone?' he asked Endika.

'I'm not thinking about it, not now anyway.'

When the slaughter was finished Estebe inspected the bodies to verify that they were all dead then ticked off the names on his copy list. Men had gone into the church and dragged out religious effigies. A statue of St John and one of the Virgin were smashed on the steps. Men came back with pickaxes and sledgehammers and destroyed the statue heads before urinating with laughter on the remains. Religious paintings were removed from the inside walls and thrown in a heap. Confessional and other wooden furnishings were thrown on the pile and set alight.

Estebe was unhappy with this turn of events. What should have been a series of military style executions was turning into mob-rule. He approached the sergeant. 'This is turning into quite a shambles.'

'It shows the level of hate towards the Catholic Church,' the sergeant replied. 'All they ever do is take our money and make us out to be the devil incarnate. They still think they're part of the inquisition. Them and their wealthy fuckin' consorts.'

Estebe nodded but said, 'Before they get even more carried away, it might be as well if you broke this up.'

The sergeant called his corporals and ordered them to do as Estebe suggested. One of the men engaged in looting complained that they wanted to finish the job but the soldiers were adamant and waved him and the rest of the throng away with their rifles.

'We should probably destroy these lists?' the sergeant asked.

'I'll need to keep one copy. It's important to keep a record of who and when. You might want to destroy yours.'

The sergeant went over to the smouldering pile of furniture and threw his death list into the fire. Estebe started his car, waved to Endika and further down the road noticed that the individual who'd complained about finishing the job was carrying a golden chalice.

**

Miren stood looking out of the kitchen window, having finished tidying up after breakfast. Being an overcast Friday morning, she thought sadly of the letter she would normally have got from Gechina on that day. No point in going to the Post Station this morning.

The smell of baking quickly filled the air when she placed a tray of biscuits she'd made into the oven. Outside, she fed the hens and returned with a bunch of dog roses and a selection of bougainvillea flowers, placing them in a glass vase at the centre of the kitchen table.

In a while, she heard the sound of a horse and cart and went out to see Arossa tying up the horse.

'You weren't stopped on the way?'

'No, but it crossed my mind when a few cars passed that I didn't recognise,' Arossa replied, handing Miren a small parcel from the cart. 'That's for you.'

She opened it immediately and was delighted with the enamelled image of Kasen, Sabine, Luken and herself.

'That's beautiful, Arossa. You're so good.'

They sat drinking tea and munching the warm biscuits while Miren's eye kept drifting back to the photograph.

'How's Luken these days?' Arossa asked.

'He's fine but finding it harder than usual to get money out of customers. He wants me to help, saying that men customers might be more amenable when prevailed upon by a woman. Now that women are supposed to be entitled to equal rights.'

'I wouldn't count on that just yet.'

'I'm certainly not. Anyway, I don't have time with work at the hospital. And Sabine needs special looking after. I have to keep impressing on Kasen the fact that he now has a sister and must share things. He's been too used to having everything his own way. Luken is very good with her, he treats her like one of his own.'

'I'm sure she'll grow up as normal as can be.'

'How's Estebe keeping?' Miren asked and immediately saw Arossa's expression turn dim.

'Doesn't say much these days. With the escalation of the war, the memories and pain of his fighting days have come back. It's almost impossible to talk to him. He's still working with the town council, doing administrative work. Dealing now with the building of bomb shelters. At least it keeps him occupied.'

'It's impossible to talk nowadays without bringing up this war,' Miren replied. 'I wondered how long it'd be before we spoke about it…'

'It's impossible to live without thinking about it, Miren. Is that a new radio?' Arossa gestured to the set on the sideboard.

'Luken bought it last week and connected up the aerial wire to an iron thing outside. We can hear lots of stations, both Euskera and Spanish. We can even get French and English ones. You certainly get to hear what's going on in the world. I'll show you.' When the receiver warmed up she turned the dial to a Donostia station.

They listened to the music broadcasts and later, sat up on hearing a news report:

'It has now been confirmed that the road from Euskal Herria into France has been closed. This follows the recent, daily migration of thousands of refugees across the border. Soldiers under the command of Nationalist Forces are now stationed at border checkpoints and are refusing transit. Refugees are urged to return home. The northern advancement of the Nationalist Army from across Nafarroa is continuing…'

Miren sensed an immediate change, the joviality giving way to an instinctive gloom.

'What's going to happen next?' Arossa asked.

'Who knows? Where are those people going to go, they must be scared out of their wits. The border is scarcely a hundred kilometres from here. There were reports a few days ago of strike leaders being shot, just for calling a strike. Luken and Endika are building a shelter under the stable but I don't know if it'll be any use if soldiers come over the hills.'

'Do you know of anyone who's left the country?'

'Señora Aguirre, Juan Joseba's wife, you know, the barber? I called up to her one day and she was gone; I later heard that she'd gone back to France. Apparently she's from Paris.'

'Was he the man who was killed in the hospital?'

'That's him.'

'I don't know her. Have you thought of leaving, Miren?'

'We have but I don't see any reason why we should. Don't really want to, everything we have is tied up here. This house and Luken's business.'

'Estebe won't leave under any circumstances. He tells me if I want to go he'll understand. I have some relations in Lapurdi and in Mexico but I haven't seen them in years, I hardly know them.'

They took a walk outside. A young ibex with its curved horns appeared, grazing in the woods overlooking the garden while they quietly approached to get a better look. The creature eyed them suspiciously then turned and walked away as they got nearer.

'They don't normally come up as far as here,' Miren said glumly. 'Maybe they've heard about the advancing Nationalist Army.'

They sat on the grass in the shade of the pine grove. Arossa gazed skywards. 'I remember when I heard that the Great War had broken out. It was this time of year as well, a beautiful day like today, blue skies. What a pity we can't stop time and just hold everything as it is now.'

'At least you haven't lost your ability to dream, Arossa.'

In a while they returned. Miren pulled up an assortment of vegetables, put them in a bag and left them in the back of the cart as Arossa untied the horse at the rear of the barn and climbed aboard.

'Are you okay going home on your own?' Miren asked.

'I'm fine going home, Miren.' Arossa smiled. 'It's only when I get there, the trouble starts.'

Miren watched as the cart lumbered slowly down the hill and thought on how difficult it must be for Arossa at home with Estebe now behaving like a house devil. He hadn't always been that way.

Chapter 11

At the sawmill, Endika loaded a dozen rough-cuts of timber onto the lorry and drove out to Luken's house. The recent executions of men in which he had played a large part dominated his mind. Reflecting on the importance of ensuring that all those targeted had been killed, he reckoned that even one escapee would be a disaster, having seen who had carried out the executions. Endlessly trying to avoid the details, he reminded himself that a war had arrived and the bloodbath could just as easily have been the other way around. We could have been on the receiving end. Whenever such deliberations surfaced, he switched his thinking as best he could, to the women and children who had been slaughtered in Otxandio. He swore to do everything he could to help win the war while struggling not to shed any tears.

He reversed the vehicle up to the stable door, shutting down the engine as Luken emptied a handcart of soil along the side of the house.

'I heard about your involvement at Arzagela,' Luken said.

'Had to be done.'

'The first time you killed someone.'

Endika hesitated before answering. 'I don't want to think about it.'

'How can you avoid it? I had some involvement as well, don't forget, having brought that list over.'

They took a brief, solemn stop for coffee. Sitting at the kitchen table, Endika said, 'I've trouble sleeping, as I expected, but I wouldn't have done it unless I thought it was defensible. One thing I hadn't expected was the smell, a lot of them shit themselves. Blood and shit. In time maybe, I'll get back to normal —'

'It'll be a long time before this country and everyone in it gets back to normal.'

'In the morning, I don't go through normal waking anymore. When I open my eyes I'm fully awake, ready to do whatever.'

'I'm sure you feel an underlying tension all the time now. Like me.'

Endika shrugged. 'What more can I say about it?'

'You did what you believed was justifiable. Remember when we got involved in the Casa del Pueblo, our purpose was to make this a better country. Where the rich and powerful couldn't lord it over us. As the French say, égalité, liberté, fraternité. That hasn't changed has it?'

'I don't suppose so.'

'Well then, it was never going to be easy. Come on, finish your coffee. We'll go out and get stuck into this digging, it'll help take your mind off it.'

Back outside, Endika gestured to the raw soil that Luken had dumped, 'What's this?'

'A raised vegetable bed for Miren,' Luken replied. 'I suppose she could plant flowers instead.'

'That's an idea, that'd be nice,' Endika, his arms folded, smiled sarcastically over the bare earth. 'It'll look good and there'll be a lovely smell of roses and things.'

'If we're still around to smell them!' Luken replied, amused at the triviality of the conversation. 'That's the first time I've laughed in a month.'

They removed the timbers from the lorry and stacked them inside the stable. Endika climbed down the ladder to where Luken had started to burrow out a horizontal tunnel. 'You've a lot done already.'

'You've come at the right time, I'm about ready to install the first uprights. I'm running out of areas to spread the soil. What's starting to come up now is only subsoil and useless for growing anything. I'll have to dump it in the old quarry.'

'Be as well to do that after hours. When you've a big enough load, I'll borrow the lorry.'

They installed two uprights on either side of the dug-out and manoeuvred a plank on top as a lintel. The perspiration soon broke out as they hacked their way into the earth.

'You heard about Señora Serrano and her sister?' Luken asked.

'Estebe told me.'

'The copper at the station knew Papá, they were in the French Army together. He remembered us as kids. The women were never found. I dread to think what happened to them, there were traces of blood on the rugs. All because she was married to a man of wealth, I'd say. Never met the sister but she was a lovely woman herself. Pity you never met her, things could have been different.'

That evening Luken lay awake alone, thinking about the killings that had taken place in Arzuela. Since he had procured the list with the victims' names, he had effectively played an active part in a major act of violence and the gravity of his actions had only hit home since talking to Endika earlier in the day. Although he hadn't fired any gun, his participation in the act was every bit as blameworthy as if he had. He wondered when he would be called upon to undertake similar acts in the future. One thing was for sure, there was no going back now, he was in over his head.

***

Sitting at the nurses' station, Miren rested after an exhausting night shift. She looked out the window as dawn broke. Besides the usual injuries from farm accidents and industrial mishaps, many Republican patients were brought in from the fighting in Guipuzkoa. The injuries were horrific, especially the shrapnel wounds from the bombing near the French border where, as well as missing limbs and torso wounds, some faces had been badly mutilated. Occasionally a man screamed with pain and a nurse rushed to his bed or mattress with a morphine injection. Easily the worst day or night's work she had ever undertaken, never so many men suffering from intentionally inflicted injuries. With so much work still to be done she decided to stay on for the day shift.

Despite the pain, some of the men had time for small talk and asked if she would go out with them or meet after work for a drink or go to a dance maybe. Taking it in good spirits, she agreed to everything that was asked of her depending, she'd say, on which bar they had in mind. Knowing full well that they'd be incapable of such activities for a long time, she urged them to hurry up and get better and never mentioned that she had a husband.

One such individual with a major back injury had been eyeing her for several days.

'Did you know I was a flamenco dancer?' he asked. 'Before this war broke out, I spent every Thursday evening teaching beautiful women like you to dance.'

'I'd well believe it, Leon. A handsome, energetic man like yourself strikes me as being quite a lady's man.'

'Not at all, Miren! I'm only attracted to women of character and I can see that's exactly what you are, a woman of character. Some people think it just takes fitness to be a good dancer but it's not true. It needs fitness of course, but it also needs character to interpret the finer points of the dance. When I get back on my feet maybe you'd like to come to my studio and I'll teach you all the intricacies of flamenco?'

'I actually love dancing and I might just take you up on that, Leon,' she replied, doubting if the man would ever walk again, never mind go back to dancing.

Sister Alicia explained at the nurses' meeting that, although medical supplies were still coming from Bilbao, uncertainty surrounding suppliers meant that this could dry up anytime now that the land border with France was closed. Future supplies to the city would have to come by ship, a major worry due to the longer transit times. All nursing staff were urged to be careful when dispensing medication and only give the exact amount prescribed.

As the meeting finished, two military lorries pulled up outside. It looked to Miren as if they were getting another batch of wounded patients. The tailgate swung down and several troops jumped out. She and Sister Alicia went to the reception area as a sergeant pushed the door open. From the blue shirts she realised with a jolt that these were Falangist soldiers, aligned with the Fascist cause.

'Buenos días, Hermana,' the sergeant said. 'We're here to arrest any Republicans or reds you have here for treatment.'

More soldiers stormed in and made their way hurriedly to the wards.

'We only have patients here, we don't discriminate what their politics are,' Sister Alicia replied.

'That's very noble of you, Sister, but we can't be so lenient when it comes to dealing with murderers and killers.'

'What about the murderers you sent to kill the children in Otxandio?' Miren blurted out, feeling the blood rush to her head.

The soldier took a good look at Miren. 'That wasn't our doing. Republican forces did that to discredit our cause.'

'They did not, it was you. I was there and I saw it!' Miren replied.

Shouting could now be heard from the wards. Then a pistol shot rang out. One of the soldiers rushed out to tell the sergeant that a patient armed with a knife had tried to stab a fellow soldier. He was shot during the struggle. The sergeant left the two women and followed the soldier.

'Don't say anything more, Miren,' Sister Alicia said as they saw patients who could walk being marched at gunpoint out onto the trucks.

'Where are you taking them?' Miren asked.

'Don't worry, we'll look after them,' the trooper replied with a sycophantic smile.

The entire men's section of the hospital was in turmoil as the invading soldiers removed any patient who had what looked like a war wound. Older men not of military service age shouted obscenities at the soldiers and were either ignored or received a punch or a pistol butt in the face if they didn't shut up. Those unable to walk were taken out on stretchers and callously dumped into the trucks.

Leon, the man with the spinal injury, was taken out and flung off a stretcher and Miren put her hands to her mouth in distress as he screamed in pain.

The trucks filled up and were driven away.

While the other nurses went to help and reassure patients, Sister Alicia drew Miren into the office where they removed the boxes containing the patients' records and took them to the rear of the building and into the woods.

'Why are we doing this?' Miren asked.

'They'll know from the records all the patients who passed through here who were on military service. Not just those they've taken away.'

On their return, the sergeant was rummaging through the office cabinets. 'Where are the patients' files?'

Knowing that Sister Alicia would have difficulty lying, Miren said, 'They were sent to the administrative offices in Bilbao when your people starting killing innocent women and children.'

A weary nonchalant look appeared on the sergeant's face. He paused for several seconds then said, 'I don't believe you. I'm quite sure the files are here and we'll be back to find them.'

Ten minutes after he left, Sister Alicia and Miren returned to the woods, where they stuffed the papers into a suitcase. They returned to see that the nurses had removed the dead patient to the mortuary and went around calming the remaining patients as best they could. Many of the beds and all the floor mattresses were now unoccupied.

At the end of the shift, Miren waited uneasily with the suitcase for the bus to take her home. She wondered about the man who had been shot, the one with the knife; had he been the one who killed Juan Joseba? Luken had mentioned that Juan Joseba was almost certainly a Republican sympathiser and yet that man had been killed because he was a Republican. What was that all about? Had he been the killer? They would never know now.

Two other nurses waited alongside her and the normal banter that they indulged in was now overtaken by nervous chatter, each woman concerned with the possibility of more military visitations. Would the staff be investigated for their allegiances? And what about the women patients? Rumours were, women with possible war injuries were being given the same treatment as men.

Sister Alicia came along as the bus approached, and put her index finger over Miren's lips to prevent her from speaking. 'Don't say goodbye and more importantly, don't come back. It's too dangerous for you here.'

She turned to one of the other women. 'You too. It's too dangerous for you to be travelling that distance. Look after your family and yourselves.'

She watched as the women boarded the bus then nodded to the driver and the vehicle moved off.

Miren looked out the window, waved to the sister and wondered if she would ever see her again.

***

Luken went to the garage early and checked out the bookings for service. The only private customer business now was for actual breakdowns or essential maintenance, failing alternators, poor brakes and the like. People were hesitant to spend money. But commercial business was improving. The reason for that, he surmised, was that businessmen were making sure that trade got done; they didn't want to risk losing whatever business they still had if a lorry broke down. Competition was intense.

A lorry and a van were in for service and after that a trio of vans were expected. He left the supervision in Dominick's hands and set out on the road in the van.

At Urkiola, the light breeze blowing from the north combined with the elevation of the area helped to ease the discomfort. Peak summer meant that the heat was pervasive. Climbing out of the van, Luken noticed a grass snake wind its way into the undergrowth.

Along with Kerbasi at the office, he checked out the takings, the stock and possible bad debts. In a while they completed the accounts and walked to the nearby coffee shop.

'How's Miren bearing up?' Kerbasi asked.

'At times, she can't stop thinking about Otxandio and it floods her mind over again but at least with the kids she has things to occupy her time. When she's not at the hospital, of course.'

'You're a lucky man to have Miren.'

'How's your Ama?' Luken asked, surprised that Kerbasi was so forthright in expressing such an opinion.

'Health-wise she's all right but still worried about it. Health is so important with the old folks.'

'Their number one occupation,' Luken said. 'Have you been to Otxandio since?'

'No and I hear the Falangists are in town.'

'What? Shit! I've to collect the adoption papers for Sabine. Should have gone sooner. And the Ariel if it's still there. I'll pick it up on the way back. I hope the Falangists haven't taken over?'

'I don't know for sure. Men stopping for petrol have told me they've seen Falangist troops patrolling the area. You'd want to get your stuff and get out.'

After leaving Urkiola, Luken stopped at the roadside and with the engine running took out the pistol from the compartment under the driver's seat.

Otxandio was quiet, there were no vehicles in the town centre and the few stragglers around gave him suspicious looks. The blood stains on the square were still visible. Even though the town was deserted, he could feel the tension. He went to the council offices, where the front door was unlocked. Inside, the only person to be seen was a junior office worker.

'Where is everyone?' he asked.

'The senior staff are down at the town hall; all the others have gone home. I'm going myself now. What brings you here?'

Luken explained about the adoption and the young woman took him to the upstairs office where he had signed the various papers. She retrieved the file for Sabine from a wooden storage cabinet and looked through the documents. 'It's been stamped and embossed with the Mayor's seal.'

She handed him the file. 'You should go straight away.'

She disappeared downstairs and left him reading through the papers.

On his way down, he heard male voices outside. He returned to a first-floor window to see two armed Falangist infantrymen in their blue uniforms inspecting the van. One was trying to open the driver's door. Luken released the safety catch on his pistol. The soldiers spotted the open door into the offices, walked in and started searching the ground floor. When they went to the rear of the building Luken tip-toed down the stairs and out to the van. Quietly, he closed the driver's door and pulled out the choke to the end stop. He let off the handbrake, put the lever into first gear and with his foot to the floor on the accelerator, pulled the starter knob. He let the engine rip and immediately sped off. As he tore up the road, he checked the mirror to see the soldiers back out on the street. They don't have motorised transport – lucky me, he thought. That gives me a few minutes to get the bike.

On the outskirts of town, he stopped at the wood described by Miren and soon found the dusty motorcycle. On inspection, everything was untouched. I shouldn't be surprised, he thought, regular thieves are now probably preoccupied looking after their own skin rather than going around robbing stuff.

Luken picked up the helmet and goggles, pushed the bike across the thicket, lifted the tailgate on the van and, with an effort, manoeuvred it on board. On the way home, he wondered about the girl at the council office and hoped that she had been spared meeting the soldiers. You never knew what two jarheads would get up to when they got together. Especially when they were on the booze, which they usually were. It was good to have got the bike, Robinson apart. You never knew when it might be needed.

He looked in the mirror and saw the empty road behind, no military vehicles in pursuit. Luken thought of the motorcycle in the back and was glad he'd got the van rather than the saloon version of the vehicle. He tapped the Citroën dashboard, saying, 'If you were a horse, I'd kiss you.'

Later, the same day, Luken and Endika emerged from the bunker, stripped to the waist, perspiration all over their bodies. They washed and Endika fired up the stove to make coffee while Luken went to the neighbour's house to collect the youngsters.

'Now that the bunker is finished what are you going to store in it?' Endika asked as they sat around the kitchen table.

'Tinned and dried food maybe. The idea was to have protection from air raids.'

'Miren and the kids could stay there if ever those Fascist bastards come this way.'

Luken put a finger to his lips as an indication to his brother to watch his language in front of the young ones. Sabine and Kasen were playing checkers.

'Papá, can we go down the shelter now?' Kasen asked.

'Why not. But just for a quick visit.'

The four went over to the stable where Kasen climbed down after Endika, who insisted on carrying Sabine. Luken held up the hurricane lamp to show that there wasn't much to see, just a hollowed out tunnel to hide in.

Back outside, they put up a set of makeshift goalposts with Kasen and himself on one team and Sabine and Endika on the other. After a short game, the kids were each allowed to score the winning goals.

Retiring to the kitchen out of the sunshine, the youngsters used a piece of white chalk to mark out the lines for a game of hopscotch.

Luken gave out glasses of lemonade.

'She's a lovely kid,' Endika said, gazing at Sabine.

'Uncle Endika, will you bring us for a ride on your big lorry?' she asked.

'Of course I will. Where would you like to go?'

'I know,' Kasen interrupted. 'The bus station. We can pick up Ama on her way home!'

'Good timing, Kasen,' Luken said as he checked his watch.

On the way to town, he looked in the rear-view mirror to see the two kids bouncing up and down on the front seat of the truck and Endika with a big smile on his face.

The two vehicles pulled up opposite the station as Miren's bus lumbered up the incline. The stately vehicle's slow but steady hike came to a standstill at its allocated slot, the diesel engine making a clatter as it shut down.

Kasen and Sabine leaped down from the truck and ran over, waving up at Miren through the bars of the glassless windows. The driver's helper jumped out the front door and opened the second, passenger door then assisted several passengers to step onto the running board and down onto the street.

Miren followed, embraced the kids and pointed to the suitcase on the roof. The helper climbed up the ladder at the side of the bus like an agile primate and staggered back down with the loaded case, saying in a jocular voice, 'How many bodies have you in this?'

She barely managed a cold smile at the helper's intended joke. Luken thought better of enquiring as to what was in the case though Kasen had no such compunction. 'What's in the case, Ama?'

'No toys or games, only dull papers.'

Endika waved goodbye and went on his way.

On route home, Luken noted how quiet Miren was, but decided to wait until they were alone before asking why.

Sabine sat on Miren's knee while Kasen messed around in the back. After a while, he poked his head between the front seats. 'What are Fascist bastards, Ama?'

Miren looked accusingly at Luken, who said, 'Endika let it slip.'

'They're just bad men, Kasen,' she said. 'I'll tell you about them when you're older.'

'Why can't you tell me now —'

'Some things aren't right for you to know at your age!' Miren snapped. 'They're only for grown up people. You'll understand someday.'

As soon as they got home, she said, 'Okay, everyone, I've an idea. I have a load of useless papers that we have to burn. Let's make a bonfire!'

The children cheered in delight when Luken returned from the stable with a steel half barrel and set the kindling alight. He felt no need to ask Miren where the papers came from nor why she had brought them when he picked up an individual's file and read his personal details. The four of them tore up the documents while the kids delighted in throwing them into the fire.

'Who's Miguel Lopez?' Kasen asked as he read one of the files not yet burnt.

'He's a man who's gone away now,' Miren replied.

Luken watched and distracted Kasen whenever he might be tempted to read more names on the papers before casting them into the flames.

When the embers started to die down the youngsters lost interest and went off to play. Twilight fell and Luken looked at the glow on Miren's face from the fire. 'So what happened?'

She described the events at the hospital in depth, the brutal way that patients had been assaulted, one had been killed and so many including the handicapped had been carelessly thrown into the lorries and taken to a prison somewhere. Rumours at the hospital suggested that the soldiers were returning to the women's wards. Other treatment centres had apparently been checked to see if women patients had disjointed or injured shoulders – tell-tale signs of those who had been firing rifles. She told of Sister Alicia's instructions not to come back, it was too far and too risky. 'Now I've no more work.'

'That's the least of our worries.'

Miren just grunted. 'Hey, what about Sabine's adoption papers?'

'Got them this morning. Stopped for a chat with Kerbasi on the way then collected the papers in Otxandio. No trouble. I picked up the Ariel as well.'

'That's the only good thing I've heard all day.'

Throughout the evening Luken was aware of Miren's silence. When they went to bed he felt her drawing close for comfort and her desire to make love as a form, he thought, of reassurance. As they united, she wrapped her arms and legs around his body, pulling him ever closer.

Later, with perspiration-soaked bodies, they slept naked without bed covers. During the night he felt her warmth as she curled up to him and he reckoned on having done right by not explaining what had happened earlier in the day. She would forever have bad dreams about Otxandio, no point in adding to them. Nonetheless the conflict was getting closer day by day and he pondered how much longer it would be before it appeared at their front door.

He thought of Señora Serrano and her sports car; still nothing had been heard about her or her sister and he reckoned she was almost certainly dead.

Morningtime, Luken emptied out the half barrel onto the raw earth that was to become the new vegetable patch. He dug in the ashes in an over-indulgent effort to bury any scrap of evidence that was already destroyed.

Chapter 12

Arossa stepped off the bus with her attaché case and walked to the school in Relortoa, finding several cars parked inside the school gates. Unusual, she thought, seeing such vehicles on the first day back after the summer holidays. More often there'd be crowds of students milling around the yard exchanging stories of their vacation time or new pupils nervously getting to know each other.

Inside the building, she came upon two Karlismo soldiers who were rummaging through the storage cabinets.

'Where is everyone?' she asked suspiciously.

'Who are you?' one of the soldiers retorted.

'I'm a teacher, I work here.'

'Follow me.'

The trooper led her into the staff room where an improvised office had been set up. An armed soldier stood at the doorway while two military men, a Nationalist officer and a senior Karlismo, sat at a long desk at the top of the room. The curriculum manuals and other text books lay on the table in front of them. Some books had been thrown on the floor. The senior officer at the head of the desk pointed to a chair. 'Sit down.' Other teachers were seated in rows facing the officers.

The Karlismo approached and gestured for Arossa to write her name and address on a clipboard alongside the other staff names.

The senior officer spoke, 'I represent, if you didn't know, the Nationalist army and this is my colleague in the Karlist movement. We are allies in the war against the communist Republican coalition and we're here to investigate material that may have been used to promote that coalition.'

Arossa watched the men as they browsed through the books and papers making derisory remarks from time to time. They went through completed examination papers studying the contents and then noted the names and comments made by the correcting examiners. Such papers they kept to one side. Individual student names were also being recorded.

Arossa turned to one of her colleagues. 'Where are the students?'

'They were sent home.'

'Shut up! Be quiet!' the senior officer shouted at them.

Even with the windows wide open the heat pervaded the room. Arossa fanned a teenager's exercise book across her face to help cool down and watched the door soldier becoming fidgety, his blue shirt soaked in perspiration. One of the teachers gestured to the soldier to switch on the overhead fan. The old mechanism cranked up and settled into a gentle clack, creating some relief with the moving air.

Arossa wondered what the officers were looking for. This was standard material, the everyday subjects of language, mathematics and so on. What politics could they possibly read into such things? As time went on and with the silence, the tension increased rather than diminished and she couldn't relax, sensing the pressure at the back of her neck.

Two hours passed before the men finished examining the school documents and the senior officer declared, 'We are inspecting the content of your teachings here and so far we are disappointed to see that so much of it is nothing but leftist propaganda. Do you people want to see communists and antichrists taking over here?'

Nobody answered and he continued, 'This liberalism is nothing but a red, socialist idea to dishonour Christianity and ruin this country.'

He directed his attention to the elderly male teacher sitting at the front. 'Señor Ferrer, as the principal you are first and foremost responsible for corrupting the minds and souls of the young people in this secondary school.'

The man prepared to respond but the officer waved him down. 'If I want you to speak I'll tell you. I don't know how many students have passed through your hands but I can tell you one thing, there won't be any more.'

The officer read aloud from a paper on the desk, '"Above all you must develop your own reason and view of all things that come before you and not necessarily accept the teachings of anyone, no matter how important."… Did you write this?'

The headmaster nodded in assent.

The officer shook his head. 'Our children are being told not to believe the word of Christ.'

He grimaced at his watch and Arossa opined that his anxiety was due to an overrun on his allocated time. He signalled to the door soldier to remove the headmaster. The trooper took the man outside.

The pressure in her head had developed into a throbbing headache and Arossa gripped her attaché case tightly as the officer turned his attention to her. 'You are Señora Ybarra, the vice principal? I see the exercises you give are of the same substance as your headmaster. What does your husband do?'

'He works for the administration in Bilbao.'

'The government, you mean?'

'In public works, the roads, drainage and so on.'

The officer grimaced again. 'As a woman it's understandable that you were led into this morass of indoctrination. Have you any children?'

She paused and bit her lip. 'No.'

'Two salaries, no children and yet so many men looking for work. So much for the Republican's women's rights. Employing women will have to stop. Were it not for the fact that you're a woman you'd suffer the same fate as your headmaster.'

The officer turned to each staff member in turn and delivered his critique about their misplaced doctrines.

'This day marks a new start and a fresh curriculum will soon be implemented,' he declared. 'Everyone's job is terminated with immediate effect.'

By late afternoon the reprimands finished and each teacher was instructed to take a batch of papers and books of a political or philosophical type to an open space in the school yard. One of the soldiers poured a canister of petrol over the papers and instructed a teacher to set it alight. Arossa witnessed her copy of Why I am Not a Christian by Bertrand Russell go up in smoke.

As the flames gathered pace, some of the papers were blown around and the soldier gestured to a young male teacher to put them back into the fire. Arossa turned discreetly to the fellow. 'What's going to happen to Señor Ferrer, Matia?'

'Execution.'

Arossa gasped in disbelief. 'Surely he doesn't deserve that? He didn't hurt anyone.'

'The civil war has come to town, Arossa. Not just a military war but also an ideological one. You should go home as soon as you can.'

When the fire died down, the soldiers dispersed and the teachers made their way through the school out onto the street. Arossa hesitated, thinking of the attaché case she had left in the staff room. She tried to recollect what information it contained. Unsure, she hastily returned, found the room empty and retrieved the case.

'That was a brave thing to do, Arossa, going back into that room,' Matia said.

She looked around cautiously. 'I've an awful bloody headache now. I couldn't remember what other things I might've kept in it. Especially any of my husband's. Don't want to create trouble for him. Or anyone else for that matter.'

They walked towards the town centre and turned up a side kalea. In a doorway a dog panted in the shade. She quickly looked through the case to find textbooks on literature and language, a few papers and a sandwich. 'If they want to burn these books they can do it themselves next time, I'm not throwing them away.'

'Fighting words, Arossa.'

Despite feeling hungry, she couldn't eat and threw the sandwich to the dog, who hurriedly wolfed it down.

All the shops and outlets in the town had been closed and quietness prevailed except where a military vehicle was parked outside. They heard the carousing wherever they approached one and took an alternate route where possible, otherwise crossing the street.

'All Juan wanted was to inspire confidence in his students. He had only a few years to go before retirement,' she said. 'What's Señora Ferrer going to do?'

'What are any of us going to do? Looks like we're going back to serfdom.'

'And you, Matia?'

'Back to my father's farm. For the time being, anyway, until things have settled. If they ever do. Just a smallholding, barely enough to live on. He'll be so disappointed after all the extra work he took on to put me through university.'

Arossa noted that more people than usual had arrived at the bus station, many with loaded suitcases being stacked on the roofs of the buses. The normally boisterous atmosphere she experienced at such times had been supplanted by gravity. As last in the queue, she wondered if there'd be enough space inside for everyone.

When her turn came to step aboard, she turned. 'Look after yourself, Matia. I don't know if we'll ever meet again.'

Before he replied, a loud noise rang out. A number of rifles being fired at the same time. Silence spread throughout the bus and everyone stopped what they were doing. In a while the driver started the engine. Arossa and Matia stared at each other as the bus moved off but they didn't say goodbye.

***

Late on a Monday afternoon, Luken sat outside his house under the grove of pine trees drinking a tankard of cider while gazing down the slope into the Eguzkitza Valley and beyond towards the Cantabrian Mountains. He wondered how, in simple terms, the conflict would affect the day to day life of Miren and his two children. The kids were at school but for how much longer? From what Arossa had said over the weekend, apart from staunch Catholic disciples, all teachers were going to be out of a job and the schoolbooks completely re-written with a different version of history.

He went to the kitchen and returned with another tankard of cider. As he sat, a car made its way up the hill throwing a cloud of dust and dirt in its wake. He recognised it as Estebe's Renault and thought it ominous to see him during the working day – normally he'd be in the office on a Monday.

The car turned into the plot and Estebe leaped out. He hurried over and with an animated look, said, 'You've got to leave the country right away!'

'What!? Leave the country?'

'Miren is in big trouble. Someone saw Sister Alicia and her remove the records from the hospital. The sister is under arrest, possibly even being tortured. They know Miren took the records home. As far as the Fascists are concerned, hiding Republican records is the same as being Republican, an executable offence. And she certainly wouldn't get any support from the church after the fracas she had with Father Mikel. You have to get her out of the country, now!'

'How did you find out?' Luken asked, trying to steady himself.

'One of the surgeons in the hospital, he came to the office specially. You'll have to go and get her and the children. You know it's impossible to get through to France by road so you'll have to bring them to Bilbao and leave by sea. Women and children are already being evacuated...'

'Jesús Kristo! Take them where?' Luken asked, getting more jittery by the second.

'Anywhere, it doesn't matter where. The first place they can get to outside this country. You can join them later. Arossa and myself will come up later to help. Go!'

Luken took the keys from the kitchen, jumped into the van and sped off down the hill.

***

'We've only got one suitcase,' Miren said, folding up the youngsters' clothes.

'Just as well,' Luken said. 'You probably won't be allowed anymore.'

'What are we going to do with the mare, Luken, with Yulene? And the hens?'

He looked out the window to see the children in a state of excitement, playing around. 'We'll just have to leave them with the neighbours—'

'I never thought it'd come to this,' she said, the tears starting to creep down her cheeks.

He went over and held her. 'You know I'll be with you in a few days no matter where you are. The four of us will all be together, you know that, don't you?'

Miren nodded and wiped away the tears. 'I don't want the kids to see me like this. I wonder how long it'll be before they realise it's not an adventure we're going on.'

'We're probably better off going sooner rather than later,' he replied. 'Who knows how the war is going to take shape. It's good that Estebe found out about the records. Next time we might not be so lucky.'

Luken heard the sound of the Renault drive into the plot and went outside. Arossa and Estebe appeared.

'Where's Miren?' Arossa asked.

'Inside, go on into her,' Luken replied as he turned to Estebe. 'Any more news?'

Estebe shook his head. 'I haven't been to the office since. The most likely ship out of Bilbao will be to Bordeaux or at least France but if it's going to England tell her to take it.'

'I wonder how much that'll cost…'

- 167 -

'It doesn't matter, just make sure she's on it. Pay a sweetener if you have to.'

'Have you made any plans yourself?'

'Like I said before, I'm not going anywhere,' Estebe said. 'Arossa might move to Bilbao, her father has a metal fabrication business, as you know, and he'd probably be regarded as a right centrist. He's generally kept his head down where politics are concerned.'

In the bedroom Arossa embraced Miren. 'I've spoken to my father earlier and he'll help you on your way. His factory is in the port area and he has contacts in the shipping business. If anyone can get you on a ship, he can.'

'What are you going to do?'

Arossa shrugged. 'I wish it was otherwise but I'm guessing the Fascists are going to win this war. I'll take my chances and move to my father's place but I don't know about Estebe. You know he's well known for his liberal opinions so it doesn't bode well for him. He insists he's not going to leave, he survived the Great War, he says, but I don't know if his luck will see him through this.'

'We're going to miss the two of you,' Miren said.

'Likewise with us,' Arossa replied, handing her an envelope. 'You might need this.'

'What is it?'

'Money. A woman travelling without a man is always vulnerable, especially during a war, and some men will try to take advantage of you. Keep it hidden, it can buy you a favour or two. Times might come when you need a favour and without money there's only one other way. Come on, you'd better make a move.'

They brought out the case and a few extra bags and put them into the van. The children climbed into the back as Arossa handed each a sugar stick.

'Look after yourselves,' Estebe said.

'You too,' Luken replied. 'You're the best friend a man could have.'

'Who was the surgeon that told you, Estebe?' Miren asked.

'Doctor Eguren.'

'I thought as much,' she replied. 'He's a good man.'

The two couples embraced each other in turn.

'Write to us,' Arossa said to Miren sitting in the passenger seat as she reached in. Striving to hold back the tears, the two women clasped hands warmly.

'Of course I will.'

Luken started the engine and the van hurtled off down the hill, leaving a miasma of dust in its wake.

***

The journey to Bilbao port was unremarkable, save for the occasional passing military vehicle.

'It's all happening so fast,' Miren said. 'Arossa gave me a load of money.'

'Why'd you take it?'

'She insisted, saying at times like this I might need it to buy favours. If I hadn't got money there's only one other way I could do it.'

'Jesús Kristo!' Luken said, throwing discretion to the wind in front of the kids.

'What's going to happen to our home, Luken?'

'We'll come back when it's all settled, you'll see. I promise. All wars come to an end.'

'Let's hope it's not another Thirty Years War. I wonder what's happened to Sister Alicia? I hope she's all right.'

As they crossed Bilbao, Luken scrutinized the large-scale movement of people and traffic. He stopped to get directions at a store and pick up the latest newspaper.

Inside, the store was quiet and deserted; he took a newspaper and a few chocolate bars for the youngsters.

Suddenly, a man came rushing out from behind a curtain at the rear. 'Have you not heard? There's been a bomb attack from the air. Spanish planes have launched a bomb attack. Some houses and shops have been destroyed. I'm closing in case they come back.'

The shopkeeper refused Luken's offer of money and ushered him to the door, giving him directions to Arossa's father's business.

'You're not going to believe this,' he discreetly said to Miren so the kids wouldn't hear. 'The city suffered an aerial bomb attack here earlier.'

'God!' she exclaimed. 'That explains why people are on the move. Maybe the ships will be full up.'

'Don't worry, it may not be a passenger ship.'

The day-to-day bustle on his last visit to the city was now supplanted by a tension and visible cheerlessness, even amongst those who were seemingly not heading for the port. He felt the tension building in his chest. Everyone it seemed was preoccupied with their safety.

He drove on, bypassing the signposts to the passenger terminal where throngs of people were making their way. Some women were simply carrying overcoats and clothing over their shoulders, as though they had fled their homes with no time to pick up anything other than what was near the front door. Or maybe they'd already made their bookings and were taking a chance to come back. Other people were carrying suitcases, and all with grim expressions.

The tall chimney stacks in the peripheral industrial areas were still belching out their choking smoke and it drifted across the surrounds. This is an easy place to get lost in, Luken thought. Having to ask further directions from pedestrians, he sensed Miren's frustration, exacerbated by the children's endless questions about the voyage.

When he found the right address, Luken entered the workshops and was directed to a small office located on a gantry on the first floor.

'Señor Abaroa, I've been expecting you,' the elderly man said, handing Luken a number of papers. 'Arossa's mentioned you before and always talks well about you and your wife. We don't have any time to talk if your family is to get away today. A French cargo ship with at least one available passenger cabin is sailing to Bayonne. I made a booking for you. You'll need to get clearance from the ship's officers first, they're expecting you too. Then go straight to the ship before it gets any later. Come back to me if they don't get away.'

'How can I thank you, Señor Larrañaga?' Luken felt the tightness in his chest start to unwind on the news that the ship would be docking a mere forty kilometres across the border.

'Don't, just get going. Let's hope we'll meet again sometime.'

Luken detected no resemblance between the man and Arossa but sensed a warmth beneath the beard and the dark skin. A man, he reckoned, who had worked hard all his life and was devoted to his daughter.

'Well?' Miren asked.

'You're going to Bayonne.'

'That's good. At least it's not some God-forsaken place.'

Señor Larrañaga came out to meet Miren and urged them on their way.

Luken pulled up alongside the huts used for processing the paperwork for import-export businesses and was directed to the ship's officer.

'On recommendation from Señor Larrañaga, one woman and two children require passage to Bayonne,' the officer said while reading the applications. 'Bring them in. You know we can't carry any male refugees?' Luken nodded and he continued. 'With the naval attacks on Irun and Donostia we're now taking a long detour and probably won't arrive in Bayonne unto around six o'clock tomorrow evening.'

The officer looked Miren and the children up and down, apparently satisfying himself that they were bona fide refugees. He took the payment fee then stamped and signed the papers and handed them back. 'You've just fifteen minutes to get onboard.'

He led them out of the hut and pointed to the location of the vessel. It turned out to be a bigger ship than Luken had expected. 'Would the crew be able to deal with any Spanish attempt to board and take over that ship?'

The officer looked put upon and said, 'This merchant vessel belongs to the French Government and any attempt by foreign forces to interfere with its passage would be treated as an act of war. Furthermore, we're in radio communication with the French Navy who we can call upon for assistance at any time. In the meantime, we also have our own supply of defensive weapons in case of any attempt by some tin-pot militias to take control!'

Given the vehemence of the officer's retort, Luken almost regretted having asked the question in the first place though the reassurance he had been given made the question worthwhile.

The family walked up the gangway and were welcomed by the first officer. Luken was allowed a five minute period onboard before departure. The small cabin had a porthole and contained a single bed and one chair. A smell of sweat and stale cigarette smoke hung in the air.

'You know what to do in case I don't get there before you,' Luken said. 'Get whatever transport you can. Remember the signs in France might show St Jean de Luz or Donibane Lohizune…'

'I know, I know,' Miren replied. 'I've been to St Jean before, don't forget. We'll go to Guillaume's hotel on the Avenue Labrouche. And you're going to call him in the meantime. The biggest problem will be keeping these two occupied until we get there.'

'Once you're out in the bay, you can go out on deck with them,' Luken said. He embraced her and told the kids to behave themselves and look after their mother. He noticed Sabine clinging to Miren.

'Why aren't you coming, Papá?' Sabine asked.

'Because only Mamás and children are allowed on the ship. I have to go by motorcycle…'

'Why didn't you tell me, Papá? I could have come with you!' Kasen interrupted.

'Well, it's too late for that now,' Luken said. 'Tell you what, I'll pick you up in Bayonne…'

The first officer burst into the cabin. 'Señor Abaroa, you must get off the ship immediately!'

Luken kissed Miren and bade farewell to his family then hurried back to the gangway.

Looking up at the ship from the dockside, he felt the tension build again as he weighed up the risks of Miren and the kids setting out on the high seas on an elongated voyage to avoid the Italian warships now bombarding the towns close to the border.

He turned to wave back at Kasen on the deck as the ship turned about one hundred and eighty degrees and set off from the shore. Despite their good luck in avoiding the over-crowded passenger ships, he resolved never to let them undertake such a dangerous trip without him again.

***

On the return journey to Durango, Luken drove at full speed with the windows down so he could hear and watch out for any aircraft overhead. None appeared.

He reflected on Sabine and how she worried whenever he or Miren had to part company from the family; understandable, given how she had lost her birth mother but maybe in time she'd get over that insecure feeling. Estebe and Arossa came to mind and he blessed his good fortune in knowing both of them. What would have happened if Estebe had not got that crucial piece of information from the hospital surgeon? Suppose the soldiers had come to the house to arrest Miren? Unthinkable.

Twilight had fallen when he stopped outside Endika's apartment, noticing the Berliet truck parked nearby. Inside, Endika turned anxiously from the electric stove where he was making coffee. 'Did they get away? Estebe was here, told me all about it.'

'Well on the way by now – to Bayonne. I have to leave as well, I'm taking the Ariel over the mountains.'

Endika nodded. 'The time has come for us all to move. I've decided to throw my lot in full-time with the Casa del Pueblo. No point in hanging around here any longer.'

'A brave decision. We never knew when this day would arrive, I suppose, only that it was coming sometime.'

'Great that she's going to Bayonne, not so far away. You shouldn't have much trouble getting there.'

'Hopefully,' Luken replied. 'I should arrive by noon tomorrow. Who are you linking up with?'

'I've been told to join up with a group in Arantza, I'll come with you as far as the Bidasoa river.'

Luken drove to his garage and left the van inside. He removed the pistol and the box of cartridges and hesitated before throwing them with a few basic tools into the bags on the motorcycle. Once a mechanic, always a mechanic, he thought, filling it up with petrol. Taking a final look inside at the facilities and the vehicles before locking up, he pondered on who might commandeer the business in his absence. The Falangists? The Requetés? Who knew?

He raced back to the house and pushed the motorcycle into the barn. The untouched tankard of cider that he'd left earlier had a collection of dead flies floating on the surface. He flung the cider into the grass and took the tankard into the house. Pouring out another bottle, he turned on the radio. A total of eight bombs had been dropped on Bilbao that day but radio transmissions from Nationalists further afield threatened annihilation of the city unless Republican forces surrendered immediately. Only eight bombs, Luken thought – that explains why we didn't see any damage. Just a warning and threat of worse to come.

As night fell, Luken took a few blankets and a hurricane lamp and, at the last minute, the pistol, and slept in the bunker below the stable. The fusty smell didn't bother him, but he noticed the temperature, at about twenty degrees, he supposed, was the same, day and night, never seeming to change.

Despite the utter quietness, only a sleep of sorts came, a drowsy partial sleep as he thought of Miren and the children, speculating on what was happening with them at that exact moment and questioning if he had been foolish to let them travel without him. Other things played over in his mind, including the possible visitation of military men to his house.

He woke to the sound of an aircraft flying overhead. Rather than rush out to see what was going on, he sat up and waited.

A few minutes later the aircraft returned, this time firing off a volley of canon fire with the immediate thud of splintering timber. It didn't sound like they hit the barn, he thought, it's not that close. Maybe the house.

He heard the distant drone of the engine as it fired off more shots. Maybe it had attacked Pérez's house.

The airplane flew past again but without any more canon fire.

In a while, Luken pushed open the trap door and cautiously went outside. He strode over to the house to see that the roof had been badly damaged. He faintly heard music and remembered that he had left the radio on overnight.

Inside he turned off the Spanish folk songs and inspected the rooms to see that, apart from a few bullets that had penetrated the upstairs floor, only the roof had been smashed.

Downstairs, he realised that he hadn't eaten in twenty-four hours. He boiled a kettle of water and poured it over a bowl of oatmeal, throwing in some dried apricots. He scalded some coffee beans and ate the cereal when it cooled.

Thinking back on the aircraft, he surmised that the pilot had strafed the house with the intention of teasing out the occupants so that he could mow them down when they ran out into the fields.

He took the hens in a sack and the mare to the Pérez's farm, intending to ask them to keep or sell the animals. Their house had been damaged, as he suspected, and there was nobody around. He turned the mare into the field with the other horses and released the hens into the chicken run.

On the radio again, no further news updates came through, only repeats of yesterday. He turned the dial to hear a female vocalist he didn't recognise singing La Tarara, an old folk song that he loved in his youth. He listened for a few minutes, feeling a strange sense of isolation.

He wandered out into the sunshine and sat on the side of the waterwell gazing down over the valley and recollecting his last hunting trip, when he had found Ander's shallow grave. Everything had changed at that moment, he thought.

Back in the house, he noticed the chalk marks on the kitchen slabs where the kids had played hopscotch. Listening to his own footsteps, he thought of the transition he was about to undertake to a different country and a different future.

Abruptly, he heard the sound of carts and motorised vehicles out on the road. And they were moving at speed. Just a week ago such movement was unthinkable.

In the bedroom he threw a clean bag onto the bed and started packing. The clothing items were only practical ones: jacket, trousers, shirts. The suit that he had scarcely worn since his marriage and other luxury or sports items like the jai-alai outfit had to be abandoned.

Out behind the barn, he took the banknotes out of the tin under the rock. He paused and chose to leave some behind and put the tin back into the ground and shifted over the covering rock.

Back in the bedroom he sadly lifted and contemplated the silver cup, his grandfather's weight-lifting trophy, a family heirloom that would no longer be passed on. He squeezed in the shaving gear and whatever aspirin tablets Miren had left behind. She had already taken the enamelled family photographs but left a paper one which he threw into the bag.

The sound of the passing traffic had stopped but then he heard three enormous thumps on the door. His heart rate took a hike and he moved silently into the side room with the pistol in hand, partly concealed behind his back. Looking sideways through the curtains, Endika appeared.

'Are you ready?'

'A minute.'

Returning to the bedroom, he stuffed in his passport and a map and put the pistol into his inside pocket. He closed the door and, about to lock up, decided no, if they come and the door is locked they'll just smash it in and then continue smashing everything else. Nonetheless, he kept the keys.

Endika had driven the Berliet lorry into the entrance to the plot. 'What's going to happen to that?' Luken asked.

'Who knows?'

Luken stuffed his belongings into the side panniers and started the motorcycle. Endika had a rucksack. Out on the road they turned east towards Elorrio, passing the occasional group of refugees. They took the mountain roads towards France, staying well south of Irun. Through Endarlatsa they turned off the road and drove up through a mountain track to avoid any patrols. Down the far side of the hill they came to a bend in the Bidasoa river.

'Good thing we're not doing this during the rains,' Luken said. 'We'd never get across.'

They pushed the bike through the river but stopped less than half way over, realising that the water was still too deep to manage. Trying to carry the bike didn't work either; with the weight and the rush of water, they almost collapsed.

'We'll have to dismantle it.'

'What?!' Endika said.

'There's nothing else for it.'

Removing the panniers, Luken took out the tools and detached the wheels. In semi darkness they lifted the machine across the water and returned for the remaining parts. Too late to start the reassembly in such poor light, they rested overnight.

Sitting against a tree, Endika handed out the bread, cheese and wine.

'How long do you think this war will last?' Luken asked.

'I'd be confident it'll be over by this time say, two years. I can't see people accepting Fascism as a government, not after what this country has been through.'

Luken gave out a long sigh. 'I really don't know, wars have a habit of lasting longer than anyone expected. Do you feel aggrieved about me leaving the country?'

'I did at first when Estebe told me; I thought you'd stay back and carry on the fight. Now, if I had a family, I think I'd do the same.'

'If it wasn't for Miren and the kids I would stay. I don't want to leave this country, especially after setting up the house and all the work I put into the garage. We'll see what happens in the weeks and months ahead. There might be an opportunity to come back. Or maybe do something to help while I'm away. We can always keep in touch through Guillaume.'

Deliberating about their expectations for the months ahead, they reminded each other of years past and the antics and silly games they got up to in their youth.

'Remember that first time we went to Bilbao and stayed out overnight?' Endika asked.

'Papá beat the shit out of us. The first time we got really drunk. We were only sixteen at the time.'

'Yeah, we wandered into a brothel but hadn't any money,' Endika laughed. 'We'd spent it all by then.'

The conversation eventually petered out and they drifted into a sleep of sorts.

Morningtime, after reassembly, they pushed the bike up through the French forest and onto Chemin de Licarlin where, after a few false starts, the engine kicked into life.

'We'll always have to stay in touch,' Endika said.

Luken nodded. They embraced and sadly wished each other well, though making a point of not over-indulging their adieu.

Luken rode across the mountain and down Chemin de la Foret. Endika went back across the river and lumbered his way up the mountain, the start of his trek to his comrades in Arantza. A long journey on foot, though he knew the way.

Chapter 13

The unease ran through Luken's veins, thinking about Miren and the kids while riding down the north side of the Pyrenees. Had their ship been approached by Fascist militias? What might have gone wrong? Anything and everything. The sooner he got to Bayonne the better. Not being familiar with the terrain and combined with the twisting ride, after a few side-turns he didn't know whether he was going in the right direction.

Arriving at a village signposted as Saint-Jean-Pied-de-Port, he realised he had taken a wrong turn and had come too far south. He went into a café, stood at the bar, ordered a large coffee and ate the last two croissants on sale at the counter. Two old men sat at a side table, doing likewise. On leaving, the waiter gave him directions to St Jean de Luz.

Outside, a gendarme was inspecting the bike and immediately Luken braced himself.

'Your motorcycle?'

Luken answered in the affirmative and explained that he was on his way to Bayonne.

'Why did you come this way?'

'The main road through Irun is impossible to get through and I got lost coming through the mountains,' Luken handed him his passport and a business card. 'I have to pick up parts to repair customer vehicles.'

The gendarme returned the card and inspected the clothes inside the panniers on the bike.

'Why are you taking all this?'

'I don't expect to make it back tonight.'

The officer grew more suspicious. 'You won't have much room for motor parts in there.'

'They're not particularly big, they couldn't be. A water pump, carburettor kits and distributor caps. They can be strapped in a box on the back if needs be. I'd hardly be taking a gearbox or something like that.'

The officer read through Luken's passport and papers. 'Come with me. You can leave the motorcycle there.'

Luken felt his pulse rate take a jump, not knowing what was going to happen next. One thing was for sure, he wasn't going to be searched. He felt the pistol inside his jacket.

At the tiny police station, the gendarme instructed him to sit at a bench along the side wall while he read through a large desk diary with a list of names.

Luken told himself to stay calm and avoid showing signs of nervousness. The officer kept watching him as he made a phone call.

When put through to someone Luken took to be his commanding officer, the gendarme requested what information might be to hand regarding 'a Luken Abaroa.' He hung up and waited.

Recollecting which pocket contained his keys, Luken estimated the distance back to the bike and how quickly he could get there.

Neither Luken nor the gendarme made small talk. A further ten minutes passed without any conversation.

When the call came through, Luken imperceptibly prepared himself for action. The officer gave nothing away in the conversation. His countenance relaxed as he hung up. 'You're free to go.'

Rather than give way to a visible release of tension, Luken kept his demeanour. 'I should think so.'

'Why's that?'

'I haven't done anything!'

The gendarme smiled. 'C'est bon. You want some coffee before you go?'

'I had some in the café already. Merci.'

They walked back up the village and the gendarme looked the motorcycle up and down.

'Nice bike. Ariel.'

'An English make, great machine,' Luken replied, kicking-starting the engine. The two men nodded to each other as he sped off.

That could have turned quite nasty, he thought. That was the second time in a few weeks I've run up against the uniforms.

As he crossed a bridge on the south side of the village, two figures appeared below at the river. He stopped to see two women in the shallows, washing clothes. They were abrading the articles up and down the corrugated surface of their washboards, rinsing them out in the river and then tossing them into a basket sitting on a rock. With straw hats against the sunshine they chatted away to each other all the while, oblivious to his stare.

Moving off, Luken reflected on the village, its remoteness in the mountains, its distance from strife and conflict and the two women launderers happily jabbering away. Even the copper had given the impression of being a decent man, apparently doing his job the way a copper should. You could do worse than live in a place like that.

As he descended down the slopes his thoughts kept returning to Miren and the kids. He peered at the clock on the motorcycle tank and reckoned they'd be arriving at Bayonne within three hours.

Though he had the goggles, the leather helmet had been left behind and the frisson of the wind flying through his hair helped to ease his residual tension. He swung onto the main road and several kilometres further east took the left turn for the coast road then stopped at Urrugne, where he stood and relaxed on the cliff edge overlooking the sea.

He looked out across the Bay of Biscay curving around to the land from whence he had come. With the stillness in the air, the only sounds he could hear were the wavelets lapping against the stony shore. Despite the war and the vindictiveness in Euskal Herria, he still believed that a settlement would someday come to pass and felt certain he would return in time. It was the only country in the world where he belonged. The country that he had to go back to. He thought of the places he was familiar with, where he was content to live. His happy years growing up, the friends and the decent people he was acquainted with. And he knew Miren felt the same way. Someday, one day, they'd be back.

He checked the time, started the motorcycle and sped off through Ciboure and St Jean de Luz. With no time to spare, he rode straight on to Bayonne.

**

Busy as he expected, a merchant vessel had docked at the quayside and disgorged its passengers, though Miren's ship was not due for another half hour.

A wire fence surrounded the docking area. Inside, travellers were ushered through a series of huts where immigration officials were actively checking arrivals' travel papers. Some were released and others detained in a sequestered warehouse.

Outside the fenced area, children were running around, hawkers selling food and men offering accommodation or transport in taxis or on horse and cart. Groups of people were greeting each other, friends or relations of those who had managed to escape. Others were taking whatever transport they could afford.

The ship arrived and docked and after an hour's delay, Miren and the children were cleared through. As soon as they saw him, the kids ran over, blurting out their experiences on the trip.

'The captain let me drive the ship, Papá, and use his binoculars,' Kasen said.

'Me too, Papá,' Sabine said.

Luken embraced the three of them and felt a surge of relief that they had arrived safely.

'So good to see you,' Miren said. 'I thought the trip would never end, especially not knowing what might have happened to you.'

'I'm fine, maitasun, I got here fully intact.'

'The children were invited up to the bridge for a while and allowed to hold the steering wheel, or whatever you call it, for a few minutes.'

Turning to the youngsters, Luken asked, 'Any pirates try to get on board?'

'No, but we looked out for them,' Kasen replied.

'So it was an uneventful trip?' Luken asked Miren.

'Thankfully. The food wasn't good but we won't complain about that. We met another family whose children were happy to play with us.'

Luken took Kasen on the back of the motorcycle and let Miren and Sabine follow in a taxi to St Jean de Luz.

The streets of the town were busy with refugees carrying whatever possessions they had managed to keep. Maybe these are the lucky ones, Luken thought, just like us, escaping whatever horror might have been in store. Come to think of it, we're a lot better off, looking at what they have.

At the Hotel Eskualduna, he took the baggage up to the room while Miren brought the kids to the café and ordered food and drinks. He quickly lifted a loose floorboard and hid the pistol below then emptied out the baggage and sorted the clothes into the dresser and wardrobe.

'How was it coming over the mountain?' she asked on his return.

'Actually, it was a lovely ride! Though I was pulled in by a cop in Saint-Jean-Pied-de-Port. He didn't find anything and let me go.'

'You didn't tell me that Marie was working here,' Miren said as she noticed the waitress serving at a table.

'I eh… didn't think of it.'

Marie came over when she recognised Miren and the two women greeted each other, touching cheeks and kissing the air in the French manner. They swapped brief résumés on their lives since last meeting and agreed to chat later.

'I must see Guillaume,' Luken said. 'We can't stay here long, it'll be cutting into our cash.'

A radio at the bar was playing local folk songs while they ate their onion soup and roast chicken and relaxed.

Retiring early, they traipsed up to the second-floor room. A double bed sat head-first against one side wall beside which a mattress lay on the floor for the children to sleep on end to end. Floral wallpaper decorated the walls and a small table with two chairs was pushed against the window. A wardrobe stood next to the door.

When the kids fell asleep, Miren said, 'It's a great relief to have a room to ourselves. Where do we go from here?'

'First of all, let's get a place to stay.'

'That wasn't what I meant, I mean, what are we going to do beyond that?'

'It's too early to say, Miren. Let's get settled in and we'll take it from there.'

Next morning, they walked along the narrow streets and out onto the beach and sat down on the sand, looking out at the waves. The children played at the water's edge while scattered individuals and groups sat around, some with colourful parasols to shade them from the sun.

'In spite of all the trouble at home we were well able to get by,' Miren said, glumly. 'Now here we are, refugees not knowing when we can go back, if ever. All my fault for bringing home those patient files. The Falangists would probably have caught up with them anyway, they don't seem to have a problem finding people they want to kill. You know what they do with women they think are communists or "reds"? Apart from the beatings and rapes, they make them drink castor oil and walk them out on the street so they defecate themselves in public.'

She looked out at the sea and continued slowly and distractedly, 'Looks like I'll never participate in the Sun Festival again. I'm going to miss that. My family have been involved in that for generations and now that's all over.'

'Don't blame yourself, maitasun,' Luken said, taking her hand. 'You prevented bloodshed and saved a lot of lives. That's what a nurse does, doesn't she? Anyway, it's not just you. They'll find out, if they haven't already, that I was involved in the Casa del Pueblo.'

'But that was all peaceful, non-violent…'

'Don't be under any illusions, Miren. Anyone who has anything even remotely to do with socialism or even liberalism is up for execution.'

'You've never told me much about it. What things were you involved in?'

'Giving out leaflets, encouraging people to stand up for their rights. Meetings. Talks about the way the country was going and what we could do.'

'I don't understand why you couldn't have told me all about it,' Miren replied as she picked up handfuls of sand, throwing them towards the sea. Most of the sand blew back over her legs. Luken saw that she'd become downcast, the novelty of the sea voyage to France now well forgotten.

'I didn't tell you much because I didn't want to worry you. Come on, Miren. We're away from all that. We're all in good health and have each other, haven't we?'

'I'm not thin-skinned, as you know. You should have told me. You know I support the cause.' She stood, brushed the sand off her dress and called to the kids, 'Come on, let's see if we can find an ice cream. And get out of this heat for a while.'

Miren took Sabine by the hand and walked slowly north-east along the beach. Luken with Kasen followed at a distance, feeling despondent himself, though trying not to let it show.

He wondered how the strain of moving was going to affect them. Already the difficulties were starting to surface. The realisation dawned on him that they were little better off than the refugees he had looked down on the previous day. A weekday and here they were, wandering around as if on holiday. All the effort he'd put in to the business, for what? It had all come to nothing. He had no work and the kids were out of school; the lessons were in French and they didn't speak French. What was going to go wrong next? The only saving grace he could think of was knowing Guillaume.

He forced a brave face as Kasen asked an endless string of questions. Why had they left Durango? How long were they staying here? When would they be moving to a new house? Aware that his son was feeling disoriented, having been uprooted from his friends during the school holidays, Luken realised that an extra effort would be needed to help him integrate into their new life, wherever that might be. And Sabine too, even more so.

They ate their ice cream and on the slow stroll back to the hotel, Miren passed a woman whom she recognized. She turned and caught up, 'Pardon me, Señora. Aren't you Juan Joseba's wife?'

'Who are you?'

'I worked at the hospital where he was a patient.'

'Now I remember, you were at the funeral.'

'Never got a chance to talk to you. I called up to your house one day but you'd already left. I'm Miren Abaroa and this is my husband Luken. My son and daughter Kasen and Sabine.'

'I remember. Juan Joseba talked about you,' Señora Aguirre said, addressing Luken. 'You've obviously left Euskal Herria.'

'I was sorry to hear about Juan Joseba's murder,' Luken said. 'He was a decent man.'

The woman hesitated and, Luken reckoned to prevent herself becoming emotional, immediately pressed ahead by asking, 'Where are you staying?'

'At the Hotel Eskualduna, for now.'

'I'm living with my mother on Rue de Midi. Maybe I'll call around to you tomorrow?'

'Yes, do, anytime.'

They went their separate ways and Luken said, 'At least there's someone from our own area who we can talk to and who knows people here.'

'I should've asked her about schools,' Miren said.

'All in good time.'

They walked further down along Boulevard Thiers and Sabine dawdled behind to look into a town house window. Luken went back to see and hear a music school with young musicians practicing on mandolins and guitars. He waited, seeing that Sabine enjoyed what she was hearing.

'Can we go inside?' she asked.

'Not now, but we'll come back another day.'

Back at the hotel, he took a wash while Miren tidied up the room and read Sabine a story. Kasen read his own book.

That evening they dined in the hotel and, back in the room, when the youngsters fell asleep Miren spoke softly, 'Señora Aguirre, Juan Joseba's wife, when I get to know her, I'll see if she can look after the kids from time to time. We'll need to talk and work things out.'

He was pleased to hear that Miren was trying to adapt to the new circumstances – essential, he thought, given the future they faced. He looked down at her as she drifted into sleep and reminded himself of how fortunate he was to have such a forward-looking woman in his life.

Next morning he woke first and slipped downstairs. Coffee was already brewing while Guillaume was setting the tables. 'You had to come sooner than I expected, Luken.'

'We were fortunate to get word in time, another day and we'd have been caught.'

'What about Estebe?'

'He's the one who found out and told me.'

'When's he comin'?'

'He's not, said he's going to stick it out.'

'Good luck to him,' Guillaume replied, then hesitated and looked out the window. 'I hope he hasn't got a death wish.'

'I wouldn't think so. He's fully armed.'

'Even so, if those fuckers get their hands on you, they'll show no mercy.'

Guillaume brought over a brew of coffee and sat down. 'This is the first time I met your wife. She's a brave woman, taking the kids out on a freight ship like that.'

'She's not easily put off and we didn't have time to think about it.'

'Luken, the first thing I want to say to you is to find work. There's nothing worse than sitting around here for weeks and months on end, hoping for an end to the war. I've seen it happen with men during the Rivera regime. They just go to pieces, thinking, I'll go back, I won't go back… and it's nothing to do with money.'

'Any idea where I might get work?'

'There's a garage on Route de Bayonne, the owner comes in for lunch sometimes, I know him fairly well. I'll have a word next time he comes in. There's a few other garages around but I don't know them, you could call in and ask.'

Regular customers had arrived and the aroma of freshly baked rolls and croissants filled the air. Two men came in and stood at the bar. They ordered brandy alongside their coffee and from their loud conversation it was obvious that they were well liquored up.

'They're just in from their trawling mission,' Guillaume said. 'Probably out two or three days. Apart from fishin' they're now ferryin' people over from Euskal Herria for which they charge two hundred and fifty francs. A lot of money, you might think, but not for the risks they're takin'.

They've been over at their usual haunt at the Port de Socoa gettin' smashed.'

One of the trawlermen addressed the patrons, 'If anyone is thinkin' of goin' to Spain by sea, forget it. Mussolini's warships are blowing the shit out of Irun and Fuenterrabia. If you have to, keep away from Basque trawlers, a lot of them have been seized by the Fascists.'

The café had turned silent as everyone stopped to listen. The second trawlerman lit up a small cigar, saying, 'Whatever you do, make sure you've nothing on you that says Republican. Even if you haven't you still might get pulled in. Some of the bastards are trigger happy and don't care who they kill out on the water.'

The men turned back to the bar and ordered more brandy. Nodding towards the trawlermen, Guillaume said, 'They may be rough, but they're both decent men. They work hard and come in here regularly; well worth knowing if, among other things, you wanted to get a decent bit of fish. Which I do, of course.'

'Don't suppose it's a good idea to ask if they could get me a job?' Luken asked.

'I wouldn't think so.'

Miren appeared with the kids, having waited until the other hotel guests had finished using the communal bathroom before giving them a good bath. Clearly washed and scrubbed, Sabine's hair was tied in a ponytail while Kasen's was neatly combed to one side. They sat and Guillaume took their breakfast order.

Luken explained what the two fishermen had revealed. After eating and cajoling the children to eat the ham and soft cheese, they took a walk across town to the port.

'Things don't seem as bad when you've eaten,' Miren said.

'Yep, nothing like a full stomach to perk you up.'

The kids amused each other running after the seagulls and firing loose stones off the pier into the water. Back at the Place Louis XIV, they sat at an outdoor café drinking coffee. The sky had clouded over and the rising autumn wind started picking the faded leaves off the trees.

Sabine approached Miren, 'Are Mamá and Errita here?'

'No, *querida*, they're not.'

'You keep saying they went away to another place. If they're not here, where are they?'

'We don't know where but they know we're here.'

'How do you know?'

'They came to me in a dream,' Miren replied after a flash of inspiration.

'What did they say?'

'They said they were happy and they want you to be happy too. But they were sorry they couldn't be here.'

Sabine's attention drifted off as she considered the answers. Miren watched as she returned to Kasen and his seagull chases.

'Quick thinking there, on your part,' Luken said.

Miren noticed her hand was shaking as she lifted her coffee cup and although feeling insecure and on edge with the uncertainty of the future, the idea occurred to her that the time had come to tell Sabine the truth about her mother and sister. 'We have to tell her.'

'What, about Gechina and Errita? Now?' Luken asked.

'Not here, back in the room. She's coming to an age where she knows the answers we're giving her can't be true. Even if Kasen keeps saying he doesn't know, someday he's sure to let it slip. This can't go on forever. Come on, we'll go back.'

They walked the short distance back to the hotel where Marie was busy freshening up the bar and, after initial greetings, said, 'I've something for you.'

She went to a storage cupboard and returned with a bag of toys. 'These were my daughter's but she doesn't play with them anymore.'

Miren took the delighted youngsters to a quiet table at the rear of the café where they were allowed to play until the lunchtime business started. Marie sat down for a time and advised her of possible schools, some of which had a smattering of Basque and Spanish. Her daughter Brigette attended L'école Saint-Joseph and she would talk to the principal to see if Sabine could be fitted in. Though a year older, Brigette agreed to being friendly with Sabine.

After lunch, in the room, Sabine rushed over to pick up one of her cloth dolls. Before she could start into make-believe, Miren sat her on the bed beside her.

'I've something very sad to tell you, Sabine. Your first Mamá and Errita have died.'

'Where are they?'

'They have a special grave in Euskal Herria. One day they just died. Remember the day when we found the dead bird in the garden? The Pardillo?'

Sabine nodded.

'Remember we made a special place, a little grave, for the Pardillo? The same thing has happened to your first Mamá and Errita. It was just like that, their bodies like the little bird, stopped working. They can't play or see or eat anything. They can't come back to life even though we want them to.'

Sabine thought for a moment, held the doll close, 'Can I see them?'

'Nobody can see them.'

Sabine thought again, looked at the doll in her hands, 'Why can't I see them?'

'Because they're in a grave. Like the little bird, once somebody goes into a grave, we can't see them anymore.'

'Why did they die?'

'There's no reason, it just happens.'

'Can I see the grave?'

'We can visit it someday but not today. And we can talk about it again.'

Sabine went quiet and went over to the toy house that she had made beside the wardrobe and started playing with the other figures.

Feeling relieved at how Sabine had handled the bad news, Miren decided to avoid using untrue references to things like dreams or other fantasies and would try to base her answers to whatever Sabine's questions might be in future on fact. For the rest of the day she kept a special eye on her while Kasen encouraged her to participate in his games, having been told by Luken what was happening.

Later in the day Señora Aguirre appeared at the hotel and asked for Miren. Guillaume directed her to the table where they sat and discussed their exile.

'You must have left at short notice,' Miren said. 'I called up to your house not long after the funeral and it was deserted. The hens were walking around enjoying their freedom…'

'I hadn't time to give them away,' Señora Aguirre replied. 'I'm sure they made a good meal for a hungry fox. I didn't feel safe there and left straightaway after the funeral. I'm glad I did since they now regard wives and even the adult children of "reds" just as guilty. Leaving, in a way, was opportune, as my mother here can no longer look after herself properly. I had intended bringing her to Euskal Herria but now I'm here. What about yourselves?'

Miren explained at length the reasons for their exile and the loss of her sister and niece. Señora Aguirre offered her sympathy. 'You must be heartbroken?'

'I am, we were so close.'

Señora Aguirre gave out a deep breath. 'How long will you stay at the hotel?'

'Until Luken gets a job and we can move into our own place.'

'Why don't you come and stay with me for a while? There's only two of us there and plenty of room.'

'That's very generous of you, Señora Aguirre. Let me just talk it over with Luken.'

'How is he with living the life of a refugee?'

'Not as bad as me; he's more optimistic. He'd a garage business as you know and had to just leave it behind after putting all his life's work into it.'

'I'm sure he's annoyed about that.'

'Annoyed and disappointed.'

Luken was more than happy to accept Señora Aguirre's offer and they moved in a few days later.

Chapter 14

The Excelsior Garage, a franchise for Simca cars, stood on Boulevard Thiers and the owner, Monsieur Vilaret, was cranking up the petrol pump in front of a Simca 5 when Luken approached.

'Sorry to bother you, Monsieur,' Luken said, 'but if you happen to be looking for an experienced mechanic, I'm available.'

'Sorry to disappoint you,' Vilaret replied, 'but with so many refugees coming over from Spain I'm approached maybe five times a day by men looking for work. It's becoming so troublesome that I'll have to put a "No Vacancies" sign in the window.'

'I'm surprised. You're the first man I've asked for work.'

'Tell me what experience you have.'

Luken described the vehicles he had worked on, his motor business and explained that were it not for the difficult political situation he'd still be working in Euskal Herria.

Vilaret acknowledged Luken's experience and skill, indicating that he'd be in touch if an opportunity for a position arose, especially in a supervisory capacity.

After pumping petrol into the car he went to the office and recorded Luken's address. Walking away, Luken supposed that he was going to get the same answer at whatever garage he presented himself. Nonetheless, Monsieur Vilaret himself seemed like a kindly fellow, the sort he would be happy to work with.

In the afternoon he walked out to see the garage that Guillaume had mentioned, on the Route de Bayonne. The Euskara Garage was much bigger than the Simca establishment, a concessionaire for Hupmobile and Mathis cars, American brands which he wasn't familiar with but still felt confident in handling. Resisting the temptation to walk in and enquire after a job, he decided to wait until Guillaume set up the introductions – better to have a referral from someone whose opinion was trusted.

His wish was granted a few days later when Guillaume approached. 'You're in luck, Monsieur Pelletier says he'll give you a try. He's just gone back but you can call him, the number is 491.'

Next morning after the phone call, Luken took the motorcycle and rode out to the garage on National Route 10.

'Have you any experience on Hupmobiles?' Pelletier asked.

'Where I come from there aren't any. But I've worked on a few Chryslers. I'd have thought they'd be similar?'

'Bien sur, the principles are much the same although innovations come along which can make a difference. Guillaume tells me you're familiar with the Citroën range?'

'Done a lot of work on Citroëns. And speaking of innovations, the Traction Avant is a particularly advanced car.'

'That's good because we've applied for the Citroën dealership for the area. In fact we've been told it's coming our way. That should help to expand our offerings, not many people can afford these American machines. So when can you start?'

Luken agreed to turn up the following day and they shook hands. Riding back to town, he had mixed feelings about the opportunity, glad that he had the job but disappointed that he had to start all over again as though he was going back seven or eight years in his working life.

***

Miren sat sipping lemonade with Señora Aguirre in the shaded back terrace of her townhouse.

'I was thinking we should call you Madame, not Señora Aguirre. Seeing as you're French.'

'Just call me Anna from now on, Miren.'

'Had you been living here long?'

'We came here in 1922. I met Juan Joseba in Paris just after the Great War but there was little work for him there and he always wanted to get back to Euskal Herria. I wasn't keen on living there initially so this was to be a compromise. But there were too many barbers here and he felt there was an opportunity in Durango. Talked me into going with him. My Maman wouldn't come and stayed here. Pity we didn't stay here, he'd be still alive if we had. Juan Joseba always believed in democracy and now he's paid for it with his life.'

'I'm sure you still haven't got over it?'

'No, not for a long time yet. He was a good man.'

'Did you know I was the one who found him?'

'No, I didn't know that.'

'Horrible. I was doing my rounds in the middle of the night.'

'You must have been terrified, not knowing what else was going to happen?'

'I was shocked that someone could be killed in a hospital of all places. There was another incident, if you could call it that,' Miren said and went on to describe the forced removal of patients and her own part in the event, taking away the records which had in turn led to the family's exile.

'We live in tough times, Miren,' Anna said and went to the kitchen, returning with a pot of tea and a St Honoré cake.

'This is absolument délicieux!' Miren said, licking her fingers. 'The first treat I've had since we got here.'

'We must keep some for the children,' Anna replied.

'Would you like to go back to Paris?'

'Not now, there's too much trouble there and, except for one, I've lost touch with my old friends. I hate the fog and the cold in wintertime Paris. Unlike here, much milder in winter and it's nice being beside the sea. What about you?'

'I don't know. Who knows what Euskal Herria will be like in years to come? I still love the country and loved where we lived, it was so beautiful in the Eguzkitza Valley, as you know.' Unexpectedly, Miren felt the emotion well up in her chest and the tears ran down her cheeks.

Anna reached over and clasped her hand. 'Such times as we live in, I felt the same when I got here. Not until I got in and actually closed the front door did I feel safe. Couldn't hold back the tears.'

'Here I am, crying before a woman who hardly knows me,' Miren said, wiping her eyes with a handkerchief.

'Well, we're certainly not strangers, Miren.'

'I'm trying to keep a brave face all the time and at times I feel like screaming.'

'Scream away as much as you like here, I don't mind,' Anna replied and they both gave out a laugh.

Anna went to the kitchen and returned with a jug of water which she poured around the base of a small lime tree at the corner of the terrace. She picked off a few dead leaves. 'This little tree was here when we arrived and I'm sure it'll still be here long after we're gone.'

One morning after Luken had left, Miren arose and sat by the window in Anna's townhouse. Although small, the room was tastefully decorated with yellow embossed wallpaper and a compact oak wardrobe alongside a matching dresser with enough drawers to accommodate their clothes. A double and single bed were pushed head-first against the opposite wall. She looked down at the children still asleep in the single bed and reckoned they were happy enough despite the recent upheavals.

When the three of them had dressed she took an empty metal container and a fine-toothed comb and drew Kasen to her. She combed through his hair, picking out the occasional head lice and dropping it into the container.

'We used to throw them into the fire,' Kasen said to Sabine. 'They make a great cracking sound.'

Sabine looked into the container to see the hopping creatures.

'Can they bite you?'

'They're harmless,' Miren said. 'But if they do, you can always bite them back.'

'Ugh!' both kids said.

Miren continued, 'We'll have to get some Schwarakopf and wash our hair. That'll keep 'em away.'

'What's Shar kop?' Sabine asked.

'It's new, a special liquid for washing hair,' she replied.

On finishing Sabine's hair, Miren said, 'Come on, time for breakfast.'

In the kitchen, she opened the stove door while Kasen shook the lice into the fire and everyone, including Anna, listened and laughed to hear the crack of each creature passing into oblivion.

***

A large showroom in the Euskera Garage connected through a door to an open area for carrying out service and repairs, much bigger than Luken's place in Durango, and more comfortable to work in.

He soon became acquainted with the automobiles and in time became familiar with his workmates, most of whom were sympathetic to his plight as an exile. Jacques the supervisor, he felt, was not quite so sympathetic, as to why he could only guess. Luken felt that he was always being watched. But he didn't overindulge such thoughts, given the confidence he had in his ability to do the work. Being happy to settle into the routine of regular work, he enjoyed time off in the evenings and especially at weekends.

On one occasion, he felt the resentment rise when he overheard Jacques say to a customer, 'We don't normally employ foreigners but we took a chance on this one and, so far, so good.'

Though perceiving his supervisor's attitude as demeaning, Luken let it pass but in the coming weeks, made a point of repeatedly using the expression, "so far, so good," whenever he was asked for a progress report on a particular job. In such instances, Jacques turned stone-faced.

Another day one of his workmates said, 'Did you know that Jacques is Pelletier's son in law?'

'That's news to me.'

'Jacques was never a good mechanic, just a good manipulator.'

'Are you not just being sarcastic?'

'Whenever something goes wrong he makes sure he never gets the blame. If a customer's car breaks down after it's repaired, it's a faulty part he was sent or it's the way the customer is driving. It's never him.'

This was something that Luken suspected but didn't wish to hear, preferring to keep his head down. At the same time he had noticed Jacques quibbling over the smallest of errors with every one of his fellow workers. Further, if there had been a recurring problem with a car, the man made a point of analysing it down to the smallest detail and always seemed to point the finger at the repairman rather than trying to understand the nature of the problem. As though the mechanic should have seen the problem and solution at the outset rather than recognising an intermittent fault that could have had a number of obscure causes.

Monsieur Pelletier called in on one of his occasional visits to the workshop and approached Luken. 'How are things working out for you?'

'Fine. I'm getting the hang of the American motors, interesting stuff. I must say the engines are huge compared to European cars.'

'Good. From your experience can you see any way we might improve things here?'

Luken scratched his head. 'Maybe we could re-use some things that are thrown out. There was a new dynamo fitted in a Mathis last week. That could have been stripped down and new bushes fitted, I thought.'

'You should speak to Jacques about that,' Pelletier said and called over the supervisor, 'Listen to him, he has some ideas that could make the workshop better and save us a few francs.'

Luken explained in depth about the dynamo – rather than incur the expense of buying a new item, the faulty one could have been dis-assembled, the windings and rotor cleaned and the spent parts replaced. Something he had done on various cars in the past.

As soon as Pelletier went on his way, Jacques' attitude changed from showing interest to antipathy. 'Get back to work.'

In the evening times, he discussed his job with Miren, explaining his difficulties with Jacques. Although prepared to continue working at the Euskera establishment, he now felt his supervisor's scrutiny as a constant source of irritation.

'Well, look at it this way,' Miren replied, 'you're fortunate to have got that job. Think of all the other men still coming across the border with no hope of work. Most of them would give their right arm to have a job like yours.'

'I understand that but it doesn't make things any easier.'

Over the following days and weeks Luken felt he was being watched even more intensely. Every job report he filled out was being dissected along with his time-keeping.

In the meantime, he had gained the esteem of his fellow mechanics, who respected his attention to detail and extensive knowledge. Sometimes one of the men asked his advice.

Another time, a workmate said, 'Jacques sees you as a danger to his position, you know that? He sees you as a foreigner come in to take his job.'

Luken shrugged and said nothing.

The months passed and the grating relationship between Luken and Jacques showed no signs of easing. One day,

Jacques and a customer looked on as Luken adjusted the carburettor on the customer's car.

'This man was on the run from Spain,' Jacques said. 'So we gave him a chance and taught him everything he now knows. He's as good as any of the men.'

Luken immediately felt the hair on the back of his neck bristle at his supervisor's condescension. He said nothing with the customer present, preferring to leave it until later when a cool head was needed.

When the client had driven his car away, Luken followed Jacques into the office. 'What was that all about?'

'What do you mean?'

'Telling that man that I'd learnt everything I know from you and that I was on the run.'

'What's wrong with that?'

'For a start it's not true, I didn't learn everything I know from you. And I'm not "on the run," like a criminal, but a political refugee.'

Jacques looked put upon. 'I never thought you were so sensitive.'

Without showing it, Luken felt the kettle boil in his head. 'The only thing you could teach me is how to be a complete shit like yourself. You follow me around like a leech, you know what a leech is? It's one of those slugs that attaches itself to your leg to suck the blood and the only way you can get it off is by burning it with a cigarette. If I had a cigarette now…'

'Who do you think you are?' Jacques said indignantly. 'Talking to me like that…'

'You're all full of wind and piss,' Luken replied casually and waited for Jacques to stand up from his desk for a direct confrontation.

In the event, he stayed seated and Luken walked out of the office. He removed his overalls, stuffed them into the panniers and rode the motorcycle back to town.

'What the hell did you walk out for!?' Miren asked when he explained that he'd left the job.

'I couldn't work for that blockhead anymore.'

'Oh Jesús! Did you hit him?'

'No.'

'Why couldn't you go and talk to Monsieur Pelletier?'

'It wouldn't do any good, Jacques is his son in law —'

'For God's sake, you and your bloody temper. Why don't you go back and say that you just lost your head for a moment?'

'You mean apologise.'

'Call it whatever you like, just get the job back. Your work was okay otherwise, wasn't it?'

Luken shrugged.

Miren took a deep breath. 'Just as we were getting on our feet, this had to happen. We've been living with Anna long enough. It's taking advantage of her generosity and she has enough to do looking after her mother.'

She sat fuming on the chair by the window and reckoned that Luken was not going back to Monsieur Pelletier. Observing the passing stragglers, mostly refugees, on the narrow Rue Joseph Garat below, she said, 'The hotel has got so busy with people like us coming over that Guillaume has offered me a job as waitress. Now it looks like I'll have to take it whether I like it or not. At least the kids have settled in school. What are you going to do for work?'

'Keep looking.'

***

Luken considered Miren's urgings but couldn't bring himself to go back to Pelletier's garage, even though he approached the front door. At the last moment he turned the accelerator and sped further up the road. I've probably been spoiled, having worked for myself, he thought. During my apprenticeship years ago, I might've put up with the likes of Jacques, but not anymore.

He checked other garages for work, one a motorcycle establishment on Boulevard Victor Hugo which specialised in Alcyon machines. But, like Vilaret with the Simca franchise, no positions were available although Monsieur DeLargey made note of Luken's address and agreed to call if anything came up. And like Vilaret, he seemed a kindly fellow, Luken thought, as he admired his Ariel motorcycle. DeLargey explained that his business had originally been a forge and blacksmith but he'd switched as the motor trade expanded.

Over the subsequent weeks Luken went further afield, trying Bayonne and Biarritz but by now most of them had the 'Pas d'Emplois' sign up: 'No Vacancies.' He reckoned that waves of emigrants had come to such places and beyond.

His hackles were raised when he heard the expression, '… un autre bendejo,' in the background when he tried a garage in Bayonne. Another Spanish fool.

Each weekday Luken brought the kids to and from school. Afterwards, he took Kasen to football and Sabine to music lessons.

Endika rang the hotel whenever he got the opportunity and Miren or Guillaume took the call. It was tough going living out in the mountains but he and his comrades were determined to fight on. Apart from the usual creature comforts what he missed most was not being able to have a good bath.

As the weeks went by, boredom and lethargy set in and Luken found it difficult to motivate himself to look for work. All his efforts were in vain. Strange, recalling those years, he thought, when he'd considered living in St Jean. Now that I'm here, no jobs.

In his efforts to avoid gaining a reputation, he spent most evenings in different bars around town and kept away from the hotel. He frequented Le Bar Basque where, since the Spanish civil war had ramped up, many foreign and French national reporters hung out. With trouble in Madrid, many embassies had moved their Spanish diplomatic offices to St Jean and embassy personnel also frequented the same bar. Though he took a drink there, Luken noted who asked the most intrusive questions and made a point of avoiding them on future visits as he recalled Guillaume's words about the Fascistas Españoles who were covertly operating in the town.

One night, to avoid going home drunk, he took a rest on the beach and fell asleep along with a multitude of other camped émigrés. Aroused at dawn by two gendarmes on foot patrol, he was told about the temporary accommodation centre and ordered to move on.

Close by, a man with his wife and three children started to fold up their blankets and covers. The woman broke up some bread rolls and gave them to the youngsters.

'Have you been long here?' the man asked.

Luken shrugged. 'Too long.'

'We arrived three weeks ago and tried to get into the accommodation centre but it's always full. They keep telling us to come back the next day.'

'We're lucky that we found a woman to put us up,' Luken said. 'But I can't get work, my biggest problem. I keep looking, hoping that some opportunity will come along. What are you going to do now?'

'Go to the centre. We get our name down every day. When someone leaves they move you up the list but I don't know how many are ahead of us.'

They shook hands and wished each other luck. Luken thought the man was, or had been, well-to-do. Although dishevelled he was wearing a business suit and had an air of restraint.

He turned to look at what he guessed were three or four hundred refugees on the beach as he walked up to the promenade and supposed it was going to get worse before it got better.

At the house, he saw Miren noting the state he was in but said nothing since he arrived just as the children were waking up. Nonetheless he felt her tacit disapproval was even worse than if she had scolded him explicitly.

Chapter 15

After breakfast Luken had a wash and a shave and took a walk.

Abruptly, the thought crossed his mind that he was becoming an alcoholic. He stopped dead in his tracks. A woman pedestrian behind bumped into him.

'Desolé!' he apologised to the old lady.

This can't go on, he thought. Miren and the kids deserve better. It's time to take drastic action. Moving again he picked up the pace this time, breaking into a stride around the streets, like a challenge race.

He thought of possible opportunities in other parts of France but he had no contacts outside St Jean and with the unemployment and political trouble playing out nationwide, it was difficult no matter what way he turned. Maybe it was time to go abroad, to America or England? One way or another he felt the imperative to find work, wherever it could be found.

Mr Robinson came to mind but, in the rush to leave home, he hadn't taken his contact details. In fact, he couldn't remember noting Robinson's address in England. Maybe Kerbasi could call to the house, if it wasn't already occupied, and pick up Robinson's business card. It was time to call him anyway and see if he had heard anything further from Endika and Estebe.

Back at the hotel, Marie and Miren were busy serving the lunchtime customers. Miren approached as he sat at the end of the bar. 'There were some interesting characters here before you arrived. I think they're from Iruña and one of them is staying here.'

'So what?'

'They're émigrés, I'd say. I think they're solicitors.'

Miren was dressed like Marie in a white blouse and long tight black skirt and as she went about her duties he couldn't help but notice other men watching her. Still an attractive woman and with that fresh, eager look about her, he thought. And the human contact she's making in the job is definitely giving her a lift. Do I deserve her?

A news broadcast on the radio at the bar announced that a large number of army officers loyal to General Franco had been taken from Republican jails in Donostia and executed. As many as sixty officers had been killed in retaliation for the recent killing of left-wing sympathisers in Irun.

A lull descended on the crowded café. They'd probably be hearing these reports daily now that the war had geared up, Luken reckoned. He took a glass of wine as a man sat on the next stool, looked at his watch and, gesturing towards the radio, asked, 'Did you catch the news?'

'Sixty Franco officers killed in San Sebastian.'

The man's seemingly good humour immediately vanished. 'When is it going to stop? All of this killing.'

'Apparently in reaction for a group of Republicans who'd been killed earlier,' Luken said and to avoid appearing partisan, kept the conversation apolitical. 'There doesn't seem to be any end to the brutality.'

'That's for sure. Do you live here?'

The man, dressed in a suit with a white shirt and necktie, was dark skinned and almost bald. Luken reckoned from his accent that despite his meticulous French, he was probably from Euskal Herria, though not his own area and probably from the upper classes.

'For now, anyway; I'm looking for work,' Luken replied and supposed in turn that the man was paying close attention to his words, trying to assess his accent.

'But you're not from here?'

'Viscaya,' Luken said, his home province. 'Yourself?'

'Navarra,' the man replied and reached out to shake hands, giving his name, 'Pello.'

Luken returned the compliment and asked, 'Staying long?'

'A week or so. I'm in the legal business and meeting a few new clients. Never been here before, nice town.'

They continued with the small talk for a time and after lunch Luken retired to the room before collecting the youngsters from school.

Evening time, as they sat in the room reading, Miren said, 'That man you were sitting with, he's one of those solicitors. I heard them again talking about leaving.'

'Where are they going?'

'I couldn't quite hear – but it's taking a week.'

'Sounds like England,' Luken replied and sat up abruptly, realising what he had just said. Maybe an opportunity here.

***

Over the subsequent days, Luken wondered how he could gain Pello's confidence while taking his customary exercise around the town.

He eventually broached the subject as he crossed paths with the man on one of his walks. 'I'm having so little success finding work I'm thinking of going abroad.'

'Would you not try elsewhere in France?' Pello asked.

'Too many refugees looking for work and I don't know anyone outside of this area.'

'Where would you go?'

'I was thinking of England.'

'D'you know anyone there?'

'There is one man I know, in the motor trade. He's retired now but I'm sure he has contacts who would help.'

'It's a big decision,' Pello answered, more as a question than a statement.

'You can only go on so long without work.'

They parted company and Luken hoped he'd sown the idea in the man's head.

The following day Pello approached Luken at the bar and discreetly said, 'I know someone who might be able to help but I can't talk here. I'll see you down on the beach if that's okay?'

The tide was out as the two men walked slowly across the empty seashore. A high wind swirled the dry, loose sand knee-high.

'You strike me as being too bright not to have work, Luken. In fact, I'm sure you're a political refugee.'

Luken was surprised and when he didn't reply Pello continued, 'You know what makes me so sure? The fact that you brought your wife and children here. If it was just work you needed, you'd have left them at home until you got a job. You must have brought them here so that you couldn't be blackmailed into going back. I could be completely wrong and you happen to be a spy for the Fascists but that wouldn't make sense. You wouldn't have had to bring them over in the first place since you'd be allowed back anytime.'

'That's very perceptive of you, Señor Pello,' Luken replied as he watched him gauging his own reaction. 'You're an émigré yourself?'

'You might've seen me talking to a few other men at the café,' Pello said. 'We're all going to Ireland. We have some contacts there. What you could do, if you're interested in coming, is to seek refugee status in Ireland. It's easy to get to England from there. We've room for one more but you'd have to share the costs. There was another group here some weeks ago on route to England. They weren't staying at that hotel but anyway you've missed them, they've already gone.'

'How are you going to get there?'

'I can only tell you that when we're all satisfied that you're bona fide and you've paid your share.'

By this time, daylight was fading. The wind died down and a light drizzle started as they turned and walked up to the promenade. Rather than go straight back to the hotel they called into a quiet bar and ordered two beers.

'When?' Luken asked as he wiped the sand particles from his face.

'I can't tell you exactly but soon. You'll have to decide within the next three days. You'll want to talk to your wife?'

'That'll be the hard part!'

Pello laughed, 'You sound like a normal couple.'

'Is there anything else you can tell me?'

'If you come there'll be four men all together. Those with families have already moved them abroad.'

'Why are you leaving?'

'I fell foul of the right wing committees because of my legal work for defendants who they regarded as communists. I wasn't prepared to hang about any longer.

I'm quite sure I'd have been arrested and God knows what after that.'

Ambling back to the house, Luken's mind was racing with questions about the journey and what might happen at the far end. They must be going by boat, he thought and decided to wait until morning to tell Miren so he could tease out any misgivings in his own mind. He hated the thought of leaving the family behind but bringing them over without an established base would be foolish. What if it didn't work out? What then? He lay awake going over the possibilities. Suddenly, he remembered Padraig in Dublin. Then, it didn't seem so daunting. Another good reason to ring Kerbasi. And maybe some word about Endika. He'd call him first thing in the morning and see if he could dig out Robinson or Padraig's phone numbers. He thought of the stagnation of having been out of work for so long. But now, time to move.

***

He rose early and went to the hotel to use the reception phone. Instead of Kerbasi's normal greeting, a gruff retort came down the line, 'Who wants him?'

Instantly, Luken reckoned the garage had been taken over and after a moment, gave the most common Spanish name he could think of. 'Jose Ramon Ferrer, a customer.'

Kerbasi came on the line and, realising that he had to speak in code, Luken said one word quietly, 'Abaroa.'

'What?'

'Abaroa.'

After a pause, Kerbasi spoke eagerly, 'Ah, Señor Ferrer, what can I do for you?'

'I'm in St Jean de Luz.'

'Okay, it stopped and then started again. It might be dust in the fuel line.'

'Hotel Eskualduna. Call me back.'

'Why don't you bring it around, I'll be here until seven this evening. Adios.'

Reflecting on the call, Luken wondered whether the Fascists had taken control over Kerbasi's garage or maybe it was a patrol, randomly checking out the businesses in that area. Either way, best to wait for Kerbasi to call him at the hotel. Too risky otherwise.

The call didn't come through until nearly eight o'clock.

'The garage has been taken over by the Falangists,' Kerbasi said. 'But I'm allowed to keep on working. They're using it to house their own vehicles. Armoured cars and trucks. They're in the café now, gettin' drunk. I won't be here any longer than a week, if even that. They're asking questions all over the place, getting people to rat on one another. What about you?'

'This place is full of refugees and I can't get work. I'm thinking of going abroad to Ireland or England. Can you do me a favour? Call into our house and get the business cards I left in a desk, if they're still there. Look up a number for a Citroën garage in Dublin, and also, see if Robinson's card is there. Have you heard from Endika?'

'He's holed up with his comrades in the forest near Gorbeia. They go out on their sorties and attack the patrols. Two of them have been killed but Endika is okay.'

'Tell him we're thinking of him next time you see or hear from him. I'll be here all day tomorrow, ring anytime.'

Noon the following day, Kerbasi rang to say that the house had been ransacked, anything valuable taken and everything else thrown about the place. He couldn't find any business cards. Other, even worse news was that Estebe had been arrested two days ago and nothing had been heard from him since. Also, the Falangists were going through all the paperwork in Luken's garage in Durango and he reckoned it was too dangerous for him to stay in Euskal Herria any longer. They'd probably unearth something that implicated him in the Casa del Pueblo. He was taking his mother and escaping across the mountain border the following day.

'Look after yourself, Kerbasi.'

'You too, Luken, and give Miren my best wishes.'

Luken walked around outside on the street for several minutes, his head racing with anxious thoughts of Endika and Estebe.

Back in the hotel, he picked up the phone and asked the operator to put him through to the Citroën head office. Soon the call came through and he was given the contact number of the dealership in Dublin. Why didn't he think of that in the first place? After all the trouble and risks he'd made for Kerbasi. He immediately booked the call.

After twenty minutes, the crackly call came through. When greetings were dispensed with, Padraig, speaking in French, asked, 'Is this a social call?'

'Not quite. You might have heard of the trouble in Euskal Herria, Padraig. An all-out civil war is now taking place. The long and short of it is that I had to leave with my family. We're now in France but I can't get work and I'm thinking of coming to Ireland. I thought maybe you could help.'

'We hear about it on the radio. Have you or your family been hurt?'

'Nothing like that but I have to get work and there's none here.'

'I'm sure we can offer you work, Luken, especially with your experience.'

As he hung up, Luken thought, that's the only good news I've heard in a long, long time.

***

Miren was on lunchtime duty at the café and noticed that Luken didn't finish his food, unusually for him. In fact, he looked downright gloomy – nothing unusual in that nowadays.

'I need to talk to you,' he said.

She was about to sit until he interrupted. 'Not here, at the square whenever you can.'

During her break, she saw him sitting outside the café, Chez René, on Place Louis XIV.

'I want to go to Ireland,' he said.

'Ireland! You want to go to Ireland?'

'There's no work here. I've been offered a definite job —'

'You had a definite job and you left it!'

'I couldn't get on with that fool who ran the place.'

'Who offered you this job in Ireland?'

'Padraig Lestrange is his name, you'll remember we wrote to him? I met him at the Citroën conference in Paris. We got on well…'

'That was just a social occasion.'

'It was more than that, I could see eye to eye with him. With Jacques there was always going to be no end of problems.'

'When would you have to go?'

'Two days' time.'

'Two days' time! How would you get there?'

'With the men you saw in the café, they chartered a boat and that's where they're going.'

'What kind of a boat?'

'A trawler,' Luken guessed.

Miren rubbed her forehead, took a deep breath and said, 'Kasen, Sabine and myself, what are we going to do?'

'I'll apply for residency, get a job and then send you money so you can all come over.'

'It's always about you first, isn't it?'

Luken raised his voice, 'Well, you could go over first if you like. Your English is better than mine and you could get a job nursing…'

'And you'll look after the kids I suppose, in between your drinking!' Miren raised her voice in equal measure.

'I don't drink that much…'

'Don't talk rubbish. I'm not that stupid if you don't mind. I have a nose.' Miren stood and walked away. 'I need to think about this.'

She went to the house, donned a woollen jacket and went back out.

On the promenade, scarcely aware of the strong offshore wind, she intuitively drew the jacket around her. Nor did she notice the other walkers squinting into the wind. She looked back on her rapport with Luken. They'd known each other since their teenage years and from the start a natural spontaneity had developed and grown between them. And even though over the years they'd parted company for a time, they'd invariably got back together despite having spent time with other prospective partners.

They'd had arguments from time to time, some of which got heated, calling each other all the names in the world – 'Stupid bastard!' 'Stupid bitch!'

Later they'd end up laughing at what they'd said. 'So I'm a stupid bastard, am I?'

'Sometimes. And I'm a stupid bitch too. Everyone does stupid things on occasion.'

In spite of his temper, she knew he would never be given to physical outbursts against her or the kids. Nonetheless, it was obvious he was putting on a brave face with his frustration and trying to hide his late-night drinking. Normally an active man, his present predicament made his disappointment all the more maddening.

Making matters worse was not knowing how long the civil war was going to go on and whether they could ever go back. He was probably better off going to Ireland and giving it a try, she thought, and if it didn't work out maybe things would improve here.

She pondered briefly on going abroad first herself but it wasn't a good idea, she decided, leaving Luken in charge of the kids with otherwise nothing to do. But, events were happening so fast, there was so little time to think, just like when they'd had to leave home.

***

They left the children with Anna and, as their last evening out together for some time, Miren decided they'd have a more lavish meal than usual, this time at the Madison Hotel Restaurant. The proprietor, Monsieur Lalande, showed them to their table in the centre of the floor and, recognising them as newcomers, presented them with a free bottle of wine for their first visit. He went about attending patrons at the other tables and paid a cursory visit during the different courses.

Although spartan, with plain wooden floors and wooden chairs, the décor exuded a charm with its starched white tablecloths and a small vase of seasonal flowers, freisas, on each table.

'This place has a reputation for exceptional food,' Luken said. '*Le moins cher parmi les meilleurs.*' The cheapest among the best.

'So, your mind is all set on going to Ireland?' Miren asked as they sipped their red Bordeaux.

'It's worth a try. The downside is leaving you and the kids behind. But it wouldn't make sense for all of us to go together, there are too many unknowns. I'll have to improve my English vastly. Ireland got its independence some fourteen years ago and I'd expect opportunities for new businesses. You have to admire the way they got their independence. Maybe Euskal Herria could learn from them.'

'That's for another time, Luken. Tell me more about this Padraig fellow.'

The starters arrived and Miren tucked into her onion soup. 'They've caramelised the onions and added sherry. Delicious. They even soaked the croutons in melted cheese.'

Luken had a small portion of cassoulet, white beans stewed in duck with a few sections of sausage.

'He struck me as being a decent man, been in business for a long time and certainly seems to know the motor trade. He was held in high regard by the big cheeses in Paris.'

'Why would he want you to work for him?'

'Because of my experience on continental cars. It seems in Ireland they're trying to break away from the British and American influence.'

For the main course Luken had a tender cœur de charolais steak, while Miren went for the traditional coq au vin, braised chicken with wine, mushrooms and onion.

They sipped more of the red Bordeaux and savoured the Crème Brûlée for dessert.

Later they took coffee in the lounge while watching other diners and visitors pass by.

On the walk back down the promenade, Miren said, 'I'll tell Kasen and Sabine tomorrow. We're going to miss you; I just hope there's no problems on the trip over.'

'I'm sure it'll be fine,' Luken said, moving closer to take her hand. 'I'm looking forward to the day when the four of us are all together under our own roof.'

Miren turned and kissed him. 'Did you know that you're an exceptional man, Luken Abaroa?'

'Oh! I'll take your word for that. What makes you say it?'

'You just are.'

'You're quite a lady yourself, aren't you? Self-possessed and not easily intimidated.'

'C'est moi,' she replied and kissed him again. That's me.

Darkness started to fall and she noticed the homeless émigrés setting up their overnight coverings and tents on the beach. They stopped to look and she said, 'That could so easily have been us. What's to become of all those people?'

'I don't know, I just don't know,' Luken replied.

***

Next day when she finished work at noon, Luken was playing a card game with the kids in the front room of the house. Miren kept a serious look about her and called them over, taking Sabine by the hand, saying, 'We've a few things to tell you. Papá is going away and we'll be going after him.'

'Where?'

'Ireland. He's going first to get everything ready and we'll be following in a few weeks' time. We'll have our own place and more space to play in.'

'Why can't we go back to Durango? We'd loads of space there,' Kasen said.

'We can't, too dangerous. There's lots of bad things happening there now, as you know, Kasen.'

'Why can't we go with Papá?' Sabine asked.

'Because our place isn't set up yet. We'd only get in his way.'

Miren turned to Luken. 'They're going to a fête at the church this afternoon since it's All Souls Day. Bring them over to the church, their school friends are all there. I'll start to pack for you. I don't think I've ever made so many snap decisions in one day.'

Luken took the youngsters and left while she gathered and folded his clothes and put them in a suitcase. She ran a bath and took a quick wash.

When he came back she was dressed in her night attire, sitting and looking out the bedroom window.

'Don't tell me,' he said. 'You were just going to have a lie down and get your thoughts together.'

'Correct.'

He reached out and took her hand. She stood, they embraced and kissed. She opened the buttons of his shirt while he started to peel the nightdress off her shoulders. He stopped. 'Wait.'

He went to the bathroom and returned after a quick wash then closed the shutters.

'This will be our last time doing it for a while.'

'Better make sure it's memorable one!' she laughed. 'It's a good thing we're here on our own, it won't matter about the noise.'

They continued undressing each other and threw back the bedclothes. Climbing onto the bed, Luken kissed and massaged her breasts and in a while turned onto his back then drew her up. She straddled his pelvis and took him inside. Miren leaned forward, put her hands on his chest to maintain balance and felt his skin still soft after the wash. She moved back and forth and let the physical sensation carry her away. She climaxed with, still, an unfulfilled craving and recommenced thrusting back and forth.

'I wonder what Father Mikel would say,' Luken said, 'if he knew we were doing the "act of procreation," as he called it, like this.'

Miren burst out laughing. 'Stop! You're putting me off!'

After the second crescendo, she lay back down, saying, 'Jesús, I'm wrecked after that. What with all the running around as well.'

Luken laughed out loud as he moved between her limbs.

Later, she asked, 'Why did I have to have such a fabulous consummation just as you're about to go away?'

'Let's just enjoy it. In the past, we should have planned on doing this when the kids were out rather than waiting until they were asleep and then trying to do it quietly.'

'We're not very good at planning,' she replied, stepping out of the bed. 'Look, the sheets are soaked. And we both need another wash. That was good fun.'

She ripped the sheets off the bed and threw them into a corner, saying, 'Come on, we haven't much time, Anna will be back with her mother soon. They're at the fête as well.'

Darkness still prevailed the next morning when, without waking the children, Luken dressed and embraced Miren.

She handed him a book. 'Get as much of that into your head as you can on the way over. It's an English language book. Watch yourself and hurry up and get on your feet.'

They kissed and with a heavy heart and suitcase in hand, he slipped quietly down the stairs.

*****

Miren was the first member of staff into the café that morning and immediately set about preparing the tables and tidying up the work area in the kitchen.

The telephone rang. 'Is that you, Miren?'

'Who's that?'

'Arossa. I'm calling from Bilbao.'

'What are you doing there?'

'We moved here after you left. It's not safe for us in Durango. The bad news is that Estebe has been arrested.'

'We heard from Kerbasi about that. What for?'

'On suspicion of communist activities.'

'He wasn't involved in anything like that, was he?'

'Not that I'm aware of but that doesn't mean he wasn't.'

'Have you seen him since?' Miren asked.

'No, but I'm asking my father to see what he can do. He knows some men in the Spanish Nationalist regime so he might be able to help. He's just doing this for my sake. You know that he and Estebe didn't get along.'

'You'll have to keep trying. How are you?'

'I'm okay but unhappy at having to abandon our home. God knows what's going to happen to it. I'm staying in my father's house. How are you, Miren, and what's been happening?'

'Luken couldn't get work and has gone to Ireland, he just left this morning. A businessman he knows offered him work there. I'm hoping to follow when he gets settled in.'

'That's a big move for Luken,' Arossa replied. 'At least it'll keep him out of trouble. What about the kids?'

'They're fine, going to school and learning French. Have you heard anything about Father Garai or Sister Alicia?'

'Health wise, Sister Alicia is okay. She was released after questioning and sent to a convent in Iruña, one of those places where they don't have contact with the outside world.'

'She'll be disappointed with that, not being able to practice nursing.'

'Father Garai was arrested and sent to jail. Too liberal. Badly beaten,' Arossa said.

'I'm sorry to hear that, I hope he's okay.'

Miren noticed that the rest of the staff had arrived. A few customers had also come in. 'I have to go. Give me your number, I'll call you back.'

She reverted to working and reflected on the call. She had only met him that one time when they were leaving but knew Arossa's father was an old man, nearing retirement. He had done well with his steel business so Arossa shouldn't have any immediate worry. But who knew how the war was ultimately going to materialise?

Despite his small stature and calm appearance, Estebe was a tough man. She wondered how he was bearing up with his incarceration. And it was good to hear that Sister Alicia was still alive, and Father Garai. With his gentle and thoughtful outlook, the last thing he deserved was imprisonment. Of the three of them, she thought the one most likely to survive was Estebe.

Chapter 16

'How did Miren react?' Guillaume asked while starting the car.

'Not too happy at first but she came around to it,' Luken replied. 'I forgot to remind her about the Ariel motorcycle, she can ride that. Maybe you could encourage her to use it?'

'She'll make other women jealous on that bike.'

'She'll always associate it with what happened in Otxandio but I keep telling her if she hadn't been there that day, who knows what might have happened to Sabine. She could have been given to anyone.'

Further along the road, Guillaume handed over a wad of banknotes.

'What's this for?'

'In case you get stuck.'

'I don't need this —'

'Keep it! You can pay me back when you get on your feet,' Guillaume retorted. 'I know Ireland is a strong Catholic country so the church will probably be praisin' Franco and condemning everyone else as Communists. As they're doing here.'

'I don't usually go to mass,' Luken replied.

'Probably as well if you do over there, until you get to know how the land lies. Anyway, you have the phone number of the hotel, you can ring us anytime and we'll get a message to Miren, if she doesn't get it herself.'

The lights were on at the Quai de Lesseps when they arrived in Bayonne. Men were lifting crates of goods onto the trawler and a crane was dropping down barrels of diesel fuel. Pello and his associates were watching nearby. As they got closer Luken saw that the trawlermen were those he had seen at the hotel café from time to time.

They parked by the dockside and Guillaume introduced the men as André and Thierry.

'Haven't we've seen you at the hotel?' Thierry asked.

'Probably,' Luken replied.

'So, you're going away and leaving that fine woman of yours behind?'

'Not for long I hope.'

The men returned to their loading duties.

Luken turned to Guillaume, 'Did you know they'd be doing this?'

'No, but I'm not surprised.'

'It'll be some time before you get more fresh fish!'

'That's okay, I've plenty in the ice box. They're not the only fishermen around.'

Luken took his case from the back seat. Standing by the ship, they looked on until the loading had finished.

Guillaume gestured to the trawler, 'You should have some entertainment with those two on board.'

They embraced, wished each other well.

'Look after yourself,' Guillaume said.

Luken went on board, picking up the odour of fish and diesel fuel. As the sun came up, the trawlermen started the engine and cast off.

Guillaume drove away as Luken looked on, wondering if he was taking the right course of action. Thinking of the commitment he'd made to himself, just a few months ago, not to be apart from Miren and the kids, now here he was doing just that. But what could he do? St Jean had nothing for him. Fate had dismissed his resolution contemptuously and he just had to get work. Ireland had got its independence and there was bound to be opportunities there.

The trawler sailed down the Adour river and out to sea. The crew set about tidying up while the four passengers leaned on the taffrail looking out to sea.

'I meant to ask you why we were going from Bayonne rather than St Jean?' Luken asked Pello, who responded in Spanish.

'We don't want to be seen or recorded as having left, not until we get refugee status. Remember to ask for asylum when we get to Ireland. You're a political refugee, not a criminal and certainly not a holiday-maker.'

'What do you think our chances are?'

'It's an independent country, not involved in any war, so it looks good. It's even better for you now that you have someone who offered you a job. You won't be a drain on the state.'

Luken reckoned from the quality of Pello's accent that he was from a well-to-do or possibly an aristocratic family. Miren had said that he spoke good English so, as well as being a lawyer, here was a man who had taken the trouble to perfect three languages.

'Are you leaving any family behind? Luken asked.

'My wife and children are in Paris but they'll be following when I get settled. As for my parents and siblings, they're going nowhere. They disowned me some time ago when I started defending liberal victims during the Rivera regime, don't want to know anything about me.'

'That's sad.'

'The price we pay, Luken.'

The smooth sailing out of port gave way to pitching and rolling as they hit the high seas on the Bay of Biscay. As the sea spray sprinkled his face and the fresh saline sea air invaded his nostrils, Luken observed the crew at their instruments, monitoring the compass bearings and compensating for any sideways drift.

Pello and the trawlermen explained to the rest of the passengers that there was a danger of being intercepted by Spanish vessels that had been commandeered by forces loyal to General Franco. Under no circumstances would they accept such a boarding party. A stash of arms including pistols and rifles were hidden in the engine bay and every man was expected to do his bit if necessary. With one exception, they all had experience in the use of firearms. The exception was then given a basic lesson in how to load and use a rifle.

Over the subsequent days, they fell into the routine of sleeping, eating and looking out to the horizon. They drank coffee, smoked and talked about the difficulties they had got themselves into at home, their families and the hopes they had for when they arrived in Ireland. Another passenger, Antonio, mentioned that he'd looked out his window one evening and seen a wounded man lying in the street, a Republican sympathiser as it happened. He'd taken him to hospital and for that he was on the wanted list. The other passenger, Francisco, explained that, like Pello, he had also defended people of various political beliefs, even fascist sympathisers during the Second Republic, but that wasn't good enough. He was convinced the firing squad was inevitable.

André and Thierry each sat with the passengers from time to time and recalled stories of other Spanish migrants they had helped escape. One particularly harrowing story related how they'd helped a woman and her seven children to escape to France. Her communist husband had been summarily executed in front of the entire family and, rather than become a victim herself, she'd fled in the middle of the night.

Luken spoke whatever English he knew when talking to Pello and studied Miren's English book when the humour took him.

On deck, he noticed the relentless rush of the waves against the hull helped to drown out the never-ending hum of the diesel engine. The trawler stayed close to the well-trodden shipping lanes while an occasional vessel passed in the distance, usually a freight ship or tanker.

***

As they approached Cobh in the south of Ireland, Luken looked up to see the houses on the hillside and the towering cathedral presiding, it seemed, over the houses, the town and the port itself. Even here the Catholic Church is showing its predominance, he reckoned, feeling more than a little apprehensive, arriving in a country he'd never been to before.

As André and Thierry tied up the trawler against the quays in Cobh harbour two immigration officers appeared with a scornful look on their faces.

The passengers had difficulty keeping their balance on land, having spent six days at sea.

The senior officer sought out the skipper and instructed him that fish, lobster or any other sea creatures could not be landed at that point.

'No fish,' André replied.

'We're here seeking asylum,' Pello said.

The officer's jaw dropped, 'What? How many of you?'

Pello declared that the four passengers had been subject to persecution under the Fascist regime of General Franco and were seeking refuge in Ireland.

Luken reckoned that the immigration men were flabbergasted. Being at their mercy, he felt the tension among the other émigrés as well as himself.

'This is unusual,' the officer said with a sympathetic smile. 'Migrants normally come here to get out of the country, not to get into it!'

He turned to Pello, 'What about the crew?'

'They'll get supplies and go back to France.'

The second officer had gone aboard and inspected the boat. Everyone including the trawlermen were directed to an office where their travel papers were inspected.

The senior officer left the room for what seemed, to Luken, like two hours and returned following what he guessed were multiple telephone calls, judging from the voices in the adjacent room.

'You're in luck,' the officer declared. 'My department have given permission for you to stay, temporarily at least. But you must apply for full refugee status, give all details about who you know here and keep us fully informed of your whereabouts at all times. You'll also need the approval of the Gardaí who should be here soon.'

Luken felt the tension immediately drain out of him while Pello translated the full details. The trawlermen were free to sail back but their travel documents were being retained until their boat was refuelled and ready to depart.

The immigrants returned to the trawler to collect their belongings. Three Gardaí arrived in a car and asked the same questions as the immigration officers and took written statements. They went onboard and inspected the vessel from top to bottom. The fishing nets were superficially checked and Luken wondered about the rifles, other firearms and 'anything else.' André and Thierry must be old hands at this stuff, he thought, when the lawmen left the ship, empty-handed.

They proceeded to the Post Office to make their phone calls. Luken in turn rang Miren but, unable to get a connection, instead sent a telegram assuring her of his safe arrival. He tried Padraig. The operator put him through though on a poor, scratchy line to Dublin.

'When did you arrive?' Padraig asked, after they'd exchanged greetings.

'This morning.'

'Have you booked in anywhere?'

'A local hotel. I won't stay on long, Padraig, there's a queue for the phone.'

'You're better off taking the train to Dublin, much quicker than me driving down. I'll collect you at the station.'

Pello, Antonio, Francisco and Luken took lunch at a café and afterwards Luken ambled around, observing the terraced houses facing towards the sea, each painted in bright but different colours. He continued up through the winding streets and, despite the cold, felt how good it was to be on land.

*****

At Kingsbridge station he recognised Padraig who, after due salutations in French, insisted on carrying his suitcase. They crossed the bridge over the river Liffey, stepped onto a stationary open-topped tram and went upstairs.

'I've been on trams in Bilbao,' Luken said. 'But I've never seen a tram with an upstairs like this before.'

'We call them "double-deckers",' Padraig said. 'I've arranged for you to stay in my place for a while, if that's okay with you? It'll take the pressure off you looking for a room, give you more time to get a decent place. I don't think you'll have much trouble anyway, everyone has a room to rent.'

'It's very decent of you doing this.'

'Think nothing of it. I'm the one who needs help, experienced men are hard to come by.'

Padraig, Luken thought, was well advanced in his years, much older than he remembered him. Nonetheless, he looked dapper with the trimmed moustache, suit and necktie and bowler hat. He thought of a picture he'd seen in a newspaper years previously of Lloyd George, the British Prime Minister.

The tram moved off along Albert Quay in the direction of the city.

In the chilly, sunny afternoon, Luken took in the view. Gazing over the rail as the tram travelled alongside the Liffey and crossed O'Connell Bridge, he saw a few cars, a multitude of bicycles and green buses moving by.

'Before we get something to eat I'll bring you for a quick look around town,' Padraig said.

Stepping off at the wide O'Connell Street, Padraig eagerly pointed out a few landmarks across the city centre: Nelson's Pillar, Clerys department store and the Savoy cinema.

Inside the Red Bank Restaurant, the maître d' showed them to a table.

'I come here once a week,' Padraig said. 'Since my wife died I don't bother going on holiday trips anymore so I don't have to put money aside. I'm happy to stay in Dublin and enjoy what I can here.'

Luken chose a filet of cod while Padraig ordered a risotto.

'Good thing we came here on a Friday,' Padraig said. 'It's the only day of the week when you're sure of getting fish. I'm sure you noticed the cars on the way here. They're mostly British, Ford, Austin and so on. Some of our customers insist on something different like continental cars. That's where you and your experience come in. In the meantime, you don't mind working on British cars?'

'Au contraire, Padraig, I'll be happy to work on anything you have. I'm sure they have their own peculiarities and innovations. I'll be glad to get my hands on any kind of work for that matter.'

Afterwards, hailing a hansom cab, Padraig instructed the driver to take them to his house on North Fredrick Street.

Luken unpacked in one of the upstairs bedrooms and looked out the window for a while to observe the fine old Georgian houses and the pedestrians passing by. He went down to the sitting room where his host turned from lighting a fire in the hearth and asked, 'Did you ever drink Irish whiskey?'

'I might've tried it once. Where I come from it's pricey, we tend to drink brandy.'

'Here, it's the other way round.'

They sat and drank and talked about their families. Padraig explained that his mother was Irish and his father French. They met when his father was based in Dublin as part of the diplomatic service. French was spoken when he and his sister, now living in Paris, were growing up, while the French surname, Lestrange, and his fluency in the language had helped to ingratiate him to the Citroën management.

Discussing the political situation in their respective countries, Padraig mentioned the dreadful killings that were alleged to have happened in Spain and Luken assured him that they were indeed true, he had witnessed some himself and described the horror of Otxandio. He noticed how Padraig was shaken to hear of the attack on civilians.

Padraig spoke of the uncertainty in Irish politics. Though independence had been established, the northern part of the country had been partitioned and remained British. Many in the south were unhappy at the arrangement, wanting to keep the country united, and there was still an undercurrent of instability with an occasional outbreak of civil strife.

He checked his watch, put the bottle of whiskey on a card table and said, 'I have to go around to the garage and lock up. I shouldn't be long but have another drink yourself.'

The glow of the fire warmed Luken to drowsiness and when his host returned forty-five minutes later, he was asleep in the armchair, the glass still in his hand.

Chapter 17

Estebe sat on the floor in a cell of Onderreta Prison. Eight other prisoners shared the cell and he felt the heat as intense as the tension. Now, after ten days, oblivious to the stench of perspiration and unwashed bodies, he still hadn't been brought before any court or investigator. Some mornings one or more prisoners were taken out to Ondarras for execution and the jail went quiet. Other times, he learnt, groups of prisoners were taken to Hernani Cemetery for execution.

On certain days, after a storm or a high wind, he heard the sound of the waves breaking on the beach – a stone's throw from the prison. Recalling visits to the beach with his family years ago, he noticed that no holidaymakers could be heard coming to the beach now, only the military trucks coming and going. The only audible sounds that could be heard at the prison were the screams of those being tortured. From time to time, Estebe thought he heard some youths, who had come along for a swim, being turned away by sentries at the jail.

Monte Igeldo was visible through the high, barred opening in the cell wall and he remembered climbing up to the top with his companions. Not particularly high but it had been fun taking a gamble on who would get there first or who, finishing last, would be prevailed on to buy the fizzy drinks or, in later times, the beer.

He was anticipating a rough time and the real possibility of death. But when the time came he'd argue his case and hoped his inquisitor would be someone with a brain and not a trigger-happy fanatic looking for the flimsiest of evidence. Either way, it was going to be a tough journey since, he knew, the Fascists treated their own soldiers with appalling brutality, severely beating misbehaving volunteers and having them whipped on all parts of their bodies, including the genitals.

Two lorries pulled up outside and the soldiers shouted at the prisoners to climb out. Soon, cell doors were opened and men were shoved into wherever there was judged to be space. Women prisoners in the second truck were being marched upstairs to the cells on the third floor. Guards inspected Estebe's cell and judged it to be full, for the time being.

'What do you think is going to happen to you?' an inmate asked.

'Probably execution,' Estebe replied.

'Why?'

'For sympathising with the hungry and destitute.'

'And how did that manifest itself?' the prisoner asked. Estebe reckoned he was an educated man by his choice of words.

'Well, I might have said in an unguarded moment, something like, "Isn't it poor that in this day and age we cannot feed our own people?"'

'And a priest overheard you?'

'Quite possibly, the wrong kind of priest. Or a cop maybe. What about yourself?'

'Strike leader. I called out the workers in a tyre factory.'

Two armed guards, accompanied by a jailer, called out a few names as they walked past the packed cells. As each prisoner responded the jailer opened the cell. Estebe's name was called and he was marched into a room where two more guards stood.

At the top of the room, a cell that looked as though it had been used at one time to hold inmates now contained shelves and cabinets that were packed with files and folders. Piles of newspapers were stacked on the floor. Estebe was directed to a seat in front of a steel desk below a barred opening in the wall. He supposed the desk was positioned so that the light was behind the interrogator and directed on him. Feeling the anxiety building inside him, he recognised that this was going to be the hardest time of his life, facing the prospect of execution or being kept locked up and mistreated indefinitely at the whim of an unknown jailer.

A Nationalist officer in a captain's uniform entered the room, sat at the desk, looked through a file and said, 'Estebe Ybarra, the sooner you tell me about your Republican cohorts, the sooner you'll know your prison term. At least then you'll know your fate and you can put aside the fear you certainly have here, now.'

'I don't have any Republican cohorts.'

'Strange that the records in your offices were all burned earlier this year, isn't it?'

'I'm no arsonist.'

'We don't believe it was an arsonist attack. People you worked with have suggested that you're at least a Republican sympathiser, a red.'

'Just because I express sympathy for the poor and subjugated scarcely makes me a red, does it?'

'So Spanish people are subjugated, are they?'

'Some of them are, those working in the factories and on farms, amongst others.'

The officer was a man of about thirty years, scrawny and thin, and had a large moustache which Estebe reckoned he'd probably grown to make himself look older.

'I'm sure our factory owners, including your father in law, would take issue with that,' the officer replied as he sat back in his chair. 'You're well on in your years, Estebe. Co-operate and we'll make it easier for you.'

'I don't know who you spoke to but they were lying. What proof have you?'

'I'll ask the questions. What about this man Luken Abaroa and his wife? We know you're a close friend of his, where is he?'

'I don't know, I went up to his house to return some tools and there was no sign of either him or his wife.'

'We know he's been stirring up trouble, urging workers to down tools and start an uprising. Treason, in other words. We've seen his printed papers. Another strange thing, records disappearing at the Donostia Hospital where his wife works. She is someone we also need to talk to. We know she removed records including those of Communist and Republican patients.'

'I'm not my brother or sister's keeper, captain. I wouldn't know where either of them are.'

'What about others that you know? Can you tell me about any other reds, others that you've worked with or in your area? There's no need for them to find out where the information came from.'

'I can't help you.'

The officer sat upright and nodded to one of the guards, who kicked Estebe's chair and gestured for him to move.

On the way, he was kicked and pushed from behind so that other prisoners saw they were goading and humiliating him. He was led to a room at the rear of the building and received a punch in the jaw as he turned to face the guards.

The force of the assault sent him sprawling backwards, though he didn't fall. The room had an open filing cabinet, two chairs, a long table and, alongside the wall, electrical apparatus that he didn't recognise. A junior officer, his uniform loosened, sat in a chair. Estebe was told to remove his clothes and lie on the table. To avoid being assaulted again he did as instructed.

Four leather straps at the corner of the table were fastened to his wrists and ankles as he lay naked, face down. The third guard connected two wired metal clasps to each ankle and turned on the electrical device.

The officer brandished a probe which he momentarily jabbed into Estebe who felt a jolt though not as severe as he expected. 'You have to tell us what activities you were involved in and who else was with you. That was just a taster, didn't hurt much, I know. This is a new invention, called a picana. The wonders of electricity; it uses high voltage but low current, which means the pain can be prolonged over a period. Good news from your point of view, my friend, because it means that if you soon change your mind we can stop immediately and you can walk out of here without any marks on you. So, you want to give us a few names and save yourself a lot of prolonged pain?'

Estebe said nothing and shook his head. The officer applied the probe to various parts of his body. A guard threw a container of water over his back to increase the conductivity of his skin while the officer turned up the voltage to increase the shock. Estebe clenched his teeth to avoid screaming. The probe was removed for a minute and the officer asked again for names. He repeated the procedure, pain and pause, until eventually Estebe screamed in a vain effort to relieve the pain. In time he lost consciousness.

He awoke to find himself dressed and loosely bound to the upright of the chair, back in the captain's room.

'Sit up.'

A guard removed the cords holding him to the upright then handed him a can of water.

'How are you feeling now?'

'I've had better days.'

'I see your son died earlier this year. That must have been heart breaking. Did he have the same views as you?'

'What does it matter, he's dead now.'

'You know what they say, what's in the cat is in the kittens. We had a visit from your father in law. He appealed for clemency regardless of what you might be accused of, telling us that you were a good man and as part of your work with the authorities you'd helped in no small way to get his factory established.'

Estebe shrugged but said nothing.

'More importantly, from your point of view, is this,' the officer continued, picking up a newspaper to read out an article:

'"…*Ander's father Estebe, now back living in Durango, fought for France during the Great War and later represented Action Française*…"'

He put down the paper and went on, 'Action Française is an organisation that we have an affiliation with, so that will help your case when it comes before the tribunal later this week. All of this information will be passed on and you're looking at a long jail sentence rather than execution.'

As he languished in the cell that evening, Estebe reflected on the irony of a factually incorrect newspaper report having saved his life.

***

Endika and one of his comrades sliced open the skin of a juvenile Roe deer, removed the entrails and threw them into a thicket. Despite the risk of firing off the shots and being located, food was running low and he felt the risk had to be taken. Going without food for extended periods weakened alertness and judgement, just about the worst thing that could happen since they were fighting a guerilla war in the wild.

Fortunately, as a young animal, the meat would be more tender than the sinewy haunches of a mature deer. Not that they wouldn't eat that, but a week of eating nothing but old buck meat was tough on the digestive system. They put the edible portions in sacking and carried them back to camp.

A portion of meat was set aside for immediate consumption while they dragged out the salt barrel and started processing the rest.

Afterwards, Endika sat outside the cave thinking about the next meeting with Kerbasi. The occasional trek across the mountains was becoming more dangerous as the war progressed. Squads of Requetés with their red berets had been sighted in some of the villages and reports were coming through of heavier military vehicles being seen in Iruña. Nonetheless, it was important to find out the latest news from someone trustworthy, who had access to the latest broadcasts.

Despite being coded, radio communication messages to and from the camp were kept to a minimum after suspicions arose that some messages had been intercepted. An eight-man company similar to their own had been attacked near Saratxo and most of the members killed, the remainder captured.

For now, his brief was to desist from further attacks, keep the area monitored and report enemy activities up the command line and to counter attack if fired upon.

As leader of the troop, he felt confident that he was keeping discipline in line although there were two individuals, one in particular, whose lack of attentiveness, especially during patrols, was a cause for concern. He made sure that the two men were never on the same detail. Boredom, he opined, was the biggest problem. Little real military activity had come their way and frustration was growing on hearing about the Fascist advance while having no opportunity to fight back.

Although participating in regular patrols and target practice in the remote valleys, foraging for food, setting rabbit traps and fishing nets took up a lot of time. In the meantime, they sat around waiting for command instructions while cleaning their weapons, the Mauser rifles and Tiger carbines.

Encouraged that Luken and his family had all got away to safety, Endika wondered what his brother was now doing. He hoped for the day when he could put all this war business behind him and lead a more settled life, whenever that might be.

Chapter 18

The garage in Parnell Street opened straight out onto the city thoroughfare. The busy street was occupied by red-bricked two storeyed buildings with latticed windows, mostly retail outlets, tobacconists, newsagents and grocers with rented accommodation on the upper floors.

Padraig introduced Luken to Eddie, the supervisor, and each of the mechanics. Shown some of the cars that were in for service, an Austin Tourer and two Ford C Tens which he recognised, Luken said, 'Ford make these also in Barcelona.'

'Have you worked on them?' Eddie asked.

'No, but no problem. Difficult for me is the English.'

'Understood,' Padraig replied. 'I know of a woman who gives English lessons, you'd probably benefit from a course with her—'

'Sorry, Padraig,' Luken interrupted. 'Please, speak more slowly in English!'

Padraig laughed and repeated his suggestion.

Luken soon settled into the job, pleased that he could be of particular help with continental cars, and found his co-workers helpful with the language difficulties. Happy to hear them ask about his family and hometown, he kept an English-Spanish dictionary to look up whatever word when needed.

He rented a room on the second floor of a terraced house on Hardwicke Place. Luken recognised that although the houses were similar to those on Padraig's street, he was living in a run-down part of the city. The houses, he reckoned, must have been elegant in their heyday but certainly not now.

Within a few weeks, the daily routine kept him busy between work, familiarising himself with the local cars, exploring the city and its environs and attending English classes. Feeling no such disappointment as he had when having to start at the bottom of the job ladder in St Jean de Luz, Luken reckoned that he simply had no time for such luxury. He went to a cinema or to the Abbey Theatre, where over time, his understanding of the spoken word improved.

As the winter hardened and the cold wet weather became uncomfortable he bought an overcoat, hat and scarf. Despite the country being at peace, the shortage of commodities was another surprise. Apart from a lot of foodstuffs, everything else, it seemed, came from or through England and the political difficulties between the two countries were exacerbating supply.

As time went on he sorely missed Miren and the children. Nonetheless, he stopped using Padraig's telephone, not just because of cost but also the lack of privacy. Instead, he went to the General Post Office and took his turn and made the call from a booth.

One day he felt a shiver of excitement when he heard Miren's voice on the crackling line.

'We're getting by okay,' she said, speaking in Spanish. 'The kids miss you, especially Sabine. She became quiet after you left … hardly let me out of her sight. She's not too bad now but still needs reassurance that we'll soon be reunited with Papá. I started playing cards with Anna, she's

- 246 -

teaching me how to play bridge with… Her Mamá died a few weeks ago … died in her sleep. She's still quite upset as you'd expect. Endika is still living and fighting in the mountains, I get an odd call from him at the hotel… Arossa has heard nothing about Estebe but her father is trying to get to see him. I needn't tell you how worried she is… By the way I had a call from a Mrs Robinson in England. Her husband is in hospital and won't be going back to Spain. She said to keep the motorcycle — '

'It won't do us much good now,' Luken said and described his new job, his lodgings and the English language course.

'There's still hundreds of refugees coming over,' she said, 'most by sea. Some of them are making a living here by fishing and it's causing a lot of resentment with the local fishermen…'

Luken tried to dampen his frustration as the line broke up.

'...many refugees have left St Jean,' Miren continued, 'and gone to Bayonne where they're offered better facilities. I've heard that Durango has been completely destroyed, and something like two hundred and forty people killed. They're calling it the "Town of the Dead" … German bombers have also wiped out Guernica, they've even used incendiary bombs and burned people to death. God knows how many have been killed there. The Fascists had the gall to blame it on the Republicans. Italian troop brigades are now helping the Fascists…'

The line went dead and Luken felt frustrated as he hung up, sensing the utter chaos in his homeland, even more so with Miren, Kasen and Sabine residing in a town scarcely a hundred kilometres away from it all.

***

In the evenings he sat with the other tenants around the fireside in a common room on the ground floor listening to the radio, each contributing towards the purchase of fuel. They addressed him using the English version of his name, Luke, and he was not unhappy with that. His grasp of English was still limited and he had difficulty understanding what was being said when the men spoke rapidly. From time to time, one of them stopped and explained, especially when an amusing story or a joke was being told. Surprised to hear of the number of people emigrating to Britain, one of the men mentioned that reports put the figure at one thousand every week.

On the street he watched children playing with circular steel hoops, recovered from discarded bicycle wheels that had had their hubs and spokes removed. They raced each other by running the hoops on the street and ran after them, making them go faster by striking them with a stick. He was amazed at how happy and healthy they looked despite many having no shoes and being so poorly dressed. He recalled the flour thief and his daughter in France and wondered what might have happened to them since.

He stopped to see a line of girls using a long skipping rope. Two girls at either end swung the rope while another ran in and skipped over the rope as it hit the ground. They repeated the chant as each girl ran in to take her turn:

    'Vote vote vote for De Valera!
    In comes Aoife at the door
    Aoife is the one
    And we'll have a lot of fun
    And we don't vote for Devo anymore!'

For appearances only, each Sunday, he attended the mass service in St Francis Xavier Church on Gardiner

Street. Outside the church, he chatted to one of the men from the lodgings and they went to Donnelly's pub where they enjoyed several bottles of Guinness stout.

One Sunday he was taken aback when the priest giving the sermon spoke at length about the civil war in Spain. It was not so much a military war as one of good and evil, he declared. On one side there were the so-called Republicans who represented Anarchy and Communism. This was Moscow's illegitimate son perpetuating the words of the anti-Christ.

I can't believe what I'm hearing, Luken thought.

'On the other side,' the cleric said, 'the forces of General Franco are fighting for the cause of God and righteousness. If the evils perpetuated by Russia are allowed to succeed, it will consume the free world, Ireland included. In essence, it is a fight between Christian Spain and anti-Christian Bolshevism.'

Luken felt the anger rising in his gut. I've come two thousand kilometres to get away from this rubbish, he thought, and here I am listening to this… this drivel!

Aware that his face had reddened and his body was shaking, he felt the urge to shout up at the priest that he was talking nonsense, that he had his facts wrong, it was the church that was promoting evil.

But knowing that he couldn't, all he could do was force himself to calm down.

'To combat such tyranny,' the priest went on, 'an international movement is now taking shape. An organisation has been established in Dublin to assist General Franco and volunteers are invited to participate. Anyone taking up the cause has the blessing of the church and is guaranteed absolution for all wrong doings committed in the past.'

Outside, one of his co-lodgers approached and asked, 'What do you think of that, Luke?'

'He got it the wrong way round.'

'So you won't be volunteering?'

'Definitely not. I'd love to go up and tell that priest what's really going on.'

After a few drinks Luken reflected that no matter where he went, war was never far away and even the one he escaped from was following him.

At the same time, radio reports told of the activities of Irish Republican groups who had been attacking state installations as part of a campaign to tear down the border with Northern Ireland and he hoped it would never turn into outright civil war.

During the weekends and especially on Saturday afternoons Luken sought out local sporting activities and went to see whatever matches were being played. He found Gaelic Football interesting and one rule he thought particularly amusing was that there was no 'offside'. A fellow spectator described how a player could receive a passed ball anywhere without being in a penalised position. Having played soccer earlier in life, he decided to give the game a try, seeing as it was the most prevalent sport locally.

At the local club, the manager pointed to the goal posts. 'You can see that they're like rugby posts. Some people regard the game as a cross between soccer and rugby. If you kick the ball into the goal mouth, you get a goal. If you kick the ball over the cross-bar you get a point. A goal counts as three points. So, if a game ends with a score of two goals and four points on one side and one goal and seven points on the other side, it's a draw. Ten points each. But, like soccer and unlike rugby there's a goalkeeper. And unlike soccer you handle the ball, as I'm sure you've seen.'

Luken was accepted at the club; the manager and players demonstrated further regulations. He got his own kit, turned up for training and in time was selected for his first competitive game.

In the dressing room four or five players were already kitted out and offered encouragement. Out on the field he was assigned a defensive position, one that he was happy to accept until he had garnered more experience. The ball was thrown into play and he took up position.

It turned out to be a free-flowing affair with both good play here and mistakes there and he soon figured who the most skilled players were on each team. Early in the second half he was thrown the ball and being unmarked and in an opportune place he raced down the left side of the pitch and kicked the ball over the cross-bar to score a point. Towards the end of the match a similar chance arose but this time an opposing player heaved into his right side and he sent the ball wide.

Back at the clubhouse, disappointment prevailed that the match had ended in a draw. Sitting on a bench removing his boots Luken was approached by a player who looked annoyed. 'You should've got that point.'

Another player spoke out, 'Look who's talkin', many's the chance you missed, Tomo.'

Tomo, staring at Luken, said, 'Maybe if we had an Irish player we would've won that match.'

Not to be spoken down to, Luken stood up and returned the stare, saying, 'And maybe if we got another player like you we'd lose the match.'

'Good man yourself, Luke! You tell him!' another player said.

Tomo retorted, 'Why don't you go back to your own fuckin' country.'

'Why?' Luken retorted back as the blood rushed to his head.

'Hundreds of men have to leave this country and go to England for work, why should we let the likes of you in?'

Luken thought for a moment and said, 'Hundreds of Irishmen go to my country to fight on the wrong side of the war, maybe you go and get your fuckin' head shot.'

With that, the rest of the team burst into laughter, not least with Luken's limited command of English.

When they went to a local hostelry the players gently advised him not to take Tomo's words to heart. He thanked them, remarking that he'd expected something like that would happen sooner or later.

On his way home Luken realised that although he had sometimes sensed resentment about his race or nationality it was the first time that someone had openly confronted him in a spiteful way. Mulling over the incident, he recognised that it was the first time he had used foul language at someone in English too, and apart from Tomo it hadn't seemed to bother anyone else. Quite the opposite, the rest of the lads were glad to see him use it. On balance, he thought that only a small proportion of people that he had met resented his foreign presence in the country and he felt happy to live with that.

***

A telephone call from Pello, Luken's fellow refugee, came through at the garage. He was anxious to meet and they agreed on Wynn's Hotel the following day.

Luken sat in the restaurant admiring the stained glass windows, the fine wooden panelling and the luxurious carpet. Set out for serving breakfast, the room was almost full of people who were tucking in to their first food of the day. He decided to wait for Pello before ordering. The cutlery, like the tea and coffee pots, were antique Irish silver. Pondering on the purpose of the meeting, Pello had seemed to be in bright spirits on the phone but otherwise had given little away. Maybe it was just a friendly get-together from a fellow Basque. On the other hand, there could be bad news from the old country, there was never any shortage of that.

He laughed to himself while overhearing two men at a nearby table who appeared to be commercial travellers. One was reading a newspaper and said, 'I don't understand this Spanish civil war business, do you?'

The other man, while forking a piece of bacon into his mouth, replied, 'As I understand it, Franco is on the Catholic side and the Government is communist more or less.'

'And what about the Nationalists?'

'They're with the Government.'

'I see. And what about the Socialists?'

'They're with Franco, I think,' the other replied, consigning a piece of egg and sausage into his maw.

Luken was about to lean over and correct the men's perception of loyalties when Pello appeared.

They ordered breakfast and recounted events in their lives since arriving in Ireland. Pello had stayed in Cork where distant relations had helped him and now, his wife, get settled. He was studying Irish law at university and hoped to take up practicing in a few years' time. Meanwhile he had got a job at the Metropole Hotel where his knowledge of Spanish and French was proving valuable.

The conversation turned serious when Pello brought up the subject of the meeting, a recent visit he'd received from the Gardaí. He had been questioned up and down about his presence in Ireland. Why had he come here and what had he been doing since he arrived?

'I explained that I'd told the Gardaí and immigration people in Cobh when we arrived exactly why I'd come here. But that wasn't enough, they wanted to know where I'd lived in Spain and what evidence I could show that I was genuinely "persecuted".'

'Why would they want to know that now?' Luken asked.

'I suspect the Fascist authorities have been in touch with the Irish Government to see if they could have us extradited. Ireland has always been on friendly terms with Spain. Have you heard from the Gardaí?'

'No, nothing.'

'What about your residency application?'

'I sent it in months ago but haven't heard back.'

'I've an interview with the Immigration Department next week. You should get a solicitor to follow it up, someone who specialises in Immigration Law...' Pello stopped in mid-sentence and looked Luken straight in the face, 'I have to ask you this, Luken. What church do you go to?'

'Catholic.'

'That should help your application, you should make a point of getting to know a priest or two. I've no doubt the Immigration Department will be checking all our religious affiliations. The Catholic Church has a lot of influence here. You'll remember Antonio on the trawler? He wasn't too happy when I told him to put his Jewish religion to one side and be seen going to mass. Until he gets his residency finalised at least. The reason I'm travelling around the country is to firm up on contact with yourself and the other two. We need to keep in touch while these things are going on.'

Walking to work, Luken's head raced over the possibilities in the coming months. He wondered which countries were not on friendly terms with Spain. The only place he could think of was Russia, which he didn't want to ever consider as an option. One thing was for sure, there'd be no end to the anxiety he felt anytime soon. In the meantime, he needed to follow up on his residency permit and get Miren and the kids over as quickly as he could.

Back in his room that evening, he counted the money he had saved and realised that he still had a way to go to pay for their passage.

At the garage he discussed his situation with Padraig, enquiring about solicitors and asking if there was a possibility of extra work. Padraig pointed out that with the recession it was difficult enough keeping the place going and it wasn't just Ireland but international. The 'Economic War' with England wasn't helping, especially with the tariffs. He suggested sounding out customers for work; they might have some in the evenings or at the weekends – the bakeries or hospitals for example.

He had no immediate luck seeking further work and anyone he approached said that workers were two a penny.

***

Arriving fifteen minutes early, Luken sat on a bench against the wall in the corridor of the Government Department. Suddenly aware of his perspiration, he rubbed the palms of his hands down the sides of his blue suit trousers. He repeatedly checked the knot of his necktie to ensure it was tight against his collar and reflected that it was not nearly as tight as the knot in his stomach. A murmur of voices sounded from behind the glass-panelled offices, though the words were indecipherable.

He stared at the coloured pattern of squares on the linoleum-covered floor; they reminded him of the lengthy chess games he played with Endika in his younger days. Competitive games that went on for hours and hours and in which Endika was overall slightly more successful than himself. He'd always get fed up with the amount of time the game took and give up.

Reciting answers to the questions he anticipated being asked in the forthcoming interview, he wondered, what if he gave the wrong answer, would he be shipped out of the country straight away? Surely not.

In a while, the door opposite opened and a dark-haired man in his late thirties appeared. Introducing himself as a Mr Trainor, he invited Luken in past a reception area through an inner door to an office. An older man who presented himself by the name of Synnott sat at a plain wooden desk. Trainor gestured to a chair.

Similarly dressed in suits, both men sat opposite and had what Luken regarded as a blank look about them.

'I know this is a difficult time for you but try and relax as best you can and we'll get through this quickly. Why did you leave your own country, Mr Abaroa?' Synnott asked.

'Because it was no longer safe for me or my family.'

'Why was that?'

'I helped workers with bad wages to ask for better pay and conditions, a criminal offence for the Fascist people. Also, my wife is a nurse and she removed the names and addresses of wounded Republican soldiers in the hospital where she worked, a bigger offence for them. Please, you must understand that my English is still not very good.'

'It's okay, we understand,' the younger man smiled.

'Do you have a copy of an arrest warrant?' Synnott asked.

'I don't understand, what is an arrest warr...?'

'It's a paper that the authorities present you with when they take you into custody.'

'No! The only arrest warrant the Fascists use is a gun!'

The two Irishmen gave a short laugh.

'This man has a sense of humour,' Trainor said. 'I see you play Gaelic Football. What position do you play?'

'Yes, I enjoy very much. Usually left corner-back but I hope to get a forward position.'

'Which club?'

'St Joseph's.'

'On the North Wall? Very good club...'

'Why did you leave France?' Synnott interrupted gruffly.

'No work. Many people are coming from Spain and there is not much work in France.'

In spite of Synnott's opening friendliness, he continued in a belligerent manner. 'Why didn't you go to somewhere nearer home, perhaps Belgium?'

'Because I don't know if I can get work in Belgium. I was offered a job in Ireland. Mr Lestrange knows of my experience on European cars. He invites me over to Ireland.'

Synnott sifted through papers on the desk and pulled out a letter which he read through. 'Lestrange certainly speaks well of you. Tell me this, how do we know you won't get involved in Communism when you're here?'

'Because I have no interest to get involved in Irish politics. I come here to get work and bring over my family. Maybe go back when things have settled in my country.'

Despite Synnott's statement that the interview would be short, the questions continued for nearly two hours.

Questions about his wife and children, his parents, his business and work experience, his religion and his socialist activities. At the end, the men shook hands and Trainor led him out to the front door.

'Will I be allowed to stay in Ireland?'

'I can't say, we have to submit the papers to our chief, he makes the final decision, but I would say you have a good chance. You should hear from us within a week or two.'

Walking home, Luken's unease diminished as he looked back on his most gruelling experience since landing in Cobh, but he supposed he'd made a good impression, especially with the younger man. His next destination, he decided, was a public house, where he knocked back a stiff drink in the form of a double whiskey.

***

Fortuitously, for Luken, Christmas was not far away and when it came around, the operations manager at the Post Office mentioned the possibility of a few hours evening's work with the additional bulk of Christmas cards and the influx of overseas parcels. Some postal workers had taken leave, ironically, Luken thought, to fight in Spain and extra men were now being used on a temporary basis.

Sympathetic as usual, Padraig loaned one of his vans after hours to help with deliveries.

While many of the destinations were well-to-do households, Luken gained an insight into the poverty in other parts of the city. Some were difficult to find, with an address without a number, typically on a back lane so that he had to ask around to find the recipient.

In one such place, a single room lay at the back of a tenement flat. When the woman occupant opened the door,

Luken was appalled to see that there were no floorboards; she was standing on dry earth. A curtain sectioned off the bed from the living area. A small table and two chairs stood by the window while a sideboard with a picture of herself and a man who he supposed was her husband sat against the side wall.

Her eyes brightened when he handed her the parcel, 'It's the only time I ever get anything.'

'It's coming from America.'

'My brother. He went there in 1922, on the run from De Valera.'

Luken nodded to the photo, 'Your husband?'

'He was killed by De Valera in the same year…'

'Mr De Valera himself?'

She shook her head. 'One of his gangsters. They were defending a bridge when they were ambushed.'

The woman went on to describe the incident at length, during which Luken had to ask her to slow down because of his limited English. He guessed that from living alone, she couldn't help but keep talking whenever someone paid a visit.

'Would you like a cup of tea?' she asked.

He hesitated momentarily then said, 'Yes… please.'

She folded and lit a section of old newspaper around the crown of the single ring Primus stove on the table. Just as it was about to burn out she pumped the plunger so that it sent up a dazzling blue flame. Soon the kettle boiled.

He sat, noticing a bible and a few other books and ornaments on a shelf. When he took the tea she cut and buttered a slice of bread and jam and presented it to him on a plate from the sideboard.

'You've very dark,' she said bluntly. 'Where are you from?'

After explaining his refugee and family situation she shook an index finger at him, saying, 'You must get your wife and children over as soon as you can. It doesn't do to have a married man living in a foreign country on his own.'

Smiling, he said he'd take her advice on board. She spoke of how difficult it was since her husband had died. The widows' pension had been introduced the previous year but it was hardly enough to live on and she had to take in sewing work whenever she could get it.

'On account of the economic war with England,' she said, 'everything is getting so dear and paraffin is so scarce now. And white bread likewise. But, one thing I won't do is go to the soup kitchens.'

She saw him to the door, pointing her finger at him. 'Now look after yourself and get that wife of yours over here.'

'I will do that … Mrs Kelly,' he said, remembering her name from the parcel at the last moment just before she nodded and closed the door.

Even though he had a long way to go to perfect his English fluency, Luken supposed that the woman was well spoken. Looking back, he thought from her attitude that she didn't seem that old, probably looked that way from living in poverty and yet, for all her ill-luck, she still kept her pride and generosity.

On his way to the rest of the deliveries he was surprised to realise how much squalor there was in Dublin. Since his arrival in the country he had only been aware of his own place there and paid little attention to the human environment but the dirt floor in the woman's tenement room had brought home the widespread deprivation.

Chapter 19

One evening Luken was sitting in the common room chatting to his co-lodgers when one of the men handed him a newspaper. 'An article in that might interest you, Luke. Big time. There was talk in Dáil Éireann, the Irish Parliament, about your people. One of them might even be you!'

'What!?'

'Yep, have a read of it.'

"...A member of the Dáil, Dalton Bell, stood and described the arrival of some immigrants – naming one, Señor Pello – on a trawler from France as being wanted by the Spanish authorities. The claim was made by Franco's Envoy that state resources in the form of gold had been stolen and the immigrants, of a Communist persuasion, were fugitives from the police. The envoy demanded not only that they be extradited but also that the names and addresses of their parents be handed over. Mr Bell urged the minister to comply with the envoy's request not only to ensure that the thieves were sent back to Spanish justice but also to keep Communism out of Ireland..."

Luken felt a shudder, a short-lived fright, but still read through the rest of the article, feeling as if a grey cloud had come into the room and halted directly over his head.

"...The Minister for Foreign Affairs replied to Deputy Bell, referring to a discussion with senior Gardaí who explicitly re-assured him that the trawler the immigrants had arrived on was thoroughly searched and no such gold was found on board. The minister further pointed out that it was unlikely the extradition request would be granted. It had been and would continue to be the policy of the Irish Government to grant asylum to bona-fide refugees—"

'You've turned pale, Luke,' the man said.

Luken took a breath, stood up and walked around the room re-reading the article. 'They've got some nerve asking for our parents' addresses.'

'What's up?' another lodger asked.

After describing the essence of the article, Luken explained his situation with his residency application and how he was still awaiting a final decision from the Irish Government.

'It'd make you wonder,' one of the men said. 'When you think of all the Irishmen that have been given refuge in other countries, why wouldn't the Irish Government do likewise here?'

'I have a friend working in the Department of Foreign Affairs, Luke,' another man said. 'I'll have a quiet word with him. He might not be able to do much but at least maybe he could forewarn you of any news, good or bad.'

'Do you need any references?' the first man asked.

'What references?'

'It's a letter from a solicitor or a lawyer to say you're of good character, you respect the law and so on.'

'No, but thanks. I have everything I need like that.'

Hardly able to sleep that night, Luken turned and turned knowing that sleep would not come and cursed his ill-luck.

Next morning at work, still out of kilter with anxiety and lack of sleep, Luken was called into the office.

'There's a trunk call for you,' Padraig said and left, closing the door behind him.

A crackling female voice came over the noisy telephone line. 'Kaixo, Luken!'

'Am I glad to hear you, Miren! How are you, *querida*?'

'Same as usual… disappointed that you're not here, this is the second Christmas you've been away and we miss you so much. What about your residency, any hint of it?'

'Had my second meeting last week with the Immigration people and…'

'How did it go?'

Despite his own reservations, Luken decided to put a positive twist on the interview. 'It went very well, I gave them good answers to all the questions they asked. I should know in a few weeks. How are Kasen and Sabine?'

'Both fine, Sabine is more or less fluent in French now… Brigette, Marie's daughter, has been really helpful bringing her along. Kasen isn't quite as good, though he's doing okay otherwise, especially at sports... What about you?'

'Staying in the same place and made some money with extra Christmas deliveries at the Post Office, temporary work.'

'That's great, I've been able to save some money too.'

'How much?'

They counted the sum each had accumulated. Miren had enough for the journey from St Jean to Bordeaux and on to Paris. Luken could pay for the voyage from Paris to Dunkirk and on through Britain to Dublin.

Walking home after work and oblivious to the kids playing on Parnell Square, Luken hoped that he hadn't sounded too optimistic about his residency. Miren, nonetheless, sounded in good form. What the hell was he going to do, what was the whole family going to do, if the residency didn't come through?

Later that evening, he sat stewing in his gloom in the common room, scarcely noticing the other men's activities, reading, listening to the radio or playing checkers. In time, the men drifted off to bed and Luken fell asleep in the armchair.

Another man, who'd been working late, came in and shook him by the shoulder. 'Luke, do you know there's a letter on the hall table for you?'

Luken recognised the letter by the harp symbol on the brown envelope – the government stamp. Pausing momentarily to gather his feelings, he counted to three then ripped open the envelope and read the contents.

"A chara,

We are pleased to advise you that your application for permanent residency in Ireland has been granted and you are free to remain in this country at your will …"

Without finishing the letter, Luken's immediate impulse was to find a phone and ring Miren but, time-wise, it was too late, she'd be finished work and back home at Anna's house where there was no telephone. And French time was an hour ahead, so she'd probably even be asleep. Instead, he re-read the letter in full and started planning the trip. After calling her first thing in the morning, he'd go to the nearest travel agent and pay for the journey.

For the second night in a row, Luken slept poorly, contemplating the events of the coming days.

***

At 6:15am, followed by Sabine, Miren and Kasen each carried a suitcase down the stairs in Anna Aguirre's house.

Madame Aguirre had tidied the kitchen after breakfast and Miren noticed the redness of her eyes when she came out to bid them farewell. She shook hands with Kasen and, embracing the little girl, said, 'I'm going to miss all of you but especially you, Sabine.'

At the front door Miren kissed and embraced her. 'You've been so good to us, Anna. I don't know what we'd have done without you.'

'You've been such good company I feel as though I'm losing a family.'

'You'll have to find a new bridge partner.'

'I'm not too worried about that, I'll find someone. I won't go to the station, I'll only get too upset. Don't forget to write to me.'

'I promise you, I will.'

Outside, Guillaume, Marie and Brigette were waiting. Sabine immediately went over and hugged Brigette, who handed her a small white woollen doll with an embroidered slogan, 'Je t'aime.'

On their way to the railway station, four hundred metres away, Sabine and Brigette walked in front chatting away while Guillaume carried one of the cases. 'Marie and myself are goin' to have a hard time replacing you.'

'There's plenty of muchachas still around, Guillaume,' she replied. 'It shouldn't be that much of a problem. I'm going to miss Marie and you and the café myself, it was fun working there, some of the customers were great characters.'

Marie, walking behind, turned to Kasen. 'Are you glad to be going to Ireland?'

'I'll be glad to see Papá again, but I'm fed up moving,' he replied nonchalantly. 'We're only settled in when it's time to move again.'

'I'm sure this time it'll be more permanent, now that your Papá is working and has a residency permit.'

'Maybe, but it also means I'll have to learn another bloody language!'

On the busy platform, Miren presented the tickets to the inspector, who duly indicated their compartment.

As they bade farewell to Marie, Guillaume and Brigette, she couldn't help but feel the emotion of departure welling up in her throat. Nonetheless, considering the kids, she forced herself to keep a straight face.

'Give Luken our best wishes,' Guillaume said. 'And tell him to send us a telegram when you get there. Let's hope we meet again sometime.'

'And make sure you write,' Marie said, handing the kids a ten franc note each.

'Don't worry, I will,' Miren replied as they kissed in the French manner and Sabine and Brigette gave each other a final hug.

They scrambled down to their seats and soon the locomotive tooted its whistle and the train moved off.

Miren stood on the passenger deck of the S.S. Scotia at Holyhead on the west coast of England while Kasen and Sabine watched the rotating escalator buckets drop tons of coal into the ship's fuel store. Running to the stern of the ship, they looked on when it pulled away from the quay and set out on the Irish Sea. At least this was a short trip and the last one, Miren reflected, just a few hours to Dun Laoghaire.

Though fatigued, she stayed on deck as long as she could bear the biting wind. The children hardly noticed the cold as they ran up and down to the bow while the ship ploughed through the waves. Thankful that none of them were seasick, she avoided the stuffy communal passenger and dining rooms. Speculating about living in a country she knew next to nothing about, she had considered the possibilities endlessly since leaving St Jean de Luz. How would the kids take to Ireland? How would she take to it herself? What would happen if Luken lost his job? At least now the speculation was coming to an end.

Looking back, as exiles, Luken and herself were lucky to have escaped prison and other unspeakable horrors. She recalled seeing newspaper pictures of the thousands of children who had been evacuated from Bilbao to England and elsewhere as she watched her own, now laughing and running up and down the deck, inviting her to play hide and seek, hiding behind the equipment chests and lifeboats, oblivious to the destruction now taking place in their own country.

*** *

Miren, Kasen and Sabine walked down the platform of Amiens Street railway station to see Luken waiting at the gates. Amidst the groups of families and friends merrily greeting each other, the two kids ran ahead to meet him, each eager to tell their story about the voyage. Seeing Luken before her and, noticing his obvious weight loss, Miren felt overcome with joy.

'I thought we'd never get here, we missed you so badly,' she said. 'It felt like an eternity.'

'That makes four of us,' he replied, embracing her. 'Did you have any trouble with immigration?'

'I got all the papers at the new Irish Consulate in St Jean. Very convenient. Once the immigration officer was satisfied that you were here he just checked my visa and let us through.'

'Great to have you all here,' Luken said, reaching out and again embracing Miren, this time clasping Sabine and Kasen all together.

They made their way out from the station darkness, down the ramp into the sunshine where Luken had a van waiting. On the way, he mentioned that the accommodation was basic but temporary – he had moved from a one-room bedsitter in the north of the city to a two-bedroomed flat on William Street in the south.

'Sounds good,' Miren replied, gazing up and down at the houses and shops in Dublin city centre. Bicycles, buses, cars and the occasional hansom cab passed by. The children were quiet, each perched on a case looking out the back window of the van.

The front door to the flat stood beside a high archway through which motorised vehicles were brought to have electrical work undertaken at a workshop to the rear. Inside the front door, a narrow hallway led straight to the stairs. The sitting room and kitchen were effectively on the third floor, above the archway, and had a view to the front and rear respectively while the bedrooms, on the fourth floor, also had a view to the front and rear.

Aghast at the dirt and dust and the rickety state of the staircase on the way up, Miren said, 'This is bad, Luken. It's freezing cold. Where's the toilet?'

'On the ground floor, under the stairs.'

'What? We have to go down four storeys to the toilet?'

'Afraid so. Like I said, this is temporary, to get us started. We can look around for somewhere better over time.'

Luken plugged in an electric heater and gestured towards the open hearth. 'We can light the fire and get the place heated up. Look, don't worry, we'll be out of here in no time.'

'What about this?' she asked, pointing to an old Goblin vacuum cleaner.

'Faulty. A customer asked me to look at it.'

Miren allocated everyone a task. She took out sets of sheets and blankets and made up the beds for the kids in the upstairs bedroom. 'At least the sheets are clean.'

Without any food in the place, they ambled to a café downtown for a meal of cod and chips and afterwards took a short walk around for a view of the city centre. Kasen was amazed at so many trams stopped at the termini at Nelson's Pillar, a granite column forty metres high with a statue of Admiral Nelson himself on top. Luken promised he'd take him up it one day – inside there was an inner staircase that visitors could climb.

Back at the flat the youngsters soon fell asleep. Luken lit the fire and sat with Miren on the sofa while they talked about things that had happened during their time apart.

'I had a tough enough time, never got a minute to myself with the work and chasing around after the kids,' Miren said. 'Endika rang me at the hotel occasionally and there was no mistaking his anger. He felt that once the Franco forces had taken broad control, he could do no more in Euskal Herria. He's now fighting with an anti-fascist organisation in France. Speaking of which, anti-Franco signs are now posted all over St Jean so there's still a lot of anger there.

'Arossa is still distraught over Estebe's imprisonment since she's unable to find out what prison term he was given – no period was set at the trial. Decisions are made arbitrarily, depending on the presiding judge, and reconciliation is not something they have any interest in. Prisoners are being treated like slaves, sent out to work on forced labour gangs.

'Word at the hospital in Donostia is that Sister Alicia has been sent to a convent in Iruña. I tried calling her a few times but they wouldn't put me through. I suspect she's being denied contact with the outside world as punishment. At least she seems to be still alive.'

Luken described the work he had done since arriving in Dublin and his improvement in English. Apart from the family, he'd badly missed Endika too, not being able to see him for the occasional drink and chat.

The room had warmed by now and he stood to go over to the vacuum cleaner. 'I better have a look at this ... apparatus.'

Miren grabbed his hand before he moved. 'Leave that, what about your own apparatus, how's that working?'

He pulled her up, 'Are you glad to be here?'

'Of course I am. But it feels a bit odd, now that we're together again. We've been apart so long, it's as though we're kind of... strangers almost.'

'I was looking forward to it so much,' Luken replied. 'Now that you say it, I feel the same way.'

'Well, we're here now. We'll just have to get used to each other again!'

The following morning Miren awoke to the sound of a piano. Luken had already gone to work and left her undisturbed. Kasen appeared at the door and Sabine soon followed. She went to the window and drew the curtains aside, asking, 'Where's that music coming from?'

Chatham Row, the street opposite, ran perpendicular to the apartment and was visible from end to end. The three of them gathered at the window.

'It's from somewhere outside,' Miren said. 'Someone's practicing. Come on, we'll get dressed and have a look. And we have to get food as well.'

Fully attired, they raced down the stairs and down the steps outside the front door. They ambled across the street to Chatham Row, discovering that the music was coming from the Municipal School of Music. Sabine went into the forecourt and looked through a window to see who was playing. Lingering awhile, Miren reckoned that it was Beethoven's piano sonata No. 3 that was being rehearsed, one she'd practiced herself in her youth. Maybe we can get a piano here someday, she thought.

After searching around, they went into an oriental café. As it was their first day in Ireland, Miren decided to spoil Kasen and Sabine by letting them have whatever fizzy drink and confectionery took their fancy and took the plunge by having a sweet white coffee and a large sticky bun herself.

Back on the street they crossed into St Stephen's Green and spent a good hour exploring the walks and watching the ducks and swans. The creatures emerged from the lake and approached, demanding pieces of bread other visitors were handing out.

'Can we bring bread next time we come?' Sabine asked.

'Of course we can.'

On route back to the apartment, they called into a grocery store where Miren procured several bags of essential foodstuffs.

That evening, in front of a blazing fire, Luken recalled various items of interest during his first year in Ireland, the mixed fortunes of people he had met, from the wealthy to the hard-at-heel, the relationship he'd struck up with Mrs Kelly, and the anti-cinema stance that, strangely, the church took. The clergy seemed to think that films were an encouragement for their congregation to turn away from their religion.

While Luken attended work, Miren looked around for local schools. Following an interview at Synge Street Secondary Boys School, the principal recommended that Kasen undergo an intense course in English.

'We're now at the end of March,' he said. 'There's only three months left in the school year, so given his level of English he wouldn't learn much. Your son would be better going back a year and catching up on his language skills in the meantime.'

'That seems a long time to hold him back.'

'Well, it's only until next September. He could get hold of the textbooks and perhaps sit in on the classes in, say, the final month of the present school year. And seeing as his French is so good, he could attend the French classes and sit the exams in June.'

Miren explained, in Basque, the principal's suggestion to Kasen, who reluctantly agreed.

'Don't have much choice, do I?'

'That would be a start at least,' Miren replied to the principal. 'You must give me a list of the books and where I might get them. He has already started a course in English.'

Walking back towards William Street, Miren noticed the sullen look on the Kasen's face.

'What did we have to leave St Jean for?' he asked.

'Kasen, you know your father couldn't get work there.'

'This place is a long way to go for work. What if he lost his job? Maybe we'd have to move again. Where would we go next time? Then I'd have to learn another language!'

'Come on, Kas. Try and be positive, you'll have six months to get a good grip on English, and you'll still have plenty of time off. And anyway, having a third language will be an advantage for you.'

'How?'

'It'll be helpful when you look for a job.'

'Big deal!'

Rather than argue the point further, Miren said nothing, deciding to let the matter run its course, confident that in time, Kasen would fit in.

The principal at Loreto Schools acknowledged that Sabine had a natural inclination towards languages and music and mentioned that the music teacher was also a French speaker so Sabine would be able to sit in and possibly catch up on music.

'Nonetheless, her English has a long way to go,' the principal, a senior Catholic nun, explained with a smile. 'But, she's welcome to sit in on the classes and we can see how she progresses over the coming months. I wouldn't expect her to pass all the examinations so she might have to repeat certain subjects.'

'Does that mean holding her back for a year?' Miren asked.

'I'm afraid so but remember that by this time next year she'll probably be further ahead of her fellow pupils. And since she speaks French she'll be at an advantage.'

As they walked home, Miren turned to Sabine, 'What did you think of that?'

'Huh! It means I'll be at school for an extra year!'

'Well, as the sister said, you'll be ahead of the other girls next year.'

'I don't know what the other girls will be like,' Sabine replied glumly.

'I'm sure you'll soon make friends with them. And you'll be bigger than them so they won't be able to bully you, even if they wanted to.'

'I wish we'd stayed in St Jean.'

'Well, there's no going back, Sabine. Not now.'

The following Saturday afternoon, Miren took Kasen and Sabine to watch their father play a Gaelic Football match for his team against University College Dublin.

They cheered with the crowd whenever the team scored a point or a goal. Sabine started to lose interest but when Papá scored a point, she perked up. Kasen was enraptured by the game, seeing how it compared to soccer.

'You did well, Papá,' he said as they walked home afterwards. 'You scored three points.'

'I might have scored a few more if I was in a better position,' Luken replied.

'Could I play Gaelic?' Kasen asked.

'They probably have a team in Synge Street,' Luken replied. 'Ask when you go for your first French lesson.'

'They'll be pleased when they hear you want to play,' Miren said. 'Now, that's something to look forward to, isn't it?'

'I suppose so.'

One Sunday afternoon, Luken took the family to the Adelphi Cinema to see The Adventures of Robin Hood.

On arrival, Miren was surprised to see a long queue that stretched to the end of the street and around the corner. At two o'clock, the doors opened and inside they were all amazed to see the size of the theatre, which sat over two thousand people. Luken sent Kasen and Sabine to the confectionery kiosk to fetch ice cream tubs. As soon as they returned, the secondary movie, Murder by the Clock, started.

'The seats are great, very comfortable,' Miren whispered to Luken as she popped a spoonful of ice cream into her mouth.

'Yep,' Luken replied. 'It only opened a few months ago. Best cinema in Dublin.'

During the performances, Miren observed the rest of the family watching the show, especially Kasen to see how he responded, concerned about how negative his reaction had so far been to his new home. Despite his limited English, she reckoned he could follow the story, simple as it was, with Errol Flynn's swashbuckling antics and sword duels. He's enjoying it, she thought.

That evening in the sitting room, when the kids had gone to bed, she remarked on what they had seen on the cinema newsreel.

'I was wondering which of us would bring this up first,' Luken stood and went to the window. 'Franco has declared final victory in Spain. Germany has invaded Poland and, France and Britain have both declared war on Germany.'

'I'll have to call Arossa and see how she is,' Miren replied. 'I wonder what's to happen to the old country now?'

'Nothing good, for sure, Franco has a great hatred for Euskal Herria.'

Miren thought for a moment. 'What are the British and French going to do, send troops to Poland?'

'For a start I'm sure there'll be a big build up in armaments and recruitment. I don't know much about the British ability to take on Germany, but I wouldn't hold out hope of France doing much. It seems more real when you see it on film rather than reading about it in the newspapers.'

'What will the Irish Government do?'

'I don't know, as far they're concerned, this is a neutral country.'

Miren rose and went to look out the window beside Luken. 'Strange, on the way home, Kasen only talked about the Robin Hood film and didn't say anything about the newsreel. It's all very worrying.'

***

When the end of the school term approached and Kasen sat in on the final month's lessons, he was taken aback to see the treatment given out to other pupils.

'The Christian Brothers beat the hell out of the boys who haven't done their homework,' he told Luken one evening. 'They give them six whacks of the cane on each hand. One of the boys was crying. They ignore me, seeing as I'm an onlooker. I'm not looking forward to next year when I'll be treated the same.'

'Well, you'd better make sure you do yours when the time comes,' Luken replied.

Miren, however, felt disappointed. It was tough enough, she thought, trying to keep the boy motivated. While he enjoyed playing in the football games, the last thing she wanted was to have him discouraged in his attempts to settle in. She wondered about the possibility of changing schools, maybe finding a better one during the summer holidays. At least Sabine was getting along all right.

***

Bringing home the groceries, Miren reflected on the convenience of city living but, after such a long time in Dublin, realised that she had yet to make new friends. The only acquaintances she encountered were women collecting their daughters or granddaughters at Sabine's school. Though nice enough, they always seemed to be in a hurry.

The apartment was getting to be a nuisance as well, with no garden or outdoor facilities.

At the intersection of Exchequer and William Street, a newsstand poster proclaimed,

'FRANCE TOPPLED'

The woman newspaper vendor called out,

'Herald or Mail or Evening Press!'

'Herald or Mail or Evening Press!'

As she stopped to buy a paper, Miren heard a horse scream in pain. She turned to see that the animal had fallen onto its side on wet cobblestones. The horse's four-wheeled cart had overturned and its contents of coal had been thrown onto the street. Her immediate reaction was to drop the groceries and run over to help the horse back on its feet. Three pedestrians, all men, went over and unleashed the cart and helped the driver to get the horse standing again. She recalled that it wasn't the first time she'd seen a horse fall on cobblestones.

'The poor 'aul horse,' the vendor said.

'They shouldn't have to pull heavy carts on wet cobblestones like that,' Miren said, wondering what had happened to Yulene, the mare she'd left behind in Euskal Herria. Probably sequestered into the war effort. Or dead.

'D'you know what? You're right, missus,' the vendor said.

Making her way home, Miren thought on the symbolism of the fallen horse, comparing it to the fall of France.

After dinner, while the kids went about their activities, Luken and Miren read the newspaper from cover to cover.

'Looks like we're in for another world war,' he said. 'I wonder what Spain's going to do?'

'God, it's so depressing. When is it ever going to end?'

'If it's anything like the last one, in four, five years, maybe more.'

Later, in bed and unable to sleep, Miren sensed that Luken was still awake.

'How do you feel about living here, now?' she whispered.

'How did you know I was awake?'

'I can feel slight movements on your side of the bed.'

'You mean about living in the apartment or in Ireland?'

'The apartment.'

'I hate having to walk to Stephen's Green just to get a decent breath of fresh air, especially at the weekends.'

'It's claustrophic living here,' she said. 'There's nowhere to sit out when the weather is fine.'

'And it's a pain having to go way downstairs to the piss-house every time you want to take a leak!'

Miren gave a short laugh. 'What would you think about moving to the country? Now that we're in for another war, it'd be a lot safer. Less chance of being killed by a bomb if the war comes to this country.'

'I don't know about that, look what happened in Durango. Anyway, I was thinking about it myself, I miss the open countryside.'

'Now might be the time to move, with the school holidays coming up. I'm not happy with Kasen at the Christian Brothers, I don't like their attitude. They have an arrogance about them, they sound like a crowd of sadists. We could look around for a better school. And it'd be at the beginning of the annual semester for him and Sabine, instead of them being plunged into the middle as happened on the last two occasions.'

'And we'd have the summer to look around and find a nice place,' Luken said. 'Somewhere for the long term.'

'Okay, let's do it,' Miren said, and, delighted that Luken was thinking along the same lines, she scarcely slept that night thinking of the possibilities.

***

From across the road, in the sunshine, Miren looked over at the thatched two-storeyed cottage on Bawn Lane. After a wearying three weeks inspecting various properties, this seemed to be the most homely. It looks idyllic, she thought. Three steps led up to the front door of the whitewashed cottage. Four latticed windows on the ground floor and two dormer windows looked through the thatch on the first floor, down onto the quiet tarmac road.

Luken parked the car a little further down the lane and returned as the agent arrived.

Inside, the cottage had all the essentials, a large kitchen and living rooms while upstairs Miren was enamoured by the dormer windows, which sat at floor level so that one could look down on the road while in bed.

'What do you think?' Luken asked when they went outside to see the overgrown rear garden.

'It's just what we want.'

'You can smell the sea,' he replied, sniffing the gentle onshore breeze.

'It's a long way to go for your work,' she said, as more of a question than a statement.

'We can't have it both ways, if we want to live in the country.'

'Would you be happy to live here?' she asked.

'Now that another war has broken out in Europe I think we're better off out of the city.'

'Is that a "yes"?'

Luken looked into her eyes and nodded.

Chapter 20

From the kitchen window Miren looked out across the grass patch. Kasen and Sabine were leaning over the low parapet surrounding the waterwell, throwing in stones to hear the splash. The drop, ten metres down, was a source of anxiety. She dried her hands, went out and fetched an old disused gate and, with Kasen's help, arranged it over the well, placing two heavy bricks on top to keep it in place.

'That's your good deed for the day, Kas.'

'Can we not throw stones in anymore?' Sabine asked.

'Not anymore, we might have to drink that water sometime. You can go down to the sea and throw in as many as you like.'

The children soon lost interest and disappeared out onto the lane, where she worried less about them as it was a cul-de-sac, had almost no traffic and ran down to the seashore. Sitting on the parapet, she looked up at the sky, wondering about the war, and hoped that it wouldn't spread any further. A few weeks earlier, German bombers had dropped explosives on north Dublin, apparently mistaking the city for Belfast. Thirty people had been killed and nearly a hundred injured. Some people in Rush had even heard the aircraft as they passed overhead. Not just locally but nationwide, the idea that the war was far away from Ireland was being severely tested.

She shuddered at the memory of the aircraft flying over Otxandio and dropping their weapons of death. The screams of the women and children and the faces of Gechina and Errita floated into her mind and the tears streamed down her face.

A car pulled up outside. She rushed back to the kitchen and wiped her face with a towel. From the living room window, she saw Luken and Padraig talking and handing the kids a chocolate bar each.

After greetings, she made tea but noticed Luken observing her eyes. The three adults sat around the kitchen table while the kids went down to the seashore. They drank tea and ate Basque butter biscuits.

'Did you make them, Miren?' Padraig asked.

'I did, do you like them?'

'Delicious,' he replied, munching his way through a third biscuit. 'So how do you like living here in Rush?'

'It's a big improvement on the city, we've more space and it's so much quieter. We always preferred the countryside to the towns in the Basque Country…'

'You can call it Euskal Herria, Miren, Luken's told me all about it.'

'It's hard to get used to the fact that everyone thinks we're Spanish or Italian.'

'Bloody cheek of them!'

'I meant to thank you so many times for inviting Luken over, Padraig. It's been a life saver.'

'It's me who should be thanking you for letting him go. How're the kids fitting in?'

'They're glad to be settling in the one place. Sabine's teacher is pleased that she's so good with languages. Amazed that she can speak both Spanish and French and coming along in English. I'm pleased that Kasen is now in a school that he actually likes. He wasn't keen on Synge Street.'

'The Christian Brothers!' Padraig exclaimed. 'I know, they've a terrible reputation for beating the lard out of the kids. How do you find the Irish weather?'

'It's taking time to get used to it, we knew about the rain and the cold in winter but the surprise is that it changes so often in the same day. But considering what we left behind it's a small price to pay…'

'We haven't quite got over it,' Luken said, looking at Miren. 'Luckily, neither of the kids saw any bloodshed back home.'

'That's good. No doubt that would've been shocking,' Padraig said.

Ambling down the long patch of land that came with the cottage, they inspected the glasshouse that needed refurbishment and talked about the potential for growing vegetables and keeping chickens. The youngsters appeared and Kasen said, 'There's a dead seal down at the beach.'

Miren left the men and kids to walk down and inspect the carcase while she returned to cook dinner. She would have liked to prepare an Oilasko Kazola, a Euskadian casserole, but, she reflected, as well as a shortage of ingredients, other items such as peppers and chorizo were not even known in the Irish larder. Instead she prepared a piece of bacon, cabbage and potatoes all the while wondering if Luken would ask about her red eyes.

Soon, the men and children returned and were driven by Padraig to the Harbour Bar by the pier where the men drank a pint of stout at the bar. Miren had a bottle of ale in the snug with the kids who were each given a bottle of Club Orange and a packet of potato crisps.

***

Despite her best efforts to procure work in the nursing world, Miren found there was already a surfeit of qualified women. Other work for married women like herself was difficult if not impossible to come by. Instead, she decided to improve her knowledge of English.

When the evening course started at the local secondary school, she was surprised to see that the students were mostly men. One of the women confided that as part of the Catholic ethos, women were expected to stay at home and look after the family while men were given priority in every other walk of life. 'I'd say the only reason we're being given the opportunity is because there weren't enough men to fill the gaps.'

'Why would men want to do a course like this?'

'They might get a job teaching, I suppose. I'm Sheila by the way.' The lady reached across the desk to shake hands.

After the first lesson, the two women chatted in the school yard and Miren briefly explained why her family had come to Ireland.

'We had to get away from all the conflict and turmoil.'

'I think I've seen you walking around the town,' Sheila replied. 'Would you like to come back to our house for some tea? We live a short distance away, just on Shore Road.'

'I'd love to.'

Sitting at the kitchen table and looking out the rear window, Miren said, 'It's great to be here, so quiet away from the city. We had a flat on South William Street but neither of us liked city living.'

'Well, I hope you settle in and make a good home for yourselves,' Sheila replied as she poured out the tea. 'And you're welcome to call in here anytime.'

'That's very nice of you, Sheila. Isn't it terrible, this war business?'

'It is. Did you see those pictures of the North Strand in Dublin? Wasn't it awful how those poor people were killed and injured? It's still very worrisome, you never know what's going to happen.'

'It is indeed.'

'Please God, the tide will turn soon. I'm sure you notice the shortage of things and how the prices have gone way up?'

'I do but at least here you can grow your own vegetables. I notice so many people have something growing in their gardens.'

'True for you. Normally I'd offer you a piece of cake to go with the tea but with the shortages I've had to cut back even on that. I must show you what we do have in storage.'

When they finished their tea, at the rear of the property, Sheila pointed out the hen run and a wooden storage shed containing foodstuffs such as onions, apples and sacks of potatoes.

Miren listened to the sound of the hens cluck-clucking in the background, a sound she loved, while Sheila handed her four eggs wrapped in a piece of old newspaper.

'Are you sure you can do without these?' Miren asked.

'Of course. Take them as your welcoming present!'

On the walk home Miren reflected on what a nice person she had met in Sheila and resolved to set up her own kitchen garden.

***

Just after sunrise one day, Luken, Padraig, Kasen and his school friend, Sean, put their equipment, life jackets and lunch packs into the small fishing boat anchored on the beach at Skerries harbour. The boys climbed in while the men lifted the anchor and pushed the boat down the short distance to the water and jumped in. Padraig clipped on the outboard motor and pulled the starter cord. He maneuvered the boat around in a semi-circle and made towards the open sea. The others assembled the fishing rods, fitted the reels, line and hooks. They passed the harbour promontory and turned south-east into a light onshore wind.

'We'll have to make a wish this morning, Dad. Our first time fishing in the Irish Sea,' Kasen said.

'Wait till we catch something first,' Luken replied and, turning to Padraig, asked, 'What kind of fish can we get on a day like this?'

'You never know, pollack maybe, over the reefs. We'll try that first then move to the mixed floor, might get some codling. There was a good easterly wind for the last few days so if we're lucky we might even get a few bass.'

'It's very decent of you, inviting us out like this,' Luken said.

'Will you stop thanking me. Think nothing of it, next time I'm sure you'll be able to do this for yourself.'

Kasen and Sean were equally delighted to be out at sea, putting ragworms on the hooks and then washing their hands by drifting them in the water.

After forty minutes they arrived at the periphery of Lambay Island, cut the engine and set down anchor. They cast out using the rods and dropped other lines overboard and waited.

'Do any fishing in Euskal Herria?' Padraig asked.

'River trout, it was good,' Luken said. 'Though we never did sea fishing. Fish is popular there, much more than here. The Basque fishermen used to go to Newfoundland to fish for cod. They'd dry and salt them and bring them back.'

'That was a long way to go, why did they have to go so far?'

'Better fishing grounds, I suppose.'

Time passed slowly and when a squall came down they donned their oilskins. A line started bobbing and excitedly, the boys reeled in a half-kilo pollack.

When nothing further came they moved to the rock-strewn sea floor and dropped anchor. They sat around drinking tea and fruit juice until midday, then ate their sandwiches.

All the lines started bobbing at the same time and Padraig yelled, 'Mackerel! They're in early this year.'

The hook on each line had a mackerel dangling. They removed the flapping fish and threw them into a tin container, then chucked the lines back overboard and even without bait, yet more fish took the hooks.

After the second catch Padraig said, 'A whole shoal have come in. Only goes to show you how thick mackerel are, they can't tell the difference between food and steel. Let's leave it at that. A lot of people here don't like mackerel, you can hardly give them away.'

'Why?'

'It's an old sea-faring fable, they say mackerel eat the bodies of the dead sailors. I'm not mad about them myself, I think you have to eat them fresh. By that I mean today.'

'We certainly won't be eating all those today,' Luken said, as the two boys looked into the container.

A mist came down, Luken started the engine and they headed for home. The mist soon thickened and Padraig used the onboard compass inside the canopy for navigation.

About fifteen minutes later, they heard a low-pitched sound, distant at first but gaining in intensity. Initially they supposed it was a ship but then realised it was coming from the sky, an airplane.

'He's flying very low,' Padraig said. They stopped the engine and gazed in the direction of the sound, now deafening. Suddenly it appeared out of the fog and passed overhead. The backward thrust of air shook the boat. It flew forward into the fog and landed on the water.

'It's a flying boat,' Padraig said. 'What the hell is he doing here?'

'It had the Royal Air Force sign on the side,' Sean said.

'Maybe they're in trouble,' Luken said, starting the engine.

Padraig steered the boat in the direction of the aircraft, which had now stopped its engines. They came upon the Shorts Sunderland Flying Boat within a few minutes and were awed by its size. They observed the two propellered engines from under each wing before turning to the front where the pilots looked down from the cockpit at a height. The boys marvelled at the machine gun protruding out of the nose but Luken was less impressed. 'What's an armed British aircraft doing here, landing in Irish waters, a neutral country?'

A door opened in the fuselage as their boat approached. A man appeared in a leather bomber jacket and asked, in a Scottish accent, 'Where are we?'

'Skerries, County Dublin,' Padraig replied.

'Dublin!' the man, obviously a flight officer, said. 'We got lost in this damn fog. How far offshore are we?'

'About three miles. You shouldn't have to wait too long; the local forecast is for clearer weather this afternoon. Any chance of a quick tour?'

'I'll ask. I see you've been fishing.'

The airplane was steady in the water while the boat bobbed up and down.

The man returned. 'We know Ireland is a neutral country but not knowing your nationalities I'm afraid we can't. But the lads can come aboard for a quick visit.'

Kasen and Sean took off their life jackets and climbed up the short ladder, jumped through the open door and onto the lower deck. The man explained that he was the navigator and showed them the instruments at his station.

'Who drops the bombs?' Sean asked.

The navigator smiled and gestured to the front of the plane, saying, 'The captain does but we can't go up there, it's out of bounds. He has a button on the joystick that he presses when the aimer signal gives him the go ahead. We've no bombs onboard today.'

The captain and his co-pilot were engaged in animated conversation over the radio. The boys were fascinated by the interior, the ribbed fuselage, the gun turrets at the rear, the galley kitchen and the ladder to the upper deck.

After the tour the navigator brought them back to the door and they duly hopped onto the fishing boat.

They thanked him and Luken asked, 'Want a few mackerel?'

Surprised, the navigator said, 'Why not. We can have them for our tea! I'll get something to put them in.'

He returned with a tin container and was given a half dozen fish.

'Where are you headed for?'

'Can't tell you but you can guess from my accent.'

They wished each other well and Padraig turned the boat around and headed for shore.

Luken wondered if there was an ulterior reason for the flying boat landing. Maybe it was part of a covert surveillance operation. You never know in wartime. He felt the anxiety rising in his system while recalling the rumours he had read in the newspapers about the possibility of a foreign invasion. Nobody knew whether it might be a British or German invasion. A British one was one thing but a German invasion would be calamitous, seeing as it was a Fascist state discreetly, if not secretly, in collusion with Franco. Must ring Pello, he thought, and see if he has any further news at his end.

No information was being released by government sources and over time, the rumours had been gathering momentum. The more he thought of it, the worse it seemed. Here they were, out on a simple fishing trip and still, war had to rear its ugly head yet again. Was it ever going to stop? War, war, war. Fucking war. Did men ever think of anything bloody else?

His thoughts were suddenly intruded upon when Kasen said, 'They won't believe us at school when we tell them about the flying boat.'

Luken took a deep breath of the sea air and despite feeling both angry and worried, decided he was reading too much into the situation. Nonetheless, he knew and felt it in his bones that he would have to live with his anxiety until the war came to an end.

They took the rest of the journey at a slow pace, mindful of their doubtful positioning while watching out for the shore.

In a while, the fog started to ease and Padraig recognised the coastline.

Back on shore they anchored the vessel on Skerries beach and packed into Padraig's car for the journey home. The fog had now completely lifted and they saw and heard the flying boat start its engines and take off.

Padraig laughed, took a slug of whiskey from a flask and passed it to Luken, saying, 'Only in Ireland.'

'What do you mean?'

'Only in Ireland would a British Flying Boat land and pick up half a dozen fish!'

Back at the house, Miren was delighted with the fresh fish. 'You got so many of them.'

'We could have got a lot more if we wanted,' Kasen said.

Miren looked into the tin container. 'I'm giving some of these to Sheila.'

She wrapped three of the fish in a newspaper and handed them to Kasen. 'Here, bring these over to her house and ask her if she can spare an onion.'

While Kasen went off, she set about making a casserole, first heating the oil in a saucepan. She filleted the fish, chopped up the carrots and leeks, then waited until Kasen returned with two onions before cutting them up and throwing them into the pot.

Later that evening, Miren recalled having recently given up on the possibility of ever making a Basque casserole again, but this evening she'd adapted the recipe to suit the ingredients and what a treat the meal had been.

***

The journey from Rush into the city meant an early start for Luken. Due to petrol rationing, he could seldom borrow a car now from the garage to get home.

With the bus full, the journey took nearly an hour. Luken read the newspaper articles on the bombing of Pearl Harbour by the Japanese Navy and the entry of the US into the war. At the same time he wondered if the neutrality of Ireland would continue to be respected, especially with its strategic position on the west coast of Europe. He dreaded hearing rumours, especially at work. Censorship of radio and newspaper reports was still obvious, with reference being made to the war as 'The Emergency.' Adding to the confusion, customers at the garage who had returned from abroad reported foreign media versions of events in Ireland. Some recalled that the Irish Government was about to throw in its lot with the Allies, others had read stories about the Taoiseach, the Irish Prime Minister, refusing to budge on Ireland's neutrality.

Apart from the petrol rationing, other goods were now even harder to come by, including coal and other fuel. He thought of the hunting and fishing trips Kasen and himself were now taking at the weekends to supplement food that was unavailable in the shops. At the garage, business had fallen off and although the repairmen were retained, everyone had been obliged to take a cut in wages.

When lunchtime came around, Luken slipped out to the GPO where he waited in turn to make a phone call to St Jean de Luz.

'Good to hear from you,' Guillaume said.

'I won't stay on long, I rang mainly to give you the number of the garage where I work so you could pass it on to Endika next time you hear from him.'

'I haven't heard from Endika in a long while. Give me the number anyway. I rang Arossa recently, she's allowed to visit Estebe once a month, though no word about when or if he might be released. So how are things with you?'

'Fine, the whole family are fine, but the war is having its effect here. All sorts of shortages, especially fuel.'

'Same here, some cars are now modified to run on gas.'

On his way back to the garage, Luken wondered about Endika in the hope that nothing had happened to him. Had he left the anti-fascist organisation and joined the regular French army to fight the Nazis? Or maybe the Resistance?

As he walked in, Padraig approached. 'I've something to show you.'

They went to one of the rear storage rooms where he demonstrated a large used storage tank. The tank contained American kerosene which, he explained, had come his way through an Irish American relative.

'What are you going to use it for?' Luken asked.

'Heating.'

'Do you not use coal or turf?'

'I do, but you can pick up a paraffin heater quite cheap. It won't be a replacement but handy to have as a fallback. Take a few gallons for yourself, I'm giving the lads a ration as well.'

Over the subsequent weeks Luken visited a number of fuel merchants until he found one selling a second-hand paraffin heater. The Valor tall cylindrical device was faulty and going for a knock-down price. The tank was leaking but back at the garage he remedied the fault by braising a section of brass around the leak and bought a replacement wick.

***

Returning a customer's car, Luken became distracted. He missed his own country and, for all its troubles, wished he could at least contemplate a time when he might go back. Since Miren and the youngsters had come to Ireland it hadn't been so bad. But now, from time to time and especially when alone, he got a craving to be back among the undulating hills of Euskal Herria and in particular missed the variety of food, finding the Irish food bland and unappealing, despite Miren's best efforts. He knew she also missed the old country, seeing her scouring the newspapers for news from overseas. Despite the cessation of civil war in Spain and given the subsequent unforgiving nature of the Spanish government, there was still little chance of returning soon.

As he turned off into Fenian Street a woman walked off the pavement in front of him. Although he stopped, she collapsed onto the street from the shock. He jumped out of the car to see that it was Mrs Kelly, the lady he had delivered a parcel to at Christmas time. He helped her up with another woman as other pedestrians came along to help.

'You were goin' too fast,' someone said.

'He wasn't, she just walked out in front of him,' the helper said. 'Come on, Mrs Kelly, I'll bring you home.'

'I have to get bread.'

They sat her in the passenger seat of the car while she got her breath back.

'Where's the shop?' Luken asked.

She gestured up the street while he said to the helper, 'I'll bring her up and take her home. I know where she lives.'

The helper looked suspiciously at him and asked, 'Are you all righ' with that, Mrs Kelly?'

She nodded. 'I know him.'

On the trip to the shop and back to her home she hardly spoke. He carried in her few groceries, bread, milk and sugar. When she sat down he noticed how drawn and thin she was.

'You don't look very good, Mrs Kelly.'

'It's the cold in this place, I can't get any turf.'

'Let me make you a cup of tea.'

Still breathless she said, 'There's no paraffin either. I have to use Byrne's upstairs. Just cut me some bread, I'll be all right.'

Even though it was September, Luken himself felt the cold in the room. He sliced the bread and spread a generous layer of jam.

She ate the bread slowly. 'Go on, get back to your work. I can't talk much. Call in and see me another day.'

'I wish there was more I could do for you.'

'You've done enough already, go on.'

Driving away, Luken thought of the poverty she was living in and wished there was something more he could have done for her. His mother had never had to live in such misery.

The following Saturday, a freezing cold day, after doing their usual deliveries three bakery vans were left in at close of business for standard service. This had to be done on Sunday, outside normal commercial hours, to minimise time off-road. Luken reckoned the work could have been undertaken in the evening time, standard Austin Six vehicles were easy to work on, but he didn't raise the point since he'd have an opportunity to borrow one for the best part of the weekend.

The vans arrived late and two mechanics wasted no time in doing the service, each then borrowing a van. Luken did likewise and loaded the Valor heater and two gallon tins of paraffin into the third van. Even inside the darkened garage his breath was visible, condensing in the cold, and as he closed the van doors he thought of Mrs Kelly.

When he got to Fenian Street, the four-storey building was mostly in darkness save for a number of windows whose tenants had money for electricity. He left the heater quietly outside Mrs Kelly's door, tapped gently and when she opened it slightly, said, 'I've something for you.'

In case she wouldn't accept charity, he barged into the room with the heater as soon as the door opened wide enough. The only light was a candle on the table at which she had been reading. She had a shawl wrapped around her shoulders and asked, 'Where are you going with that?'

'I'm not going anywhere, it's staying here.'

'Where did you get it?'

'It was broken and thrown out so I fixed it and brought it around to you.'

'Where'd you get the paraffin?'

'It fell off the side of a ship,' he smiled, realising there was more truth than fiction in what he'd said.

'Go on with you, Luke! Where'd you get it?'

He ignored the question and set about lighting the heater. Soon the warmth permeated the room and she exclaimed, 'God, isn't there great heat from that?'

Luken agreed and showed her how to adjust the wick and how to fill the tank. They sat around the heater looking at the flame through the red perspex panel.

'Isn't that great altogether,' she said. 'I'll be able to dry clothes around that, won't I?'

'You can but be careful they don't catch fire.'

'I've seen them heaters for fifteen shillings and sixpence in the ironmongers. They'll be getting dearer now, like everything else.' She went behind the curtain to the bed. Luken heard her rummaging through some objects, storage boxes, he supposed. She returned with two bottles, one of whiskey, the other of port, went to the sideboard and took out two glasses. 'The whiskey is for you, I'm more of a port person myself.'

They sat and went back to looking at the heater while taking their drinks.

'This is very decent of you, Mrs Kelly.'

'What are you talking about? You're the decent one, not me. It's a good thing you brought that in at night, some people here might get an idea of it. Drink that up now.'

'What's the book you're reading?' Luken asked, nodding to the table. She handed it to him: Lone Cowboy by Will James.

'It's an autobiography,' she said. 'What being a cowboy was really like.'

She went on to describe the book and showed him some of the illustrations.

'We've a few books we finished with, I must drop them into you,' Luken said.

'Have your wife and children come to Dublin?'

'They have, we moved to a cottage out in Rush.'

'That's miles away, you'd better finish that and go on home to her. Maybe come during the day next time.'

He knocked back the rest of the whiskey and, slightly inebriated, drove home.

Chapter 21

When summertime came around, Kasen, Sabine and four school friends took to the beach. They rushed into the sea, some screaming at the coldness of the water until they crouched down and immersed themselves up to the neck.

The sunshine beamed benevolently down on the fun-seekers in the water and others, likewise, enjoying games and tanning themselves on the sand.

The youngsters formed two teams, each side attempting to punch the ball over their opponents' heads and score points.

On finishing the game, they went for a trot up and down the length of the beach to dry off. The losing side was obliged to pay for the sweets and minerals for both teams, which they sat around and enjoyed, jeering and poking fun at each other.

'Gerry, you're not fit,' one of the boys on the winning team said to an opponent. 'It's no wonder you keep dropping the ball. You should get up early in the morning and start doing a couple of dozen press-ups.'

In reprisal, Gerry fired a half-finished tub of ice-cream at the boy, who ducked at the last instant, avoiding a hit on the head. Dissatisfied, Gerry made a lunge for the youngster, who jumped up and ran off. Both teams laughed to see the chase down the beach.

Later, they broke up and went their separate ways. On the way home, Sabine turned to Kasen. 'What are you going to do when you finish secondary school, seeing as you've only one more year?'

'I was thinking of volunteering for the Allies.'

'What!? To fight in the war? You're too young.'

'America will take you on at seventeen with your parents' consent. Now, after the Allied landing in Normandy it looks like they're going to win. I'd love to be a fighter pilot.'

'You said you were going to go to university.'

'If the Allies don't win the war, there won't be any university. We'll all be slaves. What about you?'

'I've got to like French, I might do that. Or journalism maybe. But you need to have honours-level English in the Leaving Certificate.'

'You'll have plenty of time to catch up.'

'I'm not sure, don't know whether I will or not. We don't see much of Papá these days. What do you think of Mamá's new friend?'

'Seems like a nice woman, good that she gets to meet new people. Are you coming to see us play in the semi-final on Sunday?'

'Yep, I'll be there.'

***

As soon as Sheila arrived, Miren made tea. They sat around the kitchen table and discussed aspects of the English course. In particular, the poem 'The Deserted Village,' by Oliver Goldsmith, certain expressions in which Miren had difficulty comprehending. Sheila explained some of the idiomatic phrases and each worked out their opinion of the poem.

Miren heard a sound in the hall and went out to retrieve a letter. The letter was from the principal of their school. She read the contents aloud.

'One of my colleagues mentioned your Spanish background and your name has been suggested as a possible instructor in the subject. Would you consider such a position? Spanish is already offered in other schools and indeed has been a Dublin University study since 1884. If interested please contact me by return.'

'Why, that's great news, Miren,' Sheila said. 'There's an opportunity for you.'

'But I've never done any teaching.'

'You probably don't need to. It'd say it's simple, elementary stuff.'

For the remainder of the day Miren went around on a cushion of air, both surprised and elated that she had been thought of in such a way. The kids were suspicious when they were given special treatment on arriving home. For once, Kasen wasn't asked if he had taken off his shoes and left them in the kitchen. Sabine wondered why she had been asked what she wanted for her tea – normally it was just put in front of her. For her part Miren decided to wait until Luken came home to make the announcement.

'But you don't have the qualifications to teach, Mamá,' Sabine said when all the family sat around the table.

'They must know that already,' Miren replied. 'I gave them all that information when I signed up for the course.'

'What qualifications would you need to teach it when you already speak it?' Kasen said.

'Go and talk to him, see what's needed,' Luken said.

Miren sat in the upstairs corridor in the school before being shown into the office.

'We know your eagerness to improve your English here, Mrs Abaroa,' the principal said. 'And seeing as you live locally we thought, why not see if this lady is willing to take it on? As you're a fluent speaker we don't need you to have a formal qualification, for now, at least. This will be a very basic course, with no examination at the end of the year, the first year, anyway. It's for those who really want to learn Spanish. Now that the war and the emergency is coming to an end it's time to anticipate normality again. I'm sure you've noticed the relief that people are now talking about?'

'I certainly have.'

'Anyway, we're hoping to upgrade the course to academic standard after that and perhaps you can help us in that regard. Anyway, the course isn't starting until next September so we'll work out a curriculum together. That'll give us plenty of time. You know, a basic vocabulary of everyday things, dressing, washing, going to the shops and so forth. I think you should consider doing an advanced course in Spanish yourself. How would you feel about that?'

'I thought of doing a higher course in English.'

'No reason why you can't do the two if you have time. But I'd say you'd be as well to get the academic paper in Spanish first, especially if you wanted to pursue a career in teaching.'

'It's certainly worth thinking about. My children are at a stage where they don't need so much attention.'

'Well then, let's take it as accepted, shall we?'

'Thank you for giving me this opportunity, Mr Nolan.'

***

A call came through from France for Luken in Padraig's office.

'Well brother, how are you?' the voice said through the crackle.

'Endika! It's been so long. I'm good, how about you?'

'I'm okay. Calling you from Guillaume's, I won't stay on too long, it'll be costing him a fortune. I'm living in Martignas-sur-Jalle, a town between Bordeaux and the coast. I gave up fighting for the PCF. I've had enough bloody killing and I'm lucky I've escaped capture over the years. I got injured a few times, nearly lost it a year ago. Spent months recovering in a fucking cave.'

'So what are you doing with yourself now?'

'Working in the wine trade but it's just seasonal. When this work is over I think I'll move back to St Jean.'

'Guillaume might be able to fix you up with something.'

They went on to talk about Luken and his family settling in to their new life and a little more on Endika's situation. He was staying away from all political activity and now there was a new love in his life.

'You'll have to meet her,' said Endika. 'Kerbasi kept his head down and got a job in Bayonne. Looks like he's settled there permanently. Any possibility you might come over for a visit?'

'Not at the moment, Endika. Though I often think about it, there's too much going on, workwise. Doesn't look like we'll be able to visit Euskal Herria for some time yet, eh?'

'No, not with that bastard at the helm.'

At length they agreed to stay in touch. After the call, Luken was pleased Endika had given up fighting and was looking forward to a more settled life.

***

On a Tuesday evening, Luken and his family sat in the sitting room of their house and listened to a broadcast on Radio Eireann. A government spokesman advised the populace that the Second World War in Europe had been declared over, following the unconditional surrender of Germany.

'Even though we knew this was coming, it's great to hear it,' Miren said gleefully, and went to the kitchen and soon returned with a trayful of drinks and mixed plates of confectionery and savoury treats.

Sabine had a glass of orange juice while the others each had a bottle of stout. Luken also took a small whiskey.

Sabine turned to Kasen, 'Looks like the Allies didn't need you after all.'

'Pity. It could have been ended a lot sooner,' he replied.

'Ha! Don't kid yourself —'

'Thanks be to God that they didn't take you, Kasen,' Miren said.

'I'm thinking of the Irish men who volunteered for the Allies,' Luken said. 'Men who never came back and who are still unrecognised by the government even though they gave their lives for the struggle against Fascism. Maybe in a few years' time they'll be recognised for their sacrifice.

At least now there'll be no more rumours about invasion or takeover. The government kept a neutral stance for the whole war so there probably won't be any national celebrations.'

'Still, it's time to look forward to better times ahead,' Miren said. 'Surely, it can only get better from now on.'

Despite the rain and cloudiness, on the following Sunday morning, for the pleasure of it, Luken went for a drive out on the road to Skerries and Balbriggan. Now that the war is well and truly over, he thought, the mass-relief among people is palpable. Yet, I can only feel the anxiety lifting gradually. Miren lost it straightaway. I've been preoccupied with it for so long, so even though the cause is gone, the effect is still there. Surely it'll evaporate over a period.

On the leisurely return journey the rain had stopped, a light breeze blew and the sun came out. Before entering the town he came to a disused agricultural warehouse just off the road and pulled in to have a look at the small office at the front of the building.

The windows were filthy, papers and an overturned stool were strewn on the floor. A large For Sale sign had fallen off the window. Strange, he thought, that nobody had seen fit to come and put the sign back up.

Just as he started the car an idea came to mind. He turned off the engine and went back around the building. Seemingly in sound structural condition with side doors, it also had a wide up-and-over door at the rear to allow access for delivery trucks. He walked through the overgrown grass and returned for a peek into the office window.

For the rest of the day Luken pondered over the empty warehouse and compared it to the garage business that he had left behind. It was roughly the same size and in a similar location, close to a town. The prospect of converting it to a garage seemed daunting though, especially in the difficult economic times that prevailed. And, he wondered, do I want to do this? Not without its risks, what happens if it doesn't work out? Miren will go mad if I even suggest it. You have a good job, she'll say, why don't you just stick with what you have and enjoy your life?

But he knew it was no good, the seed had been sown and he spent the rest of the day and most of that evening thinking about it.

At close of business the next day, he approached Padraig and brought up the subject of the empty warehouse. 'I thought it might be an opportunity but with the hard times, it might be foolish to start a business now.'

'Hard times can be the best times to start a business,' Padraig said. 'Especially if they go on for a long time as they are now. Prices can be at rock bottom and leases more flexible. Were you thinking of going for it?'

'Where would I get the money?'

'You must have been thinking about it so. Where there's a will, there's a way. I'll come out with you some evening and have a look. Call the agent and make the arrangements.'

Amazed that Padraig was so amenable to the idea, Luken called the auctioneer straight away.

Parts of the warehouse interior had been sectioned into two cabins but most of the area was empty save for the remnants of fruit and vegetable crates and the remains of an old motorcycle, all covered in dirt and dust.

'Size-wise, it's pretty much ideal but you'll have to put a lot of work into it,' Padraig said afterwards when they retired to the Harbour Bar. 'There's nobody operating in this part of Dublin, there's a chance here. Your best bet is to lease it with an option to buy it at a fixed price in, say, five years. You can put up whatever cash you have, I'll make up the balance and act as guarantor.'

Surprised that Padraig was already so far ahead of him, Luken guessed that his many years of business experience made all the difference.

'You can pay me back over a period,' Padraig continued. 'I'll be taking a third interest in it, by the way.'

'You don't mind me leaving the garage in Parnell Street?' he asked.

'When someone has had their own business, as you have, they'll always be hankering after it again. Better to have you onside rather than in competition. And I'm glad you came up with the idea yourself instead of me suggesting it. You'll be better motivated.'

At home Luken explained his proposition to Miren and was surprised by her calm reaction.

'I thought you were happy with the job you have,' she said quietly.

'I am up to a point but I feel it's time to move on. Remember the time I set up in Durango, you could see there was an opportunity there. If it wasn't for the civil war, that business would still be thriving. Now, with the emergency behind us, it's time to seize the day.'

'What if civil war breaks out here? There's still conflict going on.'

'Not much of that any more, Miren. The government has it contained.'

That night he couldn't sleep and sensed that Miren was awake too.

'You don't have to go through with it, you know,' she said. 'I'm sure Padraig would understand.'

'I'd say he'd be disappointed if I don't go through with it. As far as he's concerned, it's a good business proposition. Anyway, if it isn't a success, I'm sure I could come to some arrangement with him for work.'

'So, you've thought it all out.'

'As far as I can. Did you know I was thinking about it?'

'I've been living with you long enough to know when there's something on your mind.'

'So you don't object?'

'I know you wouldn't be happy if you didn't set up your own business.'

***

Standing in the second row of the choir at St Patrick's Church in Skerries and feeling a little nervous, Miren prepared for singing the Laudate Dominum. Pleased to help out in the new church since the one in Rush had a wedding at the same time, she delighted in getting back to singing after such a long time. Glad, too, that the hymns were in Latin, since she had never sung in English. She wondered, not for the first time, how badly the church in Durango had been damaged and if she would ever see it again, and how Katarin and Father Garai might now be.

After the first hymn, the choirmaster, a local priest, moved the choir onto the next canticle, Gounod's Sanctus, and Miren effortlessly found her voice. As the singing progressed, she eased into a state of relaxation as her nerves diminished.

Afterwards, Sheila approached and invited her home.

Over tea, they talked about the décor and style of the newly built church while munching on freshly baked fruit scones.

'Tell me more about the Basque Country, Miren,' Sheila said. 'I've never been out of this country and it sounds so … exotic!'

'We loved where we lived, overlooking a beautiful valley. I kept out of politics but, no matter what you did or didn't do, you were seen as being on one side or the other. I worked in a hospital and helped soldiers who were mostly Republican and that was enough to be seen as one of them. Luken was involved in what you might call socialist activities and that was seen as being a communist.'

'Maybe you'd rather not talk about it?'

'It's okay, Sheila. But you're the only one I'd say these things to.'

'Come on, it's such a nice day, let's go down for a stroll,' Sheila said.

They each put on a headscarf and, in their long cotton floral dresses and without coats, walked down through the garden to the dunes and the marram grass and out onto the beach. They removed their shoes and walked along the wet sand at the water's edge. A light breeze came off the sea while a few groups, families and couples, were sitting out in the summer sun; children were playing around and two cocker spaniels were chasing after a ball that a boy had thrown into the water.

'It looked for a time as though we were going to settle in France but there was no work for Luken. He was given an opportunity here and we took a chance on it. All the sermons we hear here portrayed the war as Christian against anti-Christian. The reality was a lot different, I can tell you. There were good and bad people on both sides but now that Franco has taken over the country I don't know what's going to happen.'

'Do you think you might go back?'

'It depends on how things turn out but we certainly won't be in any hurry. I'm mostly concerned about the kids,' Miren hesitated for a moment before continuing, 'I have to tell you Sheila, Sabine is not my daughter, she's my niece. We adopted her when her mother and sister were killed in an air raid. Sabine's mother was my sister.'

Sheila stopped walking and turned, 'Miren, I'm gobsmacked. That was a great thing to do.'

Miren smiled into Sheila's pale face and said, 'Not really. It's what any decent woman like you would've done. I have to keep impressing on her not to tell anyone. Not yet anyway, I don't want her being made fun of, as kids do. Luckily, she didn't see the bomb attack. We had to tell her what happened but it's only in the last few years that she's come to understand it. Someday, I suspect when she gets into a temper, she'll turn around and say, "You're not my real mother!"'

'I can hardly take all this in, Miren.'

'It's great to have someone like you who I can talk to, Sheila. Luken's been affected by it, though not as much as me, and he hardly admits it. I can talk to him whenever but it's good to have someone outside the family.'

'You can come and talk to me any time, Miren. Actually, it crossed my mind that you might have lost someone but I thought better of asking you.'

'I get these flashbacks. I was waiting to buy vegetables in Butterly's last week when a little boy burst his balloon in the shop. With the bang, my sister and her daughter appeared before me and I was just overcome with emotion. I had to run out of the shop and lost my place in the queue – people must've thought I was mad.'

'So you lost a niece as well as your sister?'

Miren nodded. Sheila put her arm around her shoulder, saying, 'It's good to talk about it, I'm sure. What was her name, your sister?'

'Gechina. They say she looked like me. Errita was her daughter. On the twenty-second of July I bring Sabine down here and we release two balloons with Gechina and Errita's name on them. That was the day they died. I like when Sabine asks me about her mother. I don't always have the right answer for her but at least I know what she's thinking.'

They walked on and Miren continued, 'I wonder about Kasen being picked on in school. Although he can give as good as he gets, it's the same everywhere, you get picked on if you're the same and get twice as picked on if you're different. It was like that in France but at least there were other boys there like himself. Here there's no one with his dark skin and I hope it isn't an omen…'

'It happens to us all at one time or another,' Sheila interrupted. 'Kasen's a big fella and surely he's made good friends with some of the lads?'

'He has and he stands up for himself but his slow progress in English hasn't helped. With Sabine, so far there haven't been such problems. It's interesting, you know, Kasen calls me Mam when he's with his friends but Ama, the Basque equivalent, when we're alone. Sabine always calls me Mamá, the Spanish name, regardless of who's around. Gechina taught her Spanish first. We made a point of teaching Kasen Basque in his early years. Now it's illegal there to give children Basque names and it's forbidden to even speak it.'

'Tell me this, have you come across any prejudice towards yourself here?'

'Sometimes I feel that people are being unfriendly when they hear my accent. When they find out where I'm from, they think, "Ah! Spanish, Catholic, that's okay!"'

They both gave out a laugh.

**

Luken and Kasen removed the abandoned wooden crates and cardboard boxes that had been left in the warehouse and made a fire of them at the rear of the building.

'Must get the grass cut and the rubbish removed,' Luken said, looking around the plot and noticing the discarded door and rusting machinery that had been left outside by the previous tenants.

'What about the motorbike, Papá?'

'I had a look at it, earlier. Most of it is intact. Needs new tyres, among other things.'

They heard a vehicle pull up at the front of the building and went to see a Ford van disgorge four workmen.

Luken explained what was needed. 'Getting the electrical wiring system replaced and expanded is the first priority. And a new fuse board, of course.'

He pointed out the various places where new outlets were required while the foreman made notes on a sketchpad. The men set to work straightaway, ripping out the old cables, fitting conduits and screwing down replacement sockets.

After three weeks, the electrical and water system had been completely refurbished but, despite Luken's best efforts, a telephone line was proving difficult. He met with the local administrator for the Department of Posts and Telegraphs and explained his situation.

'Look, this will be the first motor car garage in this part of the country. I expect to employ at least six men within the first year, but a telephone is essential for business nowadays. Surely you know that?'

'I do, Mr Abaroa,' the man replied, 'but it's not easy. Even with the emergency behind us, material procurement is an endless struggle and our telephone exchange is running at maximum capacity. I appreciate the benefits your business will bring and your application is prioritised, along with all businesses, over domestic applications at least. All I can say is that we'll keep trying and let you know but do keep in touch in the meantime.'

Disappointed, Luken returned to the warehouse where Kasen and Sabine were busy painting the offices.

'What do you think of it, Papá?' Sabine asked.

'Magnifico!'

'I think it'd look better in a sky-blue or yellow maybe?'

'We'll maybe do it in one of those colours later but for now let's just get it finished in white. Make the place clean-looking.'

Luken looked up as the workmen bolted the overhead sign advertising 'Esso' to the upright pole. The underground tanks for storing petrol had been installed and tested and were now filled.

Customers had already given Luken a chance by having their cars serviced in his warehouse, saving themselves the trouble of driving further afield. But now, with the high, licensed sign in place, he felt the joy of establishing a professional business. A visible statement of his intentions.

'Where did you want the other signs?' one of the men asked.

Luken pointed to the hand-written signs at the roadside. The new, impeccably printed signs were to be a direct replacement – extolling service and crash repairs at competitive prices.

That evening the entire family arrived at the garage, armed with bunting, tinsel and more signs declaring, 'OFFICIAL OPENING!' They hung the signs at the roadside where there was maximum exposure to passing motorists, while the bunting and tinsel were placed around the new petrol pumps. Kasen and Sabine held the ladder while Luken hung yet more bunting around the newly erected lettering on the building, proclaiming, 'RUSH GARAGE.' Miren played with the cash register in the outer office, familiarising herself with the buttons and levers.

The following morning, shortly after eight o'clock, a grey Morris Minor slowed as it passed then stopped and reversed into the forecourt. The driver wound down his window. 'Are you serving petrol?'

'We are, certainly!' Luken replied.

'Then give me a gallon,' the old gentleman said as he stepped out of his car at the pumps. He reached for his wallet and painstakingly counted out two shillings and ten pence in pennies and half-pennies. When he looked up, seeing that Luken had already put six gallons into his car – over seventeen shillings worth – he shouted, 'Stop! I haven't got that much money!'

Luken smiled. 'You don't need any money, this is free. You're our first ever customer for petrol.'

'Well, that's very decent of you.'

'Keep us in mind,' Luken replied. 'Especially when that car needs a service.'

'I certainly will, thank you very much!'

Miren came out of the office. 'That was more than generous of you.'

'I couldn't help it, I was feeling so elated.'

'The business won't last long if you keep that up.'

'Don't worry, it's strictly business from here on.'

Miren, for her part, put on her best smile, especially for male customers, while she handled the cash. She made a point of engaging them in day to day nonsense about the weather and wished each customer a safe trip.

For the rest of the day, Luken remained at the pumps and, buoyed by the first customer's response, gave each customer a free gallon – just one this time – proclaiming each to be his first ever customer.

And for the rest of the week, he kept it up. 'You're getting a free gallon seeing as you're the first person to buy petrol from us on a Tuesday. Remember us when your car needs to be serviced or you need to get repair work done.'

**

One Sunday morning, Miren unpegged a batch of clothes off the washing line and threw them into a basket. Holding it under her arm, she closed the glass door behind her and entered the greenhouse to see Luken at the east end, facing the sea, where he was replacing a pane of glass that had been blown in by a gust of wind.

'I'm going to use thicker glass from now on,' he said. 'Should have used thicker stuff when we were restoring it. Serves us right for doing it on the cheap.'

'It's served us well so far. I'm sure it's paid for itself by now,' she replied and sat on a nearby stool, looking around at the tall tomato plants now brimming with ripening fruit and reaching up towards the glass roof.

'I love the smell of tomato plants,' she said.

'Remind you of anything?'

'The ones back home, of course.'

'It's amazing that we still call it home. Have you thought of it recently?'

'Gechina and Errita… Every so often that day in Otxandio still jumps into my head. It's as if I was back there. I was listening to the BBC again last night,' she continued, 'and nothing has changed. If anything, it's got worse. I think about everyone who stayed, especially Arossa. What about you?'

'It's hard to keep it out of your mind. While the Generalissimo is alive nothing's going to get better.' He picked up a cloth and wiped the putty off his hands and the finger marks off the glass.

They ambled back through the rows and stopped to examine the sumptuous fruit on an individual tomato plant.

'At least we have peace in Ireland,' Miren said and immediately recalled the lines from a poem she had learned on an English course.

'And I shall have some peace there, for peace comes dropping slow,
Dropping from the veils of the morning to where the cricket sings,
There, midnight's all a glimmer, and noon a purple glow,
And evening full of the linnet's wings.'

The silence lasted for a few seconds until Luken asked, 'I presume the linnet's a bird?'

She turned and kissed him on the cheek, 'It's a little songbird. Linnet is the English word for Pardillo. I remember Sabine found a dead Pardillo in the garden in Eguzkitza and I used it to explain death to her when we were in St Jean.'

He kissed her on the lips and they embraced. Their initial touch turned to passion and they kissed intensely. She sensed an odour and laughed. 'I can smell putty, I'm putty in your hands!'

After a while, Miren heard a noise at the entrance. 'Someone's coming!'

Luken looked up as a bird walked along the apex of the roof then flew off.

'It's just a magpie.'

Chapter 22

Through the rest of the 1940s Luken worked long hours at his garage, often late into the night, and as his reputation grew, so too did his business. Car sales added extra revenue as the economy gradually picked up. He took on two apprentices and taught them the essentials of the trade and, as petrol sales improved, a full-time attendant took over from Miren and Kasen who had each worked staggered hours at the pumps.

Although Luken had long since got a telephone for the garage, as the decade rolled over into the 1950s, procuring a telephone for his house proved impossible.

Miren waited in a telephone booth in the General Post Office in Dublin City feeling a little apprehensive, exacerbated by the confined space. It was her second attempt to have the international operator put a call through to Arossa. Earlier in the day, nobody had answered. She skimmed through the letter she had recently received from her friend, reassuring herself that the phone numbers were clear.

In a while, the call came through.

'I was sorry to hear about your Papá passing away, Arossa.'

'It happened suddenly. He was about to get up from breakfast and had a heart attack. I'd urged him to retire but he didn't listen to me. But he had a good life at least.'

'I only met him once,' Miren replied. 'I hope he wasn't in any pain?'

'Not at all. I got word that Estebe is being released from the labour camps. I was allowed a few visits.'

'That's great news, Arossa. How is he?'

'Keeping a brave face but those years have been hard on him. He looked pretty wretched. At least he's being treated better than he was, years ago. Don't know yet when he's getting out. I'll let you know. How are things with you?'

'Sabine is no longer a teenager, she turned twenty last week. She still has another year to finish her degree in languages but she loves it. Kasen is doing postgraduate work in engineering.'

'How is your own teaching coming along?' Arossa asked.

'Well, I enjoy the daytime teaching the teenagers, but it's much more fun in the evening classes. The students are older and this year want to know everything about Spain and Euskal Herria. Luken's business is going very well, though he's still putting a lot of time into it. So tell me more about you.'

'Still have to be careful what you say and who you say it to. The Guardia Civil are everywhere – encouraging people to betray each other. If you were thinking of coming over, forget it, don't come to Euskal Herria.'

'Maybe we could meet in St Jean de Luz?'

After a moment's hesitation, Arossa replied, 'That's a wonderful idea, Miren.'

Later, Miren made a mental note to write to Arossa soon and wondered when and exactly where both families could get together for a visit, especially when Estebe was released.

On a Saturday morning, after breakfast the drizzle stopped. Miren watched Luken at the rear of the cottage where he removed a sheet of oilcloth from the motorcycle and pushed it around to the front. He pulled the choke and kick-started the engine. She followed him out and sat astride the rear seat. They sped away, out across town and along the Skerries Road.

The tension Miren felt at the start of the journey eased as she clasped Luken ever tighter when they raced across the straight runs past the North Beach. She looked over his shoulder and deliberately called to mind the day of death in Otxandio in an effort to exorcise the demons at the back of her mind. The motion and noise of the machine and the wind against her face and through her hair lifted her anxiety and, out of the blue, she felt her freedom in the world, freedom to confront hell without pain or anxiety.

They stopped at the seafront in Skerries and dismounted. 'Well?' he asked.

'Still a bit nervous, but I'm okay. I should have got my own goggles,' she replied, wiping the moisture from her eyes.

Luken pointed out that unlike the Ariel, the AJS used a foot-operated gearchange which in fact made the operation smoother; there was no need to take one's hand off the accelerator to change gear. Miren tried to take in the information but soon lost concentration. The previous night she had not slept very well, thinking about the journey that morning.

Inside a nearby café, they took a table by the window. Over coffee, Luken asked, 'What's on your mind right now?'

'The joy of being with you on that bike.'

He reached across the table and clasped her hand. 'Did it make you forget everything else?'

She squeezed his hand back. 'Not quite but I made a point of thinking about Otxandio and suddenly, it was no longer so … upsetting.'

They sat back to enjoy their coffee while looking out the window at the world passing by.

On the return journey, Luken eased off the accelerator and took a more leisurely pace.

The sunshine came out as they arrived at the house. Dismounting, and without turning off the engine, Luken said, 'Here, sit on the driver's seat. The sooner you do this the better.'

Seeing Miren's hesitancy, Luken said, 'You have to give it a try, come on.'

She sighed and, after a few seconds, tentatively mounted and grabbed the hand controls. When she turned the accelerator, the bike gave a roar and she asked, 'How do you work the gears?'

'Good question,' he said, turning off the engine. 'Let's leave it at that for now, I'll go through the gears with you another day.'

Miren looked on while he pushed the bike around the back of the cottage. She turned and stopped dead in her tracks to see Kasen and Sabine standing at the front door, smiling at her.

'Well done, Ama,' Kasen said.

***

Luken walked around the garage to see the progress on the cars that were being serviced and repaired. Business was going well and, accepting that he owed a lot to Padraig's helping hand, he realised that things were now at the same point they had been in Euskal Herria when he'd gone into exile. Time now to formulate new ideas and consider expansion. He had already surveyed the north-eastern area of the province and felt there was room for further representation there. The economy had picked up and car sales were improving. He looked back at the times he'd taken on the role of sales and, although he could hold his own, felt that, with certain customers, that unspoken resentment or lack of trust towards him as a foreigner.

Nonetheless, he recalled that Euskal Herria was not just well known, but notorious for resenting outsiders. A resentment and reputation borne out of generations of invaders attempting to impose their domination. In Ireland he supposed it had been the same, hundreds of years of colonial rule. No matter where he went, there was always going to be that trace of bigotry, something he would have to live with.

He believed that Kasen and Sabine were capable of dealing with the problem whenever it arose. Kasen had already spoken about a few incidents but both knew what to expect, having been counselled by Miren and himself as they grew up.

One particular incident came to mind which he regarded as amusing in retrospect although not funny at the time. He had taken up golf at the newly opened Rush Golf Club and following a few drinks with acquaintances at a local hostelry one evening, he'd gone to a chip shop on the way home. Two young men, obviously liquored up, had confronted him outside. One of them said, 'What are you doin' here, Spick?

'Excuse me?'

'I said what are you fuckin' doin' here, Spick?'

'It's none of your fuckin' business,' Luken responded, in the local patois.

The individual threw a punch but Luken intercepted it with his left forearm and clobbered him in the mouth. The second man threw a punch which caught Luken in the eye. Not to be outdone, he lashed out as best he could but, given that there were two of them, in the end he'd had to withdraw and flee.

Miren was asleep when he got home and was taken aback the next morning when she noted the eye, now well and truly blackened. Then he remembered the chips all over the place and went to explain what had happened to the chip-shop owner. The owner came out of the shop to see the potato chips walked into the ground and said, 'This is terrible. We'll have to clean this up. I think I know them. The lousy bastards. Next time you come, it's on the house.'

**

In a morning newspaper, the Irish Independent, Luken read that a number of houses had collapsed in Fenian Street in Dublin City. Thunderstorms earlier in the week had undermined cracks and defects in the buildings. Two young girls had been killed by the falling masonry and, with a start, he realised it was where Mrs Kelly lived.

He drove into the city and even though he'd been expecting devastation he was still shocked to see that, other than the back walls of the four-storey building, most of the structure had fallen into a pile of rubble. A second house had also collapsed. People had gathered around and council workers were busy removing bricks, sections of timber and household items. Visions of the devastation he had seen in Euskal Herria flooded his mind. He wondered how on earth a brick building could have just fallen down.

Families had evacuated adjacent buildings and had their belongings on the street, fearful that the same was about to happen to them. He asked after Mrs Kelly but nobody was aware of where she was or what had happened to her. He went to the rear of the building to see that the ground floor portico had remained intact even though the back door was gone. He walked through and into Mrs Kelly's room to see that the rubble had destroyed her few bits of furniture. The Valor heater had been smashed and he smelled the paraffin spill on the ground. Thoughts of the visits he had paid to the place came to mind, the chats, the cups of tea and shots of whiskey and the old lady that he had become so fond of and who he now feared for. Shifting some of the fallen masonry, he saw no sign of her.

He went around to the street and, during a lull, heard the distant sound of a bird singing. He looked up to see a yellow songbird in a cage perched on a shelf on the back wall of what was left of a fourth-floor flat. Again, he asked around after Mrs Kelly. One of the workers said, 'You could try Mercer's Hospital, a lot of the injured were brought there.'

'How are you going to get that down?' Luken asked, nodding upwards.

'Fire brigade.'

'How the hell could a house like this just collapse?'

The workman shrugged. 'Poorly put up in the first place. Bloody landlords cutting corners, probably hadn't got a proper foundation.'

Luken drove to the hospital to find Mrs Kelly in a ward on the second floor. She was asleep and he sat beside the bed. The senior nurse approached and after enquiring about Luken's relationship to the patient, said, 'She was lucky, a few broken ribs and a fractured femur. Most people have more serious injuries. You heard about the girls who were killed?'

'Read it in this morning's paper.'

'She'll be here for some time. She's on painkillers. The femur fracture at her age will take a long time to heal.'

Mrs Kelly awoke and after a moment looking around, said, 'Luke, good of you to come in. You're a wee darlin'.'

'I was half expecting you to be dead.'

'You know what they say, the devil looks after his own.'

'I didn't know you were one of his followers.'

'Aren't we all, Luke?'

'Considering your injuries, you're certainly in good form.'

Mrs Kelly smiled, 'It's the morphine, Luke, the morphine. Great stuff. What a bloody country this is, they can't build a house but it falls down in the rain. Talk about the three little pigs!'

'The three little pigs?'

'It's a nursery rhyme. A big bad wolf blows their house down.'

'What about your brother in America, do you want me to write to him?'

'Your English is very good now. You're as good as Irish.'

'That's what my wife keeps telling me.'

'If you can find my brother's address,' she replied. 'It's in the cupboard with the books. At least it was.'

She was drifting back into sleep and he said, 'I'll have a look. I'll drop in to see you later in the week. Do you want anything, maybe something to read?'

'Not for now.'

On his way out Luken left his contact details with the senior nurse and went back to Fenian Street where he searched through the remains of the room and found a letter that had been sent from New York with a return address.

He reckoned, not for the first time, that there were serious problems with so many of the old houses in the city. Disasters waiting to happen. It was about time the authorities woke up to it. What was Mrs Kelly to do when she was ready to leave hospital? Where were they going to put her up?

Over the following days and weeks he read in the newspapers of the popular furore and the outcry in the Dáil over the public housing. Temporary accommodation was at least being organised while a new policy of inexpensive housing was brought before the Government and the town councils.

***

Miren went to the glasshouse and filled a small basket with ripe tomatoes which she then emptied into a bag on the rear of the motorcycle. The new goggles were just about the right fit and after kick starting the engine she drove up the lane, across town and down to Sheila's house. She parked the bike and with the bag of tomatoes in hand, walked around to the rear, opened the door into the kitchen and emptied the tomatoes onto the worktop.

They sat, drank tea, and talked about plans for the summer festival. They were baking cakes and biscuits for charity and their respective offspring were planning on taking part in various activities and competitions, Irish dancing, football and hurling matches.

When it was time to go, Miren gestured to the tomatoes, saying, 'The glasshouse is great for growing them.'

'By the way, Miren. I don't think Father Byrne is too happy with you on that motorcycle, he thinks it's not the "done thing" for a woman. And you know what others are saying about you?'

'Tell me.'

'Did you see that "mad Spanish woman on the motorbike?"'

Miren laughed, saying, 'I don't mind being called mad but they're only partly right. I'm Basque and Irish first, Spanish second... If there's such a thing.'

Sheila put a selection of her home-grown potatoes into the bag on the motorcycle. She looked the bike up and down when Miren started the engine and said, 'You'll have to bring me for a spin on that someday.'

'I'll be delighted to, Sheila.'

A run to Donabate had now become her custom and she motored along at a comfortable pace. At Lusk she took a left and headed south.

When she was on the motorcycle, the day in Otxandio always returned with the occasional flashback and, although the emotional horror would never go away, at least now she felt a measure of control that let her look back without undue pain.

As she came to Blakes Cross, rather than stop she slowed down and turned left to go with the flow of traffic. At that moment a car going in the opposite direction overtook another. Miren was forced into the left hand verge. The bike stalled with the sharp swing left and she was catapulted off. She came down on her back and whacked the rear of her head on the road surface, immediately losing consciousness.

The driver of the overtaken car stopped and came running back. He saw she was unconscious and tried to offer comfort, placing a jacket over her. Miren had turned pale and he checked to see that she was still breathing. He hailed down another car and asked the driver to fetch an ambulance. The potatoes were strewn all over the road.

Despite realising that she could probably not hear him, the man whispered comforting words in her ear, telling her not to move and indicating that an ambulance was on its way.

Another car stopped and the occupants offered help. Nobody wanted to move Miren and men directed traffic around the scene.

The ambulance arrived and the paramedics swiftly but carefully manoeuvred her onto a stretcher and took off at speed while Gardaí appeared at the same time and took statements from everyone.

Miren was rushed through the Accident and Emergency section of the Mater Hospital. The doctors immediately had X-rays taken and noted the skull fractures. Suspecting inoperable brain damage, they had her head clamped into a static position and fitted the oxygen mask. A senior nurse fitted the intravenous saline drip.

In the meantime, the Gardaí were called and soon traced Luken at his garage.

Luken looked down with disbelief at Miren's discoloured face as she lay in a small room in the emergency section. He sat next to the bed and took her hand – warm but inert. He repeatedly gave it gentle squeezes. 'Can you hear me? What happened, querida?'

What had happened with the motorcycle? He wondered. She had always been so careful and he knew the machine was in good shape, having maintained it himself. Maybe she had to swerve to avoid a lorry or something.

He wanted to telephone for Kasen and Sabine but, not wanting to leave her side, spoke softly for an hour, reminding her of the good times, past and present, hoping for a response. They still had the best part of their lives ahead of them. An orderly looked in and left him a cup of tea he didn't drink.

He kept squeezing her hand and felt a faint reaction that persisted for a few seconds and then went limp. Her breathing stopped and he raced out and returned with the senior nurse, who took Miren's pulse. She looked him gravely in the face with a miniscule shake of her head.

Feeling empty and desolate, the tears welled up in his eyes and he wondered, what was the point of it all?

Now he had to tell the kids. Having avoided the ravages of civil war and struggled through all the misfortune since, what was it all for? Just as they'd got over all the knock-backs and started making real progress in life, now it was all worthless. With the kids nearing adulthood, they should have been looking forward to really enjoying life and spending more time together. Now that was all lost, all gone. Why had he encouraged her on that bloody motorbike?

He sat in the car feeling as if he was living in a world that was disconnected from that of the passing visitors carrying flowers and confectionery into the hospital.

'Are you all right?' a security man tapped on the window.

Luken nodded, unaware of how long he had been sitting in the car, lost in a daze. He checked his watch and realised that Kasen and Sabine would be home soon. He started the engine and moved off. The loneliest drive of my life, he thought.

***

After the funeral mass Luken was surprised at how many people approached to offer sympathy and support: women from the choir, Sheila and other neighbours, people she had befriended on the English course including the principal, Mr Nolan, and the men from the garage. Even the man who had stopped his car and came back to help at the scene of the accident. Kasen sent a telegram to Arossa, who replied that she would have liked to come but was unable to travel.

Luken felt the heartbreak around the house; his and Kasen and Sabine's lives had come to a standstill. An all-pervasive feeling of emptiness seeing her slippers that would never be used again, left casually at the kitchen door. And the wellington boots that she wore when the two of them went for a walk along the beach in winter time. And the lipstick, rouge, eye shadow and other things on the bedroom dresser.

He tortured himself with recrimination over the days following her death. Everyone telling him that it had been a genuine accident was no consolation. Even though he knew he was being unfair to himself, over and over, the anguish kept replaying in his head. The one thing he was determined not to do was to succumb to drink. The kids were going to need him now more than ever, so it was time to focus on them and their future.

One morning, Kasen and Sabine were at the table eating cereal. Luken shook out a bowl of the same and doused it in milk. Luken sensed Sabine's disapproval. He didn't blame her. How many parents could a child lose in a lifetime? First her disappearing father, then her birth mother and now her adoptive mother. He sat down and ate his breakfast.

'We're passing each other like ships in the night, as they say,' Luken said. 'I think we should sit together and have a talk. When we're finished here, let's go into the sitting room.'

Sabine and Kasen sat on the sofa while Luken drew up an armchair.

'She was buried a week ago now. How do you feel about going back to lectures?'

Kasen shrugged. 'Maybe next week.'

'Sabine?'

'The same, I think.'

'I know it's difficult to think of this now but I propose that we take turns cooking the evening meal. We're each on different time schedules during the day, between your schooling and my work, and unless we set a definite time to talk and be together we'll end up wandering around in our own little worlds. As a family we'll just drift apart.'

'How can we be a family without Mamá?' Sabine asked vehemently.

Luken shrugged. 'We'll still have one another, won't we? That's what Mamá would have wanted, isn't it?'

After a pause, Sabine sniffled and nodded.

'It means we'll all have to make a special effort that we didn't have to in the past. Mamá was always here, the lunch or dinner was always ready, the house was always cleaned up. I think we should also make a point of doing something together over the weekends. Doesn't have to be anything extraordinary, go to a film maybe.'

'I've a problem with all this,' Kasen said.

'What's that?'

'I'm not looking forward to your cooking, Papá!'

They each gave out a laugh and for the first time in over a week, Luken felt a morsel of light-heartedness creep into their souls.

Chapter 23

Over the following weeks, Luken buried himself in his work. The everyday reminders of the woman who was no longer a part of his life had become an unremitting source of sadness. He realised after a time that he only made a point of returning home when he was sure that either Kasen or Sabine would be there. Nonetheless, each of them kept up a brave face, reminding one another of the good times they had had.

One day, the telephone rang in Luken's office. Guillaume was on the line.

'Sorry to hear about Miren. We got your telegram. What exactly happened?'

Luken explained about the accident. Guillaume asked, 'How are you bearing up?'

Luken hesitated for a few seconds to gather his thoughts. 'Doing the best I can, it's not easy. It's going to take some time, especially with Sabine.'

'We'll be thinking of you. I have someone here who wants to speak to you…'

'Kaixo, Luken. This is Estebe.'

'Estebe! Great to hear from you. Tell me what's happened?'

'So sorry to hear about Miren. Guillaume told me. Miren was a wonderful woman, so friendly and yet so spirited…'

'When I think of the help that you and Arossa gave us to get out of Euskal Herria and now she had to go and die in a bloody accident...' Luken was unable to contain the upswell of emotion, but steered the conversation back to Estebe. 'Anyway, how are you?'

'I got out some time ago, I'm still in recovery, you might say.'

'You must have suffered?'

'Nothing that I couldn't bear, but I'll tell you about it when you come over.'

'I'm coming over?'

'Yes, you have to.'

'Why?'

'Can't say over the phone but it's important, Luken, you must come. Call me back when you've made the arrangements.'

Afterwards Luken wondered what on earth was so important that Estebe wanted him for. Maybe something to do with the civil war. He thought over all the things that had happened in Euskal Herria and in France but there was nothing that would warrant such a trip so urgently. Nonetheless, he decided to mull it over for a day or so. Perhaps something would come to mind, some unfinished business that he had forgotten. Had he slipped up over something, maybe something that seemed trivial at the time? At least the meeting was to take place in France, not Spain, not so dangerous.

The next morning he rang Guillaume and implored him to give him some idea about what was going on.

'It's too sensitive to talk about over the phone, Luken,' Guillaume replied. 'You can guess that it's connected with events in the 1930s but you're not the main cause of concern. Beyond that I can't say anything.'

Luken decided to take advantage of this opportunity and asked Guillaume to get a message to Endika, advising that he would come see him when he was there. He thought of Kerbasi, too, but decided to wait until he arrived to make contact.

On the flight from London to Paris, he marvelled at the speed of the turbo prop aircraft and how little time it took to get from Dublin to St Jean: two days compared to the nine it had taken when he was going in the other direction some sixteen years previously.

Though having greyed in the intervening years, Guillaume still had the pot belly and was easily recognisable when they met at the railway station in Bayonne.

Guillaume drove the twenty-six kilometres to St Jean de Luz. 'I've put you in the same room that Miren and you had when you came here first. I think you'll notice some changes.'

On the way they discussed the latest political developments in France and Ireland and how it was good to leave the wartime conflict and shortages behind. Guillaume mentioned that it'd be the next day before a meeting was convened and, along with Estebe, another man would be present. Despite Luken's insistent curiosity about its purpose, his friend refused to divulge anything.

Estebe was sitting in the café at the Eskualduna Hotel as they arrived late in the evening. They embraced in a brotherly manner and following salutations Luken supposed that he shouldn't have been surprised to see how old and wizened Estebe had become. After some fish and haricot beans with a carafe of wine, Guillaume brought out a pot of coffee.

'Sorry again to hear about Miren,' Estebe said. 'Arossa was very upset when she heard, especially when she couldn't make it to the funeral. An accident?'

Luken described what had happened and they each went on to talk about the events in their lives since they had last met.

Later, Luken looked over the hotel and his room in particular. A big improvement on what it had been all those years ago, he thought. New furniture and fittings had been installed but in a style that retained the character of the old building; more comfortable bedding had also been put in and the floors had been varnished. The echo of times past returned and he couldn't help but think with sadness of the good and the bad times they had had in the hotel.

He couldn't sleep, not knowing what was coming down the tracks next day. He went over the earlier conversation in the café, recalling the horrific treatment that Estebe had been through, the early days in prison, the beatings and the executions he had witnessed and then the outdoor days, forced labouring under the sun, building the roads and canals. The surprising thing was that he had survived at all. And there was no joviality but a certain reserve in Estebe, whether it was permanent due to his imprisonment or temporary due to the 'meeting', he couldn't guess. But after a gap of so many years he could hardly expect the relationship to take up where it left off.

After breakfast the following morning, they moved to a ground floor room, an office that had been requisitioned for the day. Luken felt a deep nervousness that he hadn't experienced since being before the officials from the Irish Immigration Department as he'd argued his case for residency.

A rectangular table sat in the centre of the floor with two chairs on either side. Guillaume and himself sat on one side and were soon joined by Estebe and another man who sat opposite.

'This is Gabirel Araña,' Estebe did the introductions. 'Gabirel was charged with investigating the murder of my son, Ander, in 1936. Luken, we recall, was the man who found Ander and luckily he did, otherwise we might never have recovered his body.'

At this point Luken felt that the meeting had the format of a trial.

'As you know, at that time there was no specific proof as to who was responsible. I'm certainly satisfied it was the Requetés who committed the act, fired the shot…'

'How do you know?' Luken asked.

'We'll come to that in a minute, Luken.'

'Recently a man came forward with more information,' Araña said. 'He's an old villager who's lived in Arakoa all his life. He's told us two things. He saw the Requetés with their rifles trained on Ander and leading him up towards the forest on the north side of the village. More importantly, from your point of view, Luken, is that he also saw Endika talking to the Requetés earlier in the day before he saw them with Ander.'

'So, the question we ask ourselves,' Estebe said, 'is why were they talking to Endika before they shot Ander?'

Luken turned the material over in his mind and asked, 'This man who gave the information, who is he and why is he doing it now?'

'He was afraid of reporting what he saw at the time,' Araña said. 'In case he'd end up dead himself, especially not knowing what the investigator's loyalties were. That was myself, by the way. You can meet him and ask him yourself…'

'How did he know who was who?'

'We showed him pictures from the time,' Araña said and handed over a wrinkled photograph of Ander, Endika and Kerbasi. 'We also spoke to the old man's wife and though she didn't see what happened she confirmed that, at that time, he'd told her what he had seen.'

Luken felt baffled. 'It doesn't look good for Endika but I'm sure there's some explanation.'

'That's an understatement if ever I heard one,' Estebe said. 'Before we take a break, that old man is here for the day and you're welcome to talk to him. In fact, I insist that you do, you'll need to satisfy yourself about what we've told you.'

Luken, accompanied by Guillaume, went to the café in the hotel where the man and his wife were sitting in a far corner. The same corner, he recalled, where Miren and the two children used to sit. Guillaume did the introductions and asked if anyone wanted a coffee or a drink; nobody did.

The man, who Luken reckoned was some eighty years of age, looked at the picture and confirmed what Araña had said. While bringing his two cows up to pasture that morning he had seen the Requetés in a clearing below the forest talking to Endika, who he pointed to in the photograph. Later in the day, collecting firewood from the fuel merchant on the west side of the village, he had seen them arguing with Ander.

'Why did you wait so long to come forward with this?' Luken asked.

'I'm not interested in politics, never wanted to have any hand nor part in it, and basically took the side of whoever was in power. I live on a smallholding and all I ever wanted to do was look after my wife and daughter. I put my family's survival down to the fact that I did just that. However, I believe that what I saw in Arakoa that day was an act of betrayal and decided to speak out in the few years I've left.'

Luken, accompanied by Guillaume, went out onto the street where they took a walk.

'This is a lot to take in, my head is bursting.'

Guillaume pursed his lips. 'Shocking stuff, especially hearing it now.'

On their return to the room, Araña had gone, only Estebe sat across the table. 'What do you think happened, Luken? I know you're a decent, sound man but you must have an opinion?'

'I'm afraid to think about it.'

'Understandable. Look at the facts. Endika spoke to the Requetés and then Ander was "arrested" by them. Endika walked away and Ander was killed. Why? They were both Republican and the Requetés were and still are, of course, fanatical Catholic Nationalists.'

Guillaume left and returned immediately with a bottle of brandy and three glasses. He poured out three measures.

'There's no reason I can think of why he would've been talking to Requetés,' Luken said.

'Neither can I,' Estebe replied with a hardened look. 'Other than he was passing on information about the Casa del Pueblo and about Ander in particular.'

'Why don't you ask him?'

'We can't ask him, but you can,' Estebe leaned over the table. 'We don't know for sure if we would get the truth but you, as his brother, might.'

Luken sensed the tension building in the room and felt the perspiration on his brow and upper lip.

Estebe continued, 'We need an explanation. We need to know what justification Endika had for dealing with the Requetés.'

Luken drank the brandy straight down and walked around the room, recounting the years with Endika, trying to recollect if there was a time when he'd shown even the slightest allegiance to any of the nationalist groups. But he couldn't think of any. He thought of the moment when he'd brushed the earth off Ander's face and the body he'd found, so carelessly buried.

'Will you do it?' Estebe asked.

'I'll talk to him and see what he has to say. There's two sides to every story.'

He noticed Guillaume look sharply over to Estebe as though waiting for some kind of action. But nothing happened. Estebe just said, 'Call Endika and make the arrangements.'

Luken turned to Guillaume, 'I thought you couldn't contact Endika by phone?'

'We can now. The house where he's now staying has a phone.'

The meeting broke up and without being told, Luken knew he could not leave the hotel alone in case he alerted his brother to what was being set up. Further everyday conversation was out of the question and he went to his room.

What could Endika have possibly been doing with the Requetés, he wondered? Maybe the whole thing was being blown out of proportion. Maybe he'd have some plausible explanation. If so, why hadn't he told Luken? That was the most incriminating part of the whole story. They'd never kept any secrets from each other, certainly when it came to wartime matters.

Looking back on the trial, as he now thought of it, there was no doubt in his mind that he wasn't going to be allowed leave that room without some degree of acceptance as to what had been asked of him. Especially with Guillaume beside him and Estebe in front.

He paced around the room, letting the earlier talks repeat in his head while wondering about the potential dangers of the next day. How dangerous would it be for himself? What protection did he have? The whole bloody business was fraught with danger and uncertainty.

With a jolt, he remembered the pistol he had hidden in this very room so many years ago. Had he removed it at some point and forgotten?

Using the small pair of scissors from his toilet bag, he went around the floorboard, below which he reckoned he had stored the gun, and quietly and gently prised up the timber a few millimetres at a time. After twenty minutes, the board came free. No pistol. He reached into each cross beam in turn.

He felt what seemed like a metal tube. The barrel of a gun? Using the tips of three fingers, he pinched the tube and drew out the weapon, the very one that Etxartea had made for him.

Luken examined the weapon and marvelled that it was still in good condition, no sign of any corrosion. The safety catch was still on. He flicked open the cylinder to see that it was still loaded and examined the bullets to see that they too were in good condition, just some tarnish on the brass tips. He laughed to himself, wondering whether it would still fire.

Good old Etxartea, he thought, never one for shoddy work.

Luken made the call to Endika in the presence of Guillaume that evening.

'I was so sorry to hear about Miren,' Endika said.

Luken described what had happened with the motorcycle and how it had thrown his life and that of Sabine and Kasen into disarray.

'I'm living with that woman I mentioned to you,' Endika said. 'You'll have to meet her now that you're here.'

'Sure, I'll be delighted to,' Luken replied and explained that he had to see him in private but was unable to give the reason over the phone. Endika suggested a site overlooking a lake on the road to St Jean de'Illac.

Next day, Guillaume drove the car with Luken in the front and Estebe in the rear. Nobody spoke. They arrived early and parked on a dirt track then reconnoitred the forest surrounding the lake. When it came near the time Estebe and Guillaume took their place within earshot in the trees.

Luken paced up and down at the water's edge and chose not to sit on one of the wooden benches that had been erected for summertime picnics. Unlike himself, calmness prevailed across the lake, not a single wavelet or a whiff of a breeze.

He recalled the last time he had waited on Endika, when he had been forced to leave his cottage in Durango, another time of great tension. Rolling over the facts that Estebe and the old man had presented, he realised that his anxiety was exacerbated by scarcely having slept since he'd arrived in France two days ago.

He heard Endika before he saw him, trudging his way through the forest path. They greeted each other warmly.

'Here we are after all these years,' Luken said.

'The last time we didn't even know if we'd ever see each other again, sleeping out by the Bidasoa river, remember?'

'How could I forget?' Luken replied and reckoned from his more rugged appearance that his brother had aged more than himself. 'I was so glad you survived the war.'

Endika shrugged. 'I saw so many men die, I can only call it luck. What was it you couldn't talk about over the phone?'

Luken took a deep breath. 'We have to turn the clock back and talk about some things that happened, in Arakoa.'

'What things?'

'Ander's killing and who was responsible.'

'Do you know who was responsible?'

Luken waited a few seconds before saying, 'An old man in the village saw you talking to a group of Requetés and soon afterwards saw the same group take Ander away. The same day he was killed.'

'I didn't kill him.'

'Endika, think carefully when I ask you this. What did you say to them?' Luken asked and in a few seconds saw Endika's expression plummet.

Immediately, Luken felt a shock as he suspected what Estebe had said was true.

'It didn't cross my mind that they were going to kill him,' Endika said morosely. 'I thought they were going to interrogate him about others he knew in the Casa del Pueblo, as they did with me. That's what they said and I foolishly believed them.'

'I never believed you had any allegiance to the Requetés but when I think of it there was a time when you suddenly became religious,' Luken said.

'I didn't have any allegiance to them. I did it to protect Gechina.'

'What?'

'Soon after Alphonso left I started seeing Gechina. We became secret friends and sweethearts. Unknown to us, we were seen by Ramon Delgado, one of the local big shots in Otxandio – and an honorary cleric – doing what we shouldn't have been doing in one of his empty summer houses. He reported us to the parish priest who had us followed. You know what that means. If we'd been taken in and arrested it'd have been the end for Gechina. A married woman having sex with a single man. The kids would have been taken off her and she'd have been sent to jail, treated worse than a whore. So they had me over a barrel. That's why I seemed so religious. They handed me over to the Requetés to tell them everything I knew.

'I very nearly told Miren on the way back from the funeral, then you appeared on the road. I promised Gechina that I'd look after the girls if anything happened to her. We'd planned on moving to France but left it too late. I was glad when the two of you adopted Sabine. How is she?'

'I'm amazed,' Luken said in bewilderment. 'You kept it very quiet. Sabine is fine, she's doing Spanish Literature in university.'

Endika continued, 'The Otxandio bombing changed everything. Gechina could no longer be compromised and I went about killing every Requeté, Falangist and Fascist I could find. Didn't care if I was killed —'

'Enough!' Estebe shouted as he came rushing out of the trees, pistol in hand. He fired two shots. Endika was hit in the chest and was thrown to the ground. Luken whipped out his pistol and fired, hitting Estebe. He fell to the ground. Guillaume appeared, also carrying a weapon. Luken put up a hand in surrender. For a second both men hesitated then let their pistols drop.

Luken went to his dying brother, held up his head, the blood oozing through Endika's hands as he clutched his chest.

'I never thought it'd end this way,' Endika said. 'Look after Sabine. Two brothers loved two sisters. Look after yourself, you're the only one left.'

Guillaume examined Estebe, then came over and shook his head when Luken looked up. The two men crouched around Endika as the light of life left him, then stood and looked distractedly out across the lake, speechless.

Luken removed his jacket and placed it over Endika's head; Guillaume did likewise with Estebe.

Feeling utterly drained, Luken sat on a bench with his elbows on his knees and his head resting in his hands.

In a while, the numbness crept over him. 'To think the two of them survived all the insanity they lived through and it had to end like this.'

Guillaume paced up and down. 'But for that second of hesitancy we could have killed each other.'

He sat beside Luken and placed a hand on his shoulder. 'Don't be too hard on yourself. If I'd been in your position I'd probably have done the same.'

After some time, he said, 'We can't take them back, too dangerous.'

He went to the car and returned with a shovel.

***

The two men sat in the hotel café, drinking their second bottle of brandy well into the night. Given his troubled state of mind, Luken felt no drunkenness and reckoned he'd feel the same no matter how much alcohol he took.

'Estebe was a lifelong friend and an honest man,' Guillaume said, 'but he couldn't be the same after suffering under that regime for so long.'

'Had he planned on killing Ander's betrayer?'

'If he did, he never told me.'

Luken reflected on losing his brother with a mixture of remorse and despair. Why the hell hadn't he tried to contact Endika before meeting with Estebe? Forewarned is forearmed. He could have worked out something. He could have presented Estebe with the facts before the event. Endika had naïvely compromised Ander to save Gechina. Under less heated circumstances, surely Estebe would have seen that. Or would he? But now, the two men were dead.

'I never expected to shoot someone like that, acting on instinct,' Luken said. 'I wonder what would have happened if Estebe hadn't acted the way he did. Maybe we could have reached some compromise, it was a long time ago after all—'

'He wasn't in the mood for compromise,' Guillaume interrupted.

'But if he had heard Endika's explanation of what happened —'

'He heard the best part of it, as I did. Whoever was responsible for Ander's death was going to get it. I couldn't understand why Estebe stayed in Euskal Herria when the Fascists took over. Then I started thinking maybe he had a wish for self-sacrifice after what happened during the Great War, the rapes and attacks on women. He was privy to things I didn't see.'

'Maybe you're right,' Luken said.

'How long are you goin' to stay?'

'I have to go and see Arossa.'

'What are you going to say to her?'

'The truth, no point in saying otherwise, is there?'

'There's talk about a possible amnesty coming up in a few years but it's still a dangerous time to be goin' over,' Guillaume said and thought for a few minutes before continuing. 'I know how we'll work this. From time to time I buy a batch of Rioja from a merchant in Bilbao. I'll put in an order and you can take the van and go collect. We'll have to get you French papers before you go, the Irish passport would raise too many questions. I'm sure I don't have to say this, but if the border guards talk to you in Spanish or Basque, pretend you don't understand. Talk only in French. I'll call Arossa and tell her you're coming, you don't want to be hangin' around.'

'I've just had the strangest recollection,' Luken said. 'At the time of Ander's death, Estebe said he saw his whole life pass by in a few seconds. It's as though it was a premonition of his own death.'

While the 'papers' were being prepared, Luken spent the time visiting the places in the town that he had frequented when he lived there.

He ambled along the promenade, down the steps and along the length of the beach, recalling Sunday afternoons with the family, picnicking, playing football with Sabine and himself on one side and Miren and Kasen on the other. And the carefree years even before that with Miren, Endika, Marie and Vincent. Swimming and volleyball.

Across the town and along Boulevard Thiers, he looked into window of the Madison Hotel Restaurant, where people were having lunch, the place where he and Miren had eaten their last meal in St Jean de Luz.

He was surprised by the improvements that had taken place; in his mind he'd pictured the town as archaic. But now the shops, the Les Halles market and the cafés had been renovated and the optimistic atmosphere was palpable, contrasting with his own grief and downheartedness.

Chapter 24

At the Spanish border, he remembered to speak French when the guards asked about the purpose of his journey. They made a quick inspection of the van, took a perfunctory look through his documents, then stamped them and waved him on, just as Guillaume had suggested. Trouble, if any, was to be expected on the way back.

Ninety kilometres down the road, he unexpectedly glimpsed the signpost for Durango. On a whim he decided to take a look and turned off the road and drove over to the town. Many of the buildings had been restored and those remaining were in varying states of repair. Where his old garage had stood there was now a new building, an outlet for farm machinery and agricultural products, tools, fertiliser and the like. The old one must have been destroyed, he thought, pondering on how things might have worked out had the country not gone to war. Having mulled over his lost business for so many years he had ultimately grown indifferent and no longer felt aggrieved at the loss.

He turned out of the town and drove up the inclines to the Eguzkitza Valley.

Though his old homestead looked occupied, there was nobody to be seen. Through the front windows the interior looked tidy, with new furnishings and modern kitchen fittings. Miren's vegetable plots were overgrown and the roof of the barn had collapsed. He wondered if the bunker was still there but decided not to check it out. Instead, the thought occurred that he might still be entitled to ownership of the house. Maybe the present occupier had rented it from the town council; it might have been sequestered by the town. He had read of properties being returned after the war.

They had worked hard to put this house in place. Why should he give it up? He could sell the Dublin garage, there'd be no shortage of buyers for that. But would he really want to, especially without Miren? And what about Kasen and Sabine? Kasen had expressed no interest in coming here but Sabine might want to. He'd still have to see them through higher education in the meantime.

Just as he was about to drive off he remembered something and turned off the engine. Behind the barn, he pushed over a rock. Badly rusted but still intact he found the tin with the banknotes wrapped in waxed paper. The waxed paper had gone stiff and fell to pieces in his hand but the notes were undamaged. Amused at what he had found, he put the tin back under the rock and pocketed the notes. This place is calling me back, he thought while gazing down at the picturesque valley and across at the mountains.

Back on the main road to Bilbao, he dreaded telling Arossa the bad news, and reminded himself of the last time he'd brought such news to her family. Then it had been her son who had been killed. Like that time, rather than try to find the words in advance he decided to wait until meeting to say it in the most appropriate way. He wondered if Estebe had said anything to her about his suspicions of Endika.

At the wholesaler's warehouse in Abandoibarra he picked up the consignment of wine and, after some difficulties with directions, found Arossa's apartment on the Calle Ledesma, near to the city centre. Turning into the street, he remembered the last time he'd been there, the side street at the back of Café La Granja, where he had taken coffee just before the war broke out.

'Kaixo, Luken,' she said, opening the door and greeting him with a smile and a kiss on each cheek. 'It's so good to see you again.'

She looked more sprightly than he'd expected as he presented her with two bottles of the best quality wine he'd picked up. She made coffee and they sat around the dining table in the living room. He saw that she had a bruise on the side of her face.

The room was tastefully decorated in the old tradition, Turkish rugs on the floor, a Rococo settee and armchairs and a mahogany dining table.

Despite the warmth of their salutations, Luken felt the tension of their unspoken business. He noticed that she was intently watching him as he started to drink his coffee.

'Has something happened to Estebe, Luken?'

'I'm sorry to tell you, Arossa, but Estebe is dead.'

He described at length the surrounding events, the meeting in St Jean, the shooting in the forest. At the end he simply said, 'I'm so, so sorry, Arossa.'

'I thought the worst. I knew he was heading for trouble,' she replied as the emotion welled up in her eyes. She buried her face into her hands and let the tears flow.

Luken could think of nothing to say.

In a while, Arossa took out a handkerchief and dried her eyes. 'When Guillaume couldn't tell me where Estebe was and said that you were coming I knew something had gone badly wrong. Before leaving, Estebe said he thought he had some fresh information about Ander's murder. We were happy in our young years but as time went on and especially after Ander was killed, he was in a state of anger all the time. But I stood by him. Now, at least I won't have to put up with his tempers anymore.' She lifted her head and turned to Luken, taking his hand. 'And now you've lost your brother as well.'

'We'd been so close,' Luken replied, his voice shaking as he fought back the tears. 'And just when we were expecting to get together again.'

'Don't blame yourself, Luken. You reacted the way any decent man would have.'

Luken shrugged, amazed at Arossa's regained composure.

'I was sorry to hear about your Papá's passing,' he said.

'He was always good to me. As you know, he couldn't stand Estebe,' Arossa gestured to the bruise on her face. 'If Papá was alive and knew what he did, he might have killed Estebe himself, he was a tough man…'

'You mean Estebe hit you—'

Arossa gently put up her hand in a gesture to allow her to continue uninterrupted. 'When Papá died I sold the house, it was too big for me and too far out in the country. I bought this place and used most of the money left over to get Estebe out of prison. So much for Franco's redemption and pacification.'

'Can you get by?'

'I'm fine, Papá left me his part ownership in the steel business. What about you? Tell me about Miren, I missed her so badly when you left.'

Luken went on to describe their years in Ireland, how they had adapted. How Miren had enjoyed living there and how the children regarded themselves as Irish. Strangely, it was Sabine rather than Kasen who expressed an interest in visiting Euskal Herria even though her childhood experiences had been more traumatic than Kasen's.

'You must tell her to come and visit me when she does. I'd love to see both her and Kasen.'

'What would you say to the possibility of me coming back to live in Euskal Herria?'

'After all this time?' Arossa was taken aback and reflected for a moment. 'I know there's talk of an amnesty but you'd have to buy your way. And more important and more difficult, you'd have to prove your allegiance to Franco, that'd be a hard pill for you to swallow. I know of one woman who did it. She wrote an article for an American magazine praising the progress in Spain under his leadership.'

'It's a possibility,' Luken replied.

He stood to take his leave and caught sight of three enamelled photographs on the sideboard. Picking up the portrait of Arossa and Miren, he thought how clear the image was. Likewise, the one of Ander, Endika and Estebe. And one of Arossa and Estebe in their young years, a happier time.

'Great photographs. I still have that picture you made for us. Miren treasured it.'

'You must write to me, Luken. And send me a recent picture of Sabine and Kasen.' Arossa stood and led him to the door.

***

As Luken arrived at the French border, a line of vehicles was waiting to cross over. He nervously waited his turn while the officers checked the contents of cars and lorries before passing them through. Lorries were the worst – they seemed intent on going through every article onboard. Some vehicles were directed to a siding when Luken supposed there was a problem with their paperwork.

When his turn came, an officer examined the crates of wine and compared each item with those stated on the invoices. The man took his time, as if trying to annoy or provoke him.

'I see you're short on some of the good stuff,' the officer said. 'Two bottles missing.'

'I gave them to an old friend in Bilbao.'

'So your boss doesn't mind you giving away some of his stock?' the man said with a sycophantic smile.

Luken paused before realising what the officer was after, then said, 'Well, a little here and there, he doesn't mind. Here, take a few bottles for yourself.'

'That's very decent of you. I'll leave them in the office.'

He went into the cabin and returned with Luken's papers stamped before ushering him on.

Luken smiled to himself as he crossed into France. What a farce that was.

Further down the road he recalled Arossa's words about declaring his allegiance to Franco. How could he do that? Write an article for, what, the Irish Independent, admiring the man? Could he be that hypocritical after all that had happened? Maybe there was some other way.

He spotted the sign for Urrugne and turned off the main road. After the village, he came to a halt at his old favourite viewing area. He walked along the cliff top then sat on a soft mat of grass and looked down at the incoming waves dashing off the rocks.

Daylight was fading as he gazed across the bay towards the country he'd come from. The idea of returning to live there rumbled in his head while he thought of Arossa's picture of the three men, Estebe, Endika and Ander, now all dead. Victims of war. Estebe, a decent man who'd strived to see the ordinary working people get a better deal, had turned into a wife beater and a vindictive killer. Endika, a victim of social and religious bigotry turned killer. Poor Ander had never got a chance, slaughtered early in life. And Arossa, who only ever wanted to teach children, the most dignified woman he had ever come across. What an awful hand she had been dealt. And himself, turned killer a few days ago, albeit in a belated defence of his brother.

But worst of all was losing Miren, the only woman he'd ever truly loved. Although she had got over the worst of the recurring Otxandio flashbacks, it was impossible to believe that they hadn't had some bearing on the day of the accident. All this horror had its roots in the war. The country had been overrun and plagued with revolution and violence of the worst kind, a nation devouring itself. It was naïve to think that he could re-possess his old homestead. Euskal Herria only held blood and tragedy for him now and he knew that he'd never return.

He thought of Ireland and the friends and people he had been good to and the people who had been good to him, Padraig and the other friendships he had formed. Those who had welcomed him and his family into their midst and treated them as equals and as one of their own. And of course, Kasen and Sabine, for whom Ireland was their first home.

Time to go back to the country that had given him refuge and sanctuary. He counted out the banknotes from his inside pocket and realised how little they were now worth. The money that he had stashed away before leaving his old house. He kept one note as a souvenir and threw the rest over the cliff when he stood up. They blew down into the sea as he started the engine then drove through Ciboure and on to St Jean de Luz.

Epilogue

University College Dublin, 1954

Luken and Kasen, both dressed in suits and ties, stood up, as did the rest of the audience, when the president, the registrar and other professors entered the stage from the wings. Graduating students stood in the front rows of the hall while eager parents and guardians resided at the rear.

The president gestured for the audience to be seated and launched into his speech. He congratulated the students on their commitment to their subjects and praised them for their hard work over the years. It might seem, he said, as though this was the end of the journey, but in fact, it was the start of a much longer one. One in which their qualifications should help them confidently along the way and encourage them to seek new ways and new ideas to progress and innovate. Such ways were what education was all about, to make Ireland a better society.

When he'd finished, each black-gowned student was called out in alphabetical order and directed up the side stair onto the stage where they shook hands with the professors and were presented with their Bachelor's Certificates in their chosen disciplines by the president.

Luken looked proudly on as Sabine walked up to receive her Bachelor of Arts degree in Spanish and French. She looks just like Gechina, pleased and self-assured, he thought.

When the conferring had finished, everyone moved to another hall where items of food and glasses of wine, beer and pots of tea and coffee had been laid out.

Sabine rushed over and embraced Kasen. 'When did you get in?'

'Nine this morning – on a boneshaker, a DC3! Congratulations, Sabine. We're proud of you.'

'Congratulations from both of us, Sabine,' Luken said. 'We're delighted for you.'

'Thanks, Papá, and thank you for coming over, Kas'. How's the work?'

'I moved to Vickers in Manchester but had to take a drop in wages, a lower-grade position. But I'm glad; it's in the R&D department, developing jet engines. I got fed up with the production engineering work, so repetitive. Hey, I'll bet you're glad to be finished?'

Luken looked on as they chatted away, brother and sister catching up on their latest news.

After they ate and drank, Sabine said, 'Papá, we're going into town for a bit of a party. Why don't you come along – just for one drink at least?'

'I'll skip it this time, *querida*. You go on and enjoy yourselves. I'll see you back home.'

As he drove home, Luken thought of the two of them and how happy Miren would have been, to have seen this day.

Acknowledgements

I would like to thank the many people who helped in the research and development of this novel, far too many to remember "just like that" but I'll get around to you all eventually. However, some were particularly helpful and unforgettable namely:

Sarah Wood, David Heitler, Alex Morgan and others in our Writers Group from the Curtis Brown Creative Class of Autumn 2019, (I think).
Also, Craig Simpson, Laurence O'Bryan and Pat McDaid.

Claude Louvigné for his kind permission to use the photographs of St Jean de Luź and its surrounds on my website and social media.

D T Murphy (David)

August 2022

For more information and pictures of the locations in the story, see my website: www.dtmurphyauthor.com

Any comments? Let me know, I'll be glad to hear from you, email to: dtmurphyauthor@gmail.com

Facebook: @dtmurphyauthor
Twitter: #dtmurphyauthor
TikTok: dtmurphyauthor

Made in United States
North Haven, CT
24 May 2023

36927144R00196